More THAN WORDS

E.L. KOSLO

Copyright

Proofing: Brittni Van - The Romance Doctor – @the_romance_doc on Instagram

Cover: Designed by E.L. Koslo

Depositphotos: jomaplaon, marzacz, Forewer, qerest, Kwangmoo, Sanychs, antart

Envato Elements licensed fonts: Barcelony and Baskerville BT

Interior Formatting: E.L. Koslo

Artwork by @irdeinfierno

Depositphotos: ElmaDesign, huhulin, floral_set, Iniraswork

Lindee Robinson Photography - Cover Model Daniel

Table of Contents

This book is dedicated to thorough research.

.

May sitting on a man's face and having him watch you with a big, black, battery-operated boyfriend be in all of your futures.

All content warnings are on my website at ELKoslo.com/words-series

Note TO READERS

Typically, I direct my readers to look at the tr!gger warnings on my website, but because of the content of this book, I want to point out portions of the story that may be difficult for some readers. Please continue reading for those, or start reading Chapter One if you'd rather skip them.

SPOILER ALERT

Isobel's story is, unfortunately, one that is all too common and involves struggles with infertility, pregnancy loss, and relationship struggles because of those things that led to a divorce. There are also mentions of fertility testing, birth control failure, unexpected pregnancy, morning sickness needing medical intervention, premature birth, a newborn in the NICU, and struggles with depression both peri and postpartum.

Adrian's story deals with the death of a parent (in the past/not on the page), guilt regarding his brother's injuries and limb loss during his time in the military and taking care of an aging grandparent with dementia.

If any of those topics may tr!gger you, please preserve your mental health and skip this book. If you have any questions about content before you read, please feel free to reach out by email elkoslowrites@gmail.com or on Instagram @elkoslo_writes.

Spice Index

CHAPTERS THAT TURN UP THE HEAT

Isobel Blom

OCCUPATION: MANAGING EDITOR

GENRE

Romance

ISOBEL

BOSTON

THE OBNOXIOUS CLICKING OF my heels echoed after me as I hurried across the marble tiled lobby of my office building. I was late, and my Uber driver would bail if I didn't get my ass outside in the next two minutes. My rider rating couldn't take a hit, or I'd be pushed back down with the idiots who drank too much and puked all over someone's seats, or who got dinged because they were morally opposed to basic personal hygiene. Since I'd sold my car, I relied on having a good rating to get to and from work—on time—most days.

"Finally," the young driver sighed as I slid into the backseat of his idling Toyota and pulled the door closed. "Took yah long enough, lady. It's rush hour, and I can't have yah killin' my rides for tha rest of the night."

"Sorry," I huffed, trying to straighten my long pencil skirt. Changing after my meeting was out of the question since the executive marketing team's presentation had run long. Those lucky bastards didn't have to go to this ridiculous team-building event that Sloane, my boss, had arranged with the publishing house genre heads. "Missed the elevator and had to run barefoot down ten flights of stairs."

"Bet that was somethin' tah see," he smirked, but quickly averted his eyes at the glare I returned. *Men.*

This was why I was keeping to myself lately. No matter the age or walk of life, men were constantly judging me based on my looks. Apparently, tall, blonde, and dimpled warranted the male population of Boston and the surrounding tri-state area to think I was a ditz or a whore. Or both. Never mind that I worked my ass off in High School to get out of my tiny midwestern town and earn a scholarship to an Ivy League university. It couldn't possibly register with them I worked three jobs—and no, none of them were stripping, although it might have paid better—during undergrad and grad school to pay for what my scholarships didn't cover. Which was a lot when you lived halfway across the country from your family, who pretended you didn't exist because you left behind the family farm to do something they considered pointless.

But none of that mattered because if you had a vagina, so you clearly couldn't be taken seriously half the time. I hated that my career was seemingly at a standstill. I hated that the genre I *chose* to edit was constantly being trashed, despite the millions of dollars in revenue it generated for the publishing house each year.

But fuck dwelling on what I couldn't change because those bastards could lick the sole of my one pair of Louboutin heels if they had a problem with me being an empowered woman.

I could survive in Boston just fine without a support network. I had friends, sort of. And I had loyal co-workers, well...I had dedicated interns. Plus, I had the support of my boss, who inspired women in the publishing industry everywhere.

"We're here," the Uber driver announced quietly, looking warily at me in the mirror. Maybe my stony glare and ten minutes of silence had changed his decision to make smartass comments about my appearance. But I wasn't expecting miracles. He just wouldn't say them to my face. I was sure the word *bitch* would be muttered as soon as my door closed, but as I pushed a strand of sweaty hair behind my ear, I didn't care.

"Thank you," I sighed, plastering on my biggest smile, and quickly gathering my things to make my way into the ax-throwing bar. I was already late and didn't want to stay any later than I had to.

"Alright, listen up, people." Sloane called the group to order once I'd settled in at a barstool, my co-workers quieting down. "The teams are as follows. Chloe and Roger are in bay one against Logan and Ryker. Amanda and I are in bay two against Julia and Mark. Kyle and Zuki are in bay three against Elliot and Hilla. Fred and Reilly are in bay four against Donna and Jacob. And last but certainly not least, Lorenzo and Kate in bay five against Isobel and Adrian."

"Oh, joy," I muttered under my breath as Adrian walked through the crowd toward me. "I get to partner with *Dickhead.*"

Yes, he was objectively handsome—tall, with broad, muscular shoulders, light blue eyes, and hair as dark as ink on a crisp white page. In fact, the first time I'd seen him, I'd stopped short, my heart beating erratically as I watched him verbally berating the copy machine on our floor. He'd somehow managed to get paper sheets stuck in every place it could jam inside the machine. That's what he got for trying to duplex print an entire manuscript—using an ancient copier that was notorious for eating anything that enters it—rather than ordering a bound copy from the printing department. Rookie mistake.

I'd thought it was adorable. The scowl on his full lips, the muttered curse words thrown into his thick Bostonian accent, but then he'd noticed me watching, delivered one sexist come-on, and I'd disliked him ever since.

Want to fix this for me, gorgeous? You're probably more familiar with this beast than I am. Then he gave me a smarmy full-body scan and said something even worse. *On second thought, I got this. Wouldn't want you to get that skirt dirty since I'd love to see you in it again.*

Adrian O'Neill was arrogant. He was an asshole. He treated some interns like they were worse than gum stuck on the soles of his expensive Italian leather shoes. He was a genre elitist. And despite all that, he was annoyingly good at his job. I'd never seen another editor quite as good at plucking obscure authors out of a submissions pile and getting them to the top of all the must-read charts. He often saw potential in authors that others overlooked. It made me simultaneously in awe of him and constantly befuddled when he continued curating this crude playboy persona.

And worst of all, he was easily the most attractive man I'd ever seen when he kept his mouth shut. He'd look even sexier with a piece of duct tape covering it. There was something about the set of his lips and how his eyes crinkled when he was about to say something stupid. He *knew* half the shit he said would get a negative reaction, but he said it anyway. The man had absolutely no filter.

He was also a misogynistic jerk. And did I mention arrogant?

"Hey, Is, long time no see," he greeted. The polished professional façade fully in place. This was the face most people saw. They didn't see the strong Boston accent and the sarcastic quips I'd spied when he interacted with people outside the office. I was certain the phrase 'wicked smart' had never passed his lips on company property. And his *you's* and *yeah's* sounded nothing other than crisp and perfectly enunciated.

When he was in work mode, he was on. Degree from Boston College with honors, a deep voice with perfect inflection, every strand of shiny dark hair precisely in place, expensive suits with expert double Windsor knots in designer silk ties.

Once, just once, I wanted to see the veneer crack and see the real Adrian. The one he'd buried deep under this giant douche persona. I knew there had to be more than met the eye, or ear, but he was so insistent on cultivating the office asshole persona that he never let anyone see past the bullshit. I recognized professional armor, as I often wore it myself.

"Adrian." I nodded, hating that the hairs on the back of my neck stood on end when his arm brushed against mine.

"Are you sure you can handle doing this in those shoes?" he asked, leaning toward me so only I could hear his words. "Not that they aren't amazing, but I can't see three-inch heels being good for your balance."

"Can you handle this with the three inches you pack below the belt? I mean, I'm sure you think it's amazing, but it can't be good for...well, anyone," I hissed, stepping away from him. I bumped into Lorenzo, grimacing as his drink sloshed over the edge of his glass.

"You alright there, Isobel?" Lorenzo asked as he reached over to steady me with a hand on my elbow.

"She's fine." Adrian's calloused fingertips closed over my other elbow, and I wobbled as my eyes darted between the two handsome men who towered over me.

"No thanks to you, I'm sure," Renz muttered as he narrowed his eyes at Adrian. There was no love lost between the two rival editors. Adrian was an asshole, which most of the interns, including my own, called *Dickhead*. Lorenzo was the office eye candy, and the interns frequently ogled his vast collection of snug dress slacks.

Lorenzo *was* nice, but his nice-guy personality left nothing about him to the imagination. A good heart wrapped in a pretty package. While that should have been attractive—especially to a woman who was nearly out of her thirties and should be thinking about settling down someday—it seemed a little anticlimactic. What you saw was what you'd get. *All* that you'd get.

There was no mystery there, no spark. No passion simmering under the surface. There were no secrets to uncover that no one else knew about. Maybe I'd been editing romance novels for too long and had become immune to the 'nice guy.' After all, the toxic hero seemed to sell, and women swooned over an asshole by the millions—especially if he had millions. Too bad the asshole in my real life wouldn't be pulling a redemption arc anytime soon.

"I'm fine," I told them both, clearing my throat. "I'll be fine. Thank you."

"I have some sneakers in my gym bag if yah need 'em," Adrian whispered as he leaned into my personal space again. My eyes flashed over to Lorenzo, but he was already deep in conversation with his partner, Kate, a non-fiction editor who had as much personality as wallpaper paste—and was just as in demand as an antiquated wall covering adhesive.

"I'm good, thanks," I responded, glancing at his polished leather shoes. His feet weren't huge, but they were also substantially larger than my size nines.

"You sure? I'd hate to see those affect your aim."

Turning to face him, I paused, taking in the lone curl of hair falling onto his forehead. I'd rarely seen his hair looking anything but like it belonged on a Ken doll, and my fingers twitched with the urge to push it back into place.

"My aim will be just fine."

He hummed, nodding before bringing his glass to his lips and taking a sip of the amber liquid inside while maintaining eye contact with me.

"Want to place a wager on it?"

"I'm not betting on ax-throwing with you. You're bigger than I am and stronger..." His grin grew as I kept talking, and I had the increasing urge to dig one of my heels into the top of his foot.

"No, no, keep going." He smirked as he did that masculine thing where he was clearly undressing me with his eyes. "I'm interested in all this sudden praise you're throwing out."

My nipples pricked with how he paused when his gaze was aimed at my cleavage. *Pig.* "Eyes up here, big boy."

He chuckled, tipping his glass in my direction before leaning close to my ear. "Which one is it? Do I only have three inches, or am I a big boy? Surely, they aren't exclusive, or your boyfriends have been seriously lacking in what they're packing."

I clenched my teeth together as I fought the shiver that ran up my spine at how his warm breath felt as it fanned over my bare neck. He smelled good—fresh and alluring, with a hint of wood smoke and something vaguely floral.

Considering he spent most of his lunch breaks in the corporate gym on the bottom floor of our building, he always looked surprisingly put together.

I hated running into him down there because my fair skin only turned bright red with physical exertion. Genetics ensured I didn't get that glow some women got when they exercised. My Scandinavian heritage meant I looked like a pink-cheeked hot mess with an excessive perspiration problem. No amount of dry shampoo would save me from that mess.

"Hmm," he hummed before he leaned away. "Care to make a wager on the outcome of this evening?"

Turning toward him, I frowned. "We're on the same team."

"I'm aware." He nodded and took another sip of his drink, his eyes clocking the nervous shifting I'd been doing since he'd set his sights on me. "Total points, bonuses for bullseyes."

"You going to keep score?" I asked, narrowing my eyes. I didn't trust him not to cheat.

He shrugged, lifting his chin toward me. "Don't trust me?"

"Should I?"

He'd given me zero reasons in our history as co-workers to trust a word he said, in a professional capacity or otherwise. More than once, he'd undermined something I said in a staff meeting. He also had the bad habit of hijacking conversations and turning the subject back to his own department.

"Fair point," he laughed, stepping in and placing his free hand in the center of my back. It wasn't anywhere inappropriate, but the jolt it sent between my legs hadn't gotten the message. "You keep track. My math is shit. But I'm sure you can handle it with that impressive Ivy League education your parents bestowed upon you."

If he only knew my parents were grain farmers who cared more about crop yields and the newest corn hybrids on the market than whether their youngest daughter got an education at one of the top English programs in the country. I may have dressed the part, but I wasn't some elitist snob like he perceived me to be. My upbringing was probably less glamorous than his. He'd likely never been asked to mix organic fertilizer by hand in his life. My job during high school had literally been shit-stirring. And not the kind he engaged in.

"Because you're clearly lacking in educational pedigree."

"According to some," he laughed, dropping his hand and stepping around me as Sloane motioned for us to move toward the cages where we'd be doing the actual ax throwing, not just the lobbing of verbal ones. I'd missed the entire demonstration, but how hard could it be?

Hold the ax, aim at the target, pretend bullseye is Adrian's face, and throw.

"You ready for this?" he asked as we stepped inside the enclosure. Kate and Lorenzo stood against the opposite wall, clearly planning their strategy.

"What are the stakes?" I asked quietly as my fingers trailed over the handle of one of the axes in the hanger on the wall.

"What do yah want?" Adrian chuckled, his palm settling in the center of my back.

"You to quit disparaging my authors. It makes you sound like an arrogant douche when you comment about how other genres are beneath you."

"I never said romance was beneath me, Is. I said that the market share wasn't as deep."

"Quit comparing the two. You stay in your lane. I'll stay in mine."

"But it's so fun to veer into your lane and cause chaos." I could hear the smirk in his voice with no need to turn around.

"What do you want?"

He paused, his fingers flexing against my back. "I don't think you're ready for what I really want."

"Try me." The smoldering look he had aimed in my direction may have worked on other women, but I wasn't some naïve intern.

"A kiss. I'd like to see if that fire can hold up or if you're all smoke."

Rolling my eyes, I turned around and placed my hand in the center of his chest, pushing until he stepped backward. "Done. No tongue."

"Deal."

He abruptly stepped back, taking an ax from the holder and stepping up to the line.

"You mind if I have first throw, Renz?" Adrian asked before he tilted his neck from side to side and rolled his shoulders back. I tried not to stare at how his dress shirt stretched across the broad expanse of his back, but his little warm-up made it difficult to look away.

With a quick wink over his shoulder, he staggered his feet and squared his shoulders, bringing his arm up to align with the target. With a snap of his arm, the ax flew, wedging itself into the center of the target with a solid *thwack*.

I had a feeling I'd just been played. Smug bastard.

As the night wore on, the soreness in my feet grew, but I refused to admit defeat as I stepped up to the line to throw my final ax. If I hit the bullseye, I could tie Adrian. But I knew he'd stopped actively trying to win a little while ago. He didn't think I had a chance and was teasing me with the close score. And I was taking the bait because my competitive streak wouldn't let me back down.

"Might as well admit defeat, Is. It's a work night. Don't want to keep you up too late."

Kate and Lorenzo had lost interest, checking their phones as Adrian and I continued to bicker between shots.

He seemed to think Red Sox fans were more devout than Cubs fans, and I was educating him on how, despite their recent World Series win, the Cubs fans were diehard loyalists who would celebrate their team until their dying breath, even if they never made another series run in this lifetime.

"Oh, come on. The Sox're one of tha originals. How can you not love the legacy of one of the first franchises in American baseball?"

"I didn't say they weren't loved. I said Cubs fans were more devoted."

"Bullshit," he chuckled as she shook his head, picking up his glass of scotch and swallowing the rest. I tried not to stare as the muscles in his throat flexed, but judging by the smirk, I failed. "Fenway is so much coolah than Wrigley. There's history heah in Boston."

I smirked at his accent slipping through, and his eyes widened, a frown crossing his features. "No, I get it. Architecturally, Fenway is nice, but I think it's easier to be a fair-weather fan than one who is enthusiastic for the underdog, even when they're beaten year after year."

"After year, after year, after year," he smirked, and I kicked my foot backward, my heel poking him in the shin.

"Don't be a dick," I laughed.

"Ah, but I've gotta live up to my name."

"At some point, you could just stop being a dick, and maybe the nickname would die out."

"And what fun would that be?" He winked. Of course, he liked that people called him a dickhead, including when it wasn't behind his back.

"Quit distracting me."

"You're the one who keeps bringing up your mediocre baseball team." Turning around one last time, I fixed him with a glare, but his cocky smile widened. "You gonna throw that ax or just tease its poor shaft all night?"

Kate gasped at his crass question, Lorenzo's face pinching into a frown as he looked between us. Our team had already won. My last throw was just a formality. And it determined whether Adrian got that kiss he wanted. Not that I had any idea why he wanted it. We didn't get along, and I doubted we ever would.

"Maybe I like to take things slow."

"Maybe you're stalling because you know you'll lose," he taunted. "Or maybe you're *trying* to lose."

Gritting my teeth, I took a deep breath and focused on the center ring, pulling my arm back and breathing out as I released my weapon toward its target.

My eyes closed before it hit, my body jolting with the sound of the impact.

"Nice throw," Renz cheered, and I opened my eyes, surprised that I'd hit dead center on the target.

"Thanks," I smiled as I looked back in his direction.

"You were a formidable opponent," Adrian drawled as I turned toward our side of the range and wiped my sweaty palms down my skirt. "Guess it was a draw."

"We both know you let me catch up. Does that mean we're both winners?"

As much as I wanted him to quit being a dick to my authors, I wasn't sure I wanted his lips anywhere near mine just to get him not to be an asshole. That seemed like a terrible idea. We worked together. He was an epic asshat, and my attraction to him was solely to his body, not his lackluster personality.

"Nah. I don't need a pity kiss. We're good."

"If you say so." I nodded, relieved. "Wouldn't want you to be embarrassed when it fell short."

"Well," Sloane interrupted from opposite the fence, smiling widely at us. "Looks like you two did quite well tonight."

"Were we keeping score for something other than bragging rights?" I glanced over at Adrian, but he only shrugged, looking back toward our boss.

"I didn't tell anyone ahead of time. Whoever had the highest score will represent Vivid at the New England Publisher's Conference next month."

"And who would that be?"

"Adrian, since he scored the most points."

"Technically, Isobel scored the same number of points, so we tied," Adrian offered helpfully, smirking at me.

"Looks like you're both lucky then."

"Am I really?" I asked under my breath, trying to sound less annoyed than I was. He'd been tolerable tonight, but I didn't want to be trapped in Eastern Maine with him for almost a week. While I enjoyed going to trade conferences, I knew we'd have to spend time together if we were being sent to represent Vivid. And I'd have to pretend I didn't despise him.

"I was secretly hoping it'd be the one of you, with the press Adrian got for Stone's latest release and the articles you've been contributing about the resurgence of romance novels into mainstream media with streaming services green lighting movies, I think you'd be good representatives. Neither of you have any releases that conflict with the conference, so it seems like a perfect fit to send you both."

Glancing over at Adrian, I tried to gauge if he was dreading this as much as I was, but his eyes weren't focused on our boss. They were focused squarely on my ass. Great.

"I'm sure it'll be more than worth our time. Have Chloe send the itinerary to Sam to ensure all the edits on my plate are covered, but I'm in."

Sloane smiled, reaching over to squeeze his arm. He grinned at her in response, and she cleared her throat before looking at me. Of course, she'd fall for his bullshit. Everyone seemed to. "Think you can make it work, Isobel?"

"Do I really have an option? Neither of us has conflicts, and it seems like a great opportunity." I tried to tack on a smile at the end, but I wasn't sure I was successful with the slight frown she directed at me before she stepped back, plastering a grin on her face.

"Great. I'll get you all the details this week and have your travel booked. I know the venue shifted, so we need to book rooms soon."

Yeah, there had better be rooms, *plural.* I was not sharing the same hotel room with Adrian. I'd rather sleep in the rental car. And the *only one bed* trope needed to stay in my author's books where they belonged.

As Sloane walked away, Adrian stepped forward, placing his hand on my back as he deposited his empty glass on the high-top table in the corner. "Don't worry, Is. I'll make sure we have a good time. Maybe you'll lighten up outside the office."

"Ugh. You're such a dick," I hissed, stepping around him. "Just because I don't fall on yours doesn't mean I'm an uptight bitch."

"Hey," he chuckled, raising his hands in defense before he stepped to the side, holding open the net for me. Kate and Lorenzo took off while we talked to Sloane, and our other co-workers were headed home or toward the bar down the street. "I never called you a bitch. I think wicked smart, opinionated women are sexy as fuck."

"You lost me at opinionated. I'm sorry that standing up for my authors and *chosen* genre makes me opinionated."

"I thought we were calling a truce," he chuckled, seemingly unaffected by my hostility.

"We tied. And you said you didn't want a pity kiss, so I thought that meant I'd still be receiving your closed-minded, sexist, crude, incorrect, and often offensive commentary for the foreseeable future."

"I can keep up my end of the bargain. I'll try to watch my mouth, but I don't want you to kiss me if you don't want to. I'm not that much of a dick."

"You sure about that?" I scoffed, pulled out my phone, and ordered a ride as he followed me toward the door. I would try to escape him outside, but it was still raining and dark.

"Trust me, Is." He smirked as he stepped in close and tucked a few loose strands of my hair behind my ear. "If you're not begging for it, I'm not interested. I can be patient. You won't keep me waiting long."

"You're likely to be in the ground before that happens," I growled as the alert that my ride had arrived popped up on my screen. I didn't look back when I pushed through the door and jogged down the sidewalk to my awaiting car.

Adrian watched me through the glass with a smug grin as the car approached where I was standing. Pressing my hand against the car window, I flipped my middle finger, hating that he had turned me into this person. While I would readily admit I was stubborn and determined, I never wanted people to think I really was a bitch. Then I'd be just as bad as he was.

I could see his smile widen through the rain-streaked glass, and he held his hands over his heart while I narrowed my eyes and faced forward. I wanted to smack him for baiting me into competing against him. It was his fault I would be stuck going to that conference with him, and he seemed to look forward to tormenting me the entire time.

Adrian O'Neill

OCCUPATION: MANAGING EDITOR

GENRE

Mystery, Action, Suspense, Thriller

Chapter
TWO

ADRIAN

BOSTON

WHILE I STOOD AT the bar window and watched the car pull away, I couldn't help the smile on my face. I knew Isobel didn't care for me. If the constant narrowed eyes and look of disdain painted across her face weren't an indication, the heated conversations we had every time we were in the same room should probably clue me in.

I knew why she didn't like me. It was my fault, but I couldn't seem to turn it off around her. The professional persona was my armor. The protection from the real world that I'd strapped on at sixteen and never taken off. At least not around anyone but my family. I was pretty sure my Ma would beat the shit out of me if she knew half the things that came out of my mouth.

My twin brother and I may have grown up without a dad—we lost him right before we started kindergarten. And sometimes with holes in our shoes—thanks to being a single-parent household—but we'd been taught manners. Too bad being the nice guy didn't get you shit in the world. It sure as fuck didn't get you respect, and it didn't remove the target from your back around the good ol' boys' club. But I was as good an actor as I was an editor.

I'd spent half of high school with my face buried in a book and the other half with a bat in my hands. Those were the only things that were gonna keep me outta the military, a construction site or a factory. My brother hadn't been so lucky. He used to joke that I was the brains, and he was the brawn, but things had changed a lot since we were kids.

My phone started buzzing in my pocket, and I pulled it out, frowning as his face appeared on the screen. Where I was all flash and good looks, he was rugged and, well...hairy. Shaggy dark hair sprinkled with grays and a full beard covered up the scars I knew he still carried from his time in the Marines.

"How's it going, Hutch?"

He huffed, probably ready to tear into me for how I could mask my accent. He'd never been able to master it, and despite leaving for almost two decades during his time in the service, I didn't think he ever would. Not that he needed to; despite multiple tours of duty in two different branches of the military, he was still a townie. You could take the boy out of the neighborhood he'd grown up in, but it would always be a part of him.

"This fuckin guy, Jesus fuckin Christ, Ad. Where are yah?"

I'd told him this morning I had a thing after work, but something must have happened at home for him to call me.

"Where's Pops? You need me to find him?"

A rough cough came through the line, and I winced, hating that every little thing seemed harder for him since he'd gotten home following his medical discharge. He'd come a long way, but his body had taken a lot of abuse at the hands of others in the last ten years.

"If you can pull yah self away from whateva cake eater shit you've been doin'. That old fuck told me he was goin' to Dunkies and took off. I already called there, and the packie at the end of the block, and nobody's seen 'im."

"Does Ma know he's missing again?"

"Are yah fuckin' kidding me with this? I'm not tellin' her shit," he laughed, then lowered his voice. "She's on an overnight. I don't want her to worry when she can't get home anyway."

"There's a Pats game on. I'm sure he's down at the bar," I sighed, grabbing my bag and heading toward the door. I knew if it weren't raining, he'd go after our grandfather, but couldn't use the cane safely with the sidewalks this wet. I also knew once he took his last dose of medicine, it meant he wasn't functioning at full capacity. Some of those painkillers really packed a punch. It also made his Bostonisms a little more pronounced. There was no doubt which side of the bay he came from once his mouth opened past 8:00 p.m.

"You're a fuckin' gem, Ad. You know I wouldn't call unless I was worried."

"I know, Hutch," I sighed, tucking my face down before I jogged toward the parking lot where I'd left my car earlier. "I'll find 'im and get him home. Do you need anything? Did you eat?"

He growled, and I knew I'd hit a nerve. He didn't like me babying or feeling sorry for him, but I knew he didn't have the best track record of taking care of himself unless he had his daughter Penny for the weekend. "I'm fine. Just find Pops, and we're square."

"I..." the line disconnected, and I clenched my eyes shut as I pressed the button on the remote to my car, the chirp of the doors unlocking echoing despite the steady downpour.

I bet Isobel wouldn't think I was quite the dick I acted like if she knew exactly how I spent most of my time. I may flirt inappropriately or say sexist things at work, but it was a sham. Half my time was spent babysitting my senile eighty-five-year-old grandfather while the other half was spent trying to figure out how to make my twin brother's life easier because I felt guilty my life had turned out so vastly different from his.

Maybe things would be different if his last tour hadn't gone so far off the rails, but I'd always felt this lingering sense of guilt that I'd gone to college and made something of myself while he spent his youth devoted to a country that'd cut him loose the second all his body parts weren't intact.

He'd missed out on a lot in the twenty-plus years he'd been in the service, and I knew it ate at him that his sacrifices were essentially forgotten after his injury. His ex-wife had dropped the bomb while he was recovering from his injuries that she wanted a divorce, and that she was carrying his former best friend's baby. Then he was told he'd never leave a desk again if he stayed in the military, and they'd offered to discharge him when he told them that'd never happen.

He'd kick me in the nuts if he knew I was still feeling so intensely guilty because he was proud and tough and didn't want anyone to pity him for anything. But I still had a hard time seeing past the imagery of him lying in a hospital bed overseas with part of his leg missing and bright red scars littering his face. He'd always seemed invincible and larger than life, and we'd almost lost him.

"Hey." The bartender, Jeanette, nodded as I pushed open the door to the neighborhood bar Pops had treated as a second home since he'd retired twenty years ago. "He's in the back with the other old fucks. They're playin' cards. He's behaved himself tonight."

"Do I need to close out his tab?" I asked, bracing myself for how much it'd be. Based on how much he'd drank, I could usually tell what kind of mood the old man would be in.

"Nah," she smiled, waving my hand away. "He paid for the two he had in cash and has been nursing a watta."

Thank fuck. I wasn't in the mood to wrestle him down the sidewalk in the rain if he was past the point of being belligerent. Pops was mostly good-natured, but sometimes things got ugly if he was deep into the whiskey.

I knew most of the people at work thought I worked out so much to look good and because I was vain—to be honest; I did like the appreciative looks I got because of my physique—but it was mostly because of Pops. The old man was the same height as me, although he appeared a few inches shorter because he stooped when he walked; but he was wiry. I'd also bulked up when Hutch was discharged because I knew Ma couldn't afford to have someone else come in when she was working, and I needed to be able to lift him when he was still heavily reliant on the wheelchair.

He wouldn't let me touch him now, but before the prosthetic and all the physical therapy he'd done in the past year, he'd needed the help. Now, he could get around fine on his own, unless it involved rainy weather or lots of stairs.

"Thanks," I mumbled, lightly patting the bar, shooting her a wink before I wove through the tables toward the back, where the old man coughs and dry laughter rang out despite the late hour.

"Ad, my boy," Pops laughed as he clapped his hands, clearly happy to see me. So, it'd been a good day. He didn't recognize me some days, and those were the hardest. Those days, I fucking hated dementia and what it did to people. Telling elaborate lies to a man I'd spent my entire life admiring just to get him to walk home at night made me feel like shit.

"Alright, Pops, time for yah beauty sleep."

His cronies chuckled; some patted my arm as I walked around the table to lend my hand to Pops. He'd never admit it, but he wasn't as spry as he used to be, his boxing days squarely in the past. It was hard to watch him get older, but I was glad he was still around. I knew he'd been lonely since my grandma passed on, but there were still enough of his old neighborhood buddies alive that he kept himself busy.

"Yeah, I guess yah right, Ad. Us O'Neill's have to keep these mugs lookin' good for the ladies. Wouldn't want them to miss out by having to look at all these ugly old fucks. Isn't that right, my boy?"

"Yeah, Pops. It's all for the ladies," I laughed and shook my head. My grandfather hadn't looked at another woman since the late nineteen fifties. Even dead, my grandmother was the love of his life. But our family had a reputation for being pretty boys, which made running around the neighborhood as a teenager fun. Especially when there were two of us. Hutch had been more the heartbreaker between us, but neither of us had ever had to work much for female company. Sometimes, it was the same female—something we stopped years ago.

"See youse assholes tomorrah." Pops yawned as he patted the shoulders of a few of his buddies while I cupped his elbow and led him away from the table. I knew he'd stay here all night if I let him, but then Ma would be worried. And she hadn't worked her ass off for decades for the men in her life to give her grief. She'd already had enough heartache to last a lifetime when my father was killed overseas.

"Bye, Jeannie," he called out, winking as the pretty bartender waved in his direction. I knew she had a soft spot for Pops. Plus, we were almost family, with her cousin technically being my ex-sister-in-law. Many of the original families in the neighborhood were related by those *five degrees of separation*.

I led my grandfather to the covered front stoop of the bar, instructing him to stay put until I pulled the car up to the curb. We could have technically walked home, but I wasn't making him do that in the rain.

As soon as I pulled up, I cursed and grabbed my umbrella, hurrying around the car to shield him as he rushed as fast as he could toward the passenger side. "Oh, I get car side service now?" he joked while I held the umbrella over his head and pulled open the door.

"Careful with the drop," I cautioned, and he gripped the handle inside the door to lower himself into the seat with a shaking arm.

"I can handle gettin' in a fuckin car, Adrian. I'm old as fuck, not a toddlah."

Biting back a sarcastic retort, I let him get himself buckled and closed the door, rushing back to the driver's side.

"So, who sent yah out after me this time?" he asked as I settled in my seat, turning the wipers back up and checking my mirrors before pulling away from the curb.

"Hutch," I sighed, hating that this was where we were. Pops felt like the rest of his family was always trying to keep him on a leash, but we'd had enough late nights, calling around the neighborhood when he didn't come home at night, to scare us all.

"Well, can't say I blame 'em," he sighed, folding his hands in his lap. "Last week was kinda bad. I know I scared your Ma. Thought she was my Aileen and acted like a shit toward her when she came home one morning."

Ma was an ER nurse, often pulling overnight or double shifts, and took care of my brother and grandfather during the day when she wasn't sleeping. I told her she should think about getting a placement in one of the doctor's offices closer to the house, but she told me she'd be bored outta her mind without the grueling pace of working in trauma care. I didn't see the appeal, but I also fainted at the sight of blood, so we clearly weren't cut from the same cloth.

She excelled at fixing the messes of people's bodies. I excelled at fixing the messes of people's words.

Hutch was more like her, joined the Marines at eighteen, served his first four years, then reenlisted in the Navy to act as a medical corpsman in a Marine combat unit for years before he moved to the Special Warfare Combat Crewman. It was during a SEAL extraction that everything had gone to shit.

"You know she understands, Pops," I sighed, pulling up to the curb at the modest row house I'd grown up in.

"Yeah, I get it, Ad. But sometimes, I feel like it's not fair that I'm still here and she's not. Your Ma is stuck with the three of us, and on my bad days, she doesn't even have me."

"Well, you're stuck with us for the time being, old man, so quit your bitchin'."

"If you'd quit acting like a prick, maybe she'd have another woman around."

Fuck. Getting my balls busted by the elderly now.

"She has Pen around. I don't think Ma cares if I settle down."

"Hmm," he hummed as he turned to face me. "You know that she always told me she wanted a house full of grandkids. If my Liam wasn't gone all the time, before he... There probably would have been a herd of you hell-raising delinquents." Pops still had trouble mentioning my dad, almost thirty-five years later. I couldn't imagine the pain of losing a child.

"Then maybe she needs to ask Hutch for another one."

"Or maybe you stop running from your problems and settle down already. Maybe I'd like to see one of your kids come into this world and put you in your place like Pen has done with your brother. And we both know your brother is too busy fuckin' around to get tied down again."

My twelve-year-old niece was a little ball-buster but was only around on the weekends. Still, I knew she had a special bond with Pops. It wasn't that I didn't want kids. I was a workaholic who had little time to meet women and, being dubbed the office Dickhead left little room in the office dating pool. Not that I hadn't thought about a certain feisty blonde a lot over the last five years since we started working in the same office. She was in the same boat as me—worked crazy hours, traveled frequently, didn't have a family, and didn't date—at least not that I knew about.

"Just somethin' tah think about. When yah grow a pair, yah let me know."

He didn't wait for me to leave the car, opening the door himself and stepping onto the sidewalk. The rain had settled into a gentle sprinkle, and I stared through the streaky raindrops on the window while he pulled himself up the front steps using the handrail. My brother swung the door open before he got to the top, his middle finger extended in my direction briefly before he helped Pops in the front door and pushed it closed.

I knew I should stick around and make sure everything was good, but I needed to catch up on a lot of work if I would be out of the office for a week. Part of me dreaded keeping up the act with Isobel the entire trip, but the other part wondered how she'd react if I didn't bother anymore.

THREE

ADRIAN

BOSTON

"Are you fucking kidding me?"

I stopped mid-stride, my eyes widening at the outburst coming from the partially open office door at the end of the hallway. I'd intended to stop by Isobel's office and confirm the itinerary for our travel plans, but I wasn't sure if I should just come back.

"Fuck, fuck, fuck me. God fucking dammit."

My lips pinched together as I listened to her little mini tirade. I could hear things being slammed around on her desk, and I imagined the little pouty look she got on her face when she was irritated—which was admittedly a lot when I was in her presence.

If her intern was in there, I didn't want to step on the hornet's nest, but as I crept forward and peeked around the edge of the frame, I saw the table across from her desk where her guard dog often worked was empty.

Maybe I could avoid a conflict this morning and return to my office to ensure my files were all marked for my copy-editing intern, Sam. He was typically on top of things with little interference, but I had this compulsive habit of micromanaging.

It was probably an older twin thing, but I was the planner, and Hutch was the one who often blew those plans to smithereens. I knew Sam thought it was weird that my files were all meticulously organized, but the only way I survived school was to ensure I had every aspect obsessively covered. It was easy to let things backslide, but that made my skin crawl. We all had our tics, and an almost compulsive need to organize things was mine.

"What the actual fuck?" Isobel sighed loudly, and I watched her throw her phone onto her desk with a dull thump. Her forehead fell to the messy pile of papers in the middle of her desk, rising and falling a few times before she sighed again and sat back in her chair, facing the ceiling with her eyes closed.

I watched her face soften as she took a few deep breaths; the tension draining from her shoulders.

"What do you want?" she asked with an exasperated exhale. "And quit staring at my cleavage."

Biting back my response was hard, but I managed, because I was not taking the bait and getting myself in trouble. I'd been more fixated on the soft motions of her throat as she breathed than the few buttons she had unfastened on her blouse.

"Just wanted to ensure we're on the same page for tomorrow. Do you need me to go pick up the rental? I don't mind. I've got some time open this afternoon."

"Fuck," she sighed, sitting forward and scooting her chair closer to her desk to pick up her phone. "About that. There won't be one. Travel just sent over an email. They weren't able to get a car. Something about the reservations not being put in for the correct dates. We'd need to come back Tuesday, and with the closing reception not being until Thursday night, there's no way to make it work."

"What are they proposing as an alternative?"

"They were going to try to get some plane tickets figured out, but then we'd be stuck in the airport all day and still have to mess around with getting a rental on the other end. So basically, we'd lose most of tomorrow when we could drive there in four or five hours. Corporate travel is so stupid sometimes."

"If you're up for it, I can drive. I mean, I've got a car. Or we can take yours, or..."

"Except I don't have one." Isobel frowned, and she finally glanced up to make eye contact with me. This was probably the longest we'd been in the same room, and I hadn't managed to piss her off yet. Although, I was sure my dumbass could come up with something quickly without trying.

"Then it's settled. I'm giving you a ride whether you like it or not."

The corner of her mouth quirked, a naughty little smirk forming as she glanced slowly at where I stood across from her desk. "Well, I have to say your tactics need a little work, but I can see that your confidence isn't lacking. Probably shouldn't tell the lady she won't like it, though. Seems a little counterproductive."

Fuck.

Blowing a breath, I tried not to take the bait, but as she crossed her arms over her chest, the movement pushed her breasts together enticingly, and my brain short-circuited.

"Well, if I were giving you that kind of ride, there wouldn't be any doubts about your enjoyment. But you would need to make sure your arms and legs were holding on tight because you might hurt yourself if you fall off."

She pinched her lips together but couldn't hide her smile or blush. I knew it was fucking stupid to say that to her, but I couldn't take it back now, and the more she fought with me, the more I craved the attention, even if it was me being a chauvinistic asshole.

"It's cute you think I'm interested in riding the kiddie rollercoaster, but don't worry, I'm sure someone will enjoy your quick and mediocre thrill ride."

Do not engage.

"Right." I blew out a breath, fighting back a retort because I didn't want to say anything else that she could turn around on me. And I definitely didn't want to offend her too much, since we were spending hours in a car together the next day. "Just email me your address, and I'll come to get you in the morning. Do we need to stop here before we head north?"

"No," she shook her head, returning her attention to the chaotic stack of papers on her desk. "I'll make sure Kristine has all the files she needs before I leave today."

I must have made a face at the mention of her intern because she narrowed her eyes and pointed toward the hallway.

"You know the way out. I'll email you if there is anything else we need to go over. I'm sure you've got things to take care of for your precious best sellers."

I couldn't shake the sense of unease at her comment, hating that things always seemed to sour when we were in the same room. I thought we'd come to a mutual agreement to try to behave around one another at the team-building exercise, but she still despised me. I wanted to say the feeling was mutual, but then I'd be even more of a liar.

I didn't want to hate her, as easy as it would be to do so. But the walls I'd constructed around myself ensured we'd never be more than colleagues who barely tolerated each other.

She'd made her distaste for me known regularly over the last several years, but I still couldn't deny I was attracted to her. I never dated within the office, but I'd shamelessly flirted with enough women to get a reaction out of her.

She claimed I was a manwhore. That wasn't a word I'd use to describe myself. I never went more than a few months between partners, but I was far from having a revolving door of pussy.

I didn't have the reputation that Hutch had when we were younger, but being the identical twin of the school Casanova—nicknamed *Big O* when we were fifteen—wasn't easy. It also meant that having the same face meant girls came after me because of his reputation alone. As a teenager, I wasn't proud enough to turn down willing partners, even if it was only my looks they were interested in.

It also didn't hurt in college that I got a lot of leeway from some of my more privileged classmates because I was attractive and an athlete. They didn't know the only reason I was even attending college was because of the scholarships I'd managed to obtain, and that I lived in the dorms all four years because I couldn't afford not to. Ma would have been fine with me commuting into the city daily, but Southie was a haul from Boston College, and I'd needed the time to study before and after classes and practice.

That was another thing I found hot about Isobel. We both loved baseball. Despite her choice of teams being a little lacking, it still intrigued me. But she was from the Midwest, so I could see why she was attached to the Cubbies. My fascination with the Sox started when I was barely old enough to hold a bat and continued through me wearing a Sox jersey and riding the pine for a few years after undergrad.

When I returned to my office, Sam was busy working at his small desk in the cubicle right outside my door, going through one of my mystery writer's newest manuscripts. I'd read the first four chapters, and the plot was solid like Evan's manuscripts typically were, but something about the character's interactions seemed clunky. Maybe Evan had spent too much time in seclusion over the last several years and had forgotten how to interact with people. Not that he was too keen on social interaction in general.

"How's it going?" I asked, leaning against the opening of his workspace. Sam sighed loudly before scrubbing a hand over his face and turning in my direction.

"It's not good. He's going to hate it, but several chapters need total rewrites. I don't see any other way around it."

"Fuck." Rubbing my fingers along my chin, I tried to think of the best way to approach this with Evan. He rarely required much hand holding, but I didn't want one rough storyline to tank his series of best sellers. "Just do a full developmental edit and send me the notes before you say anything to him. I know he's been showing signs of burnout lately, and I don't want any criticism to throw him off his game."

"Alright," Sam nodded. "I'll start over from the beginning and create a developmental file to send you."

"Just make sure you send it to me before you say anything to him. Dealing with Evan requires a little finesse." Sam smirked, shaking his head. I knew what he was thinking. "I'm capable of dealing with my authors, asshole. You can wipe off that douchey look on your face."

"Right on, boss," he laughed, putting his earbud back in and returning his attention to his tablet. I knew he thought I was an asshole, but he'd been a college athlete. He knew how things worked in that environment, especially as a scholarship athlete surrounded by rich kids. Only I wasn't lucky enough to get through it being the nice guy like he had. At least not the parts of myself I let people see.

FOUR

ISOBEL

BOSTON

CHECKING MY WATCH, I noted the time. *Way too fucking early.* That was the official time. But really, it was 6:42 am. It was still too fucking early to be awake, dressed—in hindsight, I should have worn something other than a pencil skirt—and waiting in the lobby of my apartment building for Adrian on a Saturday morning.

Saturday was the day I allowed myself the luxury of sleeping in, and this conference ruined it. Usually, I'd wake up at 9:00, walk to the café down the street for a latte at 10:00, and spend at least two hours reading something I wanted to read instead of what I was paid to read.

I couldn't complain. I got paid to do what I loved, but there was a difference between reading for pleasure and reading in editing mode. Half the time, once we got to the proofing stage, I wasn't absorbing the content of what I was reading; I was just scanning for grammatical flow and spelling errors.

My phone chimed in my pocket at precisely 6:45, so I grabbed the handle of my luggage and walked toward the front entrance, where I could see a black sedan idling in the loading zone. At least he was on time since he made me wake up this early. Just because conference registration began at noon didn't mean we had to be there at noon.

I would have been fine showing up at 2:30 and slipping upstairs to take a power nap before the arrival dinner started at 5:00.

But clearly, Adrian was one of those obnoxious morning people.

"Good morning, gorgeous. You look nice." He exited the driver's seat and jogged around the back of the car, popping the trunk and meeting me on the sidewalk.

"Hmm," I hummed, letting him take the handle from me to stow my suitcase next to his in the open trunk. His black leather messenger bag was neatly placed next to his sleek black luggage, not a scuff to be found. Knowing him, that thing was probably cleaned and polished every week. Mine was only wiped down if I spilled something on it.

"Ah, not a morning person," Adrian chuckled while he stepped around me and held open the passenger door.

"Please don't say something stupid like 'your chariot awaits, milady.' I don't have the patience for it this morning," I grumbled, bracing my hand on the door frame, climbing into the car, and dragging my purse and messenger bag with me.

Adrian closed the door and made his way to the driver's seat, glancing over at what I was sure was a frown on my face.

"Wow, remind me not to try to talk to you before 9:00."

"That'd be ideal," I agreed. "Let's just plan on that. You don't talk to me until then, and I go back to sleep. Like I should be right now."

"So, you don't want the coffee I picked up for you?"

Glancing at the cup holders, I saw two paper travel cups with steam built up at the opening of the lid. "What kind of coffee?"

"Don't sound so skeptical. I'm capable of being observant. It's a skinny mocha latte with one pump of sugar-free vanilla and one pump of sugar-free caramel. Two Stevias."

Adrian started laughing at my gob smacked expression. My shock at him, somehow, knowing my coffee order, was surely plastered across my face.

"Have you been stalking me? That's creepy. Even for you."

"Nah, I'm just that good," he teased with a wink.

Narrowing my eyes, I looked down at the other cup, turning it to inspect the label, when his hand moved to cover mine, guiding it to the correct cup.

"I asked Andrea what you order when she does the coffee runs."

"Still a bit creepy, but coffee is coffee, so thank you." This kind of thoughtfulness from him wasn't anticipated, but I'd take it.

"No problem. I was getting myself one and figured you'd appreciate it. Do we need to stop anywhere before we get on the highway?"

Turning to study his profile, I took in the neatly trimmed stubble, the crisp button-down shirt, then focused on the label of the other coffee in the cup holder to see if I could guess his order.

"Are you one of those morning people who only drink black coffee? Is that why you're such a dick? Because you drink the coffee of serial killers and don't load it up with fake sugar like a normal person?"

Adrian shook his head as he put on his turn indicator, pulled into traffic, grabbed his cup, and took a generous sip before glancing at me briefly. "No, I drink tea in the morning, with real sugar and heavy cream. No serial killer coffee for me. But it's nice to know how much of a monster you think I am."

Stunned at his confession, I picked at the label on my cup, suddenly feeling guilty that I aimed this much animosity toward him. We clearly had our differences, but he was being kind for once, and maybe I'd misjudged him a little.

"Sorry. I'm not much of a morning person."

"Yah don't say," he teased with a smirk before returning his attention to the early morning traffic. "I never would have guessed that. You have such a pleasant demeanor before dawn."

Thankfully, since it was ungodly early on the weekend, it didn't take us long to get on 95 headed north out of Boston. Four and a half hours in a car with him would surely test my patience. The small space was filled with the aroma of his cologne tinged with a hint of something sharp, likely his aftershave.

I'd noticed before that he smelled nice, but to sit in an enclosed space concentrated with it was sensory overload. Add in the thoughtful coffee provisions, and I was at a loss. He'd dragged me out of my apartment way too early to harbor fond feelings for him.

"What are your thoughts on chocolate hazelnut croissants?"

My mouth watered at the suggestion. I was a slut for croissants. "Are you asking because you have some or want to stop somewhere to buy them? Because we're less than a half-hour into an almost five-hour trip, which means we should probably keep driving."

"Because I might have a paper bag tucked behind my seat with two. But if you don't want one, I'm sure I can save it for breakfast in the morning. You never know if the continental breakfast will be dodgy at these things."

Before he even finished talking, I was leaning over the console, my fingers reaching for the brown paper bag that was barely visible in the dim lighting of the car.

"So, what are *you* having for breakfast?" I asked, opening the bag and holding it up to my face, the heady scent of fresh pastry laced with rich chocolate wafting into my nose.

"How experienced with hitchhiking are *you*?" He smirked, glancing at me. "Because if you steal my croissant, you'll need to hitchhike the rest of the way. You might want to cover up the high beams under that sweater, or you'll be sending the wrong message."

"So that's a yes to eating both croissants?"

"I brought you breakfast and coffee. Don't test me. I'll pull this car over and put you over my knee," he chuckled, reaching over to snatch the bag from me.

"You'd like that, wouldn't you?"

"Putting you over my knee?" He smirked while he pulled a croissant from the bag and placed it back on my lap. He took a large bite of his, talking with his mouth full. "I'm sure you'd like it more than I would, but sometimes all you need to put yourself in a good mood in the morning is a good open palm spanking."

"You get spanked often?" Taking a bite of the flaky pastry, I tried to hold in a moan, but was unsuccessful in my attempt. "Oh my god, this is amazing."

"Took you long enough to moan like that around me. You're welcome." Adrian shoved the rest of what was left of his into his mouth, moaning as he chewed. "Mmm. *This* is almost better than sex." He paused, licking his fingers.

"*Almost*. But to answer your question, no, it's been a while since I had a good spanking."

My eyes widened, not expecting that comment, but I wasn't sure if I even remembered sex. It hadn't just been a while. It'd been years. Probably nearing three if I had to narrow it down, and only if oral counted. I'd stopped keeping track after the first year.

It wasn't that I was holding out or anything, but with my work hours, the thought of dating made me want to pull my hair out. I'd been there, done that, and had the divorce papers stowed in my safe to prove it. I wasn't even sure how to use a dating app. My few failed attempts at dating another man had been from good old-fashioned talking to semi-intoxicated strangers in a dark bar.

Sometimes I wondered if I'd peaked early. My parents hadn't batted an eye when I got married right out of undergrad, and my sisters were already married by twenty. At least I finished my degree first. Grant had been another English major at Cornell, and we'd been the cliche couple. Met the first day of orientation, dated all four undergrad years, and had the stereotypical proposal at Christmas during senior year. Followed by a small wedding the following summer where my parents complained the entire time that I dared to get married in New York instead of Iowa.

We'd been happy, but I hadn't known anything different. It wasn't until I started my graduate classes at Boston College, when he started talking about having a family, that things began to change.

Two years later—after endless nights of bickering because sex had become a chore, a few devastating miscarriages followed by a slew of negative pregnancy tests, and a graduate degree—Grant asked for a divorce. He wanted to cut his losses if I couldn't provide the perfect family he wanted. Adrian often reminded me of a younger Grant, cocky, a little bit rude—the loveable asshole. Maybe that was why I disliked him so much. I'd been through his type once and wasn't sure I needed a repeat. Not that he was interested in me like that. But someone like him...they had the potential to break me.

"You're quiet all of a sudden. Should I be worried?" Adrian asked, staring out the windshield at the sun that'd started to just barely peek above the horizon line. "Was it the croissant sex reference? Although, on second thought, if you combined the two, you wouldn't have to choose. But you would have crumbs in the sheets, so that might be a deal-breaker."

"Just thinking." I interrupted his rambling line of commentary. He could be witty when he wanted to, but the problem was, he never wanted to. He'd rather remain on brand and be a dick. "You might want to try it sometime. Especially when you're about to start talking."

"As long as you're not plotting my murder, we're good."

"Not yet. But it's early. Anything can happen," I replied with a wink when he glanced over at me.

"Are you alright with stopping for lunch when we hit Brunswick? Or are you one of those people who power through a road trip without stopping?"

"Depends on who's buying."

"Considering we're on a work-related trip, I'd say Vivid is buying. Sloane did say we have a daily stipend."

"Well, I'm going to get some work done while you're driving, if you don't mind. I have a few proofs I need to look over." And I wanted to avoid talking for now. Our conversations usually felt more like a boxing match than anything else, so it'd be better if we didn't tempt fate.

"Go for it." He reached over and pressed a few buttons on the touch-screen in the console, and soft rock music filled the car. Somehow, I knew he'd be a Springsteen man.

Disappearing into my tablet for a few hours, I didn't realize how far we'd come until the car decelerated, and Adrian took an exit leading us toward the water. It was chilly, but still a sunny day, and the water sparkled as he crossed a bridge that took us over some half-frozen marshland.

"Where are we going?"

He smiled, nodding toward a building that looked like a fishing shack, suspended over the water with a questionable-looking dock coming right up to the road.

"I know we don't always get along, but was it necessary to drag me out of bed before dawn and drive me to the middle of nowhere to dispose of my body? You could have at least let me sleep in."

"If I were going to be doing anything with your body, it wouldn't involve disposing of it," he chuckled, pulling off along the side of the road onto the gravel shoulder. "I hope you like fresh lobster."

"I do like lobster, but don't feel like needing a tetanus shot to buy it." Two fishing boats were moored at the side of the building with chipped paint and lobster cages stacked up on the deck. "Are they even open?"

He reached behind me, pulling his jacket off the back seat. "Yes."

"Where did you find this place? Serialkillerlairs.com? This looks like a sketchy location to dump bodies from one of your authors' novels."

"Are you always this uptight?" His smile was teasing and a little disarming. Why did he have to be so damn attractive? It wasn't fair. His face did things to my lady parts. It was the mouth that made me want to kick him. Repeatedly. In the crotch.

"You didn't answer my question."

"You didn't answer mine."

He shook his head as he pulled the handle on his door, stepping out and closing the door behind him.

I stowed my tablet in my bag, pulling out my wallet and the cardigan I'd tucked inside.

Before I could reach for the car door handle, Adrian pulled it open and extended his hand to help me out. At least I'd skipped the heels this morning, my sensible flats crunching on the gravel as he pulled me from the car.

"Thanks."

"I'm not *always* a dick," he whispered, taking my cardigan from my hand and holding it open for me to put my arms into the sleeves. "Just most of the time."

I shivered, not from the cold, crisp ocean air but the proximity of his large, warm body behind me.

"Maybe there's a gentleman hidden in there after all. He's just deep, deep inside."

"*That's what she said,*" he chuckled before he stepped away and gestured with his head toward the dock. I hadn't anticipated him being a fan of *The Office*, but Adrian was full of surprises this morning.

"Or does she have to ask if it's even in?" I teased, falling into step behind him. "There's no shame if she does, but maybe your definition of deep differs from hers."

He glanced at me with an amused smirk, not rising to take the bait. At least, I didn't think he had, until he pulled open the wooden door to the building and gestured for me to enter.

"Trust me. *She* wouldn't have to question with me. *She'd* know precisely how *deep* I was." Well, okay then. "Yelp. I found the restaurant on Yelp, not the dark web. People raved about the lobster roll," he confessed while the door closed behind us. "And rumor is their blueberry crumble is orgasmic. At least according to one reviewer. She didn't have the same flair for words as some of your authors, but it was a compelling story of their positive attributes, despite the outward exterior of the building not matching the caliber of the menu."

Adrian's positive attributes were starting to not match the dickish exterior, so maybe there was something to be said about trusting what was on the inside. I wasn't even acknowledging his emphasis on the word *she* as if he meant me.

But I knew Maine was famous for two things: lobster and blueberries. So hopefully, I didn't end up with food poisoning from the former, and the Yelp reviews didn't lead Adrian astray on the latter.

As we reached the end of a narrow hallway, enormous glass paneled garage doors lined the wall that overlooked the water. The place was large and open, with high, sloped ceilings and slow-moving fans dotted throughout the dining area. Worn wood floors stretched the room, clearly restored.

It certainly kept the vibe of an old fishery, but it wasn't as scary as it looked from the outside.

"Will this work?" Adrian asked, leading us to a small table with two chairs that overlooked the water.

"You're full of surprises today," I commented, looking out over the nearly frozen bay. Having grown up in a small town as flat as the water appeared outside and surrounded by cornfields, I was still stunned by the natural beauty of New England, despite having been in the region for over a decade.

"Maybe I'm just surprising you because you buy into the perception of others. Sometimes when you get to know someone beneath all the layers they hide behind, their personality isn't what it seems."

"Are we going to pretend that you don't actively antagonize people in the office? Because if I were the only one who noticed it, you wouldn't have half the staff on our floor referring to you as Dickhead."

"I never said that. I'll own up to being a dick," he chuckled, sitting back in his chair with his arms folded across his chest. I hadn't noticed it in the dark, but an enticing patch of dark hair peeked above the buttons of his open collar. "But despite my giant dick, there is more to me than meets the eye."

While I would have expected him to be vain enough to wax or shave his chest, seeing it sent a wave of something I couldn't quite identify through my system. But my physical attraction to Adrian had never been surprising. It was his behavior that'd formed my intense dislike toward him.

"I'll take your word for it. You can keep the supposedly giant dork, I mean dick, to yourself."

The server interrupted what I was sure would be a riveting conversation laced liberally with the word dick, telling us the specials for the day.

"The lobstah rolls are amazin', but owah chowdah just won a few awahds this past summah at the local food festival. And the oystah plattah is top-natch."

Even after living in Boston for nearly a decade, it still took my brain a second to catch up to the New England accent sometimes. Adrian smirked knowingly at my confused expression, sensing I was still trying to translate what she'd said in my head.

"We'll take two rolls, two cups-a chowdah, and a small oystah plattah to share. Just a wattah to drink," Adrian ordered without hesitation, dropping seamlessly into his natural accent.

I tried to contain my blush as she walked away, but he'd totally caught me.

"That shoulda been a piece of cake to you by now," he teased, reaching forward to snag his glass and take a long drink. I watched his throat flex as he swallowed and then averted my eyes to the frozen waterfront outside while he licked the remaining moisture from his top lip.

"What if I don't like oysters?"

He let out a loud laugh. "Who doesn't like oysters? They're like slippery little slices of ambrosia."

"You probably just like them because they're supposed to make you horny."

"Now, who's the crass one?" Adrian laughed, that annoying smirk out in full force.

"Well, the high zinc content and amino acids found in oysters are supposed to increase your dopamine levels, which increases libido, and I don't think yours needs any encouragement."

Luckily, the server returned with our food before I could throw out any more of the fun, useless facts I had crammed into my brain and filled every inch of the surface of our table with amazing-smelling Maine cuisine.

"I'm not sure I even know how to eat an oyster," I confessed as she walked away.

"That's half the fun," Adrian winked, reaching toward the metal platter in the center of the table. He carefully picked up one of the small half-shells, taking a little fork from the side of the platter and slowly running it along the underside of the delicate meat in the center.

"First, you need to be very gentle with them. Oysters are meant to be savored."

Goosebumps cropped up on the back of my neck at the lowered tone of his voice and how he looked at me through half-lidded eyes. It made me wonder if explaining oyster consumption was turning into some seduction routine. Or the more disturbing thought that this was part of his usual repertoire.

"When you pick one up..." I was mesmerized by the gentleness in his quiet voice as he leaned down and studied the oyster in his fingers. "... be very careful not to tip it. The liquid around the oyster is where half the flavor comes from. It keeps the center juicy, and you know how important it is that the center stays *wet*."

Something was involuntarily getting wet at the low tenor of his voice.

"Then you don't just suck it down like a Neanderthal and swallow, although that method does have its merits." He winked with a gleam in his eyes.

"Are we still talking about oysters here?"

"Mind in the gutter, Isobel?"

"You know what you're doing," I laughed, his enjoyment at my squirming evident in his gaze.

"It's not my fault you have a dirty mind. I'm just over here trying to savor my lunch."

"Mmhmm."

"Anyway, as I was saying, before your one-track mind interrupted me..." He brought the shell to his mouth, gently tipping it back and sucking the contents of the oyster into his mouth—humming as his eyes closed briefly. His jaw flexed, chewing once before swallowing, making eye contact with me as he returned the empty shell to the table. "Slowly suck it into your mouth and feel its weight on your tongue. Have it sit there for a moment—letting the flavor flood your palate—and when it explodes, swallow."

"Sounds like your oyster might be short on the trigger if it explodes after just a moment."

"Just pick up the oyster, smartass. I'll help you." Gently placing one oyster into my hand, Adrian's warm palm covered the back of my hand as he pressed the tiny fork into my other. "Don't stab it. Slide the tines underneath the edge of the meat and slowly scrape it loose."

His larger hands guided mine in gentle movements until I felt the center give.

"Now, close your eyes and open your mouth." He grinned widely when I frowned at him. "Just trust me for once."

Taking a deep breath, I closed my eyes and slowly parted my lips, waiting semi-patiently as Adrian lifted our joined hands to place the tip of the shell at my lips.

I swallowed, my mouth suddenly parched.

"Are you ready for me?" he asked in a rough whisper, and I licked my lips, swallowing again as I let my jaw relax. "Good girl. Here it comes."

This was not how I expected spending my lunch today when I was rudely dragged out of my apartment this morning under duress. I thought Adrian would be a jerk on the car ride to Bar Harbor, and I'd be forced to sit in angry tension with him in the car for nearly five hours.

Three hours into our trip, and I was being taught how to eat oysters in a strangely erotic display of skill inside a building I'd thought was a murder shed.

As I held my breath, waiting for him to tip the oyster shell, my mouth suddenly flooded with a rush of savory flavors I wasn't sure I could describe properly. I kept my eyes closed, doing as he said and savoring the tang of the oyster meat on my tongue. He was right. The oysters were delicious.

"One bite," he instructed, taking the shell from my hand and lightly touching my chin with his finger, encouraging me to chew.

Another burst of flavor spread through my mouth; the rich nutty flavor mixed with the saltiness, causing me to groan as I bit down.

"Swallow," Adrian coaxed as I opened my eyes, almost startled by the intensity of his gaze when they focused on his across the table. "Fuckin' amazing, right?"

Nervously lifting my napkin, I dabbed at my wet lips, nodding. "You're right."

"Of course I am," he chuckled, grabbing another shell from the plate and quickly downing another before winking at me like the last two minutes hadn't been some bizarre culinary foreplay. "Make sure to save room for that crumble. Rumor has it they make their *cream* fresh."

And my mind plummeted back into the gutter at the other variety of fresh cream I knew watching Adrian teach me how to eat oysters had inspired. This unwanted physical attraction to him had become a nuisance once the dickish behavior was taken out of the picture. I had the feeling this trip would either cement my hatred—or at least major distaste—for him, or my physical attraction to him would turn into something else.

FIVE

ADRIAN

BAR HARBOR, ME

Five hours and forty minutes. Five *fucking* hours and forty minutes after we left Boston, I was pulling up to the parking lot at the hotel where the conference was being held with a semi in my pants and a raging attraction to the woman in my passenger seat.

I'd always thought that Isobel was gorgeous. Of course, I had, but I hadn't realized how funny she was outside of staff meetings or when she was biting my head off for saying something stupid. She'd loosened up when we were throwing axes at a target, showing me a whole new side of herself, but this morning was surprisingly fun.

When we'd left her apartment, I'd thought the annoyed, sleepy grump would be a pain in the ass to ride in the car with for hours on end. But then she turned on a level of sass over croissant and coffee that I never imagined seeing. And I have to say, I appreciated her fire...more than I cared to admit. She was sarcastic and quick-witted, and I found my armor dropping as I engaged with her.

Isobel clearly didn't know how to handle my teasing when it wasn't mean-spirited or downright offensive, her posture changing to one of surprise at my unintentionally flirtatious comments. But then, when we stopped for lunch, and she'd continued the playful banter, I couldn't help pouring on the charm.

I knew how to flirt with women with intention, and I knew I shouldn't be doing it over a lunch that was technically being paid for by our publisher and was not a date, but her reactions made me want to tease her more and more.

The urge to lean down and kiss the back of her neck when I was helping her into her sweater before lunch had been strong, and it'd grown exponentially after all the innuendo while we were eating. She'd been a quick study in oyster eating protocol and had easily devoured the rest of her lunch, licking butter off her fingers from the lobster roll and moaning her way through the chowder. It was the sexiest display of food porn I'd ever witnessed firsthand. Isobel wasn't afraid to eat, making me want to find more foods that brought out those little moans.

I'd been tempted to ask the server for a dessert to share, thinking there was no way Isobel could finish a blueberry crumble with all she'd eaten, but she'd hovered over that warm bowl like she was in prison, and I was going to shank her for it. I had to think of Pop's wrinkly nutsack just to keep myself from getting hard as I watched her tongue dart out to lick the fresh cream from her lips. Correction—I had to think of that horrifying scene to stop myself from getting hard-*er*.

"Here we are," I said, breaking the silence that'd settled in the car.

As I pulled up to the main entrance overhang, slowly depressing the brake and moving the car into park, I felt like this was a pivotal moment in this trip. Would she go back to not so secretly despising me once she had other people to spend her time with, or would we continue to build this tension between us until someone caved?

"Yup, here we are," she murmured, looking down at her lap.

"You go on ahead to the check-in desk. I'll bring in your bag," I offered as I looked over at her fidgeting with the strap of her bag. She seemed to do that when she was angry or nervous, her fingers fixating on whatever was closest and mindlessly playing with it.

"I'm perfectly capable of rolling a small suitcase."

"Not saying you aren't, but if you go get the keys to your room while I'm parking the car, you won't have to wait as long to escape me. It looks like people are starting to arrive."

The parking lot was gradually filling, and I knew the place would be crawling with publishing industry professionals vying for each other's attention in a few hours.

"Thank you for offering to drive up here," she mumbled, taking a deep breath, her chest heaving before she slowly let it out. A few stray hairs had escaped from her ponytail, and I suddenly had the urge to tuck them behind her ear—or just rip the hair tie out of her hair and sink my fingers in. I clenched my hands in my lap, so I wasn't tempted to touch her. I'd meant what I said to her the night of the team-building exercise that'd thrown us together. I didn't want to kiss or touch her in a stolen moment or out of pity. I wanted her to desire my hands or lips on her, but I knew it was a long shot for that to happen. It was a good thing I possessed a fuck ton of patience. Either that, or I was delusionally hopeful.

"Just pop the trunk so I can grab it. Thank you for offering, but I'd like to get up to my room and unpack. I wanted to go over the schedule before tonight."

And we were back to the professional behavior, our earlier teasing gone before I could fully appreciate it.

"If that's what you want."

Before I could comment further, she was out the passenger door, briskly walking toward the back of the car with one hand holding her sweater closed at the neck. The further north we'd traveled, the more the temperature had dropped, the breeze from the water carrying a chill. I hoped she'd packed a jacket because it seemed like a loss to spend the entire weekend indoors.

While Hutch and I typically stayed a little more inland in our explorations, we'd driven up to the Acadia National Park to hike quite a bit as teenagers during the off-season. We'd both tossed around the idea of hiking the Appalachian trail someday, but with his leg being like it was, I wasn't sure we'd ever be able to do the whole thing and rough it on the trail. But maybe we could take the time to complete part of it. With forty-one rapidly approaching, it wasn't like we could wait forever. I was already starting to feel my age sometimes.

The trunk slammed, pulling me out of my wandering thoughts and back to the confusing woman I worked with, watching her figure pass through the hotel's front doors. I knew we'd have to spend the five-hour car trip home with each other, but I wondered if this was the last I'd see of her the next four days except in passing.

Pulling into a spot in the corner of the parking lot, I shifted the car into park and scrubbed my hand over my jaw, trying to clear my head. Sloane had texted me late last night that the conference organizers had wanted to put me in a slot to speak during a workshop, one of the other presenters having to miss the conference at the last minute.

I confirmed I'd do it, but now I was second-guessing myself, not wanting to take the opportunity away from Isobel if she'd wished for it. I'd spoken at things like these a few times and had a vague idea of what I could talk about, but I knew Isobel felt like her genre was often overlooked at general industry events.

Rumor had it that she was typically a big hit at romance writing events, but this wasn't a conference geared toward romance writers and editors; this was a group of our peers from every genre. I still remembered being in awe of the presenters and speakers at the first few conferences I'd attended before working at Vivid, wondering if I'd ever get to that point in my career.

Isobel was nowhere to be found when I entered the building, joining the line at the reception desk to get checked in. Part of me wished this was being held at one of the larger hotel chains because I had reward member status at most of them and never had to wait in lines because of how much I typically traveled, but I had to admit, this local resort was beautiful. And the water views couldn't be replicated at some generic box hotel chain.

Growing up close to the ocean had always been something I'd taken for granted, but with my travel all over the country, I'd still come back to New England in a heartbeat. I couldn't imagine living anywhere else. The food, the people—despite some being dicks—and the views couldn't be found anywhere else.

When I was younger, I would have looked for any viable reason to get outta Southie, but even that changed as time passed. I thought baseball would always be my dream, but sometimes priorities change when entering the real world.

My single season riding the bench in the majors and the few brutal seasons in the minors before that pushed me to finish my graduate degree and start focusing on my career like I should have been doing. It'd been a no-brainer to retire when my grandma was diagnosed with terminal cancer. Sometimes we have to let go of childish dreams and come to terms with reality. Maybe that was why I'd clung so hard to the hardened exterior I showed everyone else.

"Your colleague has already checked in," the woman at the reception desk said after I handed her my ID and my corporate credit card. "But like I told her, your rooms are adjoining, so you'll be near each other."

Well, that changed things. Maybe Isobel wouldn't be able to avoid me so easily after all. We'd be passing each other in the hallway. Our schedules were supposed to be similar, except for the few sessions Sloane wanted us to attend that were scheduled simultaneously.

The elevator ride to our floor was quiet, my mind whirring with fantasies I knew would never play out. One, in particular, was of me throwing open those adjoining doors and letting this budding attraction play out. She would never admit it, but I'd seen lingering glances on her end. Her hatred may have been the more prevalent of her feelings for me, but there was attraction there too.

As I walked down the hallway toward my room, the door next to mine slipped open, Isobel not noticing my arrival while she stared down at the phone in her hand.

"Guess you couldn't escape me after all."

Her shoulders stiffened when she heard my voice, her eyes slowly rising to meet mine. "Guess not. Lucky me."

As she tried to step past me, my hand shot out, halting her forward movement as my fingers brushed the sleeve of her coat. "Where're you off to?"

She hesitated, toying with the zipper as I scanned her face. Her sensible skirt and ballet flats had been swapped out for some joggers and what appeared to be trail running shoes. "Going for a little hike. The concierge said there is a trailhead not far from here. Wanted to work off some energy before dinner since the weather is so nice."

"Want some company?" I asked, and she paused as she took in my outfit. While it wouldn't be ideal, my pants were loose enough that I could handle a little hike if I put on my trail sneakers. I'd also planned to sneak off during our stay here to explore the local trails, but I couldn't deny the company would make it exponentially better. "Unless you don't think you can keep up. The trails around here aren't always for beginners."

Her eyes narrowed, her face morphing into one of annoyance as she took the bait I'd placed in her path. "I think I can keep up fine with *you*."

Biting my lip, I tried to conceal my amusement at the competitiveness in her voice. "Didn't say you couldn't. Not everything needs to be a competition."

"You've got ten minutes, and then I'm leaving without you. Hopefully, you can get your primping in that quickly."

"I'm sure I can manage," I chuckled, reaching over to swipe my key card across the reader on my door. "I'm not as high maintenance as some people."

A cute little growl sounded from her throat at my dig, and she stepped around me, not turning around while I watched her disappear toward the elevator. She was so easy to wind up. "Go change your damn clothes. The clock is ticking."

Tossing my luggage on the large king-sized bed, I unzipped it, pulling out the little zipper bag that held my shoes. Yes, even my suitcase was packed using storage cubes. Organization tripped my trigger. I couldn't help it, and it made packing and unpacking easier. When you spent half your year in hotels, you tired of digging through a messy suitcase.

Isobel was pacing off to the side of the parking lot when I walked out the front entrance to the building, her mouth moving like she was muttering to herself while she stared at the phone in her hand. Hopefully, she'd disconnect for a while and attempt to enjoy the beautiful scenery of this part of coastal Maine.

The water was calm today, the surface gently rippling and dotted with thick patches of ice. The seasonal thaw would begin in a few weeks from now, and everything would bloom when spring set in.

"Did you bring water?" I asked as I flipped one of the bottles in my hand, catching it in my palm easily after the first rotation.

"It's not a very long hike," she scoffed, finally looking up at me before tucking her phone into her vest pocket and zipping it shut.

"Guess it's a good thing I grabbed two from the front desk," I smiled, extending the one I'd been tossing in her direction. "You should never go hiking without fresh water."

"I would've been fine. I wasn't planning to stay out that long."

"Hmm," I hummed as I fell into step beside her as she made her way along a path to the side of the property that led along the coastline.

"You don't have to be such a know-it-all. I am capable of doing basic things like keeping myself hydrated."

"Don't worry, I don't doubt your ability to quench your thirstiness."

She frowned, taking a few steps away. "If you weren't such a dick to me all the time, I wouldn't have to be so defensive around you."

"I haven't been a total dick to you today, have I?"

Unlike when we were in the office, I'd been trying to keep the mask off around her, resorting to teasing because that was my natural personality, not actively antagonizing her.

"No, just maybe a tiny dick."

I hummed, quickening my pace to walk beside her again. Lowering my voice, I whispered in her ear as I leaned closer. "Not the typical adjective women use when talking about my dick."

"I'll take your word for it. Although, you have been known to exaggerate quite a bit. I'll find my magnifying glass if your dick comes up again. Not that there's anything wrong with you if it can't *rise* to the occasion, I've heard it's common at your advanced age."

"You're like a year younger than me," I chuckled, and watched as a crease formed on her forehead. She was probably surprised I knew that. But she wasn't the only one capable of being observant. Her tenure with Vivid was longer, but we were nearly the same age and likely had similar experiences in our career paths.

We walked side by side down the trail, the path winding in and out of the wooded trail to hug the rocky coast. The air was crisp and cool, but it felt invigorating after spending so much time confined in the car.

"So, do you hike a lot?" I asked while she played with the edge of the label on the bottle clasped tightly in her hands.

"Some. Mostly in college in upstate New York. We didn't have places like this back home. I mean, you could find places with some hills or forests, but nothing this pretty."

"And where is home?" I asked, realizing I knew little about her besides her educational pedigree and career.

"Cumming, Iowa."

"Seriously?" I laughed. There was no way that was the name of a town.

"Yes, seriously," she huffed. "Go ahead and make the joke now, it's not anything I haven't heard before."

"Sounds like someone is a little sensitive about *Cumming*."

"That wasn't even funny."

"Wasn't trying to be funny, I'm not a total dick all the time."

"I don't even want to imagine the things that would come out of your mouth otherwise."

"I prefer to come other places."

"You're an idiot." She rolled her eyes, but she smiled so she couldn't be that annoyed with me.

"And what's in *Cumming,* Iowa?"

She slowed her pace as she began to peel back the corner of the water bottle label. "My parent's farm, my sisters and their hordes of children. Mostly boredom."

"I can't imagine you on a farm," I laughed, somehow unable to reconcile the polished business attire and conservative apparel she opted to wear with the imagery of ripped jeans, matching braids, and a worn baseball cap.

"Well, I can't imagine you in anything but a tailored suit, and yet here we are," she said, gesturing toward my jeans and button-up shirt I'd thrown a lightweight coat over.

"I'm capable of being casual. I wore sweatpants for most of my time at B.C."

"Yeah, okay," she scoffed, clearly not believing me.

"Or baseball pants. But that was only for games."

She turned to look over at me. "You played baseball in college?"

"I'm a man of many talents," I joked, earning an eye roll. "But yeah. Centerfield. All of undergrad." And those few years after, when I'd thought I might have some genuine talent.

"Ah, so you weren't a very good baseball player. They stick all the slackers in the outfield."

"Excuse me? Maybe in little league, but not in college." I corrected; my bottle perched at my lips as I looked over at her in disbelief. Collegiate baseball was hardly little league. You had to be able to haul ass to be an outfielder and have a rocket arm. My team had some solid wins in my tenure, several of us moving onto the minors after we earned a spot in the College World Series. *Not very good, my ass.*

"Oh, come on, you can unclench now. I was joking. I was a catcher throughout high school. I'm familiar with the sport."

"Ah, so that explains why your ass is so spectacular," I teased, watching a blush form on her cheeks.

"Well, my squat routine isn't what it was twenty years ago, so I don't know about spectacular..."

Exaggerating my movements as I leaned back and pretended to study her ass, I appreciated her selection of pants. They accentuated her narrow waist, tapering into the alluring curve of her ass. It was the perfect amount of bubble. I appreciated that Isobel took care of herself but still had some amazing curves. The more muscular women who lacked them at the gym weren't nearly as fun to cuddle—and do other things with. I liked my women to be a handful, apparently in personality as well, since my attraction to Isobel continued to grow.

"I'm sticking with spectacular. Maybe even bordering on magnificent."

"Quit staring at my ass," she laughed, reaching back to cover herself.

"Hey, don't cover up my view. Didn't you know I came on this hike for the scenery?"

"How about you enjoy the nature on the trail instead of making crude comments about one of your colleagues' rear ends?"

"If I were being crude, I would have told you I often imagine biting it. Or fantasizing about seeing if you really could bounce a quarter off someone's posterior."

"There's something wrong with you," she muttered, picking up the pace and leaving me admiring the view again.

"But I think you like it," I called after her.

She may have acted annoyed by my flirting and admittedly inappropriate comments, but she couldn't hide from me with that blush. It was a dead giveaway that I made her flustered.

As we reached the trailhead, Isobel kept a steady pace, veering onto a path that hugged the coast. We walked in silence; me staring blatantly at the slightly cranky woman in front of me and her looking around in awe at our surroundings.

"Can we go down to that beach?"

I shrugged, gesturing for her to lead me down the small path to a rocky beach leading out to the calm water. It wasn't ideal for swimming, but it had a breathtaking panoramic view of the coastline. Inhaling deeply, I took in the fresh scent of the ocean, closing my eyes and enjoying the slight breeze on my face.

"Should I brave it and dip my toes in?" Isobel asked quietly from her place at my side.

"If you want to lose a few. You realize that water is freezing, right?"

She paused for a moment, nibbling on the corner of her lip as she debated this impulsive decision. "I'm going for it."

"Should I be prepared to carry you back with frostbitten toes?"

She narrowed her eyes and put her hands on her hips, not looking the slightest bit intimidating. "Laugh it up, buzz kill. I'm trying to enjoy myself."

"Personally, I quite enjoy having my toes intact."

"Wimp," she muttered before she leaned down to untie her shoes, her joggers pulling snugly over her ass. Her squat routine may not be the same as when she was a catcher, but whatever she did worked.

"Man, you are an old fuddy-duddy," she laughed while she rolled up the cuffs of her pants. I surely hoped to God she wasn't planning to wade in there. February was still squarely in the winter season.

"Well, I spend a lot of my free time with octogenarians," I replied, crossing my arms over my chest.

She paused, straightening back up and turning in my direction. "Seriously? Why?"

"Why not?" I laughed at the confused expression on her face. "They're easy to school at cards."

"So, let me get this straight. You regularly seek out the elderly to take advantage of them at card games? Wow." At this point, I wasn't sure how anything I said still surprised her. Or that she took any of it seriously.

"Nah, they usually end up wiping the floor with me. Those old dudes cheat like crazy." Pop's crew ran the bridge league and the older people's poker ring in the neighborhood without mercy. Not only did they trash talk, but they had decades of experience and were brutal with their strategy. It also didn't hurt that their poker faces were exceptional because they'd spent years exaggerating the stories of their youth and were expert liars.

"That's kind of cute. You play cards with the elderly. I wasn't aware you possessed compassion toward a marginalized demographic."

I knew she was making a dig at my comments about her authors—and the romance genre in general—but I had to be prepared to take the backlash when I said something offensive.

"You'd be surprised about what else I possess."

She rolled her eyes, peeling off her socks and tucking them inside her shoes. "Of course, you're talking about your dick again."

"I wasn't, but clearly, you've been thinking about it. You keep bringing it up." *In more than just conversation.*

"Shut up," she growled while I squinted at the hint of a tattoo on her ankle that peaked from beneath the hem of her pants. How had I never noticed that before? If she wouldn't smack me, I'd roll her pants up more, so I could read the text disappearing beneath them. And maybe trace it...with my tongue.

"You're seriously doing this?" I asked, mildly concerned for the well-being of her feet, but she clearly didn't care for my opinion. I hadn't been joking when I'd told her the water would be frigid. I'd done enough polar plunges in my time to know the Atlantic during the spring was brutal. And February was practically arctic.

"Come on, join me," she urged as she extended her palm toward me. "Maybe dipping your toes in freezing water will short circuit your brain, and you'll stop being a dickhead all the time."

Chuckling, I reached down to untie my shoes and pull them off with my socks. She was trying to hide a smile as she watched me. "If you're that desperate to hold my hand, I'll join you, but I'm not carrying you back when your feet hurt."

"I'd never expect you to be a gentleman. Don't worry about that," she shot back, her eyes dancing with humor.

"Oh, she's got jokes," I laughed, grabbing her hand and tugging her toward the waterline—the feeling of the stones under my feet was like freezing little pricks against my skin. "We'll see how much you're laughing in a minute."

Isobel's giggle as I tugged her forward was infectious, and I found myself laughing while I watched her reaction when our toes hit the water. "Oh, fuck!" she shrieked, reaching out to cling to my shoulders. "It's so cold! Oh my God, it hurts!"

Chuckling, I reached forward and grasped her waist, lifted her to my chest and banded my arms around her thighs before I walked back toward the rock where we'd left our shoes. "Happy now?"

"Oh, come on," she giggled as she looked down at me. "You barely got your feet wet."

"Just put your shoes on. We've only got an hour before we need to get changed."

Isobel pouted as I leaned forward, depositing her on the ground next to our shoes. "Oh, I'm sorry," she laughed, her hand grasping the side of my neck. Before I could react, she'd run her fingers up the back of my neck and ruffled my hair. "I forgot you'd need time for your beauty routine."

Deciding to call her bluff, I left my hair in the chaotic mess she'd created, reaching down to unroll the denim at my ankles.

"Oh no, I made him mad," she laughed while she tugged her socks over her wet feet, wincing as she rubbed her cold toes.

"Sit down," I ordered, shoving my socked feet into my shoes and gesturing to a boulder on the shore behind her.

"What? Why?" she asked, picking up her shoes. I grabbed them from her and stepped forward, causing her to back into the rock, her eyes widening as she looked up at me.

"Just sit."

She stumbled backward, bracing her arms on the rock behind her while I crouched down at her feet. "What are you doing?"

"Taking care of you." Reaching forward to cup one of her feet, I slowly righted the damp sock on her foot and rubbed her toes with my much warmer hands. She'd survive, but I was sure she was feeling the sting of the frigid water. Normally I wouldn't advocate hiking in wet socks, but it wasn't like she'd left us with an option. Thankfully, the trail was on the short side and would dump us back on the other side of the hotel parking lot.

"You don't need to...*oh*..." she gasped as I did the same to her other foot, leaning forward to exhale a stream of hot air at the tips of her covered toes before rubbing them with my palms.

"Don't need you slowing us down if I'm going to do something to this mess," I chuckled, gesturing to the riot of hair on top of my head and reaching for one of her shoes.

She watched with wide eyes while I slipped on her other shoe and quickly tied the laces, reaching out to extend my hand in her direction.

Her gaze softened when she leaned forward, drawing her fingers through my disheveled hair and slowly combing the strands back into place.

"There. I don't think you'll frighten off the wildlife anymore."

Isobel's chest heaved while her fingers lingered near one of my sideburns, slowly rubbing the short strands, sending a bolt of lust straight through my system.

"And here I was, hoping to show off my manly prowess to protect you." My voice was an octave lower, my hands lingering at her delicate ankles once her shoes were securely in place.

Her eyes connected with mine as she continued to rub her fingers against my skin. My fingers twitched with the urge to cover hers, but I stayed where I was, under the spell of her gaze.

"We should go," she whispered, drawing her hand back and flexing her fingers while I stood.

"Ladies first," I smiled, gesturing back to the trail.

"You just want to stare at my ass again."

Wiggling my eyebrows as I stepped back for her to get in front of me, I confirmed her suspicions. "Damn straight, I do."

And surprisingly, she didn't say anything as I fell into step directly behind her.

Chapter SIX

ISOBEL

BAR HARBOR, ME

WHEN WE CROSSED THE state line into Maine, we must have crossed into an alternate universe. One where the guy I wanted to vote 'most likely to be muzzled' in the office had somehow turned into a charming reincarnation of himself that I had a hard time keeping my thoughts clean around.

At lunch, I'd thought naughty things about him. Bad, dirty, filthy things that I should never be thinking about Adrian, yet somehow, I couldn't stop. When he made playful comments about my ass, I found myself blushing instead of wanting to cram a red pen into his eye socket. When he offered to wheel my suitcase up to my room, I wanted to drag him inside to see what he kept under all those suits.

I'd seen glimpses here and there in the gym on the first floor of our office building, but never up close, and I usually bolted in the other direction if I saw him because I detested him.

I did.

I detested him completely.

But I also might be developing a bit of a crush on this fictionalized version of him.

One of my authors, Chase, had written his kind of hero dozens of times, the grumpy ass-wipe who terrorized everyone in his office but secretly had a heart of gold or simped hard for the *sunshiny* heroine. I *was not* a sunshine heroine. I was a tired divorcee almost past her prime, who never dated and delved into the psyche of fictional men all day.

As we headed back toward the small oceanside resort, I flexed my toes inside my shoes, knowing I'd need to soak them in warm water once we returned to our room. I mean *rooms*—separate rooms, plural—because I was not staying with Adrian in the same room. This wasn't some forced proximity trope that would force the two main characters to realize their true feelings for each other.

The only true feeling I was having toward Adrian right now was suspicion. Where was this funny, playful, considerate man while his alter ego was off terrorizing his co-workers with elitist comments about his authors and nasty comments that were borderline sexual harassment? I didn't know *this* Adrian. In the five years since I'd had the misfortune to work in the same office as him, I'd never once seen him act like this.

And it was fucking with my head. Big time.

"Are you not going to talk to me anymore? Your toes are frozen, not your tongue," Adrian teased from behind me. I could see him walking in my peripheral vision, and I may have caught him stumbling over a tree root because he'd been staring at my ass.

Do not think about his tongue. Or what it'd feel like in your mouth, or licking your...

God, it had been far too long since I'd had a man do anything remotely sexual to me, and now I was projecting years of pent-up tension on Adrian. That's what it was. I couldn't possibly *like* him. No. Just no.

He was *Dickhead.*

"Didn't your mother ever teach you it was better to say nothing than make small talk with someone who is just flirting with you to entertain themselves?"

Adrian reached forward to grab my elbow, stopping me in my tracks as a shock ran through my arm at the contact.

"That's what you think?" he asked, his voice low and slightly menacing.

"What other reason do you have for acting like you have for the past six and a half hours? I don't know who this guy is, but it sure isn't you."

"God," he scoffed as he released me and scrubbed his hand over his face, thrusting his fingers into the hair I'd recently had my fingers in. "Nice to know how you really feel about me, Isobel. I thought we'd finally come to some sort of cease-fire, but all the flirting from you today must have been fake too. I guess that's what I get for finally letting my guard down around you. Couldn't possibly be that I'm attracted to the stunning woman who gives as good as she gets. Nope, I just got something else. A square kick to the nuts."

My eyes widened when he strode toward me, his shoulder brushing mine as he squeezed around me and took off down the trail. His long legs ate up the path, my shorter ones breaking into a jog behind him, trying to keep up. I knew he'd been different today, but I still had difficulty believing that this was his real personality. I'd never seen it before. Excuse me for being a little blindsided by this sudden change in demeanor.

"Wait," I huffed, trying to keep up with him.

"Don't bother," he shot back when he hit the black asphalt in the parking lot and didn't turn around. "I guess I'll see you around, but don't worry, I won't bother trying to talk to you. Wouldn't want to upset *princess* by trying to get to know her or anything."

"Shit," I muttered, slowing to a walk while I watched him angrily stride through the hotel's front doors, leaving me behind.

Less than five minutes ago, I'd been convinced he would kiss me, but maybe I should have known better. Perhaps I was right; he was fucking with me to see if I would embarrass myself and flirt back. But his anger didn't seem to be at being caught. I'd hurt his feelings for real.

Whatever it was, I was staying away from him for the next few days, not that he seemed too eager for my company.

ADRIAN MADE A POINT to sit on the other side of the room at dinner last night, and it seemed that I was still getting the cold shoulder this morning, too, as he joined a group of men I recognized as other suspense editors from various small presses around New England.

He hadn't made eye contact with me once, not even when I passed him in the lobby. It seemed I'd hurt him when I'd called him out on the trail. I wasn't sure exactly what was going on with him, but I wasn't about to play his games. Five years of misbehavior and making me feel like I was inferior to him wasn't going to disappear in one afternoon.

Going through the motions, I plated up breakfast, taking a seat at a small table for two in the corner. Hoping to avoid having to interact with anyone, I strategically placed my messenger bag opposite me across the table, effectively signaling I didn't want to be disturbed.

Biting into the chocolate croissant I'd chosen to go with over my bland breakfast of oatmeal and yogurt, I frowned as I remembered how the ones Adrian had shared with me melted in my mouth. The warm hazelnut filling was vastly superior to the small pieces of baker's chocolate that my teeth struggled to chew through in the middle of this one. Setting it aside, I scanned the room, my eyes connecting with Adrian's. I kept my expression neutral as I maintained his gaze, trying to show him that his brush-off didn't affect me. I was a big girl, and it wasn't like I hadn't been conditioned to deal with his dickish behavior. It was par for the course at this point.

He looked away first as he laughed loudly, his mouth curving into a genuine smile as he returned to the conversation at his table full of the typical *boys' club* he gravitated toward.

I didn't know what I was expecting. Disappointment shouldn't be something new when it came to his reactions to me, but I found myself wishing that the man the day before was real. The sparks of attraction between us couldn't have been all fabricated. He'd felt it too.

Or was I just that big of a fool for trying to see the redeemable qualities in another loveable asshole? You'd have thought I'd learned my lesson with Grant.

The cocky, charming asshole was still an asshole when it came down to it, and one of those had already crushed me.

Keeping my head down, I vowed to avoid him at all costs, which almost worked.

SEVEN

ISOBEL

BAR HARBOR, ME

BEGRUDGINGLY TAKING MY SEAT at the side of the small conference room, I scanned the crowd, seeing a few familiar faces but not anyone I wanted to invest the effort of small talk into. I'd spent the last few days with my head down, concentrating on taking notes in the workshops I'd attended and spending as little time at the group activities in the evenings as I could get away with.

Adrian still wasn't acknowledging me, and the cold shoulder was starting to sting. Especially since I'd be spending the next half hour listening to him speak.

When Sloane told me via email yesterday afternoon that the conference organizers had asked him to be a presenter, I was a little insulted that neither of them thought to give me a heads-up, but I guess I should be used to it by now. Adrian was peacocking and getting all the attention, and I was pushed to the side when the self-important blowhards of the other genres realized I was an editor who worked exclusively with romance. Never mind that my degree was from an Ivy League school I'd earned a scholarship to, or that I graduated with honors. According to them, I was wasted potential.

Resentment toward Sloane had been building as I stewed this morning, hearing Adrian's door open and close before I finally headed down to the lobby. Whether I liked it or not, I was his colleague, so I couldn't exactly blow this off.

I was so absorbed in my head that I hadn't realized Adrian had been announced to the room until a shiver ran up my spine at the sound of his voice over the speakers.

"One of the most important things I've learned as an acquisitions editor is to divorce myself from the notion that authors should have impeccable grammar," Adrian started, and the room was silent. I almost felt bad for the tepid reception he seemed to get, but he didn't look fazed. "I've learned that grammar and fluidity in storytelling is something that can come with practice and some not-so-subtle hints at continuing education in the craft."

"What letting go of the technical details allows you to gauge in a story is how it makes you feel," he explained, and I saw several heads nod in my periphery. "The first time you lay eyes on a manuscript, you're a reader, not an editor. You need to approach it as such."

I had to admit; I wasn't expecting Adrian to suggest something quite so astute.

"Of course, you want to see how the story flows, how the characters develop, and that the arcs have a satisfying conclusion. But the most important thing is that the story resonates in your heart." His palm settled where I'd always thought his was absent, and he looked straight at me.

Until now, I'd thought Adrian left all this to his interns, but clearly, I'd misjudged him. I didn't like the feeling of warmth that spread in my chest at the discovery. A few sentences in, and he was softening the armor I'd tacked into place over the last few days.

"If you have the gut reaction that the story has the potential to move people, then sign the damn manuscript. Lock it down. Because you can always polish those words until the story shines."

"Conversely, a beautifully grammatically structured story with no heart might look good, but everyone knows that a bright and sparkly turd is still just a turd—only with glitter."

A few chuckles arose from the crowd, and I rolled my eyes. Only he could get away with calling a manuscript a turd in a room full of publishing professionals.

"Don't be afraid to put in the hard work and collaborate with your authors to develop their craft. Sometimes even the most competent authors need help getting a story out the best way. But don't discount the stories that are rough around the edges. Don't automatically dismiss the ones that are thought-pro-voking and cause an emotional response that is messy. Sometimes it takes peeling back the superficial to see the potential in something." He hesitated for a moment, running his hand through his hair.

When he glanced back at me, the corner of his mouth was set in an amused smirk. "And the best novel of your career may come from seeing past the bullshit. Because life is messy, and sometimes manuscripts and being an editor or publisher is messy, but don't ever be afraid to put in the hard work to create something truly impactful."

My heart pounded while he stared straight at me, those steely blue eyes locking me in place. I felt that the last part might have been aimed squarely at me.

He knew I'd judged him solely on appearance—what he wanted everyone else to see. I'd bought the act he'd been selling, but I could tell it bothered him I'd fallen for it too. Because whether I wanted to admit it or not, I'd misjudged Adrian, and all the things I thought I despised about him were proving to be the things that somehow seemed charming when framed differently. Not the sexist comments, because he deserved to be kicked in the balls for those, but

I could relate to all the word vomit and gut reaction things he said just to see if others would react.

Adrian still saw me as some spoiled Ivy League brat. But in reality, hadn't I done the same thing to fit in while I was in school? Hadn't I adopted the personality traits of my peers to blend in and stay under the radar for being different? Hadn't I combed through second-hand shops to find clothes to make me look like anything other than the country bumpkin whose mother had never worn a designer anything in her life?

Maybe the designer suits, the grooming, and the crass words that came out of his mouth were his armor, just like my sometimes cool exterior. And that realization shook me to my core because maybe we weren't so different. And perhaps the initial attraction to him all those years ago wasn't so wrong anymore, and perhaps I might *like* the person he had buried under that pile of shit. He might have been acting like himself for once a few days ago and not the persona he wore most often.

My brain was static as Adrian finished his presentation, going on to talk about other topics we dealt with daily as editing professionals, his words resonating with me despite my inability to concentrate.

He easily answered a few questions from the audience before he shook hands with one of the event organizers and headed toward where I was sitting along the side of the room. Maybe he was finally ready to stop giving me the silent treatment. I wasn't sure if the idea terrified me or thrilled me.

"Was I that bad?" he asked with a grimace while he took in my likely stunned expression. It felt like my entire perception of him—years of interacting with him in the office and feeling like a terrible human being after every exchange and watching him swagger around like he had a fifteen-inch dick—had all culminated at this moment when I realized he wasn't who I thought he was.

Everything he'd ever said to me in the office was now running through my head on a loop. Was it possible that his bravado was complete and utter bullshit? And even worse, if it was, *I'd fallen for it.* I believed he was a dickhead. I'd thought that he was a genre elitist. I assumed he didn't deserve the praise he got for his work and his over-hyped authors. But I was wrong.

I was wrong.

Fuck.

"I'm not exactly sure how to interpret the look on your face right now. I tried to tamp down the comments you always scold me for and be honest for once, and you're looking at me like I just murdered someone in cold blood right in front of you. I know we got off on the wrong foot the other day, but I was hoping to call a truce for real this time. We have to spend five hours in a car together tomorrow, and I don't want things to be strained."

In a way, he had. He'd flat-out murdered something—my impression of him. Dickhead might be a decent human being, and I didn't enjoy coming to that conclusion.

"I need a fucking drink," I muttered while I shoved my notebook into the tote bag at my feet. I needed alcohol to deal with this epiphany.

"Geez. I must have totally bombed if I'm driving you to drink."

Ignoring his sarcastic attempts at humor, I turned away from him and headed toward the outside aisle, pushing past other attendees who were still lingering despite the session being over. I kept my head down, avoiding making eye contact because I wasn't sure my brain could form coherent thoughts right now or—lord forbid—small talk. Fuck that shit.

"Is, geez, slow down. I didn't mean to piss you off by not telling you they asked me to speak." Adrian followed closely behind me, still trying to talk, but I could tell from how his voice was pitched that I was freaking him out a little. I was freaking myself out.

As I watched him speak—the audience transfixed on his every word—the only thing I could think was that he had to be the most attractive man I'd ever met. And when the total dickhead personality was stripped away from that, I wanted him. I wasn't sure I'd ever wanted another human being this much. Listening to him talk, watching his lips move, my ears picking up on the tiny little inflections of his hidden accent, I'd been aroused. Painfully so.

He followed me into the elevator, settling in along the opposite wall and staring at me with wary eyes. I didn't blame him. I was fucking scared of my thoughts right now, too. Of the images that were forming in my head of all the flirty little interactions we'd had a few days ago—hell, the last five years—and how every single time I'd felt a twinge of attraction to him, he'd killed it by opening his mouth.

"If I said something to upset you, just talk to me, Is. I'm not mad at you. The way you laid into me on the trail wasn't wrong, but it stung. I just needed some space away from you to think. You make it hard to keep my thoughts straight around you."

I'd been dreading this trip because I didn't want him to embarrass me, but he'd been downright nice in the car on the way up here, and I felt like my entire world was crumbling around me with each charming thing that came out of his mouth. Even when he was mad at me, I felt more guilty for being mean to him than angry when he reacted to it.

"You didn't upset me." My voice was quiet, but he didn't look convinced. There wasn't any easy way to explain the chaotic thoughts that were whirring through my brain.

The elevator dinged, and he stepped forward, using his arm to hold open the door. Glancing up, my mouth watered at how his dress shirt clung to his chest, the buttons pulled tight, revealing tiny slivers of his white undershirt.

"You coming?" he asked, his brows pinched together, and the only thought in my head was...

Not yet.

Nodding, I stepped forward, holding my breath as I passed him in the small opening. The scent of him was starting to set more than just my temper ablaze.

He was only a few steps behind me as I headed toward our rooms, just wanting to flee and figure out the mess of what was going on in my brain. Maybe it was the fact that today was Valentine's Day, and I was alone, but the ache in my chest wasn't just loneliness.

"You're not going to talk to me?" he asked, only a few steps behind me.

It was hard to remind myself I was here to be a professional. My job was to represent Vivid and be the face of our publisher at an industry event. I'd anticipated having a massive headache the entire time because I knew I'd have to do damage control every time Adrian opened his mouth.

But the ache I was feeling right now was not in my head. My entire perception of Adrian had been demolished with one brief presentation. I'd expected him to get up there and low-key brag about the accolades his authors had piled up, but he didn't. He didn't mention the words 'best seller' or 'awards of excellence.'

Instead, he'd gotten up in a room of semi-elitist professionals and implied that some of their precious authors wrote glittery turds. It was so charmingly *him* and simultaneously the hottest words I'd ever heard come out of his mouth. Because it meant that despite being crass and judgmental, he respected his authors. He saw them as creative professionals with value, which was sometimes rare in our profession.

"I don't know what to say right now." I didn't trust myself not to turn and climb him like a tree. Devour his mouth in a way I'd only imagined fleetingly before now.

"Are you sure you're o..."

I cut him off with my hand over his mouth as he stopped in front of his room.

"Open the door," I demanded, trying not to focus on how soft his lips felt beneath my fingertips.

"But..." he mumbled against my hand, but I grabbed the plastic key card from him and swiped it over the electric lock, yanking him through the door after me and pushing him against it.

"Don't say anything. Just..." I panted as I stared at how his chest heaved, finally inhaling and getting a full mind-altering whiff of his expensive cologne. My fingers dug into his chest, enjoying the flex of the firm muscles beneath his clothing.

"Look, Is, I'm sor—"

I glanced up at him, noticing his wide eyes, watching to see what I was doing. He didn't have the usual arrogant smirk I was used to seeing, just adding to the fire in my veins.

"Don't say another fucking word," I warned, before my hands traced down his powerful chest and stopped at his belt. "I don't think I'll survive it if you keep talking."

"Was what I said that bad?" he asked, suddenly sounding unsure. The vulnerability in his eyes should have stopped me, but it only drew me to him more. Made my impression of him dissolve as he revealed the layers of who he really was.

"No. That's the problem," I whispered, looking up at him. "It was the exact opposite of bad."

"Then why are you so upset with me?"

Shaking my head, my fingers tightened on his belt buckle, slipping the end loose from the clasp. "I'm not upset with you, Adrian. I'm upset with myself that I let you convince me you were such a terrible guy, when you're..." My voice trailed off, but I could feel his eyes scanning my face as my gaze drifted to his broad shoulders.

"I'm...?"

"You might be everything I've ever wanted."

Running on pure instinct, I pulled his belt loose, quickly unbuttoning his suit pants and yanking down the zipper before he could respond to my confession.

A dull thud caught my attention, and I glanced up as I began pushing his pants down his thighs. Adrian's head was pressed tightly against the door; his eyes clenched shut and his neck flexing with every heavy swallow. His fists were balled at his sides, his knuckles white as they pressed into the door behind him.

"Oh fuck," I practically moaned when his boxer briefs came into view, the outline of his hard cock throbbing beneath the dark material. "And I thought the office gossip had been overly generous all these years."

"Told you it wasn't tiny."

As my fingers pulled down the waistband of his briefs, he grasped my wrist, my eyes flying to his.

"Fucking Christ, Isobel. I at least wanted to take yah to dinner first," he gritted out, his voice strained. "We've spent days avoiding each other."

"It was you avoiding me, but you can feed me later. I told you to stop talking." Shaking off his hold on my wrist, I slowly revealed what he'd been hiding from me all these years. "Or maybe you have something to feed me now. I was right when I called you a big boy."

A deep chuckle came from his mouth, his fingertips sliding along my cheek and plunging into my loose hair. "I don't know what has gotten into you today, but whatever it was I said, I'm not sorry."

"Shut up."

"You could shut me up with your lips," he murmured, and I momentarily considered kissing him before I touched his cock, but that might be too far. This was attraction, not affection.

"They're going to be occupied, and I told you to shut it."

"You got it," he chuckled, his thumb caressing the edge of my jaw as I returned my attention to revealing the surprise he'd been hiding in his expensive suits.

"Is this okay? I mean..." I faltered, staring at his very aroused cock down the front of his boxer briefs.

"What do you think?" He clasped my hand, sliding it inside the front of his boxer briefs and placing it against his warm skin. Leaning down, his warm breath tickled my cheek while he used his grasp on my neck to pull me closer. "Do you have any idea how fuckin' sexy you look takin' charge? If you want to touch my cock, babe, consider this an open fuckin' invitation. Use me how you want, just touch me already. I've fantasized about havin' your hands on me for so long, and I'm desperate for it."

Deciding my mouth had done enough to feed his ego, I focused on the task at hand, shoving his pants to the floor and quickly—but carefully—yanking down his briefs to join them.

As I grasped the base of his surprisingly impressive erection, he groaned, his head thumping against the door behind him once again.

I'm not sure what I expected. Maybe for him to be just as controlling in bed as he was in real life, but his hands balled into fists at his sides again, the knuckles drawn tight.

"Watch me."

Dropping to my knees on the carpet, I watched while his eyes fluttered open, widening slightly as I gripped him harder. Flexing my fist, I began pumping his length from base to tip.

"Fuck, Is. Look at that mouth," he groaned, his eyes fixated on where I was licking my lips. I hadn't touched him with my mouth yet, but he was throbbing at the promise of what this position could provide.

I'd never bought into the idea that blow jobs were considered a submissive position. From where I was kneeling, he didn't appear to be the one in control. I held the power over his pleasure, and with the way his pretty blue irises were studying me from beneath hooded eyelids, he knew I was in charge.

"Hm," I hummed, slowly drawing circles around the crown of his head with the tip of my tongue, enjoying prolonging the tease. "Should I use it for this?"

Bracing one hand on his muscular thigh, I held him steady with the other, licking up the underside and sucking the head briefly between my lips before teasingly stroking his length with my palm.

"Fuck," he panted as I loosened my grip, lazily smoothing my fist up and down. Not enough pressure to do anything but draw a frustrated moan from his lips. "Please don't tease me."

Biting back a laugh, I continued with soft strokes, reveling in how he flexed his hips forward, trying to thrust in my grip. There was a heady sense of satisfaction knowing I was likely torturing him with my hands, as he'd often tortured me with his words.

"I'm sorry. Did you need something?" I tilted my head to the side and fixed him with an innocent flutter of my lashes.

"Fuck. You're an evil temptress," he moaned while I kissed his head, darting my tongue out to gather the moisture beaded at the tip.

I hated to admit it, but his package was just as pretty as the rest of him. Long, with just enough girth to give it some weight, curved slightly. I clenched my legs together, picturing what it'd feel like inside me, but pushed that thought aside. I wasn't sleeping with him. I just wanted to play with him a little.

It'd turned me on watching him speak, and now that he was a captive audience—with his pants around his ankles—I wanted to exact a tiny bit of revenge for these new conflicting feelings I was having.

"So, you don't want me to do this?" I asked before I leaned forward, engulfing his length until he hit the back of my throat and slowly sucking my way back to the tip.

"Fuck," he grunted, one hand shooting forward to my cheek while he looked down at me with desperation in his gaze. "You're driving me crazy, Is. I can't take it."

"Hmmm," I hummed while I backed off to suckle the tip, watching his expression grow pained as I moved when he tried to thrust forward. "You'll take this if you want me to continue. I want you to think back to all the times you've said crass things to me over the last five years. How you used that mouth to torture and degrade me. I want to make you frustrated and desperate like you've made me. And when I think you're sorry enough for your behavior. I might let you come in my mouth."

Adrian's chest heaved, and he nodded his head, his thumb stroking softly across my cheekbone. "Ah fuck, do whatever you want with me. Just don't stop."

That was all the encouragement I needed as I sucked him back in and used my hands and mouth to torture him. He groaned, cursed, and grunted his way through a prolonged tease that had me clenching my thighs together.

I could tell he was close a few times and immediately backed off, ghosting my lips along his length and leaving whispers of kisses along the head before I dove back in to get him worked up again.

Before long, he was pleading, his eyes desperate as he flexed his thighs, the muscles bunching underneath my fingertips.

"This is fucking torture," he moaned, his fingers finally tangling in my hair. "But don't you fuckin' stop. Oh, God. Just like that. Swallow that dick like you own it. You fuckin' own it, Is. Goddamn."

"Mmm," I hummed, sucking slowly before rubbing my tongue along the underside of the head and releasing him again.

"Please, oh God, please," he pleaded while his other hand stroked my cheek, his eyes imploring for me to put him out of his misery. "You're right. I'm an ass. I'm sorry. Just let me come in that pretty mouth and I promise I'll behave."

"Hold on, you don't need to sound so needy. All you had to do was ask nicely," I teased as I finally caved, needing him to come so I could go relieve the tension that had built up from watching him become desperate in my hold.

"Fuckkk," he groaned when I set a rapid pace, caressing the soft spot behind his balls with my fingertips. I took him deeper and deeper with each pass of my mouth along his length. It may have been years since I'd given head, but my blow job skills had once been epic.

Pressing my fingers firmly, I took him to the back of my throat, swallowing hard, and that was all it took to tip him right over the edge. His fingers clenched in my hair, and he moaned loudly, pulsing in my mouth. "Ah, fuck. That's it, swallow that cum."

Watching him slump against the door behind him panting, eyes clenched shut as the previous tension in his muscles eased, I began to panic.

Shit.

I just gave Dickhead a blow job on a business trip with no warning, and I think I liked it.

If the state of my panties was any indication, I fucking loved it. And I loved the dirty things he said while I was doing it.

But *what the fuck?*

Not wanting to make this more awkward than it already was, I gathered up my messenger bag, found my room key in the outside pocket, and palmed it as I pulled the strap over my shoulder.

He was still propped against the door, trying to catch his breath. It was now or never—*time to beat and retreat.*

Really, it was too bad he was an epic jackass half the time. He'd been surprisingly almost sweet in how he touched me while I had his dick in my mouth. Not what I'd expected at all. The package or the way he'd let me take charge. I'd expected hair pulling or holding my face, not the tender way he'd stroked my cheek and begged me to let him come with his filthy mouth.

But that didn't matter, because I needed to figure out how to get him away from the door so I could return to my room. I had a very pressing matter to take care of.

I reached for the door handle and his hand shot out, loosely grasping my wrist while his eyes lazily focused on my rigid posture.

"Going somewhere?"

Oh God, did he expect me to have sex with him now?

"I need to get ready for dinner tonight. But this was...fun." Cringing at how awkward that sounded, I tried to push down the lever on the handle, and his hand tightened.

"We're not finished here." Pushing off the door, he stood to his full height and stepped forward until my shoulder was pressed into his solid chest. The solid chest I'd seen glimpses of in the gym at work, but I hadn't bothered to uncover it in my desperation to pull down his pants.

"I think we are. We're good. Just...consider this a truce."

He chuckled, leaning in toward my ear, his breath warming my neck. "So, you're telling me if I put my hand down your panties right now, you wouldn't be wet, your little pink clit throbbing for release?"

Bonus points for Adrian. He knew what a clit was.

"Not anything I can't take care of by myself," I squeaked.

"But you shouldn't have to take care of yourself, Is. I *want to.* You don't know how often I've dreamed of bringing you pleasure. How desperate I am to watch you fall apart at my touch."

"It's not a good idea." My voice was still high, my body shaking from the adrenaline of what I'd just done.

"Please don't shut me out," he whispered, trying to tilt my face toward his with gentle fingers. But I couldn't do this. There was no way I could sort through my conflicting feelings right now, and if he touched me... I wasn't sure there would be any coming back from that.

"I... I need to go."

I escaped, pushing the lever and slipping through the open door before he could catch me. I had the advantage of my pants not being around my ankles, so I quickly swiped my key card against the lock. Slamming the door before he could come after me, I collapsed back against it and panted, chastising myself for whatever had possessed me to do that.

Don't get me wrong, it was hot, but letting things go further was bound to blow up in my face, and not like the blowing I had just done.

Chapter
EIGHT

ADRIAN

BAR HARBOR, ME

WAS ISOBEL FUCKIN' KIDDING me with this? She'd literally tilted my world on its axis, seemingly out of nowhere, and then just left. Fuck that shit.

Reaching down to pull up my pants and boxer briefs, I fastened the zipper and button, my belt still hanging loose, before I made a beeline for the door that separated our rooms and threw open the one on my side. I was glad we had adjoining rooms for once, because I wasn't letting her run away that easily. I could pound on her door all afternoon if she didn't answer. But considering the raw neediness I saw in her eyes when she fled, I had a feeling that would dampen her plans to touch that wet clit I teased her about.

"Open the fuckin' door, Isobel," I growled before I thumped the side of my fist against the solid wood. She could run, but she certainly couldn't fucking hide, and my mouth was watering at the prospect of tasting the result of her almost torturous blow job. She'd been completely into teasing the shit out of me, and I knew I was right when I said she was throbbing. You didn't give head like that if it didn't turn you the fuck on.

"I can bang on this all fuckin' day if I need to," I shouted while I continued to pound. "Don't make me pick the lock. It's been a while, but I can do it."

I hadn't picked a deadbolt since I'd been in high school, likely when I was along for the ride on one of Hutch's dumbass pranks, but I still remembered how, and I was pretty sure the metal clip from one of my pens would do just fine in place of a picking kit.

"I know you're in there! Get your hand out of your fuckin' skirt and open this goddamn door before I make a scene and pound on the hallway door."

I could hear a muffled curse and the unmistakable sound of the deadbolt on the other side of the door softly clicking.

Fuck yes.

Without allowing her to get it fully open herself, I pushed the door as soon as it started to creak open, grasping her hand before she could escape.

"Oh, I don't think so. Where the fuck do you think you're going?" I growled as I shouldered my way into the room and immediately swung her into my chest, bending down to grasp the back of her thighs and striding toward the king-sized bed along the opposite wall. She was fuckin' delusional if she thought I wasn't returning the favor—maybe with a prolonged little tease and orgasm denial of my own. Making her come wasn't optional. I was going to get something inside that pussy.

"What are you doing?" she squealed while she pounded a fist against the back of my shoulder that turned into a moan as I sucked on the skin at the side of her neck.

"I'm taking care of you. No way am I letting you finger fuck yourself in here alone when I can taste how much you want it myself. But nice try at running away."

"Maybe I wasn't going to use my fingers."

"Fuck that, you're gonna cover my face with it. Or do you want me to watch you with some inadequate toy before I make you come again with my tongue harder than it can?"

"Wha—?" Her question turned into a moan as I slipped one hand beneath the hem of her skirt, my finger tracing the edge of the lace covering. And that's when I felt the wet heat I knew she'd been hiding. *Bingo*.

"Fuck, you're soaked. Did my dirty girl enjoy sucking my cock? Did it make you hot?"

"Fuck you," she hissed as she bit down on my neck, but it spurred me on, my fingers pressing more insistently and rubbing against her throbbing clit. There was no way she could hide the effect her little act of dominance had, and my cock surged back to life, remembering how satisfied she'd looked when she'd maintained that defiant eye contact with me while she'd licked my dick like a fucking lollipop.

"Not right now, babe, but I'm sure we can work up to that. I believe your clit and I have some unfinished business."

Throwing her back onto the mattress, I didn't give her a chance to flee as I caged her in with one forearm across her stomach. The fingers of my other hand sought out her flimsy underwear, and I yanked them roughly down her thighs while she moaned with an arm thrown across her eyes.

"I don't fuckin' think so. You made me watch, so you're gonna watch me as I make you come. Eyes down here, Isobel."

She hesitated as she peeked beneath her forearm, giving me a wary look.

"I've got all night, babe. Watch what I do to you, or I'll just keep you pinned down so I can tease you like you teased me."

"I can do it myself." Her pout was almost cute, and I had no doubt she could get herself off, but she'd started this game, and I was going to fuckin' finish it.

"But you know it'll feel better if I do it."

"God, you're so full of yourself," she mumbled, and I laughed as my fingers crept back under her skirt, using the tips to tease her clit with barely there touches. I could do this all night. Unlike her, I didn't give a shit about the networking people did during the conference dinners.

"Bet you'd like to be full of me too. A lot," I teased before I pressed a finger inside her, searching for the place I knew could make her squirm. "But I'm gonna fuck you with my tongue first. Have you ridin' my fingers and beggin' for it."

"Oh, fuck." Her back arched as my thumb softly pressed on her clit, hovering while I added a second finger inside. She was panting and squirming against the sheets, her legs spread while my hands continued to tease her beneath the demure, professional skirt.

"Watch." I lifted my forearm and rolled up the front hem of her skirt, revealing her pretty pink pussy. She wasn't bare, but she clearly took grooming seriously with a neatly trimmed patch of light blonde hair.

"Hmm, looks like the carpet matches the drapes." Leaning forward, I blew a stream of hot air where my thumb rested, enjoying how she squirmed and reached forward to grasp my shirt collar.

"You're a dick," she growled while I teased her, never increasing the pace of my fingertips.

"Yeah. But you already knew that. And it fuckin' turns you on. Looks like you soaked the back of your skirt," I chuckled, moving my thumb and replacing it with the tip of my tongue.

She released my collar and let out the sexiest moan as she fell back on the mattress, her hands tightly gripping the sheets on either side of her hips. Part of me wanted her fingers in my hair, holding me to her, but I knew with enough teasing that it'd happen without me asking.

"Mmm, so wet," I hummed against her skin, enjoying the sucking sounds my fingers were making as they slowly fucked her. It didn't matter if she liked me as a person. She clearly wanted my touch, and I didn't plan to stop until she'd had hers.

I'd spent years fantasizing about what might be under her impenetrable professional exterior, and I was pleasantly surprised by the sensual, enticing woman she'd shown me this afternoon. Taking my time licking her pussy would be far from a hardship.

"Please stop being so soft," she panted, with her head thrown to the side, but her eyes watched my every move.

"We both know I'm far from fuckin' soft, Is. But I'm not done here. You got to tease me, and it's my turn, so lay back down and take it."

My lips curved around her clit, and I sucked softly, laving the little piece of enticing flesh with my tongue until she was squirming and having trouble holding in her moans. Isobel may have hated the tease, but turnabout's fair play and it was my turn to play.

"Fuck, more. Oh God, I need more. Harder."

Her back arched as she moaned, one hand grasping my forearm and digging in her nails while I felt her tremble beneath me. She was close, and I knew it could all be over with a little more suction and a strategically placed finger, but I hadn't been joking. This was my turn to make her desperate.

Deciding to ignore her request, I lazily drew my tongue along her lips, skirting around the throbbing nub at the top and repeating the circuit as my fingers softly stroked her from the inside. The flush on the skin I could see above her modest neckline showed me she liked it. But the little frustrated growls she let out while she tried to push her hips into my movements to get me where she wanted indicated it wasn't enough to push her over. *Good.* Then my plan for payback was working.

I watched transfixed while her chest rose and fell as I continued to pleasure her, and I wished I'd had the foresight to get her naked, but the conservative business attire was doing it for me. Once she stopped fighting me, I carefully untucked her blouse with my other hand, a gasp echoing around us as my fingers slowly traced the skin above her navel. I wanted to lick it, but my tongue was otherwise engaged with the teasing driving her insane.

"You're so fucking hot," I groaned into her, leaning forward on the edge of the mattress, finally sucking her clit into my mouth before my fingers crept beneath the lace of her bra. She had spectacular breasts but typically kept them hidden with snug, high-necked blouses at work. I'd often wondered if it was because she was one of those women who bought heavily padded bras to make their curves more pronounced, but there was just a generous handful once I got my palm underneath the thin material.

Moaning into her, I pinched her nipple with one hand and pressed harder with the fingers of my other, enjoying the way she bucked her hips into my face when I hit *that* spot. The one I knew would make her explode.

"Hmm," I hummed as I experimentally slowed my speed, returning to my previous teasing pace.

"Fuck, that," she groaned as she grabbed a fistful of my hair and held my head in place. "Quit fucking around and make me come. Playtime later."

"You promise?" I chuckled when I looked up at her from between her legs, almost laughing aloud at the look of sheer frustration painted across her delicate features. I'd seen that look aimed at me in countless meetings, but seeing it while I had a face full of her pussy was by far my favorite.

"Yes, God. Just get this over with already."

That statement uttered in a sexual context typically meant that the woman wasn't having a good time, but as I lowered my mouth again and finally stopped the teasing little strokes, the way she moaned and tightened her fingers in my hair exhibited the exact opposite. She may have been angry with me, but she was fucking enjoying it.

Isobel flushed and desperate with her back arched high, mid-orgasm, and pulling my hair out at the roots was something I couldn't erase from my mind.

She'd looked glorious kneeling at my feet with my cock in her mouth, but knowing that I'd given her an orgasm that had her crashing to the sheets breathless with a hand thrown over her eyes was fucking phenomenal.

I knew if I kept going, I could force another one out of her, but the exhausted groan she let out as I licked up her release had me wanting to kiss her instead.

Our mouths had never touched throughout this encounter, and I found myself almost desperate for it as I removed my fingers and settled on the bed beside her. Her eyes were tightly closed, but the trace of a smile on her face had me wanting to roll her toward me—with a lot less clothing—and settle her on my chest until she was ready for more.

"Feeling better?" My fingers traced along the side of her cheek, carefully tucking a stray lock of hair that'd fallen from her tight bun. With a sigh, her eyes flickered open, and her head lolled in my direction. For once, the look directed toward me wasn't irate, just satisfied and curious as she lifted a hand and smoothed back where she'd destroyed my hair. I didn't mind one bit. Each out-of-place strand was a visual reminder of her pleasure and what we'd done.

I wasn't sure what this meant, her sudden and impromptu blow job and then my reaction to her trying to run away.

On paper, we didn't make sense, like Greek fire and water—explosive and destructive. But there was something about her I wanted to uncover. I wanted to push back the professional barriers she'd placed between us due to my often-terrible behavior.

"Don't look so pleased with yourself. I'm not going to sleep with you." Her voice was slightly raspy, but the defiance bled back in as she rolled to her side, mirrored my pose, and tucked her arms against her chest.

"I didn't think you were." Nor did I expect it. We both knew she was in charge.

Brows pinched together at my acquiescence, her lips pursed as she readied to confront me, likely to kick me out, but I wouldn't let her brush me off anymore. While this afternoon may have been purely physical, something prompted her to jump me, and I wanted to find out what it was.

"Quit being a dick," she huffed, pushing my hand away from the side of her face. I settled for placing it on her hip and scooting forward, so our chests touched.

"We both know that's not going to happen either."

A ghost of a smile crossed her full lips that were red from either biting or her very competent oral skills.

"You don't need to stay here. We've got it out of our systems. We can just call it a lapse in judgment and return to work as normal next week."

I chuckled, pulling her closer. She didn't fight me, her small hand grasping my collar as her warm breath tickled my chin.

"Nothing will ever be normal about working with you ever again. You may be able to return to work like nothing happened, but I don't think that's an experience I will *ever* forget."

"Stop." Her voice was soft, but her eyes were desperate. Although, I didn't see regret, so I wasn't sure how to take this sudden return to the co-worker who despised me. "Don't try to sweet-talk me. This is *never* happening again."

"I'm sure you believe that," I responded, leaning forward to run my lips along the side of her jaw, threading my fingers through her hair while I whispered in her ear. "But we both know things will never be the same after today."

Wiggling her hand between our chests, she pushed, trying to arch away from my touch. With one soft kiss beneath her ear, I released her, watching as she placed a few feet between our bodies. I wanted to follow her and pin her arms above her head while I kissed all the skin exposed along her neckline, but I had a feeling that would get me a kneecap shoved in my nutsack.

"We're not going to talk about this. I was..." she trailed off, closing her eyes and shaking her head slightly. "I was clearly under the effects of something when I pushed you against that door, and I'm not even sure what happened here, but...it's not happening again. Ever."

She'd been seated at another table during our lunch break, but I hadn't seen her take a sip from anything but her water bottle, so I wasn't sure exactly what she was under the effects of, but I would let her keep her secrets. For now.

"What exactly were you under the effects of?"

She blushed, averting her eyes before she spoke softly. "Charm, pretty eyes, a big..."

"Dick?"

"No. A big fucking ego. Not everything is about your dick."

"But sometimes it is."

"That's just," she huffed. "It's not the point. Nothing good came from this."

"Not so sure about that. Seemed like there was some good coming involved. At least from me."

As far as what happened in her room...

"I believe what happened after that was me worshiping your pussy until you screamed my name and came all over my face. But that's just my interpretation of things."

"I didn't scream your name." Her eyes widened, and I could tell she was about to lay into me, so I quickly reached forward and covered her mouth with my palm.

"—but if you want me to be your dirty little secret, that's fine. I can be patient."

She tried to talk around my hand. Her voice was muffled until she pried my hand away.

"There is nothing secret going on here and you don't have a patient bone in your body."

The erection in my pants spoke otherwise, but I'd give her space. We worked in the same office, so we'd be bound to run into each other eventually, and until then, I'd wait until she came to me again because I had a feeling this little tryst wasn't quite over for either of us.

Leaning forward, I grasped the hand that tried to push back on my chest again, holding it still while I placed a soft kiss on her cheek, close to her lips. I desperately wanted to know how they tasted, but I knew if she wanted me to kiss her, she would have asked for it. While I *would* coax her into an orgasm she clearly needed, I wasn't kissing her without her wanting it just as much as I did.

"I'll see you at dinner. You might want to clean yourself up a bit. You're looking a little disheveled." Sitting up quickly, I fastened my belt, adjusting my cuffs as I rose, and headed toward the open door where our rooms adjoined. "I'll leave my side unlocked," I teased before I slipped through the opening, drawing her door closed behind me. "Just in case you're feeling tempted again."

"You're a dick!" Isobel yelled as the door closed, and I tried to hold in my laugh. She was right, I *was* a dick, but she'd seemed to enjoy playing with mine quite a bit earlier, so she couldn't hate me too much.

NINE

ISOBEL

BOSTON

THINGS WERE WEIRD IN the office for weeks following the conference. Adrian hadn't tried to contact me, and I wasn't sure how I felt about that. I'd assumed that once we'd become intimately acquainted with each other, he'd be even more of a jackass. The few times I'd seen him, he'd been tolerable, even surprisingly professional. I wasn't sure if my need to acknowledge what'd happened between us was driven more by my ego or by the sudden attraction I couldn't seem to shake.

I'd never been one to chase men. I was typically the one who let them pursue me, at least back when I'd made time for dating. It'd been a long time since someone chased me. Even longer since I'd bought into the whole relationship and romance thing. A relationship that failed as badly as mine did changed your perception of your entire future.

I didn't particularly appreciate that he'd been able to come back to work and interact with me like he hadn't had his mouth on the most intimate parts of my body. And there were several parts he hadn't touched that I now wish he had. He'd been the first man to touch me with that much enthusiasm since...

My phone chimed from my desk, pulling me out of my distracting thoughts. Kristine had gone to the coffee shop down the street to get our lunches, so I had some time to sit quietly and figure out why I had been so unsettled lately.

Hitting the phone to activate the speaker, I tried to put on my professional tone, not letting on that my head was a mess. "Isobel here."

"Hi, Is," the executive assistant, Chloe, who worked on the eleventh floor, answered, and I frowned as I tried to figure out why she'd be calling me during lunch. "Do you have some time available in your schedule this afternoon to come up and speak with Sloane about something?"

Quickly grabbing my work phone and pulling up the calendar app, I scanned, seeing a block of time open in a few hours. "Yeah, I can come up around 2:00.

Will that work for her?" I could shuffle some things around if I needed to, but I hated having to reschedule check-ins with my authors. Some of them could get squirrelly when in a creative state and ghost my calls, but they knew not to miss pre-scheduled calls from me.

"That fits with her afternoon. I'm still waiting on word from Adrian, but I know she wants to talk to both of you before the weekend."

My heart started to pound at the mention of her wanting to meet me with Adrian, but I managed to keep my voice even as I said my goodbye and set the handset back on the phone cradle.

Fuck.

We had sat across the room during staff meetings, but I hadn't spoken with him face to face since he had his face to my...

No.

Bad Isobel, don't think about the mind-blowing things that man could do with his tongue or how pretty his dick was. He is *a dick.*

The car ride home from Maine would have been a perfect time to talk to him about what happened because he couldn't escape, but my mind hadn't been able to rest the night before, so I fell asleep leaning against the passenger side window before we ever hit the highway. Then I was too tired to bring things up when he'd dropped me off at my building, and he hadn't pressed the issue, leaving me with a smile and a wave that confused me even more.

I was a jittery mess for the next two hours, losing focus and reading the same line edits repeatedly until I gave up and checked on the formatting for one of my authors latest books.

Chase Rodgers—known in the romance world as *Chastity Rose*—was killing it in the spicy romantic comedy sub-genre, and I was excited about her upcoming new series. She'd written a few chapters and a rough outline, but I knew once this book was published, she'd put her nose down and crank out the rough draft of the next manuscript pretty quickly.

At a quarter till 2:00, I made my way to the elevators, glad that everyone seemed to be busy and not using them now. Small talk when you were trapped in an enclosed space was beyond awkward, and since we were going to the same place, I especially didn't want to end up trapped in one with Adrian, even if it was only to ride up one floor.

Luck clearly wasn't on my side. As the elevator doors slid open and the one to the stairwell swung open at the same time I walked into the foyer on the executive floor. Adrian was adjusting his cufflinks, but stopped when he saw me standing a few feet away, gawking at him.

"Isobel." He nodded, gesturing to the glass doors in front of us with his head. My entire body tingled with awareness as he stepped behind me and reached forward to open the door. "After you," he whispered, that arrogant teasing tone amplified by his rough voice.

"Thank you," I squeaked, clearing my throat before stopping at the reception desk. "Chloe knows we're coming for an appointment with Sloane."

The receptionist waved us through with a smile, and I tried to shake my nerves by taking a few deep breaths, but when Adrian's palm settled in the middle of my back, I nearly stumbled in my high heels.

"Calm down. It's nothing bad."

Pausing mid-stride, I looked back at him hesitantly. "You know why she wants to see us?"

"I might."

His palm was burning an imprint on my back through my thin blouse, while a smirk formed on his lips. Lips I hadn't tasted yet. Not that I wanted to. "And you're not going to tell me?" I asked, my voice breathy as I licked my suddenly dry lips.

"You didn't ask."

Growling under my breath, I fought the urge to punch him in the nuts as he continued to smile at me. "I literally just asked."

"But not nicely." He teased with a shrug, failing to remove his hand from my back. "Say please, Isobel."

"I'm not saying please."

He stepped forward, his chest brushing against my shoulder. "But it sounded so hot coming from your lips the last time. Although the actual coming part was even hotter."

My cheeks flamed as I cleared my throat and stepped away. "You told me you'd keep your mouth shut."

He turned, looked behind him, and stepped even closer as he peered over my shoulder down the other end of the hallway. "Don't worry, the secret of how you sound when you..."

My eyes widened as I slapped my palm over his mouth, just as he'd done to me. "Not another word. You promised."

He clasped my hand, prying it loose as he leaned toward my ear, his smooth cheek brushing my jaw. "I promised no such thing. I said I'd keep it a secret, not that I wouldn't talk to *you* about it. Since you told me it's never happening again, I'll just have to reminisce at the memories of you on your knees in front of me. And the taste of your delicious puss—"

"You arrogant fucking assho—" I interrupted him with a hiss, and his hand covered my mouth again as he stepped closer.

"Save the tongue lashing for later. We'll be late if we don't keep moving." Adrian removed his hand, using the one on my back to urge me toward Sloane's office at the end of the hall. When I took a hesitant step forward, he leaned in close, his chest pressing against my back. "Good girl."

Fuck.

He could not start that shit with me. I'd read enough of Chase's smutty novels to see how falling for the asshole went. I just needed to get through this meeting and return to avoiding Adrian. Just because he was attractive, could captivate a crowd at a conference, had an objectively pretty penis, and could do things with his tongue that literally had me shaking did not mean that I had to like him.

Sloane's door was open when we turned the corner, and she smiled widely when she saw us approaching. Chloe was on the phone at her desk just outside the office door, but motioned for us to go in.

"You can close the door." Sloane gestured as we stepped inside, and Adrian tipped his head toward the chairs in front of her desk, indicating for me to sit before he pulled the door closed with a soft snick. "Great. Let's get started, shall we?"

"I'm ready whenever you are," Adrian responded while I took a seat, noticing his eyes lingering on my legs. Scowling in his general direction, I expected him to look away, but his smile only widened, and he winked. *Dick.*

"Well, when you first approached me after the staff meeting yesterday, Adrian, I was skeptical about what you requested, but after looking through Evan's manuscript, I think your assessment may be correct."

Still having no idea what they were referring to, I kept my mouth shut and listened to her talk about the manuscript in question for a few moments. I wasn't sure why they needed me here for this meeting, but she'd requested me specifically.

"Isobel, has Adrian explained what he requested to you?"

Giving my head a slight shake, I looked between them. "No, he's kept all this quite a secret."

"I am *good* at keeping secrets," he replied while winking again. Smug bastard.

"I'm sure you're familiar with one of his authors, Stone Evans?"

I nodded, recognizing the name. The author, Evan, had made quite a name for himself in the last several years with a few bestsellers. I'd only briefly met him once in passing, but he typically stayed away from the publishing house events and author events in general. Word had it he'd fled the city after a nasty breakup, but I tended to ignore office rumors.

"Well, he's finished a manuscript we were hoping had potential, but there are some passages that've made it through the first round of edits that just aren't shaping up like we need to see to move forward with going to print."

Glancing over at Adrian, his expression wasn't the smug arrogance I was used to seeing from him, especially around our superiors. "I need your help, Isobel."

"With what?" I clamped my lips together at the sound of my voice, my tone slightly incredulous. Adrian asking me for help and getting our boss to back him up was the last thing I expected.

"I was thinking."

"That's dangerous," I muttered, cringing when Sloane chuckled from behind her desk. She knew that Adrian and I didn't have the best working relationship. But I still should try to remain professional in her office.

"As I was saying," Adrian stated, clearing his throat, and sitting upright in his chair. His expression was almost pleading, so I kept my snarky comments to myself and let him continue. "I thought that since you have several well-established authors who excel at romance and slightly suspenseful plot lines, maybe we could arrange to have one of them consult on his novel. I asked Sloane about the possibility of bringing in a writing consultant, and she suggested using someone in-house."

"Let me get this straight. You need me to lend you one of my authors to clean up your golden boy's manuscript because you can't handle it? Why romance? I don't get it."

"I can handle it just fine, but he's having trouble grasping what I've asked for in the edits. I think he needs another creative to help him flesh out the scenes a little more. It's a suspense novel with a prostitute and a police detective who have a rather tumultuous relationship."

"Where do my authors come into play with this? Are you telling me Evan is having trouble writing a romantic subplot?" I had several competent authors who were more than capable of consulting on a project and a few who mentored up-and-coming writers, but I'd never been asked to lend one out to an editor of another genre.

"You know Evan's background, right?" Adrian asked, leaning back in his chair as he faced me.

Glancing toward Sloane, she nodded at Adrian, clearly just here as a facilitator for this request. Did Adrian think I would've said no if he'd just asked me directly? Well...I probably would have, but I didn't know what that said about my behavior toward him. Was I that unsupportive to my co-workers? Or did I just have that much animosity built up toward him?

"I've heard that he likes to keep to himself."

Adrian chuckled, his expression warming as he turned to face me further in his chair. "That might be an understatement. He has generalized anxiety disorder, so he doesn't socialize outside of his inner circle. He's not completely sheltered, but it's been a while since he's been exposed to the content he's trying to write. And he's become a bit of a recluse over the last two years after an emotionally abusive ex, so I need someone close that doesn't mind going to him. And who will work at his residence."

"He's not in Boston anymore?"

He shook his head, reaching down to grab a packet of papers from his work bag. "He relocated to Connecticut and lives on a plot of land near a state park. Sloane has agreed to provide a stipend from Vivid, rental car if needed, and accommodations to whoever you choose to send."

"How long are you planning for this *consultation* to last? I have several authors mid-contract. I don't want to break their progress just to save one of yours."

Sloane cut in, clearing her throat. "Whomever Adrian and Evan decide to request will be given appropriate extensions to their current contracts provided we get a quick resolution to this. Only half a dozen chapters need attention, so I'd estimate two weeks would be adequate time to get the manuscript up to par."

"And what do I tell my authors when they ask why this must happen in rural Connecticut? Can't he come to Boston for a few weeks and meet one of the local authors? If it's not that much material to restructure."

"Evan won't come into the office to fix the manuscript."

I scoffed, suddenly irritated that his inability to manage his talent was now leaving me to pick up the pieces. "And you're okay with letting him tell you what to do? Doesn't he have a contract with Vivid? Enforce the timeline of the document exchange. If he doesn't deliver, then let legal deal with him."

"Isobel," Sloane soothed, sitting back in her chair, and letting it swivel gently from side to side. "Evan has some clauses built into his contract that limit the time we are legally allowed to call him into the office or require him to take part in promotional events. He's threatened to take the penalty and scrap the book if we don't find a solution to this. The pre-orders have already been up for over a month, so I'd like to avoid the bad press Vivid would get if we do that."

"So, your author is a prima donna, and I need to send in a babysitter to get him to behave. Is that where we're at?"

Adrian sighed, clearly thinking that having this discussion in Sloane's office would give him the edge. "All I need from you is a list of authors and some hard copies of their books. Evan will choose who he wants to work with, and then we'll go from there."

"And if my author doesn't buy into this?"

"Then we'll choose someone else."

Turning back to face Sloane, I clenched my jaw, trying to remain professional. "At the first sign of misconduct by anyone in Adrian's department, I want my author protected by Vivid. If we're coming to the rescue in this situation, we have the flexibility to call the shots, and I want my editing team to have eyes on this document if my author's name is being attached to this project."

"Those sound reasonable. I'm sure we can include those in a written agreement between the two parties. Adrian, does that sound amenable?"

"Evan is a professional. I don't see why there needs to be a mention of misconduct. What happens if your author harasses *him*?"

"Alright," Sloane interrupted as I opened my mouth to respond. "Both authors will be equally protected in the very unlikely event of something inappropriate happening during the consultation process. It would behoove both of you to play nicely during this, because it is in everyone's best interest to get this book to print on time. Isobel, forward me a copy of that list once you narrow down the field, and keep in mind we need someone who knows how to write something graphic and spicy. Adrian, please get this settled with Evan as quickly as possible so we can arrange travel."

Sloane opened the screen of her laptop, apparently dismissing us. I still had mixed feelings about this, but I was already narrowing down the authors who lived in the Boston or Hartford areas that I knew could handle something like this. One, in particular, didn't have trouble being thrown into a new environment with someone who may be less than social. Now I just needed to convince Chase that this project was worth taking on and hope that Evan was alright working with her.

Adrian was quiet as we both gathered our things—a tense, awkward silence surrounded us as we stepped out into the hallway and walked back toward the reception desk.

I hated that he still seemed to be able to get under my skin. My reaction and defensiveness to his request for help weren't making things any easier between us, but neither was his intentionally antagonistic behavior before we went into the meeting.

The receptionist was busy as we passed by her desk, and Adrian stepped forward to open the glass door to the foyer where the elevators were located.

"Thank you," I whispered when I passed him, flinching as his hand grazed my back as the door closed behind us. This awkward tension was killing me.

This consultation project was going to upset the balance that we'd found over the past few weeks, and I wasn't ready for it. I wasn't prepared to deal with the shift in my perception of him.

Knowing he was hiding a thoughtful, sensually generous—but that was beside the point—intelligent, playful persona behind the façade of Dickhead, made things harder for me. I didn't want to like him, and he surely didn't like me—not with the looks he'd given me in that meeting when I pushed back.

Shifting nervously from foot to foot, I watched the numbers change on the display above the elevator, fighting the urge to look behind me at where I knew Adrian was standing.

"Fuck this," he mumbled as his hand circled my wrist, tugging me toward the stairwell door.

"What are you...?" I trailed off when I looked behind me at his murderous gaze. Deciding not to push the issue, I stumbled after him into the stairwell landing, the door closing behind us with a thump.

Turning to lay into him for manhandling me, he shook his head once, advancing on me, and I hastily backed up into the wall behind me. My fingers flattened against the cold concrete block as he caged me in with a hand on either side of my head.

"What tha fuck was that?" His voice was a raspy growl, his thick Bostonian accent unmasked and his face full of irritation.

"What was what?" I asked, my tone breathier than I ever wanted it to be in his presence.

"You in that meeting. I asked you for help, and you immediately implied that Evan was going to be sexually harassing one of your precious writers."

Fighting back the urge to smack him, I straightened up, narrowed my eyes, and leaned toward him. His eyes widened as I encroached on his personal space, but he didn't move an inch. "Excuse me for being cautious because your department has a reputation for being arrogant dicks about everything. If I remember correctly, *you* want *my* help, not the other way around, so I need to make sure you aren't going to come in and bully my talent and throw off all my schedules. Everyone I have regionally is under contract right now, and saving your ass isn't something I get paid for."

Adrian's jaw clenched as he stared into my eyes with that unnerving intensity he was so capable of, but I wasn't backing down or letting him bulldoze over me as he did with everyone else.

"Sloane wasn't asking you to help. That was just a courtesy. This request came from above her. If Evan tanks this release, we all lose, so why don't you look at the bigger picture here and realize the revenue my department brings helps everyone stay afloat. If he nails this one, that's one more mommy porn author you get to keep under contract, so just get me the list and quit being so condescending about it."

"Excuse me?" Did he really just say my authors write mommy porn?

"You heard me. I don't think I need to repeat myself. I may need your help now, but your job is secure because of my department."

"Why you piece of..." My voice trailed off as I tried to keep my anger in check. He was goading me, and I didn't want to give him the satisfaction of feeding into this perception he had of me being difficult.

"Ass?" he smirked, his smile suddenly seeming less aggressive and more passionate as his eyes flickered down, an eyebrow rising as he looked right down the front of my blouse.

Throwing an arm over my chest, I blocked out his view, but he took his time, returning his gaze to mine, seeming to fixate on my lips. A surge of heat licked between us as I remembered what it felt like to have his hands on me. His long fingers and slightly rough palms, how his stubble had tickled the insides of my thighs.

"If you'd just pull the stick out of that tight ass of yours for a little while, I think this collaboration could be mutually beneficial."

"I already told you I wasn't sleeping with you."

An amused chuckle rang out into the air between us as he brought the backs of his fingers to my cheek, brushing them against my heated skin. "Not where my head was, but good to know you're thinking about sleeping with me."

"You're infuriating."

"And you're intoxicating," he whispered as he leaned in, his lips softly ghosting over where his fingers had traced. I sucked in a surprised breath, my hand pressing into his chest, the muscles flexing as I wavered between pulling him closer and shoving him away from me.

"Stop." Tilting my head to the side, I tried to push away the sensations that his warm breath on my neck was invoking, and stop imagining what it'd feel like if he kissed my lips instead of my cheek.

He backed up a few steps at my request, straightening out his tie and buttoning his open suit jacket. "I should be around until six tonight if you get me the list of names. I'll get on Evan first thing tomorrow to get the ball rolling."

As he turned, picked up his discarded briefcase, and descended the stairs back toward our floor, I tried to calm my racing heart and figure out what the fuck was going on between us.

TEN

ADRIAN

BOSTON

AFTER OUR LITTLE BLOW-UP in Sloane's office and subsequent confrontation in the stairwell, I thought Isobel would continue to resist working together on this consultation project. I should have known better.

Like the professional she was, within an hour, she had a list of authors in my inbox, and someone from marketing dropped off a box of paperbacks a few hours later that I prepared to send express mail to Evan first thing in the morning.

As much as I wanted to think she was being intentionally difficult, I knew I just brought out that part of her personality. I respected she had no qualms about putting me in my place when I stepped out of line. Which I'd done with my cheap crack about her authors writing porn.

Ma was the same way as Isobel, taking life by the balls and putting herself through nursing school when she was left with two unruly five-year-old twins and a Marine widow's pension that didn't cover the bills. I was certain she'd have my balls in a vise grip if she knew how I spoke to people—Isobel especially—and acted in the office. I knew it was toxic as fuck, but I couldn't seem to break the cycle. I really should know better, but it seemed I'd never kicked the habit I'd adopted twenty years ago. Inside the office, I was *Dickhead*. Outside the office, I was the well-behaved, devoted to his family, boring older twin, Ad.

The dichotomy of my life had never bothered me before, but I'd never dated a woman I wanted to take seriously. Although, I was far from the dating part with Isobel. She could barely stand to be in the same room with me. That didn't stop me from getting turned on every time I pissed her off, and the claws came out.

"You can take off, Sam," I told my copy-editing intern while he sat at the small table in the corner of my office, intently staring at his tablet. "I'm gonna stick around and head to the gym after I get these PDFs ready for Isobel. Is the last draft of Evan's manuscript on the server?"

He stared at his tablet for a moment as he held a finger up. I hated when people didn't acknowledge me, but I knew he was trying not to lose his place in the proof he was going through.

"Yeah. I swapped out all the docs with the latest version, and I emailed you a list of the chapters that Sloane thought needed an extra set of eyes."

"Great, thanks for getting it to this point. Hopefully, whoever Is sends to help can pull him out of this funk. We can't afford to have another shitty first draft like this coming out of him. I think he's been jerking off alone in the woods too long."

Sam shook his head at my borderline inappropriate comment, but he'd long ago stopped trying to make me see the error of my ways. He didn't know I probably hated the things I spouted off more than he did.

Verbal diarrhea was a bitch. But I probably wasn't wrong. Evan rarely left the house and never spoke to anyone besides me when he was forced to come into the office, so I doubted he was pulling from fresh source material on these sex scenes. Watching internet porn was hardly accurate research to write a semi-realistic sex scene in a novel.

"Go ahead and take off. I won't be too far behind you."

"If you're sure you've got everything handled," he hedged, but I wasn't in the mood. I knew he was trying to help, but my frustration from this afternoon didn't need to be taken out on Sam. The fifty-pound weights on the floor would do the job, or angrily beating off to the memory of Isobel smirking at me with my dick poised at her lips. But I could hold off on that until I returned to my apartment. Alone. Because despite my reputation, it'd been a while.

"I'm good. Go home. Do whatever it is you young people do on a Thursday night." That made me sound old as fuck, but my bar-hopping weeknights were firmly in my past. I was too old for this shit. And according to my ball-busting brother, not getting any younger. Even though most of his life centered on physical therapy and co-parenting a surly twelve-year-old part-time, his social life was booming compared to mine.

After Sam packed up and left, I scrubbed my hands over my face, running my hands up into my hair and tugging, just for the rush of adrenaline that accompanied the pain. I needed to get my mind off the shitshow of this rough draft and whatever minefield I'd placed myself in the middle of with Isobel.

Running the last month through my head, I still didn't know where that stolen afternoon at the conference had come from. Isobel hated me, and regardless of my intense attraction to her body, I wasn't exactly the president of her fan club either.

Despite my inability to keep the inappropriate thoughts in my head, I didn't like it when people didn't like me. Ironic, I know, but knowing that Isobel harbored an intense dislike bothered me. I respected the fuck out of her, and she couldn't care less if I died in a fiery bus accident. She'd probably be the one driving the bus and pouring the gasoline on my decimated body with how much she didn't like me.

Deciding there was nothing I could do about our current animosity toward each other, I grabbed my gym bag and headed toward the elevators, knowing that if I tired myself out, I'd stop obsessing about the situation.

My personal phone didn't have any missed messages when I checked them on my walk down the hall, so I breathed a sigh of relief that I wasn't needed at home to clean up messes or hunt down any wily octogenarians. It seemed I was getting a momentary reprieve.

"You're here late." A quiet voice called out from behind the reception desk, startling me a little as I turned the corner.

"I could say the same about you," I chuckled nervously as I shoved my phone into my pants pocket and looked over at the reception desk. Andrea, the receptionist and executive assistant to the genre editors, had her hair pinned up into a sloppy bun, and a slew of textbooks and notebooks were strewn across her typically pristine desk. "Shouldn't you have taken off at 5:00 with the rest of the admin staff?"

"Yeah," she smiled, her eyes nervously flicking between the mess she'd made and my eyes. I know my office may have been meticulously organized, but I wasn't going to judge her for spreading out while she was clearly working on something. "But my apartment is a shoebox, and the restaurant below is loud, so I didn't think I'd get much studying done there."

Tilting my head to the side, I tried to recall what I knew about her. I knew she was only a year or so younger than Sam, with a bachelor's degree. I'd seen her name on the interview list for the copy-editing intern pool a few times, but she was somehow still at the reception desk. "I thought you already had your degree."

She blushed, looking down and tucking her short hair behind her ear. "I do. But it didn't seem to give me much leverage when I was applying for jobs, so I started my graduate degree this semester. Hopefully, once I'm done, I can get something more than a glorified secretary position."

Hmm. I respected that. I had a master's degree in Literary Editing and Publishing, as well as several industry certifications and part of a Ph.D. I'd abandoned when Hutch was discharged. She was right. Things were different now than when I'd been hired as a proofer straight out of Boston College. The industry was getting saturated, and it was cutthroat to get a position with more than lateral movement within a house.

Quite a few of the people in my graduate classes did freelance now since the self-publishing industry was growing in popularity, so the industry was changing. I'd just been lucky enough to discover a few authors who had secured my place at Vivid.

"Well, keep at it. Positions open here a few times a year. Just make sure you're keeping an eye on the listings as they come up. They'll get snatched up quickly." I knew there was talk about a few people transferring or retiring soon, so as people moved up to fill those positions, there would be a scramble from the university intern pool to plug in the holes with the entry-level jobs.

"I have been. Sloane sends out a memo to all the executive assistants when things open, so I usually see them before they get posted. No luck yet."

"Hang in there." Pulling my phone from my pocket, I glanced at the time, knowing that if I didn't get moving, I'd only get in a partial workout.

"Sorry," she apologized, waving me toward the elevators. "I didn't mean to distract you. Have a good evening Mr. O'Neill."

"You can call me Adrian," I laughed, feeling old as fuck when people called me Mr. O'Neill. That was Pops, not me. "I'm not that much of a dick."

She blushed again, ducking her head as I headed into the elevator lobby. Thankfully, it didn't take long for the car to arrive, and I was able to get down to the second floor, which housed the fitness center, without a million stops on the way down. The fitness crowd that came down here immediately after work should be clearing out now, but the gym closed at 9:00, so I knew I needed to get changed and get moving, or I'd be crunched for time.

While the heavy bar had a great appeal for tiring myself out, I didn't have a spotter lined up, so I settled for a moderately heavy weight on the leg press and pushed myself until I couldn't get out more quality reps. Knowing I would be feeling it tomorrow but had a manuscript to get through a developmental edit on, I went lighter on the arms, the repetitive motion of the chest fly helping to clear my mind.

After a good forty-five minutes of torturing myself through the various chest and arm repetitions, I wiped my sweaty face and guzzled down the rest of my water.

It was times like these I missed the twenty-four-hour gym down the street in my old neighborhood. I used to wake up at five and go for a run before high school and exhaust myself after practices in the afternoon with free weights.

Then I got used to a nicer facility after graduation, spending hours after classes in the university weight room during the off-season. College was lonely for me. Trying desperately to fit in with the other guys on the baseball team or in the library, trying to keep up with my studies. It would have been easy to get caught up in the party lifestyle, but I wasn't throwing away my only opportunity to make something of myself.

Guilt was a constant companion while I enjoyed the perks of being a scholarship athlete and my brother was off literally fighting for his life in places he couldn't even tell me about. We tried to keep up an email correspondence, but he'd go silent for weeks at a time and come back sounding more jaded than ever after a particularly long deployment. He didn't tell me the terrible things he witnessed overseas, and I didn't ask, but the guilt was always there that I was close to home and building a secure life for myself while he risked his every day.

Weary and sore, I took a shower in the locker room and got dressed in casual clothes, pocketed my car keys, and headed to the parking garage.

A flash of a blonde ponytail caught my attention as I made my way across the closed lobby of the building, my pace slowing as I watched a woman in a pair of tight leggings and a baggy sweatshirt grumble at her phone.

"Can I help you with something?" I asked as I walked closer, my steps faltering when Isobel turned toward me. I wasn't used to seeing her face bare, but she still stunned me as I took in the flush in her cheeks and the sweat along her hairline—she was beautiful. She'd clearly been trying to work off some aggression in the gym tonight like I had been.

"I'm good. Just trying to get this stupid app downloaded on my work phone, and the network is being slow as fuck. My personal phone died, and I forgot to charge it this afternoon. Kind of hard to request a ride home if I can't log into the damn app."

Without hesitation, my mouth opened. "I'll give you a ride."

"Yeah, I'm sure you'd like that," she mumbled before she turned away from me and continued stabbing her finger on the screen.

"Is, I'm not trying to be difficult, but at this rate, you'll be waiting here a while, and I feel guilty leaving a woman stranded after dark if I can help."

"Oh, so you need to come in and flex your muscles to protect me because I'm a helpless little woman?"

God, why did she have to think the worst of me immediately? I knew the answer to that, but I didn't like it. "I'm offering to be a nice guy, not because I think you're helpless. My mother raised me to be a gentleman. Please let me escort you home safely."

"Could have fooled me, *Dickhead*."

Flinching as she hurled that nickname at me like an insult, I took a deep breath and walked closer with my hands held up in supplication. "I know you're pissed at me, and you should be because my mouth gets me into trouble with you, but I'm not trying to be a dick right now."

Closing her eyes, she took a deep breath, and I tried to keep my eyes on her face instead of her breasts as she let it out on a shaky exhale. "Fine. I'm sorry. Just...don't. I can't handle the dick right now."

My jaw clenched as I stifled my laughter, trying to keep in the crass commentary about her last statement. She'd handled my dick just fine.

"Shut up." The way she narrowed her eyes, and the finger pointed at my chest, should have been intimidating. Instead of shriveling my balls, it made my attraction to her flare to life, which I needed to get under control because athletic pants hid nothing.

"I didn't say anything."

Her hand reached out and smacked my arm before she shouldered her bag and nodded toward the door that led to the attached parking garage. It still befuddled me she didn't have a car, but with the cost of gas and parking rising exponentially every year, I guess that using Uber was a solid economical choice. At least that was probably safer than taking the public transit at night. As a woman traveling alone, I wasn't sure I'd trust people on the T after the evening rush hour was over. While I knew she prided herself on being independent, the world could be a dangerous place for women after dark.

"Did you get my emails?" she asked quietly while we fell into step together.

"I did. Thank you."

"And have you talked to Evan yet?" Her voice was a little louder, and I could tell she was gearing up for a fight.

"Not yet." Glancing over at her profile, I could see her mouth open, so without thinking about the implications, I reached out and squeezed her palm before she could get started. "He's a morning person, so I'll call him in the morning, but I already had the box of books waiting for same day delivery when I left my office."

"Oh, good." She shook her hand out, massaging her palm after I let go, and I had a hard time forcing myself not to react to the jolt I'd felt with her palm connected to mine.

I knew she was saving my ass on this one, and while Sloane's idea for a collaboration with Isobel was sound, I still wondered if hiring an outside consultant might have been a better idea. Then the tension between us could have some time to dissipate, and I could figure out how to be in a meeting with her without getting a fucking hard-on like a teenager.

"Are you sure this is going to work?" she asked while she followed me up the ramp toward my parking space. One of the only perks I negotiated in my last contract was a reserved parking space included in my benefits package. Parking downtown was a bitch.

"At this point, what harm does it cause? Even if whoever he picks doesn't work out, this may light a fire under his ass to get this manuscript past the rough draft."

"Why wouldn't they work out?"

Rolling my eyes, I crossed to the passenger side of my car, pulling the door open so she could slide into the seat. She opened her mouth to ask again, but I held up my hand as I started to swing the door closed. "Hold that thought."

Taking a few deep breaths, I tried to psych myself up to spend another half hour trapped inside a vehicle with her. It'd been torturous to ride back to Boston from Bar Harbor. The only saving grace was that she hadn't worn a skirt on the trip home as she had on the way up there. Honestly, though, my focus had been drawn more to her calm face while she was sleeping more than anything else. Something I don't care to acknowledge because it would probably make me sound like a complete simp.

She was checking her email as I slid into the driver's seat, pressed the button to start the ignition, and reached forward to turn down the music.

"You don't think my authors can keep up with Evan? Then why did you need my help? Several of my authors are just as talented. Just because they don't have the same mainstream success doesn't diminish their abilities."

Clenching my fingers on the leather of the steering wheel, I bit back the quick retort, realizing that one of us had to start diffusing the tension before things got heated.

"It's not that they can't keep up. It's him. I'm unsure how he'll handle having someone else look at his work. He barely tolerates me sometimes, but I know how to handle him."

"He *is* a prima donna, then?"

Laughing at her continued use of the term, I tried to figure out a way to describe my most prolific author. I knew she hated it when I started going into rankings and sales, but behind all that, there was a quiet man I wasn't always sure how to reach.

"Evan is special, not because of the accolades, but because his mind innately plans out a coherent plot line with little effort. Where some authors take months to construct a book and start cranking out words, he rarely takes longer than six weeks to draft and have a manuscript in my inbox. While we treat it like any other project, he doesn't *need* a developmental edit most of the time." I paused to formulate my thoughts as I signaled to pull out into traffic. I knew where she lived, so she didn't need to give me directions, but I still pulled up the street map on my car navigation. "When Sam did the first read-through on this project, he asked me if Evan had sent me his initial unedited draft instead of the rough draft."

"Well, that's never good. I can see why you're worried."

In my peripheral vision, I could see her fidgeting with her phone grip, but for once, she was listening to me instead of trying to pick a fight.

"While I know this isn't ideal for either of us, Sam and I have only gotten so far with our suggestions. We need someone to work with him who knows what they're doing. Someone who speaks author. I know we like to joke that editors are the unofficial co-writers for any book, but sometimes we can't access that creative process like they can."

"I'm sorry. I thought you had ulterior motives with this one. I know Evan doesn't have a reputation for being difficult. I just thought you were manipulating me to make my life more difficult after..."

Biting my tongue until I pulled to a stop outside her building, I turned in my seat. "I get you think I'm an arrogant asshole, and I'll own that, but I would never go to Sloane to force you to do something. We need your help, and when she suggested working with you, I guess I underestimated exactly how much you hate me."

"I don't hate you." She refused to look at me, continuing to spin the grip on the back of her phone while she stared at her lap.

"Could have fooled me. Once we got back to the office, it was like nothing ever happened while we were together in Maine. You shut me out before we even got in the car to come home. And if the silent treatment in the office wasn't a sign, the glares aimed in my direction every time I opened my mouth were a pretty good indication." I didn't want to continue this fight, but we would have to rely on working together for the next few weeks at the minimum—probably longer as our interns collaborated on the edits for the new pages.

"I don't know what you want from me. And I hate that I feed into your bullshit attitude. I don't like the person I am when I fight with you."

"Can you look at me?"

She hesitated, continuing to spin the grip in her fingers. Knowing it'd probably piss her off, I grabbed the phone and placed it into my cup holder before I tilted her chin toward me.

"I don't want anything other than your professional help. There's no manipulation here. I need you, and I don't want to spend the next few months with you hating me. Is it possible to come to some sort of cease-fire? I'm not the only one picking fights here."

"Stop the arrogant peacocking, and I'll try to bite my tongue." As her eyes met mine, I tamped down my physical reaction because I wanted to be the one who bit her tongue.

A charged moment seemed to pass between us while she looked up at me, her eyes darting around my face and briefly settling on my lips. The physical attraction I'd been fighting felt like another entity in the car, wrapping around us and sending a line of goosebumps up my neck. She kept fighting it, and I knew she'd deny it, but she wanted me too, despite all the antagonistic behavior.

"I'll try," I promised, reaching over and pressing the button to unlock her door. She sucked in a breath as I leaned across her body, and I knew I could have easily leaned back and pressed the unlock button on my side, but watching her reaction to my proximity was more fun.

"Let me know when you hear something." She shoved her phone into an outside pocket of her bag, her eyes nervously darting around the car's interior, anywhere but where I was watching her intently.

"You got it. I'll call him in the morning, but I'll lean on him if I don't hear back by the end of next week. Thank you again. I do appreciate this."

"Night," she mumbled before she pushed the door open, darting across the sidewalk and swiping a key card on the electronic lock outside her building.

As I pulled back into traffic, I wondered if this temporary truce and working together would ever address the elephant in the room. I knew what she looked like when she came, and I wanted to see it again. Desperately.

Chapter ELEVEN

ISOBEL

BOSTON

Evan didn't take long to decide which one of my authors he wanted to work with, and I was pleasantly surprised he chose Chase. She'd also been my first choice because I knew she was easy to get along with and had never met a stranger. I was a little afraid for Evan because of his introverted nature, but if anyone could teach a masterclass on writing a steamy sex scene, it was her. Chase's writing methods were a little unconventional, but maybe pushing Evan out of his comfort zone would spark something.

Adrian had played nicely during the weekly staff meetings, keeping his snide comments to himself for the most part. Unfortunately, he'd actively antagonized Chase when she'd been in the office for me to pitch this idea of consulting to her. But a few well-placed barbs, aimed directly at Adrian, and she'd calmed down enough to agree to help.

She'd left the city a week ago to help Evan, and it took all my willpower to let her do what she did best without my interference. We'd exchanged a few texts, and I'd forwarded information from Adrian, but things were quiet on her end. It'd seemed important to Adrian that this intervention work, so I was letting it play out naturally.

Kristine, my copy-editing intern, was less enthusiastic about being forced to work with Adrian and Sam, but it wasn't her decision. I'd just have to find creative ways to keep Adrian's mouth shut in her presence. Sam could probably handle her prickly attitude. He possessed more tact than his abrasive supervisor, not that it'd take much.

But, of course, Adrian just couldn't resist riling up my intern and intentionally provoked her in my office when I was trying to explain to her why she needed to play nice during this collaboration. As much as I hated to admit it, Sloane was smart to call in someone internally, because all our authors had signed NDAs in their contracts regarding internal communications from the publishing house.

Which meant that even if she wanted to—not that I thought she would—Chase wouldn't be able to breathe a word about the reason she was helping Evan polish up his book. The last thing we needed was it getting accidentally leaked to the press that one of our top performing authors was having trouble with his manuscripts to the point where another department was being called in to salvage his work for print. Not to mention that his readers were less likely to take his book seriously if they thought he wasn't capable of writing what he was putting out without someone more experienced holding his hand.

Now I was left standing in my office, staring down at the man who couldn't control the filter on his mouth long enough for me to convince my intern to play nice with his.

"What the hell do you want?" I asked after Kristine's silhouette had stormed past my window. "Surely you aren't that much of an asshole that you came down here to pick another fight. Because I'd hate to talk to Sloane about cutting you out of your author's novel because you couldn't play nice with an intern."

"What the fuck, Is? That's out of line. He's my author and I am not letting you hijack his work. You've never overseen a thriller in your career."

Stepping around him to push my office door closed, not wanting to give the gossips any fodder. "And you were out of line suggesting that my direct report was anything less than a professional. That's twice now that you've picked a fight inside my office, once with my employee, and don't forget how you insulted one of my authors. That shit isn't going to fly with me. I know you apologized for what happened when we talked to Sloane, but this is becoming a nasty habit for you. That aggressive bullshit better stop now, or I will no longer be providing my assistance on this project."

His eyes were comically wide as I laid into him, and he shifted, awkwardly pulling at the seam of one of his pant legs while his eyes were focused somewhere on my face, but certainly not my eyes.

"What?"

"I don't want to get slapped for telling you the truth, so let's just move on."

Taken aback by his comment, I opened my mouth but wasn't sure exactly what to say to him.

"It was hot," he whispered, his eyes filling with mischief.

"What—?"

"When you put me in my place just now. *That* was hot." He continued to stare at me, the atmosphere in my office shifting as it had in the car the other night. While neither of us had directly addressed our mutual physical attraction to each other, it was clearly still there, even if I didn't want it to be.

"You didn't come down here to flirt with me. What do you want?"

He leaned forward, cupping his chin, and slowly rubbed the stubble he surprisingly hadn't shaved off this morning. "I think it might actually work. The new pages, they're..." He trailed off, and I watched him swallow, his Adam's apple bobbing heavily. "They're hot. Like *I didn't know Evan was capable of writing this* kind of hot. I can tell he had help, but it's still his writing. I know I made a crack at Chase being flirty, and I'm sorry for that, but I think she's getting through to him."

"Oh." Well. That was good, at least for Evan and Chase. It meant they might finish up quicker than expected. "That's good. Then we can stay out of each other's hair if they complete the rewrites early."

"Right," he nodded, his gaze traveling lower and running down my body like a caress.

"Right." Snapping to get his attention, I pinned him with a loaded look, not knowing how to deal with his blatant ogling. Clearly, he was attracted to me, but we'd agreed that weekend had never happened. It was a one-off that I wasn't planning to repeat.

"I think we should sit down and go over the pages together. I know they're vastly improved from the originals, but if everyone else is working together on this, shouldn't we?"

"They've already gone through four sets of eyes by now, and I trust Kristine and Sam to make sure they catch any further issues. I don't think we need to sit down together. Anything you need regarding the document can easily be handled via email."

He frowned, clearly not liking my dismissal, but the two of us spending time alone together was a terrible idea. While I hated myself for it, I couldn't repress my attraction to him anymore, and the temptation of having him near wouldn't help that.

"I know we can communicate by email, but sometimes it's easier to brainstorm and have a discussion in person where I can see your reactions to things and get real time feedback. Isn't working that way a little distant?"

He wasn't letting me off the hook. But I knew he had to have an ulterior motive to get me alone. I didn't want to talk about my impulsive behavior, or the fact that he was the first man to give me a satisfying orgasm in years. "We can sit down in my office next week once we've got the final documents ready for the proofers."

"You seem to be giving me excuses as to why you won't work with me. When you've been insisting this entire time you want our offices to work as a team on this release. This is me being a team player. Are you capable of being a team player, Is? Or was that little display of dominance in front of your intern just another way to get back at me?"

"You seem to think I want to spend more time with you than necessary on this project."

He smirked, knowing I was having a hard time coming up with reasons to avoid what he wanted.

"That was still avoiding the question. But nice try at blowing me off. We know how much you enjoy doing that."

My cheeks ached as I clenched my jaw, gnashing my teeth together. My blood pressure started to rise, my heart pounding as I fought the urge to tell him exactly where he could shove that blowing comment.

"What are you doing tomorrow night?"

My pulse raced as I thought about his request. Tomorrow was a Friday, so after 5:00, we were off the clock. This didn't sound like a professional invitation. It sounded more like a come-on, and I hated that my nipples were standing at attention at the prospect. It'd been a while, but I wasn't sure that opening the door to something like this was a good idea.

"You can send me your notes, and I'll review them this weekend."

Adrian's smile widened fractionally as he stepped forward, his palm settling on the outside of my arm. "Or I can use my expense account to order dinner, and we can go over this together. You said you wanted this to be a collaboration, so I think we need to discuss where *we* might make some changes. If everyone else is working together, it only makes sense that we spend time together to ensure this document gets the attention it deserves. I know you'd rather do that here in your office, where you think I'll behave myself. But I secretly think you like it when I misbehave. Come on. Work with me. One working dinner won't kill you."

As his thumb caressed the front of my arm, I felt like he wasn't talking about the document. He wanted to give this tension between us attention, which was a scary prospect to indulge in. Office affairs were messy, and while my quickened pulse and the increased wetness between my legs in the last few minutes confirmed that my body still wanted him, my brain was screaming to run in the other direction.

I opened my mouth to shut it down, but the heat in his gaze made me change direction. "I'm not coming to your fuck pad. We'll do this at my apartment. I get to pick the restaurant. You go pick it up. And I'm still not sleeping with you."

Completely ignoring my last comment, he nodded. "Done. Text me with the details. I'll be there at 7:00. Do you like red or white?"

"You're not getting me drunk if we plan on getting work done."

"Not drunk," he smiled, stepping forward and leaning toward my ear again. "Maybe just enough to loosen you up. You're a bit *tense*."

Adrian quickly realized he was borderline outwearing his welcome and retreated, smirking at me as he turned in the doorway and gave me a slow once over again, making my skin break out in goosebumps.

"I'll see you tomorrow."

This had to be the dumbest decision I'd ever made. Next to getting married and then divorced before I even hit thirty. Hopefully, this didn't wreck me like that had.

Chapter TWELVE

ADRIAN

BOSTON

To my surprise, Isobel texted me bright and early Friday morning with her dinner order, along with a very specific list of wines I could bring if I wanted admittance to her apartment. I knew I was treading a dangerous line between professionalism and my attraction to my co-worker, but this was a risk I felt I'd kick myself in the ass later for if I didn't take it.

The attraction had been building since my first interaction with her when Vivid hired me, and it'd simmered for five years. Five years where I'd thought she was an uptight shrew who couldn't take a joke and five years where she'd bought my world's biggest jackass routine.

I had a long route to convince her that my attraction wasn't just another thing I'd done to mess with her, and I was tired of watching her from afar. Without our brief dalliance at the publisher's conference, I would have continued to think my attraction was one-sided, but once she flipped the switch on me, I couldn't turn it off.

She was guarded, no-nonsense, and sexy as fuck in a way that I couldn't resist. I was tired of the meaningless hookups or younger women hitting on me because I dressed like I had more money than I did. I wanted a real woman. Someone who had worked hard and made something of herself, and Isobel checked all the boxes.

Sam had sent me all his notes on the pages we'd received so far, and I was amazed at how quickly Chase and Evan had been able to restructure the scenes. I thought he'd fight it, and it'd take weeks of drawn-out collaboration, but with Chase's help, Evan's writing had a spark behind it I'd never seen before. It reminded me of Evan's earlier work, not the sex part, but the inspiration behind his writing—before he'd met Simone and she'd driven him into a life of seclusion with her toxic manipulating bullshit.

My mind started racing with possibilities of the two of them continuing their writing collaboration past this book, but I felt Isobel would be dead against it. She guarded her authors like a junkyard dog, and I had no desire to be bitten.

At least not in anger.

Maybe in sexual frustration.

Because I was feeling lots of that since we left Maine.

Isobel's door was closed when I walked the floor after my weight-lifting session during my lunch hour, but she hadn't canceled on me yet. I knew I'd fought dirty by goading her into meeting with me outside the office. I needed to see if this pull I felt toward her was only because she didn't seem to want me, and I was rising to the challenge. Or if it was because once she let her hair out of those tight buns and sleek professional ponytails, she was attracted to me too, telling me it was definitely not one-sided.

I debated on changing after leaving the office at 5:00, but I needed to take a trip to a specialty wine shop on the other side of downtown if I was going to fulfill her demands. After fighting rush hour traffic and barely finding a spot to park on the street, I hurried to pick up our food.

The restaurant had my order packed in an insulated travel container in just enough time for me to make it to Isobel's apartment. Despite giving her a ride to and from the conference and then home from the gym, I'd never been inside.

Balancing the bags containing our meals, I buzzed the intercom, waiting for it to connect and hoping she would let me in. It'd be a bitch move to let me plan all this and bail, but I couldn't blame her for punishing me for my past misbehaviors.

I began to worry when the buzzer disengaged, and the speaker went silent. Shifting nervously as I scanned the windows above for signs of Isobel peeping out at my discomfort, I steadied the bags again and pressed the button for a second time.

A few long seconds later, the speaker crackled to life. "Keep your pants on. I'm coming."

Laughing at the way she sounded out of breath; I couldn't hold in the obvious joke. "I think you'd enjoy it more if my pants were off."

The intercom went silent, and I wondered if I'd pushed too far, but the lock on the door to my left buzzed loudly, and I heard it disengage as Isobel's voice floated over the line. "Doubt it, but I'll let you up anyway. You better have my wine. You know I'll need it to deal with you. I'm in 306."

Thankfully, her modest brick building had been updated and had an elevator, so I didn't have to trek up three floors with my arms full. At least it was leg day, so my arms weren't tired, but I hadn't expected to get a second workout for the day with our dinner. Although I wouldn't be opposed to a third if this working dinner went how I wished it would. While our brief tryst had been quick and slightly frustrating, I could tell Isobel would be a handful in bed. And I wanted to fill both hands.

I took a deep breath before transferring all the bags to one hand and knocked on her apartment door. She kept me waiting once again, my pulse picking up as I waited for the door to swing open. When it did, I wasn't expecting what I saw.

Isobel was fresh-faced, with her wet hair piled on top of her head in a messy bun. A soft-looking turquoise sweater hung to mid-thigh, and her long bare legs peeked out underneath.

"Eyes up here," she chuckled while I perused her casual outfit, my hand flexing against the handles of the bags so I didn't do something reckless, like drop to my knees to explore all that smooth bare skin with my lips.

"No big boy this time?"

She rolled her eyes, pulling the door open further as she stepped to the side, my shoulder brushing hers when I stepped into the apartment. "You don't need your ego inflated any more than it already is."

It was a stark contrast to her office as far as the color palette, but just as chaotic. A fireplace surrounded with built-in bookcases lined the far wall of her small living room, stuffed full, with no visible order to them. I thought of my bookcases at home, with the titles neatly stacked upright and organized chronologically by release for each author who were placed in order alphabetically. Hutch often teased me for my OCD tendencies, and I typically spent at least an hour combing my shelves for the one book he tried to hide out of order after he'd been over to my place.

As I scanned her modest living space, the only similarities we seemed to hold were the number of books we owned. She'd surrounded herself with creature comforts, cushy-looking furniture, plush pillows, pops of bright color mixed with the warm tone of the exposed brick walls, and several lamps interspersed to give it a homey feeling. It made me glad we'd decided to work in her environment, not mine. I knew she'd never be able to resist giving me shit for my stereotypical bachelor pad filled with leather couches, sleek furniture with clean lines, and stark white walls.

My apartment was a little smaller than hers, but they were day and night, sort of like the two of us. We both had sharp edges, but hers were rounded where mine were jagged.

"Quit being weird. You can run a full stalker analysis on my living room later. My food better still be warm."

"I would tell you to keep your pants on, but I can't tell if you're wearing any," I smirked, nodding toward the long hem of her sweater.

"I'm wearing shorts, you ass." She swatted at my arm before she turned and moved toward the kitchen while my eyes studied the creamy expanse of skin exposed on the back of her thighs.

Every exchange of words between us lately seemed to be laced with sexual tension.

"Did you get my—?" she trailed off as she looked back at the table, and I pulled out the bottle of wine at the top of her list. It wasn't a fancy blend, but I was glad I'd stopped at the specialty shop because it wasn't something I could have picked up at the street market near our office.

"Yes, I got your wine. Where are your glasses?"

Isobel pulled open the container with her meal and inhaled, a satisfied smile crossing her face as she let out a tiny moan. I could appreciate a woman who liked food as much as she did.

"Do I need to leave you two alone?" I teased as she reluctantly returned the container to the table and walked toward me.

"While I'd love to have the satisfaction of kicking you out of my apartment, you brought my favorite wine, and you got me carbs, so I'll let you stay...for now. But I reserve the right to push you out the door if you start that arrogant bullshit you get away with at the office."

"Fair enough," I chuckled, stepping to the side as she passed me. I followed a few steps behind, watching while she pulled cutlery from a drawer next to her tiny dishwasher. She opened an upper cabinet, pushing up onto her tiptoes, the muscles in her calves drawing my eyes as they flexed. "I'll make sure not to tell you how much I'm enjoying your shorts. If you could call them that."

My eyes slowly trailed up the back of her legs, lingering on the swell of her ass as it peeked out from beneath the hem of her shorts. She may have joked about not being in shape like she was in back in high school but combined with the curves of her hips and the long lines of her legs, she was hotter than she realized. The clothes she wore at work hinted at some insane curves, and the glimpses I'd gotten of her while we were in Maine were enough to want more, but I wasn't sure where we were now.

"Are you still staring at my ass?" she asked, glancing over her shoulder with the stem of a wine glass balanced between her fingers.

"Are you surprised? We've had this conversation before. You know I'm fond of the scenery."

Isobel rolled her eyes as she pulled down a second glass, gently setting both on the counter. I knew being around me bothered her now. We hadn't talked about what had happened at the conference. Not really. Just me teasing her and pissing her off. I didn't like that there was this tension between us. I wanted to get to know her better. While I may not have been in touch with all my emotions, I knew that the feelings she stirred up in me weren't just physical attraction. That was currently a large part of it, but she was kind—to everyone but me—and she was funny.

"Keep it in your pants, Casanova. We're here to work. You just insisted on inviting yourself over. Try not to look so needy."

Taking another step forward, I placed my hand on the counter next to her, careful not to touch her, but close enough that she could touch me if she wanted to. And damn, I hoped she wanted to. "You could have said no to me.

It wouldn't be the first time. I think you want to talk about what's happening between us. Or maybe the problem is you don't just want to talk."

"There is no us, Adrian. I was temporarily shown a different side of you, and I had a lapse in judgment. It won't happen again."

Testing her boundaries, I traced a lone curl at the back of her neck, my fingers lingering at the collar of her sweater. "You keep saying that, but I've seen how you look at me. It was more than just a lapse in judgment."

Her shoulders heaved as she took a deep breath and turned to face me, her expression guarded as she looked up into my eyes. "Being attracted to someone doesn't mean I like who they are as a person. And you haven't convinced me that the bizarro world Adrian was real. As soon as we got back to the office, you were back to the arrogant comments."

"Was I?" I asked, knowing I'd been tamer lately besides our confrontation in the stairwell. "Or have you convinced yourself that I was?"

Her palm settled into the center of my chest, causing me to pull in a surprised breath, my hands clenching at my side with the urge to touch her.

"You called my authors *mommy porn writers*. Not exactly on your best behavior."

Narrowing my eyes and clenching my jaw to hold in my gut reaction, I took another deep breath and tried to relax. "And you were implying my author was going to sexually harass yours. Was that you being on your best behavior?"

It was her turn to clench her jaw as she reached behind her and grasped the wine glasses, brushing past me to put them on the table beside the bottle of wine.

"Not going to admit you sometimes say things in poor taste just as I do?"

Her movements were agitated as she grabbed an electric wine opener from the counter, centering it on the bottle and pressing the button to remove the cork from the bottle.

"Don't even try to compare me to you. When I met you, the first words out of your mouth would be considered sexual harassment by most people. I didn't even know you."

Thinking back to when I'd first met Isobel, I frowned while I tried to remember what she was talking about. I know I'd noticed her before she noticed me, but what could I have said that caused her to hate me this much?

"Fine. Since you don't even remember what you say to people," she huffed while she poured wine into one of the glasses, then turned toward me using the half full glass to gesture in my direction. "You told me you could handle fixing the copy machine by yourself, because you weren't sure my sexy skirt would allow it."

Fuck.

I remembered her walking in on me berating the copy machine my first week at work. I chuckled as I recalled the look on her face when she'd caught me, slightly amused, a bit arrogant and a lot knowing.

"And you're laughing about your shitty behavior. Real attractive, Adrian."

"That's why you hate me?" I laughed, shaking my head.

"You were a dick from the moment you met me."

Stepping forward and grabbing the wine bottle from the table, I poured myself half a glass, earning narrowed eyes from Isobel.

Too bad. I paid for it. I could at least have a small glass.

"Did you look at my hands?"

"Why the fuck would I have been looking at your hands? You were simultaneously hitting on me and being a douchey jerk," she scoffed.

"I won't apologize for calling you sexy, because you *are* sexy. I may not have a filter, but I know when I turned around and found you watching me from the doorway, I was stunned by you."

"Are you trying to flatter me to get me to overlook your behavior? That may work on the administrative assistants you fuck, but it won't work on me."

I tipped my glass back, taking a generous sip of the red wine, my eyes widening as I let it sit in my mouth. It was surprisingly tart, but had a full-bodied flavor and hints of cherries and something smoky I couldn't place. It was good.

"And do you remember the skirt you were wearing? What color was it? Because I remember. It was white. And I had toner all over my hands. I accidentally jostled the cartridge while I was trying to dislodge a piece of paper that was stuck. I didn't want you to help me because I was afraid it would ruin your skirt. And that would have been a travesty."

Reaching behind me, I grabbed a fork from the counter where she'd left them and the bag my meal was in, walking past her to the large plushy couch.

"And I have never once *fucked* an administrative intern. I think someone has been listening to the office rumors. If you actually paid attention, you'd see I'm usually very nice to the assistants and the interns." She narrowed her eyes at me, and I knew what she was getting at. "Except for Kristine. But she usually starts it."

"And you could end it without baiting her," she growled.

"I can try better next time. Now can we eat dinner and then get through proofing these pages? Or would you rather continue to hash out a miscommunication from over five years ago?"

Placing my takeout container on the table, I unbuttoned the front of my suit jacket and sat down, sinking into the cushion immediately. Yeah, my leather couch was not this comfortable.

As I settled my meal in my lap, I could see Isobel hovering in my periphery, her wineglass in one hand and her takeout container in the other.

"Sit."

"I'm sorry." She spoke so softly I almost didn't hear her, but when I glanced in her direction, I could see the remorse painted across her features. I didn't want an apology. She probably wasn't even wrong to think I was a dick, but I hadn't meant to offend her with my comments either.

"Don't be. I have just as much to apologize for. We both know I've been a dick around the office more than I should be. Your dislike of me probably isn't far off the mark, but I genuinely didn't know that's why you don't like me."

The couch dipped slightly as she sat down next to me, almost an entire cushion between us.

"We've seen each other half naked. You don't need to act so awkward around me," I teased, and watched a blush creep up her neck.

"That's exactly why I'm awkward around you. I know my avoidance of you hasn't exactly been subtle. But I don't know how to act around you anymore."

"Just keep teasing me and putting me in my place. I know my big mouth is one of my worst traits. Trust me, I've tried to turn it off, but it just keeps popping out things I regret saying later."

"Well, maybe you should work on that."

"Well," I started, watching her tentatively taking small bites of her food while keeping her eyes on me. "Maybe you should work on not jumping to conclusions when I say stupid shit."

"I can try," she conceded. It was progress.

"That's all I ask."

ISOBEL

BOSTON

"Did you read over everything they sent?" I asked, closing my food container and setting it on the coffee table. I still couldn't believe he'd found my favorite wine and brought me dinner. I knew it was what I'd demanded of him, but I didn't think he'd follow through.

"Yeah. And I looked at the notes from Sam's first pass through. It's so much better than the first draft. I wasn't being facetious when I said Chase had worked some magic on Evan."

Shaking my head, I laughed. "Could have picked a better way of phrasing it in front of Kristine. She was ready to rip your balls off. And I might have let her."

"Aw. And here I thought you liked my balls where they are."

"Don't," I warned, tipping my glass in his direction. "I may tolerate your bullshit occasionally, but don't start."

"I didn't say anything bad."

"This time."

"Fair enough." He paused, rising from the couch to deposit his now empty container on the edge of my kitchen counter. He walked back toward the door and bent down to retrieve his computer from his bag. His snug dress pants tightened across his ass, and I shamelessly ogled him like he'd done to me earlier.

"Quit staring at my ass."

Smothering a giggle, I tipped back my wine, setting the nearly empty glass on the corner of my coffee table.

"You didn't deny it," he observed with a smirk while he returned to his seat on the other end of the couch.

"Am I supposed to? You know you like all the appreciative looks your suit porn gets."

His grin was borderline obnoxious as he opened his laptop, refraining from responding to my comment. He had to know how despite his mouth being a problem; he was often a source of gossip among the women of the office. Typically, because we were all bemoaning that a man that attractive had the emotional intelligence of a gnat. But Adrian had fooled us all, thinking he was a colossal douchecanoe when he could be a thoughtful, considerate human being.

Maybe I needed that last swallow of wine after all.

"Wasn't aware I was the star of your pornographic menswear fantasies, but I can't say that I'm mad about it. You're often the focus of my nocturnal emissions as of late."

He laughed as my eyes widened, my mouthful of wine nearly becoming a choking hazard as I sputtered.

"Do you need a napkin?"

This smug bastard.

"You keep your emissions off my couch, mister."

"Oh, I'm sorry, is this an emission-free zone?"

Why did our conversations always lead to something suggestive? Maybe it was because the thinly veiled mutual attraction we shared seemed to be fully out of hiding. Or maybe because I could still remember the taste of him in my mouth. Whatever it was, I was in trouble.

"Sorry, this couch is pristine in more ways than one. You keep your dirty thoughts away from my baby and keep your pants on." He chucked as I lovingly petted the soft material of the first possession I bought when I moved into this apartment after the divorce.

"Do we have to keep yours on?" Adrian asked, with one eyebrow raised slightly. His tongue made a slow pass between his lips and my mouth went dry at the sight of it, but I wasn't letting him suck me back into the orbit of his sexual brain fog. I made impulsive decisions around him, and I needed to keep this professional for my own sanity.

"Just pull up the document and stop flirting with me."

Quickly reaching forward, I grabbed my glass—tipping in the last few drops lingering in the bottom, rose from the cushion I'd been slouched against, and carried my partially empty container to the kitchen counter. I eyed the bottle of wine on the table, debating on a refill, but we needed to get something productive done tonight regardless of his flirtatious advances. The consumption of more alcohol would just make interacting with him cloud my brain further.

I grabbed my tablet off the table before I returned to my end of the couch, quickly typing in my passcode and sitting down.

"If you want to see my notes, you need to sit a little closer than that."

My pulse skipped as I shifted across the empty cushion between us, his arm perched across the back of the couch, seemingly welcoming me into his side. I may have known what he tasted like, but we hadn't exactly cuddled after what we'd done in our adjoined hotel rooms. Or what he'd done to me, despite my best efforts to escape. Couldn't he just let a girl fellate and flee? Sometimes you just wanted a mouth full of—

"Can you see alright, or do I need to make the font larger?" he asked, interrupting my line of thought. He'd leaned toward my ear, his warm breath stirring the stray hairs against my neck, the sensation not entirely unpleasant.

"Are you calling me old?" I whispered, my voice tense at his proximity. The warmth from his side radiated through my sweater, sending a shiver up my spine. Despite spending the day in the office and coming straight here, he still smelled amazing, and I was finding it hard to concentrate on the words on the laptop screen propped on his legs. His strong, muscular legs, that had flexed when I grasped them, while my lips surrounded his—

"You're shaking. Are you cold?" he whispered back, shifting slightly in my direction.

I didn't dare look at his face. He could read me too well. He'd know by the flush on my cheeks and the dazed look in my eyes that my thoughts weren't entirely on work.

"You seem tense."

I *am* tense—was what I wanted to say, but admitting that would only lead to more questions. Questions I didn't have the answers to. I was wondering about my sanity lately, too. I was never this scattered when it came to work.

If Kristine wasn't so meticulous about putting things into our shared calendar, I would have been lost this past week. I didn't like that I was letting a man distract me from my professional life, but I couldn't seem to stop thinking about him. Adrian was slowly endearing himself to me when we were alone, although I still had a hard time trusting that he was being sincere. This all seemed too easy to be real.

"I thought maybe that glass of wine would relax you," he murmured, and I felt his fingertips brush against the back of my shoulder blade. "But maybe you need something else."

"Stop," I whispered, trying to focus my attention on the words on his screen. I'd looked over the shared document on the server earlier, before my shower, so I knew what was already noted, but all my brain could focus on was the deep, gravelly sound of his voice when he whispered that close to my ear. "Just pay attention to the document, not me."

"It's hard to concentrate with the potent scent of your shampoo. It smells almost as sweet as the taste of something else on my lips."

"*Adrian.*" My voice was exasperated as I leaned forward, trying to calm my racing heart.

"Fine, I'll stop," he coaxed, his palm settling between my shoulder blades, and causing my arms to break out in goosebumps. *Still not helping.* "Sit up. Please."

Clenching my eyes closed, I counted to ten in my head, willing my body to relax. It wasn't his fault my thoughts kept drifting to the way I'd fundamentally changed things between us. As much as I wanted to displace the blame, I was the one who'd come onto him. I was the one who'd touched him first. I was the one who started this slow descent into madness after our brief tryst.

I was also the one who'd reconstructed the boundaries after everything that happened, somehow expecting them to keep my feelings from changing.

"I know you've seen all these, but I wanted to make sure you were good with the changes I'd suggested after this went through Sam and Kristine. She had some solid suggestions on word usage and the impact of the way Evan had phrased some things. Are you alright with this going back to him next week?"

"You mean her comments about the use of phallic nouns?" He smirked, but didn't respond. Kristine had suggested Evan start coming up with other words than *dick* in one of the sex scenes. Scanning the side margin to double-check that Adrian hadn't added any additional notes since I'd studied them earlier. "What do you think about the changes they've made to the rough draft so far? I know you've gone through and made your own notes, but most of them were technical in nature."

"It's better. I'm still not convinced it needs this much detail, but the scenes in question do flow better."

I knew most of his authors glossed over spicy material, so writing explicitly was likely new to him, but he wasn't exactly a prude.

"You can call them sex scenes, Ad. It won't diminish your author to have a little spice in his novel. I think in this case it helps draw the reader into the relationship between the two characters. Adds some suspense and conflict," I noted. "And Kallie's job is sexual in nature, so including detailed interactions is keeping in line with her backstory. She uses her sexuality to exert control on the rest of her life."

Adrian tensed beside me. "Evan's achieved suspense and conflict just fine without a romantic subplot before."

"And with a little help, he's done it just fine here." Just because there was an angry couch fucking didn't diminish the suspense of the book. It added a little more excitement.

"I guess." Adrian nodded, glancing over at me, his posture still tense. I could tell this was pulling him out of his comfort zone.

"Quit being so dismissive," I teased, pushing my shoulder into his side. "You realize sex is part of the human experience. People fuck. Seeing it on the page shouldn't be shameful or dirty."

"Well," he smiled, a little bit of his bravado returning. "I agree with the shameful part, but being a little dirty is the fun part of sex."

And there was the teasing again. Even if hearing it made my heart skip a beat.

"Was that an admission that maybe I'm right?" I gasped, dramatically placing my hand in the center of my chest. His eyes narrowed in on the action, the neckline of my sweater dipping dangerously low.

"Don't look so smug. Chase helped him get this into shape, but I told you the bones were good." His voice still held an edge of vulnerability, but I knew he was trying to defend his author. I'd never doubted the quality of Evan's work, and I knew I was sensitive when people criticized my authors.

"It was just the actual boning that was terrible." A slightly obnoxious laugh escaped before I clamped my bottom lip between my teeth, sensing Adrian wasn't quite as amused with my comeback.

"Why is everyone in the romance genre so sex obsessed?" He had a point, but like I'd told him. Sex was a part of real life too. Sure, sometimes fictional characters had a bit more of it in frequency and intensity, but despite my own personal dry spell, people fucked.

"Maybe because sexuality is something you shouldn't be ashamed of. Every level of spice is relevant in romance, but there's a huge market for spicy reads. That's why Chase has built up such a following. If you haven't noticed, there are plenty of women out there who aren't ashamed to own that they like reading about sex."

"You mean Evan's novel isn't a really spicy read?" he asked, a little wrinkle forming between his dark eyebrows.

"Hardly." I was trying to tone down my amusement, but he really was clueless when it came down to what was popular right now. He'd been off in his mystery bubble, not realizing that while his authors were successful, mine were as well. He may have thought the revenue from his projects kept my department afloat, but in most fiscal quarters, it was the other way around. "It's maybe midlevel spicy, but you clearly didn't read the books you sent Evan."

"Why would I read a romance novel?" he frowned. I knew I'd given the marketing department specific books to send up to him, but I hadn't realized he'd not looked at any of them before forwarding them on to Evan.

"You might learn a thing or two."

We were treading back into dangerous waters by continuing down this path, but I was enjoying putting him in his place too much and him being the uncomfortable one for once.

"I think I'm competent in the sex department. I don't need to be taking notes from some desperate single woman's erotic fantasies," he snipped, reaching forward to place his open laptop on the coffee table. When he sat back, he shifted away from me, his hands tense on his thighs.

"Excuse me?" Was he really going to continue to believe this bullshit? To be honest, I was almost certain some of my popular authors had sex lives that rivaled their characters. While I was sure some of it was imagination, there were some writers who were extremely committed to research. I knew Chase was one of them. She'd studied the local kink scene for months before her last book, and while I knew she didn't have a sexual relationship with her Dom resource, I knew she'd observed some scenes she'd written firsthand.

"Chase is a talented author, and she's built a following, but I don't want to read some self-insert fantasies." He couldn't even look at me, his shoulders tense as I reached forward and placed my tablet on the table, bringing my leg up onto the couch cushion between us so I could look directly at him.

"Wow. Tell me how you really feel about my work."

"It's not about you personally, it's just..." he heaved a sigh, his posture tense but also a little defeated. I was sensing he realized he'd misspoken, but I wasn't letting this go that easily.

"Nope. Stop talking. Whatever shady bullshit that is about to come flying out of your mouth can just stay in there."

"I'm not trying to be offensive, but people write what they know, right? It'd make sense that the romance authors are writing out experiences or fantasies and using their characters to bring it to life."

"Evan is a detective now?" I asked, willing him to look at me. He had to stop this hypercritical mindset. Both our genres could coexist without it being a constant competition. Because let's face it, if it came down to a dick measuring contest, the romance genre would win every fucking time.

"Um, no, but—"

"Well, applying the same logic, that'd mean he's using his novel to write out his fantasy to be a police detective."

"It's different for—" he started, but I wasn't doing this with him.

"Fuck that, it's not different," I argued, my voice rising as my anger started to boil. "Why don't you pull the stick out of your ass and realize that a romance author can write fictional characters and not be projecting their own fantasies into it?"

"But..."

"Nope," I interrupted again, watching as his jaw clenched. "Close your mouth. Isn't it exhausting to be this much of a jackass? Do you even process the words before they come flying out of that big mouth of yours?"

"You seemed to like this big mouth before," he spat back, finally turning to face me.

"Yeah," I scoffed, rolling my eyes. "When it's full of something and you can't talk."

"You can gag me next time," he shot back, his chest heaving as his intense eyes scanned my face.

"There won't be a next time." My hands shook as I scooted back slightly, needing to be further away from him. "What happened in Maine was..."

"Fucking hot." His voice was harsh as he shifted forward, my eyes widening as he leaned in closer. "And you liked it. *All* of it. Denying it only makes it look like you're trying to hide something. Even I'm able to tell when a woman isn't faking it, Is. And *you* did not fake it all over my face."

"And it was a major lapse in judgment. You can enjoy something and still realize it was a mistake." Placing my hand on his chest, I pushed slightly, but he only shifted closer in response.

"So, if I leaned forward and kissed you right now, it wouldn't turn you on?"

My heart was beating frantically as I shifted back again, the arm of the couch digging into my back. "That's not going to happen, so it's irrelevant."

"But now you're thinking about it," he accused. "Wondering what my lips would feel like pressed against yours. We've never kissed before. Not once through the whole thing. Are you really telling me you haven't thought about it? That you weren't thinking about it when we were yelling at each other in that stairwell?"

"That doesn't matter," I denied weakly. How had he turned the tables on me yet again?

"Doesn't it?" he questioned, his voice dropping an octave as he reached forward to lean over me, his palms braced on the back of the couch and the arm behind me, boxing me in so I couldn't escape. "You know there's chemistry here. Why are you so insistent on denying it? If sex isn't shameful, why aren't we acting on this mutual attraction?"

"Because you're an asshole," I hissed, pressing my hand against his stomach, intending to push him away, but pausing as I felt his muscles flex through his shirt.

"That's all you've got? Me being an asshole didn't seem to stop you from practically ripping my pants off before." He leaned in closer, rising above me, but his eyes were focused entirely on my lips. He was right. We hadn't kissed before, but now I *was* thinking about it.

"Well, you weren't being an asshole then," I retorted, my voice sounding weak even to my ears.

"I'm going to ask you something that's been driving me nuts," he murmured, his eyes capturing my gaze and holding it. "Why then? What changed and made you decide to attack me?"

"I hardly attacked you," I whispered. "You're the one who shoved my hand down the front of your boxers."

"Quit deflecting."

"I'm not..." I panted, my head swimming as his lips hovered inches from my face. "Fine. It was your speech. I sat there listening to you and realized that maybe there was this other side to you. That maybe you weren't a total dickhead, and I was intrigued. And you know what you look like. And it's been a long time for me—"

"Intrigued enough to rip off my pants?" he interrupted.

"They were pulled around your ankles. There wasn't any ripping."

"Semantics. So, you liked what I said?" His posture relaxed, but he didn't back up, the warmth from his body being so close making my head swim.

"Yeah, made me wish you'd stop being such a gigantic asshat ninety percent of the time." Although that number was steadily dropping when we were alone.

"To be fair, it's probably only seventy percent."

"Not from what I've witnessed," I argued, my fingers twitching against him, wondering what his skin felt like beneath the cotton of his shirt. I'd never seen him shirtless this close. And now I was desperately trying to recall it.

"And you've spent all this extra time with me outside of work?" he asked, still hovering.

"I'm doing it now, aren't I?"

"But we're working. Not the same," he argued.

"Are you telling me you aren't *Dickhead* outside the office?" I asked, my voice breathy on his nickname. Sometimes I hated myself. Why was he affecting me like this?

"Are you telling me you aren't boss bitch Barbie outside the office?"

"What?" I froze, my mouth dropping open slightly as my hand faltered, catching on the edge of his belt. "That's what you think of me?"

"Well, you're probably hotter than Barbie, but yeah. That's my impression of you at work. Cold, bossy, and a little bit plastic," he taunted, narrowing his eyes.

"My impression of you is that I'd like to leave the impression of my handprint across your face every time I'm forced to interact with you," I growled, pulling my hand back, but he captured it in his and pressed it against his belt buckle.

"Go ahead," he taunted, turning his cheek slightly and raising an eyebrow.

"I'm not going to slap you." My fingers struggled against his, my eyes widening when I felt his body responding to the movement a few inches lower.

"But you want to. So do it. I dare you. If you really think I'm as terrible as you've built me up to be in your head, then slap me. I. Dare. You," he hissed, his nose brushing mine as he leaned in.

I pulled my other hand from in between our bodies, but Adrian knew I didn't have the nerve to hit him. He sat back on his knees, capturing it in his other hand, twisting it, and pinning it behind my back while he loomed over me on the couch. "You know the saying there's a thin line between love and hate?"

"Are you quoting song lyrics from the seventies to me right now?" I hissed as I struggled against his tight hold on both of my hands.

"I don't think you hate me as much as you say you do. Your nipples wouldn't be that hard if you hated me," he growled, glancing down at where my sweater had gaped open.

"Quit looking down my shirt."

"Quit inviting me over when you're not wearing a bra if you don't want me to look."

"Are you really trying to blame what I'm wearing on your pervy behavior?" The pure audacity of this man was staggering.

"Tell me you don't want me to kiss you right now," he whispered, leaning in closer, his grip on the hand behind my back loosening.

"Is that what you think I want?"

"I think if you wanted to twist off my nuts for touching you, you'd squeeze a hell of a lot harder," he teased, guiding my hand lower, the hard outline of his cock pulsing against my palm.

Adrian stared at my lips, his chest heaving as he waited for my reaction, for a signal that this wasn't one-sided and that I felt this insane, reckless attraction as much as he seemed to. My fingers flexed against his zipper and his hold on my wrist behind my back relaxed as he let out a low groan, the sound utterly desperate.

Fuck.

Acting purely on instinct alone, I wiggled my wrist free and reached out before he could react, my fingers gripping the hair at the back of his head firmly and pulling him forward.

As his lips touched mine, all rational thought flew out the window and I opened for him, matching the frantic desperation of his tongue with my own. My lungs burned while our lips and tongues and teeth collided, the world dimmed by the pounding of my pulse.

Adrian's palm slipped beneath the back of my hair, gripping the strands tightly while he tilted my head backward, his mouth slanting over mine in the same possessive manner he'd held my hips to the bed with not so long ago when we were in Maine.

It seemed the time for talking—although it more closely resembled arguing when Adrian was involved—was over.

FOURTEEN

ADRIAN

BOSTON

"Fuck," I groaned as Isobel yanked on my hair, gasping into my mouth when we briefly pulled apart, diving right back in until my lungs burned from a lack of oxygen.

My lips ached with the ferocity of our kisses, but I was too far gone to stop. I'd wanted this for weeks and I was greedily taking in every nuance of what it felt like to be with Isobel like this.

I should've anticipated her being passionate, her spark being one of the qualities I admired about her, but I hadn't expected her to be quite this desperate, this passionate, this borderline feral as she pulled my hair and bit my lips in between frantic kisses.

It only made me want to touch her more, kiss her more, strip her bare and lick every inch of her body until she convulsed against my tongue.

Her words may have showed her intense displeasure at working together, but her body felt something different toward me. She was hungry and insatiable, and I wanted to possess her—both her body *and* her mind.

"Wait," I panted, pulling away. My heart hammered, and my cock throbbed against the chokehold of my zipper.

"No," she snarled, pulling me back, biting my lower lip and wrapping her calf around the back of mine, urging me forward. For someone who had informed me multiple times she wasn't sleeping with me, things appeared to be heading in that direction.

"Is," I panted, trying to sit up, but she followed me, her other arm wrapping tightly around my neck, her lips tracing the edge of my jaw and nipping at my skin while she tried to pull my mouth back down to hers.

"No, don't stop. Just kiss me," she whispered against my cheek. "It's been so long since I've felt like this. Let's just pretend we like each other."

That was the problem. I wasn't pretending to like her. I did like her. Which was problematic because I didn't know how to stop being an ass around her either. That was the drawback of acting like someone who you weren't for so long. Eventually, you forgot where you ended, and the faux persona began.

"Isobel," I coaxed before I reached back and captured her wrists, bringing them around to hold in front of my chest. "I'm not saying we can't keep going, but I want to talk to you first."

Her bright eyes scanned my face, her cheeks flushed and her hair chaotic as it battled to escape her messy bun. I was sure she'd be embarrassed to see her reflection in the mirror right now, but to me, she'd never looked more alluring.

"What do you want to talk about right now?" she asked, her voice tense and her eyes guarded.

Deciding not to keep beating around the bush, I laid my cards on the table. "I like you."

Her eyes widened, and a surprised laugh escaped her lips. "We'll, I'd hope you like me, seeing as your tongue was just studying the contours of my mouth."

"No, that's not what I'm saying." I shook my head, trying to come up with a way to formulate my thoughts in a way that she'd listen to. "I like who you are, not just your body, or how you kiss me like my mouth holds the secrets of the universe."

Her eyes rolled at my last comment, but I wouldn't expect anything less from her.

"I like how you make me feel. I like your sense of humor. I like how you call me out when I say something I shouldn't. I like how you're finally starting to *see* me, even though you hold me at arm's length. I like *you.*"

"Oh."

I wasn't expecting some grand declaration of her feelings, but when her expression sobered, and she continued to stare at my face with a deep crease pinched between her eyebrows, I worried I might've confessed too much.

"Why are you telling me this right now?"

It was a valid question, but we'd already blurred the lines between us once. I wanted her to know that this wasn't happening only because I found her attractive. I needed her to know that I was developing genuine feelings for her.

"Because I want you to know that if we do this, if things become physical again, I want more."

"I..."

She looked away, but I cupped her cheek, gently urging her face back to mine. "That means you'll need to talk to me. Try to get to know the real me. The me you think is an anomaly."

"What do you want from me?"

"I want you to spend time with me trying not to bite each other's heads off."

"Are you saying you want to date me?"

I nodded, my thumb slowly stroking the soft skin of her jaw.

"Like go on actual dates and do things together outside the office?"

"That is the general idea, yes."

She nodded, her eyes darting across my face, her posture tense. "And this isn't some elaborate joke to you?"

I reached down and grasped her hand, pulling it away from my zipper. I pressed it against my chest, my heart beating at a frantic pace beneath her palm. "Does this feel like a joke to you?"

Isobel licked her lips, swallowing hard. "I'm still not sleeping with you."

"I can live with that." I nodded, lifting her hand and kissing her palm. My lips trailed down her wrist and across the soft skin of her inner forearm, lingering in the crease of her elbow as I draped her arm over my shoulder, leaning in. "But that still leaves quite a few things on the table I'm hoping you're open to."

"Like what?" she asked, her voice shaky as I placed small kisses behind her ear.

"Since you seem to think I'm so out of touch with what your authors write... Have you ever sat on a man's face before? That seemed to be a position Chase's legions of fans enjoyed mentioning in some of her reviews."

She froze, her hand clutching the material of my shirt tightly in her fist. "No."

My teeth nipped at the soft skin of her neck before I shifted, my lips barely grazing her ear as I lowered my voice. "Then I think we need to rectify that. Let's take these tiny shorts off so I can show you what that feels like. Think of it as editorial research. You encourage your writers to do research, right? I think maybe we need to do some of our own."

"We...I...you..." she stuttered while I released her and hooked my thumbs into the elastic waistband of her shorts. As I drew the material down, I expected my fingers to encounter more lace underwear like what she'd been wearing in Maine, but all I felt was soft, warm skin.

"Oh, what do we have here, naughty girl? You knew I was coming over tonight, and you didn't put on any panties?"

Isobel blushed, her forehead falling forward to my chest, with her hands shaking against the material of my shirt.

"I'm taking that as a yes," I whispered, my cheek brushing against hers while I drew the material down. "Stand up, babe."

She braced her hands on my shoulders as she stood from the couch, her shorts falling to her ankles before she kicked them to the side, still refusing to look at me.

"Don't get shy on me now," I urged, tipping up her chin, and leaning in to kiss her lips softly while my other hand explored the soft, bare curves of her hips and thighs. "Can I take this off?" I asked, tugging lightly on the hem of her sweater, my fingers skating beneath the material as I awaited her response.

"You're still fully dressed," she whispered, her fingers moving to the button of my pants.

I caught her wrist, dragging it away from me. "This isn't about me. This is about you."

"But..."

"No buts, Is. Take this off so I can see you. I didn't get to appreciate what I was touching the last time."

She grasped the hem and slowly lifted the material, the soft expanse of her belly coming into view. She was gorgeous. Generous curves, and a silhouette most women would kill for with a tapered waist that flared out into a luscious ass and thick thighs. The thighs I wanted wrapped around my head sooner rather than later.

"Fuck, come here," I whispered, pulling her close. My hand skated down her spine and grasped a handful of her ass while I leaned down to capture her lips once more. She had no idea how much I'd been fantasizing about this—about her—for the last several weeks, wondering if I'd ever touch her soft skin again.

"I know I'm not..."

"Fuck that," I interrupted as I stood, pulling her against my chest while I dipped down to shut her up by ghosting my lips across hers. "I'm not as shallow as you seem to think I am. All those little imperfections you think you need to hide just make me want you more. I don't need you to look or act a certain way. I just need you. Exactly like you are."

I released her, unbuttoning the top few buttons of my shirt before I laid down on the couch, one leg extending over the arm while I braced the foot of my other on the floor next to the couch.

"You're serious?" she asked, shifting nervously from side to side as I extended one hand toward her.

"Fuck yes, I am. Get up here."

"I'm going to crush you." She sounded worried, but she took a small step forward, still hesitating to join me on the couch.

"I hope you do," I replied with a smirk, and she shook her head.

"Not everything is a joke."

"And I'm not joking. I've been fantasizing about tasting you again for weeks. Get up here. *Now.*"

She hesitated for a moment, but I internally cheered when she braced one hand on the back of the couch, swinging her leg over my torso and straddling my chest.

"My tongue isn't down there," I teased while I grasped her hips, pulling lightly to urge her forward. This wasn't the same headstrong woman who'd told me to shut up and unzipped my pants before my brain had caught up during our last encounter. "Don't be shy, Is. I've already had a mouthful of you. I know what I'm getting into, and I want more."

Her body relaxed slightly, and she shifted forward. I let go of her hips, reaching forward to slide a finger through her slit, testing to see how much our aggressive kisses had affected her.

"Oh God," she whimpered while I teased her clit with the wet tips of my fingers, her eyes falling closed and her head dropping back slightly.

"Come on. You know where I want you."

She took a shaky breath and moved her thigh over my shoulder while I scooted down slightly, giving her room to straddle my head.

"Brace yourself," I warned, curling my palm around her thigh, and anchoring her to me while I licked my lips in anticipation.

Her breasts heaved slightly as she took another deep breath and shifted forward, lining my mouth up with her.

"That'a girl," I murmured, pulling her down. My nose drew through her pussy as I nuzzled her clit, my tongue darting out to taste her. *Fuck.*

Her body was tense at first, thighs shaking as I held her tightly to me, but with each swipe of my tongue, I could feel her melt in my hold. When her hips began to rock against me, I groaned in satisfaction, thankful that she was letting me past all her barriers. When she ran her fingers through my hair and stared down at me, I was in awe watching her eyelashes flutter with each movement of my tongue.

Sucking her clit into my mouth, I laved my tongue over it while I maintained eye contact, watching with rapt interest as her eyes dilated and her nipples tightened.

"Oh, fuck. That feels so good," she moaned, letting go of the back of the couch and cupping her breast in her palm while her hips continued to rock into my movements.

Tipping my head back slightly, I couldn't keep the grin off my face as I watched her fondle herself. "You're so fuckin' beautiful."

"Quit teasing me," she laughed lightly, her palm pressing against the top of my head. "Since you're so insistent on doing this, then do it."

Oh, it was on.

She moaned loudly as I held her to my face, pulling her to me while I lightly captured her clit between my teeth. Rapidly swiping my tongue against the tip as she squirmed against my grip, I grinned.

"Fuck, too much," she moaned while I continued to torture her, the desperate tone in her voice spurring me on. "Oh, fuck. Oh, fuck..."

Her back arched, and I felt her legs start to shake. Continuing the onslaught, I moaned into her flesh as I felt her fingers grasp my thigh, digging in through the material of my pants while she arched backward, thrusting her hips into my movements.

Just a little more.

Curling my hand further around her thigh, my fingers sought the place I knew would send her right over the edge. As I pushed my wet fingertips against the soft puckered skin of her asshole, she cried out again, her clit throbbing against my tongue while I felt the familiar contractions of her orgasm start against my lips.

"Oh, fuck. Adrian, *yesss*," she hissed, her orgasm rolling through her body, thighs quaking against my cheeks.

As she collapsed forward, I reached up to grasp the sides of her waist so I could shift her backward and suck in a much-needed breath. My wet lips tingled, and my chest heaved beneath her as I watched her come back to herself. Her eyes slowly drifted open, and she looked down at me, a satisfied smile morphing to one of concern.

"Enjoy yourself?" I teased, stroking the soft skin of her waist with my thumbs.

"I'm so sorry, I should..." she scrambled backward, but I held her still before she could escape, tilting my head to kiss the inside of her thigh.

"Trust me, I enjoyed myself. There is absolutely no need to apologize. That was fucking hot."

She averted her gaze, her shoulders rolling inward as I shifted her back to straddle my hips. My cock throbbed at the sudden attention, but this wasn't about me. I could deal with myself later.

"Can you hand me my sweater?" She whispered, her arms coming up to cover her chest.

Shifting my hips, I sat up, slowly peeling her fingers from her chest and softly stroking the tip of one peaked nipple with my knuckle. "Don't hide. You're gorgeous."

Isobel's eyes were wary as I leaned in, her tongue wetting her lips while I kissed the side of her jaw softly. While I was dying to kiss her again, I wasn't sure how she felt about tasting herself on my lips.

"You've never looked more lovely," I murmured into the skin of her neck, my lips trailing lower while I pulled her up slightly, angling her back so I could caress the soft skin of her breast with light flicks of my tongue. "Freshly fucked is a good look on you, Isobel. I think I found my new mission in life. To make sure it happens more often."

"Adrian," she whimpered in protest. My lips closed around her nipple, causing her to grind down against me, and I knew I needed to stop before things got out of hand.

Pulling my hand free from her back, I reached down and grasped her sweater. Reluctantly, I released her nipple before I bunched the fabric and pulled it over her head, helping her pull it into place over her drowsy body.

Isobel didn't fight me when I picked her up to settle her into the corner of the couch with another lingering kiss on the side of her neck.

"You alright over there?" I asked while I sat back at the other end, running my palm over the wet stubble on my chin.

"Um," she stuttered, pulling her legs into her chest and looking at me with wary eyes. I tried to ignore the fact that without her shorts, all I could see was her pussy. "I should just...maybe I should get home."

"You are home," I chuckled as I watched her try to work through what had just happened.

"Oh, right."

"I can take a hint," I nodded, sitting up straight and pulling the wrinkles out of my shirt from where she'd been sitting on my chest. A few wet spots dotted the light fabric, and I could see the moment she noticed as her eyes widened. "Guess it's time for *me* to head home."

"But what about..." Isobel waved at my prominent erection, the fit of my slacks doing nothing to conceal the hard line of my cock underneath the material.

"Don't worry. I've got it in hand."

Isobel's eyes widened while I adjusted the waistband of my pants, shifting my hips so my belt didn't press uncomfortably against the head.

"Not literally. Get your dirty little mind out of the gutter," I teased. "I meant I could *hand*-le things when I get back home."

And I would, probably more than once. Using the scent of her on my face and hands to picture what it'd felt like to have her ride my tongue with vivid clarity.

"But..."

"It's fine. I don't expect you to touch my dick again. Wouldn't want to expose you to such *hard*-ship."

"It's not that, I..." she trailed off, her voice unsure while she stared at me.

Reluctantly, I rose from the couch and leaned forward, closing the distance between us as I left a lingering kiss on her cheek. "Don't worry. It won't take long when I recall the sounds that escaped your mouth a few minutes ago. Especially the way you moaned my name when I felt you tip over the edge. That will probably run on repeat in my brain for the foreseeable future."

"Ad," she whispered as I pulled away, standing and walking around the edge of the couch to pick up my discarded bag.

"I'll see you in the office on Monday. Can you try not to ignore me this time?"

"Wait..."

"Goodnight, Isobel. Sweet dreams. I'll text you if Evan sends me any more pages."

"Why are you leaving? We still have a few pages to go through and..." she stuttered, sitting up and reaching down to grab her shorts from the floor.

"Because you told me you didn't want to sleep with me. And if I stay and things get heated between us again, I won't have the self-control to slow things down, which *won't* be honoring your wishes. So, I'm being the gentleman you don't think I am and going home. Alone."

Her mouth opened and closed a few times as I pulled the front door open and escaped to the other side. Pausing for a moment after the door clicked shut, I leaned against the door frame and took in a shaky breath, trying to calm the racing of my heart.

Hopefully, this was the last time I had to walk away from her after we shared something like this. Because as much as I wanted inside her body, I wasn't risking losing her heart for a few moments of relief. I wanted all of her, and I was willing to wait for her to catch up.

ISOBEL

BOSTON

As the door to my apartment clicked shut, the gravity of what had just transpired between Adrian, and I felt like a weight on my chest. I wasn't sure I was prepared for what he was asking. Two months ago, I would have laughed at anyone who suggested I was even attracted to him more than physically, much less that I would know what his face looked like when he came, or what he tasted like, or the sinful things I now knew he could do with the tip of his tongue.

Grant hadn't been like this, he hadn't been spontaneous or passionate, and he'd certainly never told me to sit on his face. I knew that we'd been young, but my track record with relationships had left a bad taste in my mouth. It was easier to hide in the books I edited and live vicariously through women who had exciting sex lives. It'd never bothered me, at least not until Adrian had awoken this dormant side of me.

I knew women in their late thirties were supposed to have an insatiable sexual appetite, but I never expected that to apply to me. After the divorce, I hadn't anticipated anyone coming in to sweep me off my feet like this. I was damaged goods. Used up and spit out during my mid-twenties and left to become an old maid.

The handful of dates I'd been on had been lackluster. Men my age were looking to settle down and have a partner by their side while they started a family. It hadn't been appealing to me, especially since I was unsure if I could deliver on the providing a family part.

When I'd suggested fertility testing before I was served with divorce papers, Grant had made our inability to conceive seem like it was my problem, not his. After he left, I was too afraid he was right and pushed the idea of having kids out of my mind. I focused on my career, dated when it was convenient, and built up a life where the only bedroom adventures I seemed to have were explored through the pages of a book.

I envied Chase and her ability to have this big, open heart, to believe in love and men who were supportive of their partners and the happily ever after I wasn't convinced existed.

Adrian wanted to *date* me. It was the last thing I expected when he invited himself over tonight. I expected him to try to fuck me, since we hadn't the last time, and then ignore me in the office like I'd been futilely trying to ignore him for the last several weeks. But he seemed to like me, and when we were alone, I found myself returning the sentiment.

We'd had our disagreements recently, but those didn't seem to faze him. He wanted me, and God help me, I think I wanted him too.

> Isobel: I need to talk. Are you in town? Can you meet me for a drink?

I waited impatiently as I saw the three dots appear on my phone screen, taunting me as I waited for a reply to my text. This was an emergency. I needed someone neutral to tell me I wasn't being an idiot by considering this.

> LJ: I am *in town*. But I think you need to make it worth my while. How about dinner at my place? You buy and I'll supply the booze.

Placing my phone down on the coffee table, I pulled my shorts up, running my hand over the top of my head and cringing when I got to the disaster of what was once my artfully messy bun. I must have looked like a hot fucking mess when Adrian left. Real attractive. It was a wonder he kept coming back for more.

> Isobel: I'm available tomorrow. Does around 6 work for you?

> LJ: I can make it work. Come hydrated and ready for tequila shots. Sounds like it's time for the truth serum.

> Isobel: We're not twenty-five anymore, Lei.

> LJ: You can handle a few. I have a feeling it's the only way I'll get the truth out of you.

> Isobel: No withholding. Trust me, I need someone else to talk this out with me.

> LJ: Is this about Grant's post?

I paused, frowning as I looked at the message. Grant hadn't even crossed my mind when I texted Leila. And I hadn't looked at any of his social media in years, deciding to hide his posts for my own mental health. Sure, we were still 'friends' on Facebook and Instagram, but I wasn't exactly keen to revisit the man who left me.

> Isobel: I haven't spoken to Grant directly in nearly a decade. Why would one post bother me?

> LJ: Just checking.

Now I was burning with curiosity over what this mystery post said. Last I heard, he was dating a yoga instructor who was into holistic medicine and was going to some kind of wellness center for a few months with her in the mountains of Colorado.

> LJ: You know he's different now, right?

> Isobel: I don't want to talk about Grant.

> LJ: Okay. I'm here if you change your mind. See you tomorrow. I'll send you my order. Don't be late or I'm making you take extra shots.

I closed out of my text messages, my fingers hovering over the icon for Instagram, knowing it was a bad idea to go snooping. But if Leila thought his post was going to upset me, I knew I needed to put on my virtual big girl panties and find out what it said.

Typing in his familiar username, I blinked when I saw the thumbnail above his stories. It was him, the tiny yoga instructor, a dog at their feet and a little bundle in his arms.

My stomach bottomed out as I clicked on the colorful ring surrounding the picture, a boomerang coming up on the screen of two large hands cradling a little head, the soft features of a sleeping baby pulling the breath right out of my lungs.

So, it was me.

My jaw clenched as I tried to keep tears from forming in my eyes, and I knew I needed to exit out of his page and leave things alone, but I'd always blamed myself for the deterioration of our marriage.

Clicking on the first picture in his feed, I scanned the paragraph of text below, my pulse racing as I took in the words, Grant's ability to manipulate words into something beautiful shining through.

Today, we welcomed another little heart into our lives. I'm so proud to be the father of this little boy.

The words echoed in my brain as I scanned the rest of the text, the hashtag #miracleofadoption catching my attention.

Over ten years after he'd divorced me, he finally got his happily ever after with another woman, with the one thing he'd sworn to me he never wanted. The one thing I'd suggested after years of trying that had driven him further away from me and led to my grad school graduation present from him being divorce papers.

Fuck.

Maybe I needed to talk to Leila about this. Because I was tired of feeling like I wasn't enough.

SATURDAY MORNING HAD BEEN spent avoiding my phone, my Wi-Fi turned off on my laptop, and my head down as I proofed a document that was being sent to print in a few weeks. Kristine had already been through it twice, but I needed something to keep my brain occupied while I tried to figure out where my head was at.

Leila was one of the first friends I made in grad school, and she worked for a lifestyle blog in Boston as a copywriter. I'd tried to get her to come with me to the dark side of fiction writing, but she claimed she didn't have the creativity to create new worlds, just to make witty commentary on the real one we lived in.

She was there when my marriage fell apart, helping me to pick up the pieces of my shattered heart when Grant walked away with my future.

Deciding I'd been productive enough, I picked up my phone from the coffee table and glanced at the screen, my heart stuttering when I saw I had a missed text message from Adrian. I hadn't expected to hear from him until the work week started, and I was equally scared and curious as to why he was messaging me. The preview on the lock screen wasn't giving anything away.

> *Adrian: Morning, beautiful. I hope you slept well. I know I did after…*

Knowing I'd just get sucked back in by him, I ignored the message and sought a hot shower instead. I needed to process some things in my head before Leila confronted me because if there was one thing I knew, Leilani Johnston didn't hold back when she thought you needed to hear something.

Two more text message alerts were taunting me after my shower when I pulled up the Uber app on my phone to request a ride. Leila didn't know that

I'd finally sold my car, and I knew she'd feel bad that I was picking up dinner on my way to her place, but it wasn't like I was struggling. I was just tired of the weight around my neck that insuring, parking, and fueling a car entailed. I wasn't going to drive to Iowa when I visited my family, so being close to an airport and public transportation was all I needed.

> LJ: I'm using tequila to distract myself from being hangry, get your cute ass over here soon or I can't be held responsible for my mouth later.

Leila was never one to hold her tongue regardless, but as the text confirmation my order was ready at the Thai restaurant a few blocks from her place came through, I grabbed my purse and locked up my apartment, heading down to the street to wait for my ride.

As a shiny black sedan pulled up at the curb, I momentarily panicked that Adrian had come over unannounced, but when the window rolled down and a petite woman with pink dreadlocks leaned over the passenger seat, I relaxed.

"You Isobel?"

Nodding, I stepped to the back passenger door and slipped into the backseat, relaxing into the worn leather seats.

"Address still the same?"

"Yeah, the one stop okay before the final destination?" I confirmed, and she nodded before she merged into the light traffic on my street, heading out of Jamaica Plain toward South End, the much trendier district my friend had claimed as home after we'd moved away from the university graduate housing.

LEILA WAS HOLDING A pint glass with amber liquid pooled in the bottom when she opened the door to her apartment, her signature knowing smirk in place.

"You need to catch up, especially if we're going to unpack that bomb I dropped in your lap last night."

Thrusting the takeout bag at her outstretched palm, I took the glass from her. Sniffing, my eyes widened as I took in the pungent aroma of Don Julio. He'd seen me through many questionable decisions in the last ten years, but Leila kept thrusting him back into my life when I thought I'd kicked the habit.

"You're not messing around." Blowing out a breath, I took a generous sip of the liquid, the spicy flavor coating my tongue as I held it in my mouth before swallowing. But that innocent motion just reminded me of another liquid I'd held in my mouth when Adrian was seducing me with oyster play and suggestive commentary that my brain had taken and run with. Which had to be the reason I lost my damn mind and had gotten involved with him. He was becoming as addictive and toxic as the liquid in the glass in my hand. Nothing good would come from a night with him, but I couldn't manage to stay away.

"Girl," Leila laughed while she closed the door and led me into the kitchen. "With the look that just crossed your face, you've been keeping secrets. Drink up, because you're not getting out of here without telling me why the hell you're texting me for an emergency girl sesh that has nothing to do with Grant."

Wincing, I took another generous sip, hanging my purse on the back of a barstool as I sat down at the small peninsula dividing her kitchen from her open living space.

"We doing this before food or after?" I asked before I tipped the glass back, my throat burning as I swallowed hard.

"After," she said with a nod, peeking inside the bags and pulling out the container with the familiar markings of her usual order. "I don't think you want me hangry for this conversation."

We sat across from each other in the tiny booth seating she'd installed in the bay window in her living room; her smirk growing as I picked at my Khao pad, the fragrant fried rice making my mouth water.

Leilani had—unsuccessfully—tried to set me up on blind dates in the past, telling me that while I didn't have to ever get married again, it was unacceptable to settle into a life of spinsterhood in my thirties. That could be delayed until my sixties. Which was looking like a likely possibility with the way things were headed.

"Quit playing with it and get down to it." Leila smirked as she closed her container, nodding at the destroyed bowl of rice and remnants of my meal that'd been picked apart with the blunt end of my chopstick.

I wanted to laugh, and add in the classic Michael Scott joke, but then that just reminded me of Adrian, and I was trying to figure out if this thing between us could go any further.

"Remember the guy from the office I told you about?"

"Which one? The one that was too nice and had a great ass, or the one who acted like an ass that you frequently want to castrate?"

Her laughter indicated she'd answered her own question, and she was highly entertained by my poor decision-making choices.

"Is he at least good in bed? That must be the reason you're coming to me, right? You need me to smack some sense into you."

Not exactly. I needed someone who didn't know him to analyze the situation to see if they thought he was being sincere. That was the thing about loveable assholes. They had good intentions most of the time, but they still managed to hurt people without trying. I didn't want to set myself up for disappointment and buy into his words instead of his past actions.

"I haven't slept with him."

"But..." she prompted, her dark eyebrow arching into the smooth caramel hued skin covering her forehead. I was envious of the fact that she was a year older than me but didn't have a wrinkle or gray hair in sight. "You did other things though, right? I can tell. Did you *hawk-tuah and spit on that thang?*"

"Can you be serious for like one minute?" I knew she was teasing me, but I didn't know how to deal with Adrian after what happened on my couch.

"Spitting on it *is* serious."

"You spend too much time on TikTok," I laughed, knowing she was referring to a video that'd gone viral a few months prior. Shaking my head, I decided to just tell her. "He wants to date me."

"Holy fuck," she laughed. "Only you could attract the same man twice."

She met Grant when we were together. He'd been as much of an ass as Adrian could be, but he was also emotionally distant and stubborn as hell. Not good qualities in a man when you were trying to salvage a floundering marriage. From this alternate side of Adrian I was seeing, it was obvious they were vastly different in their emotional maturity. Not something I'd have thought a few months ago when I was convinced my four-year-old nephew had more emotional bandwidth than my handsome coworker.

"You can start talking or I can ply you with more of our favorite Don, but either way, you're not leaving here until we talk this out. So, open your mouth or I'm getting out the shot glasses."

Glancing at my phone on the table, I saw it light up with another text message from Adrian, and Leila's eyes zeroed in on the screen full of notifications.

"Are you ghosting this poor bastard?" she giggled, reaching for my phone. Before I could stop her, she'd typed in my passcode and started scanning. "Oh, he's got it bad. Sounds like Dickhead wants to put his dick in something alright."

Her fingers started flying across the screen and my eyes widened as I reached across the table to grab my phone from her grasp. The last thing I needed was her sending Adrian something incriminating, or worse—sexting him.

"Nice try, bish," she laughed, triumphantly tapping the screen before she dropped it into my hand.

> *Adrian: Morning, beautiful. I hope you slept well. I know I did after I handled things when I got home. Not as well as you did, but I can wait for more from you. I've waited this long. And I'll wait until I know you want me for something other than my hot bod.*

What an idiot. I tried not to laugh at his phrasing, but from what I'd seen of his bod so far, he wasn't wrong.

> *Adrian: What are your lunch plans for Monday? I made a reservation at that little Italian restaurant down the street from the office. I think we need to talk. We do still have some pages to get through. Working lunch?*

Adrian: I lied. I don't want to work, but I do want to see you again. I meant it when I said you weren't allowed to ignore me anymore.

Adrian: I'm going to keep texting you until you agree to a date. I can be very persistent when I want to be. You may as well give in now.

Adrian: Wear that skirt we talked about to work on Monday. I was sad when you took it out of the rotation.

Adrian: It's long enough you don't need panties. Just an observation.

Adrian: I'll be in your office at 11:45. If you try to escape, I'll find you.

Adrian: Yes, I meant for that to sound creepy, but I'm serious. Hiding isn't going to get you out of giving this a chance. Now that I've gotten a taste of you again, I want more.

He was clearly trying to lay it on thick, so I couldn't get nervous and try to push him away again. From any other man, I would find the overbearing attitude a turnoff, but I couldn't hide the blush as I read his missed texts.

Isobel: I'll be waiting, sans panties, at 11:45 on Monday. You had better bring your A-game, big boy.

As I read through Leila's reply, I shook my head at her brazen response. But I had no doubt that he'd think it was from me because of the big boy comment tacked onto the end. I'd called him that before, much to his inflated ego's amusement. Clearly my friend knew my go to phrases a little too well.

Adrian: Better block out your calendar in the afternoon with that kind of flirting. I'm going to need time to check the truthfulness of your statement. It's not nice to mislead a gentleman.

Isobel: Let me know if you find one. We both know you're not a gentleman.

Adrian: If I weren't a gentleman, I wouldn't have left last night.

Isobel: Behave.

Leila was bouncing in her chair as I ignored her to respond to Adrian's messages, her eagerness to see the rest of the conversation obvious with how she was watching me.

"Give me that." Leila snatched the phone from my hand, laughing as she read through the messages. "Oh, he so wants to fuck you."

Yeah… I was aware. Which was why I told him I wouldn't sleep with him. But I was having a hard time convincing myself that was the right choice.

"You're going on Monday." Her statement left no room for argument, and she would hound me until I agreed.

"I know." I was curious how things would play out between us. It was too late to back out now. He'd worked his way in, and I was intrigued enough to give him a chance.

"Let me know if his A-game involves getting dicked down in the copy room."

"Leila!"

"Hey, might as well live out those dirty work fantasies. He looks like the type to know what he's doing."

"Not exactly looking to get fired for screwing on the copy machine, Lei."

"They invented locks for a reason, Is."

She laughed as she handed back my phone, her delight at this situation pulling me out of the funk I'd been in since my deep dive into Grant's social media.

"I'm taking it by the way your expression just darkened that you looked at what I let slip?"

I nodded, biting my bottom lip, tears forming at the corner of my eyes as I finally let myself process what I'd been avoiding. "I'm not surprised." My eyes closed as I shook my head, reaching up to swipe a tear that escaped. "I mean, look at her. Of course he'd change his mind for her."

"We both know he was obsessed with you, so fuck that, Is. He's not the same angry person he was with you."

"Is that supposed to be helpful? That being with me—being *married* to me—made him angry."

Leila pinched her lips together before she sighed. "He was too upset back then to understand the ramifications of his decisions. He still texts me to see how you're doing sometimes."

"Oh great, glad you two like to talk about me behind my back. He hasn't had a actual conversation with me since the ink dried on the papers. Nice to know he's willing to spy on me through my best friend, but doesn't have the balls to ask me how I was doing after he destroyed my future when he pulled the shit he did."

Angrily dropping my phone to the table, I stood and paced behind the couch, hating that I still had this much resentment over the situation in my heart. It still felt like there were so many answers I was denied when everything happened, and now he was moving on with a new woman and a new baby. All he did for me was rip my heart out and stomp on it without so much as a backward glance.

"If you couldn't tell by the cryptic adoption hashtags, it was him, Isobel. He was the reason you couldn't get..."

Yeah, I figured as much since one of the largest arguments of our marriage happened after I threw out the idea of adoption when trying to conceive wasn't happening naturally. Along with the fingers he pointed when I suggested both of us seek fertility testing.

"But for her, he did the one thing he told me he never wanted. The exact subject that triggered him filing for divorce. He would do it for her, but not for me. What does that say about me? Where does that leave me? Why does he get his happily ever after and I don't? You think it didn't break me when we lost the first baby, then another, and then all the negative tests that followed? I thought I was barren."

Her arms wrapped around me, her chin resting on my shoulder as she rocked back and forth.

"You can still have that, too."

"Yeah. Okay," I scoffed, knowing that the part of me that wanted a family had died out and my career had filled in the void.

"Women our age have babies all the time."

"I don't want to do this by myself."

"Then don't," she whispered, squeezing me tighter. A tear tracked down my cheek and my chest heaved as I tried to swallow back the grief that had been building inside me for the last decade. "I'm here if you want to do this, obviously not with the whole dick-sperm part, but you know Auntie Leila will help teach your kid how to take over the world."

"I want a partner," I whispered brokenly while I leaned my head against hers, hating that I still held this weight on my chest over ten years later.

"So go find one," she laughed. "Dickhead seems to be auditioning for the part. And you know he'd make pretty babies."

"Oh, God. He is not father material." But I wasn't convinced that was true. From the parts of his personality he'd revealed to me over the last few months, he wasn't what I originally thought he was. He could be kind and compassionate. If I let him in, would he make a good dad? Did he even want to be one? He was over a year older than me and remained a bachelor. But that didn't necessarily mean anything. I wouldn't know the answer to that unless I asked. Which meant putting myself out there.

And putting yourself out there was scary as fuck.

"Sometimes people surprise you."

And as she rocked me from behind and I let the tears fall from my eyes, I realized she was right. Sometimes people surprised you and maybe it was time for me to open my heart again.

Chapter

SIXTEEN

ADRIAN

BOSTON

As I settled into my cramped spot in the corner of the elevator, I scanned the faces entering the car, the corner of my lips rising when I saw a familiar pair of legs just outside the door. The hem of an ivory-colored skirt hugged every alluring curve of the woman I'd been eager to see since I left her apartment on Friday night.

Isobel pushed through the people surrounding the doors, squeezing inside the crowded car, and glancing over her shoulder, eyes widening when she saw me watching her. I couldn't see from where I was trapped in the corner if she'd listened and left her panties at home, but I didn't care. I was just excited to see her, especially knowing we had to sit through a staff meeting for the next hour, where she wouldn't be able to escape me.

The crowd dissipated as the elevator stopped at each floor on its way to the eleventh until it was just the two of us remaining with three floors left to ascend, Isobel standing entirely too far away.

Deciding to tease her a bit, I stepped forward and placed my hand at her waist, enjoying the way her body shuddered at the small contact. "You listened."

She nodded, surprising me by taking a step backward, her ass barely grazing the front of my pants. "I'd almost forgotten I had it."

"I hadn't," I whispered, grazing my lips along the shell of her ear. I was barely touching her, but the contact was enough to awaken the erection I'd been literally trying to beat down for the last two days. "Did you do the other thing you promised?"

"You'll just have to find out later," she whispered, the tips of her fingers slowly grazing the material of my pants. It was truly astounding to me that such a subtle touch had me hard as stone and wanting to make poor decisions in an elevator car.

"Maybe I will." My voice was hushed while I trailed my fingertips up the soft material covering her thigh.

"I hope so," she breathed, laying her head back against my shoulder, and glancing up at me sideways. *Fuck*. Her attitude toward me seemed to have changed dramatically after my string of text messages this weekend. Part of me was scared it'd make her retreat into hiding again, but I was shooting my shot and if that meant letting my desperation for her show, I'd do it.

We parted ways in the lobby of the eleventh floor, my eyes lingering on her hips as she walked away, knowing I'd be worthless until lunchtime.

"THE TOPIC OF THIS meeting is going to be a little different from what is listed on your agenda." Sloane's voice carried through the conference room in the same authoritative tone she typically had, but I was only partially listening as I gazed across the table, studying Isobel's profile. I'd forgotten what our staff meeting was about, but was enjoying the view. "As some of you know. There will be some restructuring coming in the next few months within Vivid. You should have gotten the links from HR for the internal positions that will be opening late summer."

The room filled with quiet murmurs, but my attention was focused squarely on Isobel and the way she kept doodling in the margin of her notebook. For some reason, I found it endearing that the romance department seemed to have a fixation on putting pen to paper. The advent of digital publishing had erased so many things that our predecessors treated as commonplace. I often wondered if sometimes the message got lost without that extra thought on whether to type or write the word.

Now we could produce finished books in a matter of months. It was astounding how prolific some authors of the past were, given that it took them years to get through the same process. Interns like Sam and Kristine didn't know what it was like to wait a year or more for an author to finish a manuscript. The consumer demand for quick releases had changed the game immensely.

"I'll need a few of you to stay back after we finish up. Isobel, Kate, and Adrian, we need to talk about the next steps with the lower-level positions opening. I believe you have some potential candidates within your groups."

Nodding, I risked a glance at Isobel, who was slyly trying to watch me, briefly glancing up and then returning her gaze to the table in front of her, an impassive expression on her face.

Don't worry, babe. I see you.

My phone buzzed in my lap, a fission of worry going through me before I looked at the notification screen.

> Isobel: Quit staring at me.

The grin that stretched across my lips was surely obnoxious, but I didn't care. She was initiating contact, and I was going to take it.

> Adrian: You'd have to be looking to notice.

> Isobel: I think everyone has noticed.

> Adrian: It's nothing new then. I usually spend these meetings watching you.

> Isobel: Creepy much?

> Adrian: I like to call it observant. I only wish I could observe the way your legs look in that skirt underneath this table.

Her eyes widened as she looked down at her lap to read my message, her cheeks taking on a rosy hue that indicated she liked what I was telling her. Or she was about to haul my ass into the hallway to give me a verbal lashing. Either one was hot.

> Adrian: If only people wouldn't notice me climbing underneath the table to take a closer look…

> Adrian: Your legs parting slightly as my fingers encircle your delicate ankle. My palm slowly traveling up your calf until it reached the slit in the hem of your skirt.

> Adrian: Your soft skin shaking as I slide my hand inward…

> Isobel: STOP IT!

> Adrian: The lace at the edge of your panties… Oh wait, we have yet to verify what's under your skirt.

> Isobel: ADRIAN!

> Adrian: I love it when you scream my name.

A small piece of paper hit the leather cover of my notebook, bouncing into my lap. I glanced around the table, but the rest of our colleagues were still engrossed in the meeting, listening to Sloane detail some new procedures that were being put into place with the marketing department.

Isobel was facing forward, her phone now lying face down on the table, her attention focused elsewhere, but I could tell she was keeping an eye on me as well.

The laugh that wanted to escape my mouth when I pulled open the crinkled corner of a piece of paper turned into a loud cough, but I reached for my cup on the table in front of me, swallowing down a mouthful of water.

> *You stop it right now. We are in a meeting. Stop sending me suggestive text messages or our date is canceled.*

Picking up my phone, I sent her one last text. Her phone vibrated against the table, causing her jaw to clench while she tried to avoid eye contact with me.

> Adrian: I'll stop. For now. But you can rest assured that I will be verifying if you listened to what I requested of you on Saturday. Because fantasy conference room Isobel might be wearing lace panties, but you better not be.

Deciding I should probably listen to the information my supervisor was bestowing upon us, I locked my phone screen and tossed it into the bag at my side, only stealing brief glances at Isobel for the rest of the time we were forced to be here.

Isobel escaped back to her office after the meeting with a slow glance in my direction. Her eyes lingered on mine for a moment, the corner of her lip twitching as she fought to keep her expression neutral. I knew I was pushing boundaries by outright flirting with her at work, even if it was by text to our private cell phones.

After years of watching her, in an observant manner, not a creepy one despite her accusations, I was finally seeing the vulnerable woman beneath the badass professional shell. She was still pretty badass, but like I hid beneath a veneer of *assinine* comments, she hid behind her professional strengths. She'd made her work her personality around her co-workers, and she was finally letting me see the real her.

The conference hadn't just changed our physical relationship. We now saw parts of each other we'd never revealed before. And while I was enjoying letting her see my true personality, I wanted to see hers even more.

Chapter
SEVENTEEN

ISOBEL

BOSTON

Leilani's words had been echoing in my head for the past several days. Maybe I could still have a baby. But I'd never know unless I did something about it. I still wasn't convinced Adrian would be a good fit for someone to solicit for insemination services, but I could address that later.

Deciding to put on my big girl panties, I pulled up the contact I'd saved for the fertility clinic a few blocks away from my office building.

As the phone rang, my palms began to sweat. I knew this decision would ultimately change the course of my entire life. Not only could I potentially be responsible for another human being, but I would also have to consider how it would affect my career. I knew there was a daycare on the second floor where we received a corporate discount, but what about the rest of it? I worked insane hours when I was on a deadline. I couldn't do that anymore with a child.

Book tours would also be something I wasn't sure I could navigate in the future. Short of hiring a traveling nanny, I wasn't sure that kind of travel was possible being a single parent.

"Hello, this is Vitality Women's Health and Hormone. Can I ask what you're calling to schedule today?"

My mouth suddenly went dry as I swallowed hard and tried to find the words to talk.

"Um, hi. My name is Isobel, and I'd like to schedule an appointment to get some fertility testing done."

"Great," she chirped, much too chipper for my frazzled nerves. "Let me get some basic information from you. Do you have your insurance card handy?"

My mind went on autopilot as I answered her questions and read the policy number off my insurance card. I should have done this years ago, just so I would know once and for all, but it was better late than never. The more I thought about it, the more I wanted to see if this was possible.

Sticking my head in the sand and pretending I didn't want this wasn't healthy for me any longer. I'd be forty in a few years, and once that happened, my chances of having a successful pregnancy were slim.

"Alright, we've got you down for an appointment two weeks from now. I'll send you a link to access our registration forms, so if you could submit those before your appointment, that would be great. Aside from that, you're good to go until we see you."

"Thanks," I said before ending the call, dropping my phone to the desk, and cradling my head in my hands.

That was how Adrian found me minutes later, but the look on his face was cheerful and excited, so I doubted he overheard my phone call. Thankfully, Kristine had decided to work elsewhere this afternoon. While she was an excellent employee, the lines of professionalism were clearly drawn between us. And she already had a very negative reaction to Adrian without adding in the way our relationship was changing.

"Hey," he greeted, taking a seat across from my desk and crossing one leg over the other in that typical masculine way men did. Lei liked to call it manspreading, but the look of it on Adrian was quite attractive. "You ready?"

Glancing at my abandoned phone on the desk, when I answered, I wasn't sure if it was his question, or my unanswered one. "Yeah. Just let me grab my bag and lock up."

Adrian watched as I logged off my computer and pulled my purse out of my filing cabinet. He sat there smirking but not saying a word.

"What are you in the mood for?" he asked, settling his hand on my back as we walked toward the elevator a few moments later. If Andrea noticed how close we were to each other as we passed her desk, she was great at pretending, because her head remained down as she studied the papers on her desk.

"Lasagna is always good, but I'm not sure if I want something that filling." I typically ate salads for lunch, preferring to eat at my desk while I had at least one document open on my computer. "What?"

"I'm gonna refrain from commenting on that one."

"Why?" I wasn't sure how he could spin eating Italian food into something that'd irritate me.

"Because you usually roll your eyes at my inappropriate commentary."

"What's inappropriate about lasagna?"

He leaned in close to my ear, his lips grazing my earlobe. "Not the lasagna part, the filling part. I'd be happy to fill you with more than cheese and carbs. My own special white sauce should do the trick."

"Wow," I laughed, shaking my head at him, but secretly charmed by his candid comments. "You just can't help yourself."

"Not with you wearing that skirt." He seemed to be fixated on this skirt, but now that I knew his recollection of our first introduction to each other, it didn't seem filled with quite as much animosity. "But don't think I haven't noticed you checking me out."

Of course, his inflated ego couldn't resist. He knew he was an attractive man. Despite his personality flaws, he was the object of several young employee's office ogling sessions. I knew what the gossip was about him—and certain appendages included in his nickname. And he surprisingly didn't have a tiny one, despite the ongoing debate. "You're so full of yourself."

"Again, not what I'd like to fill. And I'm worn out from taking care of myself. The taste of something lingering on my taste buds kept me distracted all weekend."

My cheeks warmed at his blatantly sexual comment, but knowing the memory of straddling his face kept him excited all weekend was flattering. "You really should practice better oral hygiene if it lingered that long."

"You're just setting yourself up for all kinds of inappropriate jokes today. My oral skills are just fine."

"I'm regretting my decision to join you for lunch," I sighed, but we both knew I would likely agree to it.

"Date."

"Hmm?" My hum had a teasing edge to it, but I knew exactly what point he was trying to make.

"Don't play coy with me. You're not just humoring me with lunch as a coworker. This is a date, Isobel. I made that clear in my texts. But if you need a refresher, I'd be happy to show you why I think we should date."

"Physical chemistry isn't everything." The obnoxious smirk on his face should have been insulting. He really enjoyed throwing my attraction to him in my face.

"You know this bantering turns you on as much as it does me."

"Yes, borderline hatred just does it for me."

Despite my droll delivery, he still chuckled, leaning in to whisper in my ear, his warm breath caressing my neck. "We both know you don't hate me. But I'm happy to fulfill any of your hate fucking fantasies after work."

"Oh, go fuck yourself," I scoffed, pushing him away, but he didn't go far.

"I thought we established I do," he laughed, wiggling his eyebrows.

"Same," I laughed, finally giving into the humor of the situation. And trying not to picture Adrian stroking the cock I'd had a few interactions with. We could start with dating and maybe work our way up to me reenacting my first encounter with his male anatomy.

He leaned in closer, the heat of his body pressed up against mine doing crazy things to my self-control. "Did someone touch themselves this weekend while they thought about what I did to them on Friday?"

"No." I shook my head, and he laughed, his lips slowly grazing my neck.

"Liar."

"*I* didn't touch myself. My vibrator did. I already told you I fucked myself." Biting my lip, I waited for the inappropriate comment, but it never came as Adrian growled and grasped my hand, pulling me out of the alcove by the elevators and down the hallway behind him.

Thankfully, most of the people on our floor had already left for their lunch breaks, so not many heads turned at Adrian towing me down the hallway. Fortunately, I had long legs, so I could keep up, but this was a surefire way to become fodder for the office gossip pool.

"What are you doing?" I hissed as he stopped in front of the door to the copy room, his hand pausing on the doorknob.

"What I've fantasized about nearly a thousand times over the last five years."

He pushed the door open, briefly checking to make sure the small room was unoccupied before he tugged me inside. Carefully closing the door, he locked it and turned me to face him.

"I'll take you to eat later," he promised, pulling off his suit jacket, tossing it on the small table next to the copier, and loosening his tie before he threw the tail over his shoulder. My eyes widened while I watched him carefully remove his cufflinks, stuffing them in his pockets before he precisely rolled up his sleeves, the muscles of his forearms flexing as he smoothed out the material. "But I'm too hungry to wait."

"What are..." I trailed off when he dropped to his knees, his eyes fixated on rolling up the material of my tight skirt, the cool air causing goosebumps to rise along my thighs.

"Fuck yes, such a good listener," he praised. Leaning forward, he placed a kiss on my pubic bone, his fingers teasingly drawing through my wet pussy. The wet tips pressed on my clit with enough pressure to cause my head to thump against the glass behind me. "No panties makes this much easier."

"We shouldn't be doing this," I whispered, grasping the hair on the back of his head, my fingers messing up the carefully styled strands.

"Fuck yes, we should. I wish I could've enacted this fantasy the day I met you." His voice was rough as he leaned in closer, carefully tucking my skirt up into my waistband while his lips dragged along the crease of my thigh. His large hands wrapped around me, possessively cupping my ass through the material of the skirt bunched up against the backs of my thighs.

"That would've been sexual harassment," I panted as he took one slow lick between my legs.

"And it would've been worth getting in trouble," he responded, looking up at me from his knees, his blue eyes almost glowing in the dim lighting. "But I'm glad I waited. Because now I know you want it just as much as I do."

"I..." I stuttered as he trailed his fingers back, meeting absolutely no resistance as he slid them inside because I was obscenely wet. I had been since he'd started sending me those text messages during the staff meeting.

"I know, babe. You don't need to feed my ego. I can feel how much you want me. And it is so fuckin' hot."

Before I could formulate any kind of coherent response, his focus changed, his tongue darting out to torture my clit with soft, teasing touches while his fingers hooked and massaged a place inside me that made my pulse race.

My legs were tense, thighs flexing as he continued to tease me, my body feeling overwhelmed with heat. But I couldn't cry out like I wanted to, because I didn't know who might be lurking outside the door. My teeth dug into my lower lip as his touches became more desperate, less controlled, and I could tell he was tired of stringing me along.

"Fuck," I panted, yanking his hair, knowing that I wanted more than his fingers this time. It was impulsive, and entirely reckless, but despite my earlier protests, I wanted to fuck him. I wanted him inside me. And I wanted it now. "Stop... please stop, Ad."

I pushed his head away from me, almost laughing at his confused expression. He was the most unkempt I'd ever seen him—hair a disaster. His tie flipped back over his shoulder and his lips and chin glistened with the evidence of how much he turned me on.

"You didn't come yet. Why'd you want me to stop?" he whispered, his palm wrapping around the back of my thigh with his thumb stroking my skin affectionately.

"I want something else."

He frowned, seeking but waited for me to elaborate. I just needed to build up the courage to ask for what I wanted.

"*You*. I want you."

"You've got me, babe. I'm literally on my knees for you right now." He smiled, clearly enjoying this interaction even though I'd basically cock-blocked myself, but I hoped not for long.

"I don't want you on your knees..." I took a deep breath and finally asked for what I needed from him in a hushed voice. "I want you inside me. I need you to fuck me."

"Fuck," he growled, scooting closer and kissing the fronts of my thighs, his lips dragging over my skin. It felt so good to have him touch me, and I didn't doubt he would've given me a satisfying orgasm with his mouth and fingers, but I wanted something else.

He slowly rose from his knees, drawing up the back of my skirt to cup the bare skin of my thighs while his nose dragged up the front of my blouse, his lips seeking out the skin of my neck while he pressed me into the door.

"Are you sure this is what you want? You want it like this?"

"Yes," I panted while he squeezed my ass, pulling me in close so I could feel how hard he was beneath his suit pants.

"This isn't how I imagined fucking you the first time."

His growled confession into my neck should've been sweet, but I wanted it rough. And I wanted it now.

"Just fuck me," I panted, my nails digging into the starched material of his shirt. "You told me to beg for it. I'm begging. You want me to be specific. I want you to shove your hard cock inside me and make me come all over it."

"I don't have a condom with me..." he whispered quietly into my skin, and I was glad I had been practical in my birth control selection, even though I rarely needed it.

"Doesn't matter..." I knew it was being irresponsible, but he made me feel reckless.

"Is, come on," he whined into my skin. "You know I want to. I think you can feel how much, but I can wait."

"Fine." I pushed on his shoulder, trying to wiggle out of his hold. "Nevermind, if you don't want me..."

"It's not that, but I want you to feel safe with me. Getting carried away and doing something reckless isn't how I want this. Things are safe on my end to go bare, but..."

"I got tested after my last time, but it's been a while."

He smirked, his lips slowly caressing my cheek before he leaned back, his fingertips slowly tucking my wayward curls behind my ear, his gaze lingering on my mouth.

"Define awhile."

His smile widened as I clenched my jaw, but it didn't stop the gentle caresses of his hand on my neck. "A long time."

"Time is subjective," he whispered, attention firmly fixed on my face.

"A few years."

His eyebrows rose, clearly startled by my confession. "Why?"

"Not everyone is sex obsessed, despite your commentary otherwise."

"You clearly weren't getting good sex," he laughed, leaning in to dust a kiss on my lips, his slowly coaxing mine apart. It should have bothered me that his mouth had been between my legs a few minutes ago, but it didn't, my tongue slowly pressing into his as he gently deepened the kiss. "I'd be happy to change that."

When we broke apart, I was done waiting, knowing the longer we stayed in this room, the higher the risk of getting caught once people returned from lunch.

"Pull down your pants."

"Oh, baby," Adrian laughed, not moving away from me, his lips seeking the skin just above my collarbone and sucking lightly before he tipped his head back. "Talk dirty to me."

"Shut the fuck up," I laughed, not expecting this lighter side of him.

"That's it. Just like that. Keep runnin' that mouth." His face traced down further, his nose nuzzling my nipple through my thin blouse. He teased it as his hand pressed between my legs again, his fingers slowly fucking me while my head arched backward.

"Fuck," I panted when his touch became more insistent.

"I'm gettin' to it," he laughed against my chest, seemingly not in any hurry.

"Not fast enough. God, just stop talking."

"You like it." He chuckled again, pressing his thumb into my clit to tease me. As I felt myself climb higher and higher, I didn't want his fingers. "I feel how excited you get when I tease you."

"Then quit teasing me. I thought you wanted to fuck me. All you seem to be doing is stalling."

"But feel how wet you are," he whispered, thrusting his fingers deeper inside me. "I think you like this. I think you want me to rile you up. And when you can't take it anymore, I'm gonna fuck you so hard you'll need to sit down the rest of the day. While you're trying to concentrate on work, all you'll be able to think about is my cock inside you, and at the end of the day you'll be wondering if the people walking out of work behind you can tell my cum has been leaking out of you all afternoon."

"Please, I can't..." My chest heaved as he showed no signs of stopping, my orgasm bearing down on me.

"Are you sure you want me bare?"

"I've got an IUD," I choked out, trying to keep myself from coming. *And if things continue like this, I may be asking for your sperm in a few months.*

"You could have told me that earlier," he chuckled, but it turned into a groan. "God, I want to make you come like this, but I want to feel it more."

"Yes, inside...now."

"So, bossy. I love it," he panted against my cheek, slowly removing his hand, and unbuckling his belt while I watched.

Adrian shoved down his pants, his tight boxer briefs outlining how hard he was. Unable to help myself, I grasped him, squeezing while he groaned in my ear. "Someone is impatient."

"Someone just wants you to fuck her. But you're being insufferable again."

"And you like it. It makes you hot when I irritate the shit outta you."

Adrian leaned back, slowly unbuttoning his dress shirt, and pushing his briefs down his strong thighs, my mouth watering as I took in the expanse of hard muscle he hid underneath his designer clothing. I knew he was a gym rat, but this was ridiculous. He was forty. Men weren't supposed to look like this at our age.

"Are you done gawking now?" He teased while his large hand slowly pumped his hard cock, a bead of liquid pooling at the head. "Someone wanted me to fuck her. And I'd hate to disappoint."

"We're going to get caught if you don't hurry."

"Maybe I like the thought of someone hearing you come on my cock," he whispered, stepping forward, and crouching slightly to draw the tip of it teasingly along my clit.

"You'd have to make that happen first," I whispered back, cupping the back of his neck, and bringing his mouth to mine.

Adrian didn't waste any time grasping the back of my thighs, hoisting me up and pinning me against the wall beside the door. His hand left my skin briefly, but then his mouth smothered the moan I couldn't hold in when he pulled me down onto his cock.

"Don't worry, babe. I've got you." His gruff whisper against my lips was the last sweet moment before he thrust hard, bottoming out inside me with a muffled groan.

All his hours in the gym proved worthwhile, as he managed to somehow hold my entire weight and fuck me at the same time, savagely pulling me against him while he thrust into me. All the teasing since we'd come in here had just worked me up to the point I couldn't hold back long, biting the collar of his shirt to keep quiet as I came hard.

"Fuck, that's it," he panted against the side of my face. "Gonna come inside you so hard. Fill this pussy just like you wanted."

And he did, moments later, pulsing while I clung to his shoulders.

My lips quivered as he clasped me against his chest, suddenly overcome with something deeper than my usual irritation with him. Adrian made me feel things, more than just the physical, that I hadn't felt in years. And if I thought I could escape this situation with my heart unscathed, he'd just proved me wrong.

Adrian didn't talk for once, slowly lowering me to my feet, pulling a handkerchief from his pants pocket and swiping it between my legs.

As we dressed, I didn't know what to say to him. I hadn't expected him to make me feel something other than loathing. But now Leila's comments about him were running through my head. What if he would be okay with helping me get pregnant? And even though I tried to fight it, my last thought as he kissed me softly before he helped me pull my skirt into place was...

What if he also wanted to help me raise it?

EIGHTEEN

ADRIAN

BOSTON

I MAY HAVE TAUNTED Isobel with the idea that she'd be the one who couldn't stop thinking about me, but it was the other way around. A fat cherub had shot me in the ass when we were at that conference over Valentine's Day, and I was a total goner now that I'd been inside her.

My fascination that started years ago had morphed into a full-blown obsession with one ten-minute tryst in the copy room. The same room I'd met her in and now could never step foot inside without getting a raging erection.

She'd canceled our dinner plans that night; Sloane calling her in for a last-minute meeting at the end of the day. But I hoped she wasn't using it as an excuse to avoid me again. Isobel seemed to scare easily, but I hoped my transparent pursuit of her made it clear I wasn't trying to string her along.

I lingered in the office long after Sam left, scanning over the pages he and Kristine had submitted for final approval. Part of me kept hoping Isobel would find me after her meeting, but as 6:30 rolled around, I knew I needed to get home.

I concentrated on the slow-moving traffic the entire drive through downtown, but the further I distanced myself, the more my mind kept wandering. How was Isobel getting home after work? Would she be vulnerable waiting for her ride when the building had emptied for the day? Did Sloane know she didn't have a car?

As I parked down the block from Ma's house, my fingers itched to text her, but I wasn't sure what the boundaries were. Did she want me to text her? Should I pretend something inside me wasn't fundamentally changed after what happened this afternoon? Was I acting like a pathetic douche?

I didn't have a fucking clue what the answers were to the first two, but I was thinking a resounding yes on the third one.

A thump on the passenger side window startled me and I glared at the person standing on the sidewalk. Until they crouched down, and my brother's amused grin greeted me.

"Get outta the car, you fancy fuckah'."

He was so eloquent. And to think people often couldn't tell us apart when we were younger. Half a dozen words out of his mouth and it was never hard to guess.

I shoved my phone into my pocket and climbed out, locking the car before I joined him on the cracked sidewalk. "Such a lovely greeting. I'm never disappointed by your hospitality, asshat."

"Pot meets the fuckin' kettle. Pops is in fine form today. We betta get back in there before Ma loses her shit."

Fuck.

"How long this time?"

Sometimes his lucid moments would last days, but on his bad days, he was a little unpredictable. He'd been more melancholic lately, especially when we mentioned grandma, but Ma took the brunt of it on the days when he was agitated.

"Past few days," he replied with a shrug, looking more concerned than I'd have liked to see. If Hutch was rattled, something was wrong. "I got tha tickets for this weekend from Patty down the block. I'm hopin' that'll pull him outta this funk."

"It's not just a funk, Hutch. Eventually, this is what he's going to be like all the time. Do we need to talk with Ma about that assisted living facility again?"

He sighed, clenching his jaw and running his palm down his bushy beard. "Yah think I don't know that, Ad. I live here with him every day. But Ma won't consider it. He took us in when he didn't have to and made sure we all had a roof over our heads. She's not gonna leave him in a place like that."

He was right. I knew he was. And I hated thinking that it might be the best place for him, but taking in your son's young widow and your grandsons was a little bit different than advanced dementia and a heart condition. And while I knew she could handle the medical stuff, she also worked crazy hours. Once Hutch decided what he wanted to do now that he was retired from the military for good, there wouldn't be someone home all day to help keep our ornery grandfather in line.

"Just think about it. We can convince her if it gets to that point. And you know I'll help find the best place."

"We don't need your money," Hutch sighed, and I knew they didn't. Pop's pension and Medicare should cover most of it, but my money could make sure he was comfortable. I'd take a demotion and work remotely until we could find him somewhere that wasn't a shithole. Despite Isobel's insistence that I didn't, I did have a heart. And loved my Pops something fierce. He'd protected our family without question when we needed it, and I'd make sure he had whatever he needed until his last fucking breath.

"Just know the offer is there if he needs it." I'd do anything for my family. And it's not like I lived an extravagant lifestyle. Other than half a dozen expensive suits and my car, I lived well within my salary.

"Noted," he responded, his voice gruff. "Anyway. Pen has a conflict with her mom this weekend. Anyone yah want to invite to fill the empty seat?"

I sighed, knowing we'd never hear the end of it if Pat found out we didn't fill all four seats for the game. He and Pops had gone in together before we'd even been born to get 4 season tickets to the Sox, and they had yet to spend a game empty. If neither of our families were using them, there were plenty of people in the neighborhood who'd jump at the chance to buy them from us.

"Gimme an hour and I'll let you know. I think I might have someone from the office who'd be down to fill the spare seat."

"I thought your intern was into lacrosse or some shit."

"He is. But I'm not asking him." I knew I could tell my brother about Isobel, but I wasn't ready for the shit I knew he'd give me over inviting a woman.

He nodded, slapping my shoulder before he started up the steps to the front door, using the handrail to pull himself up. His gait with the prosthetic was improved from the last time I was at home.

While he was distracted, I pulled my phone out of my pocket.

> Adrian: Are you free Saturday afternoon?

> Isobel: Trying to pencil in a booty call?

> Adrian: Not exactly.

> Isobel: Not a no either. But yes, I'm free.

> Adrian: I'll pick you up at 11.

> Isobel: And we'll be doing…?

> Adrian: It's casual. You'll need sunscreen and a hat. Wear something red and sneakers.

> Isobel: Casual as in business casual? I don't remember ever seeing you out of a suit.

I didn't remind her of when we went hiking in Maine, but I kind of liked it when she busted my balls. And did other things with them.

She didn't respond right away, so I tucked my phone back in my pocket, joining my family for dinner. I wasn't sure how many we had left with Pops, so I wouldn't take anything for granted.

THE REST OF THE week in the office seemed to fly by with stolen looks and an abundance of self-restraint, at least on my part. The truth was, we were both too busy with our own projects to sneak away to talk about whatever was going on. Evan and Chase had gone quiet, but I was too distracted to track down my wayward author now that his book was going to print.

Sloane had been meeting with each of us to get a feel for how prepared our interns were for their interviews in the coming weeks. She'd also had several meetings with Isobel privately, and while I was dying to ask what they were about, I respected her privacy. If she wanted to tell me, she knew how to find me.

Saturday morning was already a bit of a disaster. Pops seemed to be more lucid, but Hutch was stuck doing damage control with his preteen daughter and bitch of an ex-wife. Despite him being stationed overseas for a good chunk of her childhood, Penny was a daddy's girl. And when his ex's temper came out, he was left to play mediator between the two of them.

That meant I was left to wrangle Pops into his game gear and get him in the car before I picked up Isobel.

She knew about my grandfather from our brief conversation in Maine, but I hoped his presence in my passenger seat wouldn't be a total surprise. We really hadn't dived into too much childhood emotional trauma at this point, so she didn't know he'd spent most of my life as my only male role model.

It probably would've been easier to just tell her where we were going and with who, but I never did things the easy way. And part of me knew if she didn't accept Pops, dating her wouldn't work out, anyway. He was part of who I was, and while he'd likely be a bit of a cockblock on our first official date, I'd already told her I didn't want things between us to be only physical.

"Where are yah takin' me, Ad?" Pops grumbled from the passenger seat as I turned off the freeway towards Isobel's neighborhood. "I know I'm losin' my marbles, but even I know how tah get tah Fenway. Tha green monster is thattaway."

"We're pickin' someone up, Pops. Remember Pen isn't comin' today?"

He frowned, and I watched him process what I'd said. Hopefully, today he didn't have trouble remembering his great-granddaughter. It broke my heart when he didn't, but the little sweetheart took it in stride when he had trouble around her.

"Ah. Yeah. She's with the she-witch today. I remember."

There wasn't any love lost between my brother's ex-wife and our grand-father. Respect was everything to his generation. And Hutch's wife getting knocked up by her husband's best friend while he served his country overseas was the ultimate disrespect. There was no way he'd ever look at her the same way again.

"He's meeting us at the park. But I invited a friend from work to come with us to the game today. You haven't met them before."

He nodded, looking a little less wary, but I knew sometimes it was easier for him to be around new people. They didn't have any preconceived notions about who he was. And they also didn't expect him to remember shared experiences. I just wasn't sure exactly how much he'd bust my ass over our guest being a lady.

Bringing someone home with me hadn't happened since I was in high school, so I was sure he and Hutch would have a field day giving me shit.

"Is your friend a Sox fan?"

Hesitant to answer, I kept quiet, even when he turned slightly to face me as the car slowed next to the curb in front of her building. Isobel was leaning against the brick, her foot propped up while she typed on her phone.

Pops followed my gaze and then burst out laughing. "Only you could fall for a Cubbies fan, Adrian. I would say I hoped her taste in men was better than her taste in baseball teams, but she is spendin' time with you."

The worn Chicago Cubs hat pulled down over her twin braids wasn't a surprise, but it also wasn't staying. I grabbed my extra hat from the back seat and leaned forward to shove it into my back pocket.

"Yeah, yeah, old man. Just don't embarrass me."

"I think you probably do that enough by yourself. You don't need my help."

"You can walk the rest of the way," I threatened as my eyes met Isobel's through the windshield. She smiled hesitantly, her eyes darting between me and my surprise passenger.

"And miss you makin' an ass out of yahself in front of a pretty girl, not on yah life."

"Behave."

"Why would I do that?" He laughed while I checked my side mirror, swinging open my door after the traffic had cleared. She didn't live too far away from the ballpark, so we could have walked from here, but I'd splurged on a season parking space in a lot near Fen a few years ago when Pop's stamina had declined.

"Hey," Is said while I walked toward her, my eyes taking in the tight red t-shirt and frayed jean shorts she was wearing. Add in the double braid under her traitorous ball cap and she looked years younger than what separated us.

"Hello, gorgeous," I greeted, enjoying the pink creeping up the side of her neck.

I snatched the edge of her cap, carefully pulling it off before I leaned in and brushed a soft kiss across her lips. Pops had already guessed I had a thing for her, so there was no point in holding back my affection.

"Hey," she argued, reaching for her hat, but I held it behind my back. "That's..."

Distracting her with another quick kiss, I pulled my worn cap from my back pocket and pulled it down over her hair.

"You can have this back later. But you're wearing mine today."

"Should I be worried about what's on this one?" She asked, lifting the brim of my hat and trying to pull it off.

"Don't you trust me?" I teased, stepping back to capture her hand and tugging her down the few steps to the sidewalk.

"You really want me to answer that question?"

"Probably not, but let's get going so we can find our seats before it gets too crowded."

She tugged on my arm, reaching up to scratch the thick stubble on my cheek while she threw me a naughty smirk. "I thought this was my seat."

"Later," I chuckled. "After I show you what a real ballpark looks like."

Despite his protests about letting a lady sit in the front seat, Isobel insisted on climbing in the back, patting Pop's shoulder before she settled into the leather seats.

"It's nice to meet you, Mr. O'Neill. Now I know where Adrian gets his handsome smile from."

Pops grinned, smirking at me as he turned slightly. "He wishes he had my looks. Poor boy got some of those pansy ass, pretty boy genes from his Ma's side of the family. Always felt sorry for him and his brotha."

"How unfortunate for him," Isobel quipped, meeting my eyes in the rearview mirror. "I can only imagine how devastated he is that he won't get to be a silver fox like you."

She was pouring it on thick, and we both knew that Hutch and I looked just like him, but I'd let them have their fun.

"Yeah, some of the ladies around the neighborhood still think I'm a piece of man candy, but my heart hasn't been up for grabs for a long time."

Isobel mouthed *Man Candy,* and I tried not to laugh, but the wink she followed it up with had me smothering a fake cough into my fist.

"Anyway. Pops, Isobel is the one who went with me to that conference a few months back in Maine."

"Ah, so you're the one who Adrian has been chasin' for years and still won't give him the time of day. I would try to sing my grandson's praises, but I've gotta feelin' you've seen him cram those size twelves in his mouth enough times to make an educated decision."

Pops knew I didn't have the best verbal filter around the family, so I knew he was commenting based on that, but he'd be disappointed if he knew how I'd treated Isobel the last several years. I was disappointed enough in myself, but Isobel didn't throw me under the bus like she could have. Hopefully, the recent changes in both our behavior would stick, and we could see where things went between us.

"So how long have you had terrible taste in ball teams, Ms. Isobel?" Pops laughed as we thankfully got through traffic and into the parking lot a few blocks away from Fenway.

"Pops," I warned, but Isobel just laughed, indulging him.

"I know the Cubs are an acquired taste outside of Chicago, but I've loved them since my dad took me to Wrigley the first time when I was about five or six."

"You from Chicago?" he asked as I steered into an open parking spot, shifting into park and unbuckling my belt.

"No, sir." She responded with a smile. "Small farm town in central Iowa."

"Shoulda guessed," he grinned, turning to glance at her over the seat. "Only a sweetheart midwestern girl could put up with my grandson. None of the Southie girls would put up with his charming bullshit."

"Adrian's charming?" Isobel asked, deadpan. The only sign she was joking was the way she chewed on the corner of her lip while my grandfather's laughter filled the car again.

"Oh, I like this one, Ad. She's not gonna put up with nonsense."

As I made eye contact with her in the rearview mirror, her light eyes dancing, I fell a little bit deeper. Isobel was dismantling my armor as much as I was trying to dismantle hers, and the more we both uncovered, the more real things became.

What started as a drive to rile her up and explore our physical connection had morphed into something I wasn't sure I was ready to identify, but I was helpless to resist.

"She definitely is not, Pops. And I think I like that about her the most."

His weathered hand covered mine on the center console and squeezed. Isobel had just cemented my grandfather's seal of approval in one brief car ride, and it felt like another part of my life clicking into place after being untethered for so long.

NINETEEN

ISOBEL

BOSTON

Adrian's grandfather was my new favorite person. His deep, weathered voice, the ever-present smirk, and the knowledge that he completely had his grandson's number was truly impressive. It also had me aching for my family to be that close. My grandparents were all gone now, but I knew I'd never had the spark bond the men walking in the stadium gates in front of me shared. Adrian carried the heavy weight of his family on his shoulders, and while I hated that he'd masked himself for so long, part of me was thankful that he was letting his guard down for me and no one else.

I wasn't sure I wanted to share his kind and compassionate nature with the rest of the world. His dickish façade had kept people away from his heart, and it wouldn't be here for me, open to the possibility of more, if someone else had come along and claimed it.

For the first time in a long, long time, I felt my spark returning, my once dormant dreams flickering to life at the possibility of something I thought had been snuffed out long ago.

"You alright takin' a seat toward the middle?" Adrian asked as we stood at the top of the stairs leading down to the general seating area. The ballpark was still half empty, but people were steadily filtering in and finding their seats.

"Which row?"

"Fourth one down, the four seats on the aisle." The hair on the back of my neck stirred as his warm breath flowed over the side of my neck. "If you go in first, I can help Pops get settled. It's easier for him to sit in the end seat."

"Four?" I asked, wondering who else would join us. Going to the game was enough of a surprise, much less meeting his grandfather and some mystery stranger.

"Hutch isn't here yet," he smiled, pressing his hand to the center of my back, his fingers flexing against the material of my shirt. "He's dealing with some tween drama right now, but I'm sure he'll show up before the end of the first inning."

As I started down the steps—Adrian carefully leading his grandfather down the steps behind me—I racked my brain trying to place the name. I wasn't sure he'd mentioned Hutch before.

Once we were settled into the seats, Adrian sitting between me and Pops, he leaned over and squeezed my knee, whispering in my ear. "Did I not tell you I have a twin?"

There were a lot of words constantly coming out of Adrian's mouth, but the word *twin* hadn't been one of them.

"You need anything? Drink? Frank?"

"Did you forget my name again?" I teased, turning toward him, watching his face go from confused to mildly insulted.

"You're not that naïve, Is. I know those heathens in Wrigley call them dogs, but they also desecrated a classic."

I tried not to laugh but couldn't help myself. "No, Ad. I don't need a sausage to fill my mouth right now. Maybe later."

It may have been years since I attended a ball game, but I wasn't completely clueless. I knew ballpark franks were apparently a religious experience at Fenway. Even though I'd never actually eaten one, Chicago dogs were something I'd always remember. As a child, I hadn't been a fan of onions, but my dad loved them. The smell of those loaded hotdogs was something I'd always associate with summer and baseball.

"I'd be happy to help you out if you want it filled later," he whispered, mirth in his eyes. If it were anyone else, I'd be shocked at him flirting so blatantly in front of his grandfather, but it was Adrian, so it wasn't surprising at all. His sense of shame had left the building a long time ago, nowhere to be found. "My sausage seemed to fit pretty well."

"I'm sure you would, but I'm here to watch some men in tight pants handle their bats, not flirt with you over ballpark wieners."

As Adrian opened his mouth to respond, a booming, eerily familiar laugh sounded from behind my back as a warm shoulder settled against mine. "Did I hear yah say yah wanted to see some men playing with their bats? Sounds kinda kinky."

My face flushed red as I turned, not expecting the rugged doppelgänger of the man on my other side.

"Aw, did I embarrass yah, sweetheart?" he chuckled, glancing over my shoulder to his brother. "Sounded like my brother had finally found someone who shared his affliction of telling thinly veiled dick jokes no one else finds funny."

"Not all my jokes are about dicks," Adrian laughed from behind me, his fingers squeezing the inside of my knee.

"But yah didn't argue them not bein' funny," the bearded man to my left boomed before settling against his seat next to me.

"If I didn't know better, I'd think he was overcompensating for some-thing," Hutch whispered, leaning in closer, my shoulders instinctively mov-ing toward Adrian, but I was trapped between the two of them. "But since we're nearly identical, I know that's not it."

Blinking to clear my head, I gasped when Adrian's warm lips grazed my earlobe. "Am I trying to overcompensate, Is?"

Wedged in between them, I was feeling overheated, but not from the bright late spring sunshine.

Working in editing romance novels for as long as I had, you'd think I'd almost be immune to fleeting fantasies of being shared by two men, but I was woefully unprepared to deal with the situation off the paper.

Thoughts of heaving chests and more than one set of warm lips tracing my exposed skin flooded my brain, and I was beginning to think maybe Adrian had been right about my genre. Maybe we were a bit obsessed with sex. Not that I was thinking about Adrian's twin brother in that context. That would be wrong. *Down girl.*

But they did look alike. It had me wondering if Hutch's comment about *everything* being identical was accurate. Sounded like a mystery that need-ed to be resolved.

With a yardstick.

There was something seriously wrong with me.

"He tryin' tah mark his territory with this?" Hutch smirked as he playfully pulled at the brim of the hat on my head, drawing me out of my completely inappropriate line of thinking. Adrian had clearly been rubbing off on me.

Mmm...rubbing.

And it was official. Trapped between two equally built, equally desirable men, I'd lost my damn mind.

"Can you believe he wouldn't let me wear my Cubs hat in here?" I whispered conspiratorially, still trying to study his features to see the differences between him and Adrian. Other than a few greenish flecks around his irises, if Hutch shaved his full beard and cut his hair, they'd be hard to tell apart.

Which was kind of freaky. It had me wondering how many poor un-suspecting souls they'd fooled when they were younger. I could see them using their identical looks as a challenge to befuddle people.

"Ah. I get it now. No wonder yah like Adrian. You've got a thing for pussies who can't figure out how to score."

My shoulders shook as I tried to hold in a laugh, biting my lip as Adrian's warm breath ghosted over the side of my neck.

"Think I figured it out pretty well a few days ago," he whispered, his hand gripping possessively on the inside of my bare thigh.

"With a little coaching, I think it's salvageable," I snickered, trying not to moan as Adrian dug his short fingernails into my flesh.

"Yeah. Diehard fans always say that until they get some new talent, and then they're screaming for the new guy no problem the first time he hits a bomber."

"Sometimes a little home team loyalty pays off when a struggling player figures out how to drive one home," I quipped back with a grin.

"Didn't have to struggle much," Adrian's amused voice was in my ear once again.

"Yeah, but it's hard to go back to a struggling player when you've experienced the rush of an all-star."

"Hutch, you leave that poor girl alone," Pops chuckled from past Adrian's shoulder. "Besides, some women like the underdog. They try a whole lot harder to get the job done. Sometimes those all-stars get lazy. All flash and no *bang*."

My eyes watered as I tried to smother a laugh. The O'Neill men were not what I would have expected. But they were all endearing in their own way.

AS THE GAME STARTED and the day warmed up, Adrian and Hutch really got into it, shouting at the players, cursing at the umpire, high fiving behind my back when the Sox scored. It was loud, and I was sweaty, and likely sunburned, but I couldn't imagine being anywhere else.

Hutch and Pops welcomed me into their little circle, teasing me just as much as they teased Adrian. Making crass jokes and not trying to mansplain the game to me. It was strange to feel so comfortable around a man's family so soon. It'd taken most of the four years we were at Cornell to be comfortable with Grant's family. Even though Adrian and I hadn't even defined what was going on between us, I was trying not to question how right it felt.

My cheeks flamed while Adrian's fingers traced the ragged hem on my shorts. He'd been touching me all day. Not anything blatantly sexual. But it was possessive. And I liked it.

The big screen on the far side of the stands drew my attention. The infamous kiss cam scrolling across, pausing briefly to capture a sweet kiss between an older couple as they laughed.

As the camera zoomed in again on its next unsuspecting victim, I was too distracted by the men on either side of me to register that it was my face staring back until Hutch leaned in, his beard tickling the side of my face.

"Which one is it gonna be, Bel? You want me to lay one on you to make my brother jealous?"

My cheeks heated while I continued to stare at my likeness, sandwiched in the tiny stadium seats between Hutch and Adrian's broad shoulders.

"Nice try," Adrian growled, leaning over and planting his palm in the center of Hutch's face as the crowd's laughter surrounded us. "She's mine."

I didn't even have time to respond as Adrian firmly grasped the back of my neck and pulled my lips to his, claiming me with a searing kiss.

The noise of the surrounding crowd couldn't compare to the sound of blood rushing in my ears when he slipped his tongue into my mouth, stealing any coherent thoughts.

"Damn, Ad," I heard Pops chuckle from a few seats down. "Don't eat the girl's face. Let her breathe."

When I regained my ability to speak, I took one from Adrian's book, letting my uninhibited thoughts fly after I cleared my throat.

"I think I'm ready for that sausage now."

"YOU ALRIGHT WITH ME dropping these two off before we head to my place?" Adrian asked while we followed Hutch and Pops out of the stadium. We'd waited in our seats for a while after the Sox narrowly pulled off a win in the 9th, reminiscing about the impressive plays during the game. By the time we stood to exit, the crowd had thinned to a tolerable level.

"A little presumptuous of you to think I want to go back to your place after our first date," I answered distractedly, watching the two men in front of us.

"Cute that you think this is only our first date." He chuckled, bumping his shoulder into mine.

"Eating take out with you on my couch hardly counts as a first date, and—"

"Eating you on your couch is now one of my favorite ways to spend a Friday night," he interrupted with a grin, wiggling his eyebrows for effect. *Shameless.*

My cheeks flamed, but hopefully, my blossoming sunburn would conceal it, because recalling straddling Adrian's smug face on my couch was warming up other things. Things I should not be thinking about when I had to spend the next half hour trapped in the car with his eighty-something-year-old grandfather.

"I'm sure this is breaking some kind of date protocol, but would you mind sittin' in the back with Pops? He'll probably be snoring by the time we hit the freeway, but Hutch has a hard time with his leg being crammed in the back seat."

Tilting my head to the side, I studied the men in front of me again, noticing a break in Hutch's gait, his balance favoring one side. He was also wearing cargo pants on a day when most other people around us were in shorts.

"We can talk about it when we get back to my place," Adrian whispered at my questioning look, his fingers skimming the back of my hand. "He was injured when he served overseas. He's got a prosthetic." Another mystery about the twin I never knew existed. Apparently, Mr. Suit Porn's brother had been in the military. "I know we've done this all out of order, but I think it's time we sat down and talked. And not about anything related to work or how much of an ass you think I am."

Nodding, I was startled when he slipped his hand into mine, squeezing before he laced our fingers together.

"You're not a total ass," I whispered, suddenly nervous at the butterflies that took up residence in my stomach. *It was probably the hot dog.*

"Don't start overthinking, babe. I know you think I'm not capable of having a serious conversation without cramming my foot in my mouth, but I'm trying not to screw this up."

The two of us sitting down and having a genuine conversation scared me more than any confrontation we'd had in the office. It'd been so much easier to dislike him than to see him how I was starting to.

As someone I could fall for.

I'd promised myself after Grant that I'd never go for the lovable asshole again, but Adrian was making it hard to stay away.

"You're just trying to screw something else," I teased, leaning into his shoulder and looking up at him.

"Some*one* else," he said with a wink. "I'd be lying if I tried to deny it, but talk first, screw later."

Adrian was right, Pops was snoring before we got through the exit of the parking lot. Which left me to watch the excited Sox fans still lingering on the sidewalks as we headed toward South Boston from Fenway.

I'd been in Boston for years, but I'd never had a reason to venture into what the locals called Southie. A creature of habit, I stuck to my little neighborhood of Jamaica Plain or downtown, where the Vivid offices were located. After the divorce, most of my friendships fizzled, except for Leila's.

Throwing myself into my professional life made sense then, but now I was questioning all the choices I'd made along the way. If I didn't insulate myself with endless manuscript acquisitions, long hours and a hectic travel schedule, would I have met someone by now? Or was it all building up to what was unfolding with Adrian? I found it hard to believe that the man I thought I'd despised for being a pig for the last five years was suddenly the man I was supposed to end up with. But it wasn't like my romantic radar had really worked out for me before.

The overhead light startled me when Hutch opened the passenger door, turning in his seat to aim the O'Neill signature grin in my direction. Oh yeah, those two had been dangerous once upon a time. Actually, they still were.

"It's been a pleasure, Bel. I hope my dipshit brother doesn't screw things up and I'll get to see you again sometime soon." He extended his hand through the break in the seats to grasp mine and drew it toward his mouth, his eyes intent on mine. Soft lips gently caressed the back of my hand, his beard tickling my knuckles before he pulled away, chuckling.

"Don't hit me, you fuck," Hutch laughed, rubbing the back of his head while Adrian aimed a deathly glare at his brother.

"Don't kiss my... *fuck*." Adrian trailed off with a groan as Hutch smacked him in the stomach.

"Boys," Pops huffed from the seat beside me, now wide awake. "Let's pretend we have some manners in front of the lady."

He turned toward me, mimicking his grandson, softly placing a kiss on the back of my hand and leaning back with a wink.

"I've got my eye on you, old man," Adrian laughed while watching our interaction in the rearview mirror.

"It's not our fault we've got more game than you. Better step it up if you want to keep this one," Pops chuckled before he turned back to me. "Don't be a stranger. I've got a feeling my boy might already be over his head with you. Be easy on him, sweetheart."

Hutch helped Pops from the backseat, the two of them waving as they ascended the concrete steps of the row house we'd parked in front of. The siding looked a little weathered on the old building, but the front door and the trim were nicely painted. It wouldn't take much to imagine two dark-haired troublemakers spilling out of the front door and running amok in the neighborhood. Seeing it just added to the ever-changing picture of who Adrian was in my mind.

My door pulled open, Adrian leaning over the top with a soft smile. "You want to ride shotgun or pretend I'm an Uber driver?"

"You mean I have to be seen in a car with you? How embarrassing," I teased.

"I can throw you in the trunk if you're that worried about it."

"Maybe you've been reading a few too many of Evan's novels," I laughed. "Although it usually is the pretty ones who end up being the serial killers."

"No black coffee here, remember?" he shot back, holding his hand out. "I'll make you suffer sitting in the front with me. I kinda enjoyed being able to watch you squirm with my hand on your thigh all afternoon."

Unable to argue with that, I took his hand. I'd never admit it to him, but I too was craving the feeling of his palm after it'd spent most of the game possessively gripping the space where my denim shorts met my thigh.

Chapter
TWENTY

ADRIAN

BOSTON

Isobel's hand cradled mine the entire ride to my apartment. We quietly watched the sun drop below the horizon as we headed west, the city seeming to come alive after dark. Part of me wanted to take her out somewhere, sit down and tease her over dinner, but I knew we needed to talk to see if we were on the same page. She seemed like she'd be receptive to trying out a relationship, but I wanted to make sure. With my terrible habit of saying the wrong thing at the wrong time, I couldn't afford to leave this up to chance.

Being a temporary fling was exciting, but I was catching feelings. Or maybe I was just tired of having to suppress my feelings. Either way, I wanted more.

It'd kill me, but if she wanted something casual, we could call it quits now and try to go back to some semblance of a working relationship.

Although Evan was currently avoiding my calls, his revised manuscript had shaped up to be something we could fast-track to print. Usually, once inspiration hit, he was quick to turn around a first draft. And his newfound inspiration for working with Chase might ensure that.

I could throw myself into his next project and anything else that came across my desk and go back to watching her in staff meetings.

Except this time, I'd know what she tasted like.

How she sounded when she came...

The quiet little moans she made when my dick was in her mouth...

How it felt to have her coming on my cock, knowing anyone could walk by and hear her, or catch us...

Okay, maybe I was royally fucked. But I'd figure it out. And I wouldn't know anything until I asked.

"Are you hungry?"

Turning onto the street near my building, I was thankfully able to find a spot, maneuvering my car into the space quickly before some asshole tried to poach it.

"I'm still full from the sausage you fed me." Her voice was quiet as she looked over, her fingers flexing over my hand. "Maybe we can order in something later if we work up an appetite."

At first, I thought she'd been playfully insinuating something, but the look in her eyes threw me off. Isobel rarely looked apprehensive about anything. I could tell she was uncertain about why I was so adamant we talk.

"Definitely. Have to keep you fed or you'll get hangry. Don't need you getting all grumpy on me again."

"That was one time, and it was the ass crack of dawn. I'm not a morning person. You know that."

"Mmhmm."

Her nose scrunched as her eyes narrowed. I knew she wanted to say something, but she was holding back.

She'd been doing that quite a bit lately, and I had to admit I missed her ire. Part of our dynamic was riling each other up. Just because we got each other off now shouldn't change that.

Being a dickhead was somehow foreplay. Lucky me.

"Are we going to sit in the car all night?"

Fuck. I just needed to suck it up and take her inside.

"Stay where you are," I ordered while I unbuckled and grabbed my keys out of the cup holder. Her soft laughter followed me as I jumped out and slammed my door.

"I told you that you didn't have to put on the gentlemanly act with me," she teased when I pulled open her door, extending a hand to help her out.

"And I told you it wasn't an act."

"Sure. Whatever you say." She walked past me, and I couldn't help myself, playfully swatting her ass. She yelped and glared at me over her shoulder. "Gentlemen don't spank."

"You bet your sweet ass they do. I thought we'd covered this already," I challenged, following her to the entrance of my building and swiping my digital entry card. She stepped in ahead of me and stopped in front of the elevator doors. A quick glance around the lobby to confirm we were alone, and I crowded against her back, possessively gripping her hip as I pulled her flush with me. "Gentlemen most certainly spank. Does the thought of being bent over my knee make you wet, Isobel?"

Her chest shook as she tried to hold in a laugh. "No, but the thought of spanking that cocky attitude right out of you might."

Groaning quietly into her hair, I traced my hand down, cupping her pussy over the denim of her shorts. "I always knew you had a bit of a dominant streak. I can't wait for you to let it out."

"I don't know if you can handle giving me control," she teased, pressing her ass right into my building erection. Isobel seemed to enjoy fooling around—and more—while there was the potential to get caught.

"Try me."

Her hand reached back, pressing between our bodies while we watched the numbers go down on the digital panel above the elevator doors. "I bet I could make you come in your pants before we get to your floor if I tried hard enough."

"Mmhmm," I hummed, burying my nose into the back of my hat, wanting to grab her braids and tug, just to hear the moan I knew she'd give me.

"What if there's someone else in the elevator with us? Could you manage then? If someone tried to watch what you were doing to me in the reflection of the doors? I bet you'd like it if someone watched you drive me crazy. If they imagined your soft hand on them instead of me."

Her fingers crept underneath the hem of my t-shirt, toying with the button of my jeans, her breathing picking up as she released it, tugging on my zipper, but not pulling it down.

"Imagine their faces if the doors opened to you flushed and trying to play with my cock in the lobby. Such a filthy little minx." I hadn't called her anything remotely degrading before—except for my snarky comment about her being Boss Bitch Barbie—but the quiet moan that slipped from her lips clued me in that she might enjoy it. *Noted.*

When the elevator chimed and the doors slowly parted, I grinned as I took in the vacant car. Would Isobel back down, or would she continue since we were alone?

"After you," I urged, stepping forward and following her into the car without breaking apart.

I spun and leaned against the back corner while she settled in front of me. Slowly cupping my hand against the front of her neck, I felt her pulse pounding as the door closed and the elevator jumped softly as it ascended. There weren't that many floors until we got to my apartment, but that didn't stop her from reaching back and yanking down my zipper.

Her warm fingers reached inside my boxers and grasped me firmly while I grunted into her neck, pulling her tightly against me with the hand on her throat. "Fuck. Maybe I shouldn't have doubted you."

She squeezed, snickering, while I continued to groan against the back of her neck. Maybe the thought of getting caught was getting to me too as I flexed my hips into her jerky movements, fucking her palm while we continued to rise. The elevator was going to stop any moment now, and while I wanted her to win our little game, I also didn't want to get reported to management by any of the little old ladies who lived on my floor.

"*Fuck*, Is. You win. Spank me all you want," I hissed when her thumb passed over the tip of my cock, spreading the moisture that'd been leaking out as she played with me.

"You can't give up that easily," she laughed as the elevator slowly stopped. Before the doors could open, she quickly pressed the button to close them again. As long as no one else called the elevator...we were in here alone. "Although I wouldn't mind it if you begged a little more."

She reached up with her free hand, pulled mine away from her neck as she turned around, and spun my hat so it faced backward before she tugged my shorts a little lower.

"What are you doing, naughty girl?" I grinned, watching her grasp me with both hands, looking up at me while she lowered her face.

"Not a girl, but since you asked... I'm keeping you from embarrassing yourself and making a mess in your pants, big boy." She lowered her voice to a murmur. "Very. Big. Boy."

My neck arched back, hitting the wall of the elevator with a thump as her soft lips drew me into her mouth, inch by agonizing inch until I settled against the back of her throat. She swallowed once, drawing a pained curse from me before she eased back and sucked.

While the blowjob in my hotel room had been spectacularly torturous, I was helpless against her as she sucked hard and pressed her fingers to the little space behind my balls, hurtling me toward the finish line before I was ready. This time, she wasn't in the mood to prolong things.

"Fuck, fuck, fuck," I groaned, my hips flexing forward, and my cock throbbing while I tried to hold off.

"*Now*, Adrian. Come in my mouth now, and then I'll spank you later," she whispered after she momentarily pulled back, arching an eyebrow before she sucked me back into her warm mouth. Her tongue moved frantically, rubbing on the underside of me in a way that had me seeing stars.

"Goddammit," I groaned, reaching forward to grasp her braids, desperate to hold on to something as I released, spurting into her mouth before she swallowed.

My breath caught when she sucked hard again, disentangling my fists from her hair as she pulled away. Her tongue flicked out, coyly licking the tip before she stepped back, turning my hat on her head around and nodding to my open pants.

"Might want to put that away before you frighten the neighbors."

"Wouldn't want to scare them with this massive beast," I laughed, immediately cursing my lack of inner filter. I desperately wanted to smack myself upside the head, but I wasn't sure I could move my arms.

"I'm sure they'd be terrified of the teenie weenie on the loose in the hallways," she shot back, holding her hand out toward me.

This woman might as well slap a collar on me and lead me around with a leash. I was officially her bitch.

And I loved it.

As we walked hand in hand to my door, I swallowed hard, trying to sort my chaotic thoughts.

Usually, you experienced stage fright over the first kiss on a date, but since we'd sped right past that landmark and onto blowjobs in the elevator, I was at a loss for words.

And brain cells. They'd vanished as soon as she told me to come in her mouth.

"This is me." My voice shook as I fit my key into the lock, glancing at her out of the corner of my eye.

"I figured." Her cheeks were flushed, the end of her nose pink, lips puffy from...

"It's not that big, but it is what it is." Why was I suddenly choosing now to be quiet and awkward?

"Seemed big enough a few minutes ago."

Shaking my head, I pushed open the door and motioned for her to go in ahead of me. "If I'd have known you were this much of a perv, I would have seduced you a long time ago."

"Pretty sure I'm the one that seduced you, but I'll let you pretend you're in control if it makes you feel better."

"So..." I gestured to the modest open plan living room, kitchen, and nook I'd turned into my makeshift office. My large desk was staged against my one floor to ceiling window. My bedroom door was across the living room, cracked open slightly. But I wasn't taking her in there. There wouldn't be much talking if I got her near my king-sized bed.

"I know I distracted you on the way up here, but you were so insistent that we have this talk. *So, talk.*"

She stepped away, running her fingertips along the dark granite of my kitchen peninsula.

"Don't you want to sit?"

"Hmm, in a minute," she hummed, running her fingertips along the spines of the hardbacks in one of my bookcases. "Should have pegged you for the type to be so anal about their bookcases."

Since my little head was clearly still in charge, my brain picked up *should have pegged you* and *anal.*

Along with her spanking comments from earlier and her threatening to boss me around in her playful texts, I imagined her in only a set of high heels with me on my knees at her feet.

"Where'd you go?" she asked, suddenly appearing in front of me, bracing her palms on my shoulders before she settled in my lap. "You were there for one minute and then a totally blank stare. Did I break you? I thought men were supposed to have that post orgasm mental clarity."

Her palms cupped my cheeks, her thumbs smoothing the skin beneath my eyes as I looked down at her thighs. There was a faint patch of pale skin in the shape of my handprint surrounded by gently pink, sun-kissed skin. Tracing it with my finger, I tried to figure out how to lay all this on her without scaring her off.

"If this is just fun for you, I need you to tell me now. Because I could see myself falling for you. It would be so easy to fall, babe, but I can't do it alone."

"It is fun..." she trailed off as she lifted my jaw with her hands. "But it's not only about that."

"What is it about?"

"I'm not sure yet," she confessed, her eyes searching mine. She had to see that I was hers. "But if you keep showing me this side of you, it won't take much for me to fall too."

Leaning forward, I grasped her back and urged her to scoot forward. "This isn't just about how much I want you physically. Please give me a chance to prove I can be what you need."

Nodding, she leaned in and kissed me, just a ghost of her lips across mine. But it was enough to ignite the burn inside of me to get closer.

"Spanking time?" She smirked against my lips, her fingers tugging on the hair at the nape of my neck as she tried to lighten the mood.

"Not yet," I murmured as I gathered her against my chest and took possession of her lips as I stood from the couch.

My skin ached to be pressed to hers, my cock hitting deep while my fingers traced every little freckle while she writhed beneath me.

She seemed to be on the same page, leaning back to pull her t-shirt over her head as I carried her to my bedroom. "Just so we're clear, I'm definitely sleeping with you this time."

"Yay, slumber party," I mumbled against her flimsy bra, nipping at one peaked nipple through the soft cotton.

"I didn't say I was spending the night," she laughed while I clumsily toed off my shoes, reaching back to pull her sneakers off one at a time. "But I'm open to persuasion."

Her fingers crept under the hem of my shirt, pulling it up as my knees hit the end of the bed. "The bakery with the croissants is next door."

"Mmmm. Good to know. Keep going."

She reached between us to pop the button on my jeans, moving to unbutton hers while I sucked on the skin above her breasts, leaving a faint mark.

"I'll let you eat it in bed while I eat my breakfast. Pussy is especially tasty while it's still warm," I whispered against her skin while my tongue traced her earlobe.

"You really like going down on me, don't you?"

Hoisting her higher on my waist, I reached down to push my briefs and pants down, kicking them out of the way. "Feeling seems to be mutual."

"It's a nice cock. Are you complaining?" She laughed while I crawled onto the mattress with her in my arms.

"You've got a pretty pink pu—"

Her palm covered my lips. "Shut up and get inside me already or I'll just go home and do it myself."

"Not happening," I growled against her fingers. She wasn't coming on a toy unless I was the one controlling it.

Laying her against the pillows, I yanked off her tiny shorts and panties, pulling off my socks before I settled over her, balancing on my forearms.

"You still alright to do this bare?"

The spontaneity of the copy room didn't mean she wanted to do it again.

Licking her lips, she didn't respond with words, instead reaching down to grasp me in her hand and positioning me against her entrance. My hips ground instinctively, and she let out a breathy gasp, tilting her hips to urge me inside.

Hesitating, I leaned forward to kiss her, slowly coaxing her lips open while I slipped against her wetness, throbbing while I held back.

Lost in the feel of her skin on mine, I kissed her desperately, realizing I hadn't been entirely truthful earlier. I wasn't falling. It was done. I was hers.

She rocked her hips against me, her fingers moving from my neck to my shoulders, drawing her nails down the center, causing me to shudder as I waited for her to answer me.

"I want to feel you," Isobel whispered against my cheek, digging her nails into my lower back. "Make me scream your name and then I want you to come inside me."

"Fuck, yes," I breathed, tilting my hips, and pressing forward in one measured thrust. She moaned into my lips as I ground my hips into her, meeting each movement with a needy moan.

Leaning back to brace my palms on the mattress, I watched every reaction. Every flutter of her eyelids and heave of her chest. Her breasts bounced, her eyes closing and her back arching as I circled my hips with each thrust.

"Look," I murmured, glancing down to where my cock disappeared, her body taking everything I had to give her. "Watch how greedily you take me. You're so wet, babe. *Fuck*."

She lifted her head, her eyes transfixed, while I continued to fuck her. The pale skin on her chest flushed as I felt her clench around me.

"What do you need?" I asked, wrapping my arm around her lower back and using it as leverage to pull her into me. "How do you want me to make you come?"

"Just..." she trailed off while I leaned back, pulling her upright into my lap. "Oh fuck. That. Do that."

Thrusting up into her, my hands traced her skin, pulling her into me. She gasped my name, grinding down against my movements, her eyes falling shut as she rocked in my lap.

One hand fondled her breast as I leaned down, pulling her nipple into my mouth while her neck arched. One of her braids brushed against where I held her back, tickling my skin. Biting down on her nipple, I turned my hand and grasped her wayward braid, tugging until she moaned loudly.

"Fuck me," I groaned into her chest as she braced herself against my shoulders, grinding down.

Holding her head back with one braid in my fist and a hand at her waist, I rose to my knees to get more leverage. My hips thrust hard while her eyes rolled back. She was clearly enjoying this new angle. I hoped she was close when my thighs started burning. All my hours in the gym were worth it as I held her up, fucking her frantically while her moans increased in pitch.

Grunting when she fell apart, I watched her mouth fall open in a wanton moan when she came.

My cock throbbed while she fluttered around me, and the blood rushed in my ears as I panted, fighting the urge to come.

Her eyes opened, drowsy and satisfied. She reached up to pull the hair on the back of my head. "I always knew your arms were ridiculous, but that was just showing off."

"You know you liked it," I teased, laying her back against the mattress, pulling out, and rolling her to her side. I slipped in behind her, moving her leg back over mine and positioning myself before I thrust back inside.

One hand held her thigh in place while the other slipped underneath her and captured her breast, kneading it gently with my palm while I pinched her nipple between my fingers.

"This shouldn't feel this good," she whispered, my hips setting a steady pace while I traced up her thigh to strum her clit with my thumb.

"You clearly weren't getting fucked right," I whispered into her neck, biting the skin playfully.

"Why didn't we do this sooner?"

"Because you hated me," I laughed, enjoying how needy she was.

"Oh, God. You're going to make me come again."

"That's the plan," I grinned, thrusting harder as I felt her tense in my arms.

"I've never come more than once," she confessed, pressing her head against my shoulder. "Who am I kidding? I was lucky to come once."

"Fucking stupid bastards," I groaned when I felt her clench hard, right on the cusp of letting go. My teeth ground against each other as I continued pistoning my hips, trying to fight off the urge to finish before her. "Never again, babe. Never. You're mine now. It's such a fuckin' turn-on to make you come."

"*Yes*," she exhaled, shaking in my arms. Her chest heaved when she spiraled into another intense release, my fingers sliding easily against her clit. I prolonged it, pressing inside as far as I could before I let go.

My heart hammered as her body relaxed, beating frantically against where her back rested against my chest. Tracing my fingers along her waist, I pulled her back, erasing any space between us. "You don't have to worry about that anymore, Is. I'm going to take care of you."

Her hand covered the one I pressed into her stomach, her fingers settling into the spaces between mine. She may not be ready yet, but my mind was already on the future, hoping that she wanted the same things I did. I wasn't just trying to get her into my bed. I wanted all of her.

She shuddered as my thumb slowly caressed her soft skin and tilted her head to look at me. "I want that too. I want—"

"It's yours," I interrupted. "Whatever you want, it's yours."

Chapter
TWENTY-ONE

ISOBEL

BOSTON

My mind drifted while I sat in a chair outside of Sloane's office, daydreaming about the last few months with Adrian. Things had shifted after the baseball game a month ago, and it was totally unexpected in the best possible way. While I never doubted Grant had loved me, Adrian was borderline obsessed. He couldn't get enough (not that I was much better), but things weren't purely sexual.

He talked to me while we ate dinner together after work at either one of our apartments, sent me text messages throughout the day—of both the sweet and spicy variety—and he hadn't been a total dick at work in weeks. We spent as much time as possible with each other when we weren't actively working, although our lunch dates had set off the office gossip mill. I should've been horrified that my coworkers were speculating about my sex life, but frequent orgasms had a way of desensitizing you to pointless office politics.

Every day, tiny pieces of his actual personality slipped through the cracks of his facade, and he showed me he was serious about trying to have a real adult relationship outside of work by behaving in the office. He didn't intentionally try to provoke Kristine, and he even helped the receptionist, Andrea, with her coursework when no one else was watching.

He'd also successfully calmed me down when I freaked out that Chase and Evan had seemingly disappeared after his book was released and only resurfaced long enough to tell me they were writing a book together and Chase was putting her own upcoming book series on hold.

"You ready?" Sloane smiled as she appeared in her office doorway, motioning for me to follow her.

She'd mentioned when she met with me over a month ago wanting to pass down some of her duties as head of publishing while Vivid restructured to expand into a television streaming platform. Details had been vague at the time, but as the hiring process was already underway for the genre editor positions opening in a few months, she was clearly ready to fill in those blanks.

"When we talked earlier, I know I didn't have any concrete information for you, but now that we've figured out how to cover some of your day to day, I wanted to bring you in so I could pitch what we'd like to be your new role with Vivid."

Other than stepping into her job, there wasn't much advancement possible on an editorial level, so I was intrigued by the thought of taking on more while still maintaining my role as the head of the romance genre department in Boston.

"We'd like to create a hybrid position and promote one of your interns to take over the less critical parts of your job duties. Kristine would be the natural choice, but we can revisit that later since it looks like she's one of the final candidates for the position in New York."

"What would that mean for me?"

"You'd be given the title of publishing manager and oversee all the genre heads at a production level. That'd mean less time spent on your individual authors and more time making sure each department had what they needed for their releases."

Nodding, I mentally processed what I'd be willing to give up taking on this new position. "So, I wouldn't work directly with any of my authors anymore?"

"Not exactly," she hedged. "You could pick a handful to continue to be a primary contact for, but the rest would fall under your new intern supervisor and the rest of the copy-editing team."

While this opportunity would be amazing, I wasn't sure I wanted to completely leave behind the creative process. Even if it was only in a limited capacity, I loved working with authors. And with Chase dropping the bomb on me she was working on something secret with Evan, I didn't want to give up control of that manuscript to someone else. It meant working directly with Adrian again, but that would go a lot smoother than the first time.

"The management team discussed it, and whenever the next book tour begins for your department, we'd like Kristine to manage it to test out her ability to step into your role."

"Does that mean less travel for me?"

She shook her head. "No. Just a different kind of travel. You'd be based out of Boston, but we'd need you to travel to all four locations on an as-needed basis. The California office will be restructured to take on the television production, so we may be able to find someone to work under you from that pool of editors, but you'd be responsible for the department heads here, New York and Chicago."

Meaning I'd become Adrian's boss.

"If there is a conflict of interest in supervising one of the editing heads, would that be a problem?"

Sloane chuckled as she leaned back in her chair. "As long as you and Adrian can keep it professional in the office, I don't see why it would be."

My cheeks heated as her smile widened, knowing she'd easily hit the mark. "Do I have your permission to share the details of this offer with him?"

"Let's wait a few weeks until your contracts are ready for specifics, but I don't see why you can't tell him about the opportunity. A few months ago, I would've expected him to protest this kind of change in the management structure, but I don't see that being a problem any longer."

"Let's hope so."

"I've seen how he watches you. Really, how he's watched you for years. I don't think he'll have a problem with it. He respects you a great deal. I wouldn't have had you two working together if that wasn't the case. Think of Stone's book as a trial run for your professional relationship."

"I wasn't exactly in a position of power over him then."

"Not so sure that's entirely accurate," she replied with a knowing grin. "He was quick to defer to you during that process more than I think you noticed. That's a good quality to look for in a partner. It's not always easy for men to put their egos aside to let a woman tell them what to do professionally. I know I've dealt with a lot of fragile masculinity in my career."

Adrian didn't seem the type to try to get in the way of this promotion, but we were equals when things started to change between us.

"The job isn't officially yours yet, but I'd like to get the contracts drawn up for you to review if you're open to negotiating the change."

"Does the offer have a time limit?"

"It'll be a few weeks until everything goes through legal and the management panel, so think about it until the offer is ready. You're our first choice for the position, and I'd like you to seriously consider it before turning anything down."

"I will. Thank you for considering me."

"There wasn't anyone else as far as I'm concerned. You've put in your time, and you deserve it."

Nodding, I stood, reaching forward to shake her hand before I saw myself out of her office.

My mind raced during the elevator ride down to the lobby. I was meeting Adrian to have lunch at a restaurant a few blocks away from the office. He'd know as soon as he saw me there was something on my mind. Keeping the details from him was going to be a challenge, but Sloane had already told me it wouldn't be forever. I also needed to talk to him about other things.

My bloodwork and tests had come back from the fertility clinic and while I hadn't initially been hopeful, they didn't find anything that would prevent me from getting pregnant or carrying a baby to term. We hadn't set anything into motion, but after my IUD was removed, there wasn't anything holding me back from trying. All I needed was someone to *get* me pregnant, and I didn't think I'd have to look too long.

It all seemed almost too good to be true. I was being offered a promotion I'd be stupid to turn down; I wasn't barren like I'd believed, and I was falling for Adrian harder than I'd ever thought possible. If only I could have it all without sacrificing something.

I wasn't even sure if Adrian would want to have a baby with me, but I was resolved to try whether or not he was on board. At this point, I wasn't willing to put trying for a baby on the back burner again. He would either be the father of my child, or I'd do it alone.

The promotion would make it a challenge, and being a single parent would be hard, but I needed to try. I'd lived with regret for too long.

One small text from my best friend had me halting in my steps in the lobby of my office building.

> *LJ: Since when do you like the Red Sox?*

> *Isobel: What are you talking about?*

> *LJ: Kiss cam footage of you and Dickhead is trending right now on IG. Seems his little macho display of possession hit Bookstagram with the hashtag #bookboyfriendgoals.*

A link followed and my eyes widened when I opened it, a brief shot of me sitting next to Hutch appearing followed by Adrian reaching around me to palm his brother's face. Even though I'd been there, a blush rose on my cheeks while I watched Adrian kissing me in front of tens of thousands of baseball fans.

> *LJ: You lucky bitch.*

> *Isobel: Should I be worried about this?*

> *LJ: It could be worse. You didn't go viral for saying something wild like that hawk-tuah girl.*

> *Isobel: You really need to let that go. I'm more concerned about what my dad will say if he sees that.*

> *LJ: Who gives a shit. I'd be saving that shit on my phone to show your grandkids.*

> *Isobel: Adrian hasn't agreed to anything yet.*

> *LJ: He will.*

Isobel: We'll find out later. Testing showed everything is fine on my part.

LJ: I'm so happy you're doing this.

Isobel: I'm scared shitless, but I also don't want to give this up yet.

LJ: And you shouldn't have to. Pull up your big girl panties and go ask that hottie for a sperm deposit.

Isobel: Such a romantic.

She sent back a middle finger emoji, and I resumed my way across the lobby, pausing as another text came through.

LJ: Grant sent me the link. He asked me if I knew about your boyfriend.

Pausing, I sat down on a bench and tried to calm my racing heart. The last thing I wanted to think about right now was Grant.

Isobel: What did you tell him?

LJ: That if he wanted to know, you'd have told him. And that the hunky guy in the video was more than happy to give you everything he refused to.

Isobel: Should I message him?

LJ: Fuck him and that skinny bitch yoga instructor. What he did to you is in the past. All you need to worry about now is riding your hung stallion until he puts a bun in your oven.

Isobel: That was way too many idioms in one sentence.

LJ: You know what I mean. Go get your cavity filled.

Isobel: You're almost as bad as Dickhead.

LJ: Maybe that's why you like him.

My body was on autopilot as I headed toward where Adrian and I planned to meet, slowing down to watch him leaning against the side of the building, waiting for me. He truly was a beautiful man, and some part of me ached to confess everything I felt for him, but I wasn't ready to lose him.

I also wasn't letting myself dwell on the fact my ex-husband only reached out when he was worried about me moving on. Well, fuck him. He didn't deserve any real estate in my brain. He'd made his decision, and I was making mine.

"Hey." He smiled, pushing off the wall to reach for my hand. He didn't give two fucks about the office rumor mill and took every opportunity to touch me while we weren't actively working. The copy room tryst sadly hadn't been repeated. Stolen brushes of fingers and secret smiles had been the only physical contact between us once we got to our floor every day.

"Sorry if I made us late," I apologized, starting to walk toward the restaurant with his thumb tracing the back of my hand the entire way.

"You know Sloane doesn't care if we take a long lunch break as long as we don't fall behind on our work."

"She knows about us," I confessed, not wanting to keep too many secrets from him.

"I figured. She kept glancing back and forth between us during the meeting last week. I think I might have been too obvious when I complimented your willingness to be a team player during collaborative efforts between departments."

"You've been obvious for a while," I teased. "But I think it was probably the way I blushed when you stared at me across the table after bragging about me in front of all the other department heads."

"You know I love it when you blush." His gaze was affectionate as he looked over at me, my cheeks heating, which caused him to smile wider. "Just like that. Although, I like it even more when you're wearing a lot less clothing."

"Quit. We're in public."

"No one gives a shit, Is. I don't care who knows I want you. You're all I think about. You have to know that."

We arrived at the restaurant before I could respond, but his words strengthened my resolve to talk to him about my plans and his place in them.

My leg bounced under the table as we went through the motions of ordering. When the server finally left to turn in our orders, I exhaled slowly, preparing to ask him if he wanted to consider being involved beyond just dating. This decision wasn't one I could take lightly, but he'd continually surprised me, and automatically dismissing him as an option because of his previous behavior wouldn't be fair.

While I tried to formulate my thoughts, his phone buzzed on the table and he looked down, eyes widening at the notification on his screen.

"Something wrong?"

He grabbed the phone, his eyes frantically scanning while his mouth dropped open.

"Holy shit. Check your email." He didn't even bother looking up, continuing to scroll down whatever he was looking at.

Reaching into my pocket, I pulled out my work phone, surprised at the notification waiting.

Chase Rodgers and Evan Stineman have shared a PDF with you.

They were done already. Holy shit was right.

Wanting to stay ahead of things, I pulled up her name in my contacts and pressed the call button. Adrian pulled his phone up to his ear across the table at the same time. Clearly, he needed to talk to his wayward author about what was in that PDF as much as I did with mine.

"Adrian is already losing his shit over this." I didn't even bother with a greeting when she answered, just jumping straight into it as Adrian spoke animatedly into his phone. "We've worked together a long time, Chase. Pitch me."

"Sexy thriller centered on a Dominatrix and her long-term sub with a serial killer who keeps going after her clients one by one. She doesn't know who to trust until her sub disappears and she's kidnapped with no hope of escape."

"So, it's one of your feel-good rom coms," I teased, watching Adrian across the table. While he would have been skeptical of this kind of storyline a few months ago—automatically dismissing it because it wasn't Evan's usual niche—I had a feeling he would be all in on this project.

"Evan's freaking out a little bit, so please tell Kristine to be gentle with him. Whatever Adrian is saying has him almost pulling his hair out."

The server returned with our food, and I rushed Chase off the phone with a promise to send the pitch through to Sloane. Adrian ended his call with Evan moments later and grinned at me across the table.

"Eat up, babe. We've got a book to pitch. And some serious reading to do. Did you see the word count?"

"I didn't open it yet, but I'm sure the detailed sex scenes Chase is known for will push it over a hundred." She left nothing purely to the imagination.

"A little long, but I think we can make it fit."

"Yeah, we can," I teased with a wink, grasping his hand across the table. Adrian looked almost proud that I was the one making the inappropriate comment this time.

"Spend the night at my place tonight?" he asked, his hand turning to lace with mine. "This might dampen my plans for you, but I think it's probably good to read this one where we can talk about plot points in person."

"If it's as hot as I'm expecting, you probably don't want your first read through to be in the office."

"Think I can't handle a little spice?"

I shook my head, signaling the server and handing him my credit card. "Can we get this boxed up to go?"

Adrian tilted his head as I picked up my work phone to fire off a few texts to Kristine and Sloane that I'd be out of the office for the rest of the afternoon.

"We still have time to eat. It's not that time-sensitive."

"You know you're not going to sit on that document. You'll be itching to skim that PDF in five minutes, so we might as well dive into it."

He grinned, grabbing the bag of our food while I put away my card and pulled up the Uber app. "You're probably right. What's the plan?"

"You head back to the office and settle whatever you need to work from home tomorrow. I'll go home to pack a bag and meet you at your place. You're gonna want me there when you go through it."

He'd be horny as fuck at work if we read it there, and while it was fun to skirt the line of professionalism, I wasn't getting caught doing something at the office with this promotion on the table. And he was going to want to do something after reading that manuscript. Or more specifically, *someone*.

"Don't trust me to behave myself with the comment feature?"

"No," I laughed. "I don't trust you to not try to fuck me on my desk."

His eyes widened, and he almost choked on air, his Adam's apple bobbing while he tried to regain his composure.

"You don't think I can control myself?"

"I *know* you can't. And this way you won't have to. And neither will I."

I had a feeling that solo sessions with my vibrator after going over sex scenes were a thing of the past. Now I had a real cock to play with if the words made me horny.

Women all over the world had better sex lives because of romance novels. Why shouldn't I? It was time I started reaping the benefits of my job.

TWENTY-TWO

ADRIAN

BOSTON

Isobel was waiting outside my building, two duffel bags at her feet, completely absorbed in her phone when I turned the corner from where I'd parked my car.

"Hey there, sexy," I whispered, pitching my voice low and letting my full accent bleed in while I snuck up behind her. "Howse about we take this upstairs? I'm sure yah boyfriend wouldn't mind if I took yah for a spin."

She jumped forward and spun with her arm cocked back, ready to smack her assailant across the face. But she settled for swatting my bicep and fixing me with an adorably terrifying glare.

"Ad, come on, seriously?"

"And that's why you should always pay attention to your surroundings. You never know what kind of creep could sneak up on you."

"Oh, I know exactly what kind of creep snuck up on me," she chuckled, and then her face suddenly sobered. "And now I don't feel guilty about what I'm going to do to you tonight."

"I know you meant for that to sound threatening, but if you've been reading what I've been reading, I'm fully supportive of you channeling your inner Domme."

"Oh, how the tables have turned," she laughed, watching me swipe my key card before leading her toward the elevator. "A few months ago, reading something like this would have been beneath you. Now you want me to tie you up and..."

"Hold that thought," I whispered while the doors slipped closed. Wrapping one hand around her, the other supporting her head, I dipped her slightly, my mouth descending on hers with a ferocity that even surprised me.

"What was that for?" she whispered when I leaned back, her hands falling to my chest. "Not that I'm complaining, but..."

"I know I've not always been the easiest person to work with." The smirk that formed on her kiss-swollen lips made me want to shut her up again with my mouth. "Yeah, point made. But thank you for giving this a chance between us. I've never been so simultaneously frustrated and charmed by a woman before."

"The feeling is mutual," she murmured, stroking her fingers along the side of my face.

"Getting put in my place by you is a million times more exhilarating than doing just about anything with anyone else. And I'd like to keep doing it indefinitely." I paused, swallowing hard. "If that's alright with you."

Her eyes searched mine, emotions changing with each flutter of her lashes. Hopeful, worried, vulnerable...

"I know I haven't given you a lot of reasons to trust I can behave myself, but I'm trying."

Before she could respond, the elevator stopped, the doors opening to one of my elderly neighbors impatiently waiting in the doorway.

We pulled apart and awkwardly shuffled past her into the hallway, Isobel smiling up at me as we heard a raspy voice call out behind us. "At least it doesn't smell like a brothel in here this time."

By the time we made it to my door, we were both shaking with laughter. "Wow, called out by the elderly," Isobel laughed, smiling up at me. Every time she genuinely smiled at me, it made my insides light up with hope she felt the same way. Hutch would tell me I needed to turn in my man card, but I hadn't been lying when I said I was enchanted by her. Reality was so much better than the fantasy.

"I would tell you it was the first time I got my balls busted by an old person, but you've met Pops."

"Pops is one of my favorite people. You're really lucky to have him in your life." Knowing that and hearing it confirmed made me feel guilty. I'd been so wrapped up in Isobel that I'd not been able to stop by the house as much as I used to. Pops would be thrilled I hadn't fucked things up with Isobel, but his lucid days wouldn't last forever.

"You should come by the house for dinner next weekend. I know Ma would like to meet you." She'd told me as much on the phone last week, but part of me was still worried that Isobel would tire of me. I didn't want my family to get attached to her and then have her dump me. Especially Pen. She'd love her, and with her tenuous relationship with her mother, I knew it'd be easy to get attached to a woman who was strong, sarcastic and loving.

"That sounds like something you'd ask a girlfriend to do," she replied, her eyes guarded.

Unlocking the door, I ushered her inside, dropping my bag by the door. Quickly taking her bag and tossing it with mine, I turned her around and grasped her by the hips, lifting her and carrying her the short distance to my desk.

Once I had her settled on the edge, I leaned down and kissed her softly, loving that she didn't hesitate to return my kisses.

"Is that something you'd be up for, being someone's girlfriend?"

She paused, searching my face, her eyes tracing over me. "You're going to stick around, aren't you?"

Smiling, I leaned down and whispered in her ear. "Gettin' rid of me isn't an option, Is. You're definitely stuck with me."

"I hope you mean that," she whispered back, tears gathering in the corners of her eyes.

"Hey." Cupping her cheeks, I leaned in to kiss her forehead. It wasn't like her to seem this overwhelmed by something. While I could still tap into my inner asshole when I wasn't consciously trying to unmask it, I hoped I hadn't done something to question my utter devotion to her. Being a boyfriend wasn't something I'd done in a long ass time, but I thought I was doing a decent job of it, just without the official title. "What's goin' on in that head? We alright?"

Nodding slowly, she leaned back, bracing her hands behind her on the desk, putting space between us I didn't like. But I wanted her to know I could listen to her, so I took a step back, ready to talk about whatever was bothering her. Distracting her with kinky sex would be fun, but it wouldn't erase that look from her face either.

"I don't want to sound needy," she sighed, "But I need to know I can rely on you before I ask you this."

"Of course, babe. You know I've got your back. Lay it on me."

"Would you..." she trailed off. Whatever this was, it was making her hesitate.

I had a feeling this had something to do with the conversation Sloane had with the other department heads earlier in the week. The management structure would be changing after the copy-editing intern promotions were decided. We hadn't really talked about it, but one of us, or both, would lose our interns, and even I recognized her viper had the potential to be a great genre head. It'd be weird to think of her as a peer, but I could keep my tongue if I had to.

"If this is about Sam and Kristine," I started.

"No." She shook her head, breaking eye contact to stare at my chest. "This is about me."

"I'm not worried about anything happening at the office, Is. Sloane told us about her plans for the department."

"It's not that either," she murmured. "Although she told me to keep quiet about the details of my future there until they have the contracts drawn up."

Tilting her head back, I waited until she made eye contact with me. "I'm fuckin' proud of you. You deserve whatever she offers you. Don't be worried about me."

She smiled, some of the hesitation draining out of the way she looked at me. "Thank you."

"Now tell me what's really bothering you."

"I want to have a baby." Her voice was quiet, but she didn't avert her gaze this time, watching my reaction with guarded hope in her eyes.

If any other woman had uttered those words, I would have been formulating an excuse to get her out of my apartment, but not with Is. As I contemplated her confession, images of the future ran through my mind. I could see it—us going for it and starting a family together. I couldn't imagine doing it with anyone else. It was a little sudden, but it's not like we were twenty-five. We could do this.

"What are you waiting for?" I asked, knowing this was clearly something she wasn't just saying on a whim.

"I don't know. At this point, I'm probably too old to even try. And I don't know how easily I'll get pregnant. Two miscarriages and a year's worth of negative tests make it hard to believe being a mom is something that will ever be in the cards for me. The last time I tried, it ended in divorce."

A little line formed between her eyebrows, but I already knew that she'd been married before. The rumor mill in the office was thriving, and when I'd started, there were whispered conversations about her reverting to her maiden name.

"What do you need from me? I still don't see this changing things between us. You don't need to worry about me not wanting you." The frown deepened, her head tilting back, but I grasped the sides of her face, forcing her to look at me. "I'm not gonna deny you something you want this much, Is."

"With the changes that might be coming and an increase in travel and learning a new dynamic in the office, I don't know if I'll have time."

"Those sound like excuses from someone who is scared." Her eyes flared with annoyance, but she wasn't going to use this to push me away.

"I'm not..."

"Don't lie to me, Isobel. What do *you* want?" I could see the raw hunger in her eyes. And the more the idea of it sunk in, the more I wanted it too.

"I want what my parents have. I want a family." She rarely talked about her family. I knew she'd felt isolated from them being halfway across the country, but I could tell she still loved them, even if they didn't understand her need to follow her dreams professionally.

"Then what do we need to get there?"

Her chest heaved, clearly catching my intentional use of the word *we*. I wasn't kidding when I told her she wasn't getting rid of me.

"I already had some tests done. They didn't see any reason why I wouldn't be able to get pregnant or stay pregnant. I don't know for sure, but I think my problems previously were with my ex, not me. He, uh... He adopted a baby recently, and..."

And she realized *she* might not be what was keeping her from having a child when she was married to him.

It was weird, thinking of her with someone else. There wasn't any question now that she was mine. And the thought that she could still be married and have kids with another man gutted me in a way that confirmed what I wanted to do to make this happen for her. For us.

"So, what are the next steps then? Time for a turkey baster?" I joked, trying to get a smile out of her.

"Not exactly." She rolled her eyes, but she looked more relaxed as she talked to me. "I'd need to investigate donor options and IVF and probably taking hormones... I don't know if I... I don't know if you..."

"Stop trying to talk yourself out of it. And you don't need any of that. You've got me." I was volunteering as tribute. There wasn't any way I would let her do this without me. If Isobel had a child, it was going to be mine. And if it didn't happen the conventional way, I'd still want to be there for her—for them.

"Be serious for once. You don't want to have a baby with me."

"You don't know what I want," I replied, grasping her waist and pulling her toward me. She was tense at first, but then melted into my touch as my thumbs traced the sides of her stomach. "You forget I've been there. I've been that kid without a dad and a single mom who worked her ass off to give me a good future."

"That doesn't mean we should have a baby together, Adrian."

"Then maybe the way I feel about you might need to be factored in." We hadn't talked about feelings or where this was going yet, but I tried to show her constantly that this wasn't some fleeting interest in her.

"And how do you feel about me?"

That answer was easy. "I feel like you're one of the strongest women I know, and you don't put up with my shit. And even though you hate half the things that come out of my mouth, I'm enchanted by most of the things that come out of yours."

"We barely know each other. You don't want to have a baby with a woman you barely know." She was trying to use this to push me away, likely protecting herself, but she didn't need to. Barely knowing her wasn't an excuse I was willing to take. We both knew that was a lie, anyway.

"Men with faulty condoms all over the country do the same damn thing every day." As her jaw set, her usual annoyance with me flaring, I smiled, knowing she was about to lay into me.

"That is... I don't... do you even try to filter the comments that come out of your mouth?"

With how guarded she was being, I knew making her angry would finally get her to talk to me, even if it was to yell at me for being a dick again. "All I heard of that sentence was come and mouth."

"See. This is exactly what I'm talking about. You're a man child. You take nothing seriously. Why would I want to procreate with you?"

"Because despite my lack of filter, you somehow still like me."

"Do I?" she taunted, but I could see she was onto me.

"Well, you at least like my mouth for more than its talking ability. But that's not the part of me you need to knock you up."

"Whatever." Isobel blushed. "I'd still need to get my IUD removed. That would be the first step."

"Then make an appointment and find out what we need to do to make this happen." I'd even go with her if she wanted me to, hold her hand while they did whatever they needed to do. "If having a baby is what you want, then it's what I want too."

"It's that simple?" She still looked a little skeptical, but there was relief there, too. While she didn't outright ask, I knew she wasn't bringing this up because she wanted to kick me to the curb. She wanted to include me in this. And I wasn't hesitating, which I knew freaked her out a little, but too fuckin' bad.

"Yes, it's that simple. You know you don't want to do this with anyone else. You wouldn't have brought it up if you did. But you're more than welcome to kick the tires before you buy the car."

"All that comment needed was a smarmy wink and an elbow nudge," she laughed.

Obnoxiously, I turned and lightly pressed my elbow into her stomach, making an exaggerated wink. She tried to hold in the laughter, wanting to be annoyed with me, but she knew I was a charming fucker.

"That better?" I asked, leaning in to kiss her forehead, peppering tiny kisses down her cheek, loudly smacking one on her lips before I wrapped her in a hug.

"You're incorrigible," she mumbled into my shoulder, but I wasn't letting her go.

"I've been told it's one of my more endearing qualities."

"Whoever told you that is a bigger idiot than you are," she whispered.

Leaning back, I kept my arms around her waist, looking into her eyes as I teased her again. "I'll let my Ma know that the next time she calls."

Her eyes flashed with panic, but I soothed her with another quick kiss, reaching up to play with a strand of her hair. "Don't you dare—"

"I won't. But she's gonna love you, babe. And once I tell her you want to have my babies, she'll love you even more. She keeps telling Pops she wants more grandbabies."

She shook her head, leaning away from me. "Can we keep this between us until I'm actually...? I don't want to tell anyone and then have it not work out."

"Whatever you need, but I have a good feeling about this." Bringing my hand to her flat stomach, I affectionately tapped my palm against her. "But once you start showing, I'm tellin' everyone I knocked you up with my baby."

"Maybe we shouldn't tell people at the office. They'll think I trapped you with the rumors about us sleeping together, and I don't..." she whispered, but I wasn't letting her finish that thought.

"Isobel, stop. People who work together have relationships all the time. I'm not sneaking around anymore. Hell, I'd move you in here tomorrow if I thought you'd agree to it. If we're going to do this, I'm all in. And I need to know you are, too."

If I thought she'd agree to it, I'd have a ring on her finger too. But I'd give her some time to get there. We were doing things completely out of order, but that seemed to be what we did.

"Are you in this with me?"

"I don't want you to be doing this for the wrong reasons." She really had no idea how into her I was. She wasn't ready for me to tell her I loved her, but I wouldn't be doing this if I wasn't already a goner.

"Nothing about this feels wrong. I want you in my life, Is. And I want this too. The thought of you having my baby feels like it was always meant to happen. Maybe that's why you finally succumbed to my irresistible charm."

"Not going to dignify that with a response, but I want this. And while I want to gag you half the time, I know you'd be a good dad."

"Would I be a good boyfriend, too?" Circling back to earlier, I was ready to put a label on this. She needed to know for sure this wasn't a fling.

"I guess. You're not entirely terrible at this relationship thing." If she wasn't smiling when she said it, I'd be worried, but she couldn't mask her affection as well as she thought she could. "And it helps that you seem to enjoy giving me orgasms."

"Fuckin' love it," I confirmed, leaning in to kiss her. It started out slow and affectionate, but quickly morphed into something else, her hands frantically working to unbutton my shirt as I held her face to mine.

Deftly, her fingers pushed the buttons through the holes, making quick work of my belt afterward, then letting her soft hands roam all the skin she'd just exposed.

"Want to give you one right now. Hope someone is watching this window, because I'm gonna fuck you on this desk and have you coming on my cock."

Her head arched back, a gasp escaping her mouth as I reached under the skirt she was wearing, ripping her panties down her legs. My fingers found her clit, and it didn't take much to have her moaning while I supported her weight, so she didn't fall backward.

"I was supposed to be tying you up," she panted, holding my head to her neck as I bit down, sucking on her collarbone hard enough to leave a mark.

"We've got all night." Pushing my pants and boxers down far enough to free myself, I stroked my cock, lining it up with her drenched pussy. She was so wet I slipped right in, bottoming out and groaning at how good it felt. "Right now, we're practicing something else."

"Oh God," she moaned, clinging to my shoulders as I thrust hard, the desk banging against the window frame.

"If you thought I was obsessed with your pussy before, just wait. I'm gonna fuck you all the time now. Fill you up."

"Yes," she hissed, reaching down to grab my ass and pulling me into her harder.

"Have you begging for it. The only thing swallowing my cum from now on is this pussy. You're going to beg for it. I'm gonna have you so cock hungry you'll finally let me fuck you on your desk. Every time you sit down, you're going to be sore and thinking about when you're going to have me next."

"Oh fuck," she wailed, her muscles clamping down. Her neck arched with her head thrown back as she released, coming all over my cock.

"Are you ready for it?" I whispered, thrusting faster, chasing my own release.

"Yes," she panted, staring at my face, her eyes still dilated in pleasure.

"Tell me," I commanded, cupping the back of her head.

"Oh God, do it."

"Use the words, Isobel. What do you want from me?" Something primal in me needed her to say it.

"I want your come inside me," she gasped, trying to fight my hold on the back of her head, but I held her still.

"Why? What do you want me to give you? What do you need from me?" Bringing the thumb to where we were joined, I thrummed her clit, holding back a groan as I felt her clench with every deep thrust.

"I need..." she panted, her eyes unfocused. She was so close. "I need you to..."

Deciding to take pity on the fact that forming a coherent thought wasn't possible this close to an orgasm, I leaned in, biting her earlobe before I whispered what we both knew she wanted. "You want me to fill this cunt with my cum. You're so desperate for me to put a baby in you that you need it. Admit it, Is. You think about having my cum inside you constantly. You crave it like I do. I need it like I need my next breath. Need you coming on my cock and taking everything I have to give you. Your greedy pussy making me explode inside you."

"Fuck, *yes,*" she groaned in my ear, her back bowing while she shook in my arms.

That was all I needed to let go, thrusting in deep, listening to the way my desk slammed against the window frame. Part of me wanted this to leave a dent so I could look at it every time I worked from home and know that I'd claimed her on this desk.

"Holy shit," I panted, tucking my face into her sweaty neck—her blouse sticking to my chest as I pulled her close. The urge to tell her I loved her was strong, but now wasn't the time. I'd wait until I thought she was ready to hear it. Ready to accept that I didn't want to get her pregnant because the thought of her doing it without me made me irrationally angry. I wanted it because I wanted it all with her.

"Well... this didn't go how I thought it would." Her quiet voice made me laugh, and I leaned back, smiling as she cupped my cheek.

"I'm still down with you tying me up. Just give me twenty minutes to get us fed first."

"Thank you," she whispered, her hands stroking the side of my head and sinking into my hair.

"You know I'd do anything you want," I responded, meaning every word.

"I know."

"Now let's get you in bed while I make you dinner."

She shook her head, but she didn't argue.

Watching as my cock slipped out, I nodded at it, her eyes following mine. My fingers instinctively reached down, gathering up the cum leaking out of her and pushing it back inside, grinning as she laughed and then moaned when I rubbed my thumb against her clit.

"IUD isn't out yet," she teased, but I didn't care.

"You never know. Never hurts to start practicing now."

Hiking my pants back into place, I grinned, earning an eye roll. Isobel giggled as I swept her up into my arms, one arm behind her back and the other underneath her knees.

"I can walk, you know."

"Be quiet and let me take care of you."

"You're getting bossy," she huffed. But I could tell from her tone she was amused. As we passed the front door, she reached back. "Don't forget my bag. I need to keep reading to get some ideas for later."

"As long as it involves me coming inside you bare, I'll let you pick."

"Such a generous offer," she laughed as I crossed the threshold and walked to the side of the bed to gently lay her down. I grabbed a pillow and put it under her hips. Might as well give this practicing my all.

"I'm thoughtful like that." Shedding my open shirt and pants, I winked before I walked back toward my kitchen in my boxers. I wanted to throw something together quickly, suddenly anticipating reading through the manuscript that had the potential to amplify our already spectacular sex life.

If I was going to have to up my game over the next few months, I was going to need some source material.

Maybe there *was* something to this spicy romance I'd missed before.

Who needed Viagra when you had a hot as fuck girlfriend willing to reenact scenes of a Dominatrix tying up her subs to have her way with them?

TWENTY-THREE

ISOBEL

BOSTON

ADRIAN HAD BEEN RIGHT. We had barely come up for air the rest of the week. If we weren't reading or marking up scenes with comments and corrections, we were googling objects the heroine, Fanny the Dominatrix, was using throughout the story and then playing them out with our limited resources.

If we could have kept our hands off each other long enough to put on real clothes, I would have insisted on a field trip to meet Chase's friend Talia. While I'd not been to the studio she shared with her Dom, Emory, I knew she had an extensive collection of toys, courtesy of her job as a sex toy blogger.

I was sure they had every piece of equipment Chase and Evan included in this book because there was no way those two wrote this manuscript without help from the experts. But introducing Adrian to that much hardware at once might scar him for life. It intimidated me a bit to think about seeing all the things I'd only read about before.

There were only a few scenes I was hesitating on, unsure if they were a little too taboo to tie to Chase and Evan's current pen names.

"Do you think this is going to turn off Evan's reader base? I know some of them weren't supportive of the last release. I don't want to lose readers for either of them over this."

Adrian's lips quirked to the side while he tilted his head, looking contemplative. If I'd asked this question in the office, he would have blurted out something totally inappropriate or offensive by now, but I could see he was genuinely trying to do better controlling his filter.

"Those readers are already drifting. While this might entirely push them away from his work, there will probably be just as many who would eagerly devour this kind of content."

"Wow," I teased, not expecting that succinct of an answer. "And you thought only desperate housewives read these kinds of books."

"I wasn't that bad. I know spicy romance sells well. I've seen the quarterly sales reports."

"Uh, yeah, you were that bad, Captain Dickhead. I believe the words *mommy porn* and *self-insert fantasies of single, middle-aged romance writers* were words that actually came out of your mouth."

"Yeah, well. I get it now," he shrugged, moving his leg to press up against mine.

We'd been sitting up against his headboard, laptops on our laps, editing in our underwear. I'd tried multiple times to put on a bra, but he just kept taking them off me every time a particularly *compelling* scene got to him.

"Only because you're getting something else out of it."

"That's not entirely true. I think this book will sell. And you can't deny their writing styles play well off each other. The chemistry between the main characters is explosive and you can't easily predict the ending."

"Okay. You made your point. You're a changed man," I teased, reaching over to kiss his bicep.

"Damn straight I am."

"That still doesn't answer my question. Does the scene in chapter twenty stay or not?"

Adrian knew exactly what scene I was talking about, quickly scrolling up to the passage that was throwing me off.

Frances looked between the two men sitting on the edge of her bed, smiling at their eagerness.

One watching her face, cataloging her every move. Ensuring she was alright with acting out his request. They both knew she had other partners, her job practically demanding it. But he'd never been in the room during an appointment with one of her clients.

Their relationship happened outside of her sessions, his need to please her feeding the part of her desperate for affection once she shed the mask of her profession.

Dominic's open devotion after hours kept her soul fed, and her shattered heart pieced together.

She knew they both had deeper feelings for each other than they let on, but their dynamic worked as it was. There wasn't a need to whisper words they both felt when saying them aloud might alter things.

The other man practically beamed at her pleasure, desperate for the opportunity she'd given him.

It was rare she handed over control, but she trusted him to stay within the confines of their plans for the scene.

"Dom, stand and go to the chair," she ordered, pointing at an armchair she'd moved close to the bed.

> *He didn't hesitate, slowly lowering himself into the plush cushion and spreading his legs wide, his arms draped over the low sides. While this position would make some men look powerful. He looked exactly like he always did at her, waiting for his next command.*
>
> *"Unzip your pants and pull yourself out, but don't touch. I want to watch what this does to you."*
>
> *Dominic obeyed, lifting his hips to pull down his pants a fraction, his lack of undergarments displaying his half-hard cock laying against his upper thigh. He returned his hands to the arms of the chair, his posture entirely relaxed.*
>
> *"Callum," she murmured, turning toward the man still sitting on the edge of the bed. His eyes looked hungry, anticipating what was to come. He wanted to show off as much as Dominic wanted to watch. "Strip."*

"How can Dom just sit there and watch Callum putting his hands all over her? The reader already knows he's in love with her at this point. Isn't that just cruel?" Don't get me wrong, the scene was starting off hot, but I couldn't fathom sharing something.

"Is it the fact he's there watching it that bothers you, or is it that you think he should be more possessive? Because Chase did a good job displaying Dominic's understanding of the demands of her job. She gives other men their fantasies all the time."

"But her job is totally different than her time with Dom. When she's not Madame Frances, she's just his Fanny."

Adrian smirked, and I tried to hold back a laugh. "Yeah, he definitely likes her Fanny."

"Shut up for a minute and be serious. I'm talking about their connection, not her vagina."

"Should we mention Fanny means something a bit naughty in the UK?"

Laughing again, I leaned my head on his shoulder. "If you think that wasn't one hundred percent intentional on Chase's part, then you're an idiot."

"You keep trying to convince me your writers aren't sex obsessed, but so far, the evidence is proving the contrary." His deep voice was teasing, but I could see his point. The further we dove into this manuscript, the more ravenous I was for him. I wasn't sure if it was just my libido or the fact we were now going to try for a baby, or that he was too damn attractive for me to keep my hands off him. But he seemed to feel the same way.

"Just keep reading," I told him, and he cleared his throat before he spoke again.

> *"Now take off my robe," she instructed, pulling Callum's rough hand to the silk tie at her waist.*

"That's the last command you'll give me," he responded, releasing the tie and pulling open her robe. His warm hands grasped her hips, and he pulled her roughly into his chest as he kissed the side of her neck. "This body is mine now."

"I want you to see how you affect him," he whispered while he spun her, grasping both breasts in his palms as he turned her to face the man in the chair. "He wishes his hands were on you. Look at how tightly his knuckles grip the chair."

She nodded, gasping as one of his hands traced down her stomach and Cal plunged two fingers into her already wet pussy. Dominic may have asked for this, but she couldn't deny she wanted it too.

"So beautiful," Dom murmured as he watched Callum manipulate Fanny, the roughness of his hand making her head fall back against his shoulder. A flush spread up her chest as a moan escaped her lips, her eyes closing.

"Look at me," Dom whispered, and her eyes opened, drowsy with pleasure as Callum drove her closer to release.

She panted as she watched Dom, his posture relaxed, but she could tell he was holding back. He wouldn't touch himself until she told him to, and as his cock bobbed when a moan escaped her lips, she found herself wanting to see how desperate she could make him.

"Get on the bed," Callum hummed, pulling his fingers from where she was throbbing. "Hands and knees. Let him see your face while I fuck you."

Frances didn't take her eyes off Dominic as she sat down on the edge of the mattress. Callum's large arms encircled her waist and pulled her back, manipulating her body until she was on her hands and knees in front of him.

"Hold on, darlin'," he growled as he grasped her hips, roughly pulling her back, his cock throbbing against her hip.

She gasped as he entered her, watching as Dominic sat forward, watching her every move as the man behind her thrust roughly.

Dominic's eyes were riveted to where Callum thrust into Fanny frantically, his large hands manipulating her into a tight hold.

"Fuck," she panted as she felt her body right on the cusp of spiraling out of control. Callum's thrusts were brutal, but the force of them had her desperate for release.

"You wish she let you do this," Cal taunted from behind her, Dominic's eyebrow arching as he tried to remain calm. Even being actively provoked she admired her sub's restraint.

"She's going to come on my cock harder than she ever has on yours."

Dominic's jaw twitched, but still, he held back, taking his cues from Frances.

"Like there," I murmured, trying not to get distracted by the feel of Adrian's fingers caressing the bare skin on the inside of my thigh. "You can tell Dominic is upset while he watches Callum manhandle her."

"He's not upset," Adrian whispered, leaning in to place a kiss behind my ear. "He's fucking turned on."

"How can you tell?" My voice was breathy as his lips lingered, his warm breath fanning across my neck.

"Because he gets off on watching her receive pleasure."

"But why?"

Adrian cleared his throat, leaning back and turning my face in his direction. "He doesn't see her as a thing to possess. He's not jealous because Dom sees her as something he knows is his because she cares for him. He's not insecure, but there is also a primal part of him that wants others to covet what he has. Notice how Fanny watches Dominic the entire time. He knows he has her attention. Callum is just a means to an end. His body may be the one fucking her, but Dominic is the one pulling the strings. *He's* the one providing her pleasure."

"But he's her submissive. Isn't he supposed to be the less dominant one?"

"You know more about this stuff than I do, but part of his devotion to her is bringing her pleasure. He's watching her receive it and letting her act out a fantasy for him, which brings her another level of satisfaction."

"I guess that makes sense," I hummed, still not convinced you can let someone else touch you like that or let your partner be touched like that and not have jealousy play a part. "Let's keep reading."

Callum started whispering depraved things in her ear, her mind registering his words, but unable to respond as she clenched, finally succumbing to her powerful orgasm with a scream.

Panting as Callum thrust a few more times, she watched Dominic, knowing he was close too, his cock throbbed when the man inside her growled loudly, reaching his peak as well.

The sound of the door to her playroom clicking shut echoed in the quiet room, but the only thing she saw was Dom trying to hold back from coming.

He'd been trained early on in their dynamic to control his orgasms, able to come without external stimulation if she demanded it. But he'd also learned how to keep himself on the edge, riding the painful wave between restraint and release.

After she caught her breath, she climbed from the bed, not hesitating before she settled into Dom's lap, pulling him to her entrance. Callum's release dripped down the head of his cock, a filthy reminder of the man who'd been inside her moments before.

Dom's fingers dug into the arms of the chair roughly as she thrust her hips downward, completely engulfing his hard cock inside her.

> *"Is that what you wanted? To watch him claim me?" she whispered, grasping the back of his neck and riding him with abandon.*
>
> *She'd never been on the receiving end of this kind of scene, the person whose partner watched them with someone else. But now she understood it.*
>
> *Understood how overwhelming it was to have eyes on you like that. Overwhelming in how much she needed Dom to reclaim her body.*
>
> *"Fuck me," she whispered lowly, and Dom didn't hesitate, immediately grasping her hips and pounding into her from below as his head fell backward, his eyes never leaving her.*
>
> *"Make me come again," she whimpered, and his thumb moved to press against her clit, his other hand roughly manipulating her on his lap the way he knew she liked. "He was wrong. You're the only one who gets this side of me."*
>
> *He felt her clench, knowing the one thing that would drive her over the edge.*
>
> *She gasped as he sat up, grasping the back of her neck and pulling her face to his as he uttered the one word they both knew would always be true.*
>
> *"Mine."*

"I don't see what the problem is," Adrian responded, reaching down to adjust himself. "That almost made me come in my pants. Isn't that what we're going for?"

"You're not wearing pants," I pointed out, eyeing the hard outline of him through his briefs. I had to give him credit. I was tempted to touch myself as he'd read that, and he'd kept going until the end. Maybe he had a bit of Dominic in him.

"Is, quit deflecting. Why is this scene really bothering you?"

"Do people really *do that?*" I asked, unsure how to refer to what had happened between those three characters. "Do people really watch their partners do that? I thought that was something people only did in porn."

"What kind of porn have you been watching?" Adrian laughed, grasping my thigh and rubbing his fingers suggestively over my panties.

Smacking his hand away, I turned slightly to face him. "That's not the point. I'm worried this may cross a line from romantic thriller to erotica. Those are two vastly different genres."

"The plot still works if you gloss over the sex. It could fade to black or be non-graphic and get the same effect. It just makes it more compelling with the details Chase and Evan included."

"I gotta be honest. I was not expecting you to be so open-minded about this manuscript. Should I be worried you hit your head and gave yourself brain damage?"

"Maybe all the orgasms in the last month and a half have lightened me up a little," he joked. But I wasn't entirely discounting his dickish behavior, being exacerbated by a dry spell.

"A few months ago, I would have labeled you as the type of guy who was only concerned about getting yourself off."

"I'm a little insulted by that," he chuckled, putting his laptop on the bed beside him before pulling me into his lap. "I may have acted like a dick and unfairly judged your genre, but I'm clearly not as selfish as you thought I was."

"Well..." I cringed and then shrieked when his fingers dug into my sides.

"Okay. Okay. You're a sex god," I laughed as I wiggled in his lap, the feeling of him hard beneath me making it difficult to concentrate on the conversation we were having.

"That's better," he murmured as he grasped my waist, holding me still. "But to answer your question. That kind of thing happens more often than you think it does."

"I don't know." I was still unsure if that kind of thing happened outside of fiction or internet porn.

"If you want to ask someone questions, I might know a guy."

"You know a guy who sleeps with women while their partners watch?"

"I told you I was full of surprises," he replied with a shrug.

"Who is he?" And how did Adrian know him? Being a participant in a cuckold scene wasn't exactly something you talked about in casual conversation.

"And ruin the surprise?" He grinned, pulling his phone off the nightstand and rapidly typing into the screen before he set the phone back down a few moments later.

"He said he's available tonight. We can order some takeout and you can ask him some questions."

I wasn't sure how to respond to that. "Is it safe for this guy to come to your apartment?"

"He's been here plenty of times before. It'll be fine. Relax a little."

"He won't expect us to be into that sort of thing, is he?"

Adrian laughed, shaking his head before he leaned in, pecking my lips before he sat back against the headboard.

"He won't expect anything other than helping you understand things a little better. And I'm sure as fuck not sharing you."

Suddenly nervous, I ran my palms along the sheets beside Adrian's hips.

"I... uh..."

"Isobel, relax. I promise he won't intentionally make you uncomfortable. He might try to make you blush a bit, but I promise you can trust him."

"And you're not going to tell me anything else about him?"

"Nope." He shook his head, an obnoxious grin showing off the dimple in his cheek. "If I tell you, it'll spoil the surprise."

Chapter
TWENTY-FOUR

ADRIAN

BOSTON

Several hours later, Isobel nervously paced the small space between my kitchen and my bedroom, and I couldn't help smiling at her reaction. We'd quickly taken a shower after I'd confirmed our plans for later, and while she'd relaxed a bit with my hands trailing over her soapy curves, as soon as her hair was dry, she was wound up again.

"Is, babe, it'll be fine."

"That's easy for you to say. You know this guy. I do not. I've never talked about things like this with someone who's actually done them. All the adventurous things I've been exposed to have been in books."

Standing up from the couch, my arms wrapped around her waist, her head falling back to my shoulder as I slowly caressed her stomach. "He's just a normal guy. And what about the last time Chase wrote about this? The book about the Dom. Didn't she have a consultant or something for that book?"

"Yeah, but I never asked him questions. I was just introduced to him briefly at a book signing."

"What is it about the thought of talking to this guy that is making you so nervous?"

While she'd calmed down as I held her, I needed to get to the bottom of these nerves now, because once he showed up—and she discovered who I'd been talking about—her nerves were bound to multiply. To be honest, the possessive part of me didn't want him talking to her either, but I think she needed this.

I knew my past would come up with her eventually, and this scene in particular had made it hard to refrain from telling her everything. It was a completely different situation, but having him here was bound to dredge up secrets we'd both kept for the last twenty years.

"He won't judge you, Is. You're curious and he's coming to help you work through that curiosity." And I trusted him. Even if things didn't go as planned, and I knew he'd flirt with her, he'd make sure she felt safe in the conversation.

Two loud raps on my apartment door caused her to stiffen, and I distracted her the only way I knew how.

Spinning her in my arms, I grasped the back of her neck and captured her lips with mine, pouring all my feelings for her into the kiss. The next few hours weren't ones I could predict the outcome of, but I was going to be here to support her the entire time however she needed.

"He's here," I whispered, pulling back and kissing the soft spot behind her ear once before I pulled away.

Reaching back to grasp her hand, I led her behind me to the door, pausing to take a deep breath before I let in the chaos.

"Finally," he laughed, pushing the door open. "I was beginning to think you'd forgotten I was coming."

"Trust me, bro. No one is going to forget about you." He stepped past me, and Isobel stiffened at my side, her eyes comically wide as I turned to pull her into my side.

"He's..." she squeaked while her eyes bounced to him, then back to me, his smile growing obnoxiously large. Much like his ego.

"It's nice to see you again, Isobel," he grinned, reaching forward to grasp her hand and bending in close to kiss the back of it. Arrogant idiot.

"He's..." she stuttered again, and he laughed, stepping back with her hand still in her grasp.

"He's my dumbass brother," I filled in, pushing Hutch's shoulder lightly so he'd step back, dropping Isobel's hand. It trembled at her side, and I felt a pang of remorse that I'd kept her in the dark about his identity.

It wasn't every day you found out the guy you'd been sleeping with regularly for the last several months had an identical twin brother who slept with other people's partners in front of them.

Hutch, clearly reading the room, turned and headed into my kitchen, pulling open the refrigerator and peering inside before he grasped a bottle of beer.

"Should you be...?" I trailed off as Isobel pinched my side.

"Don't worry, I didn't drive over here myself, obviously. One beer won't hurt. The doc took me off the heavy-duty stuff."

"Adrian," Isobel hissed, digging her elbow into my side.

"Uh oh. Someone is in trouble," Hutch laughed while he pulled the bottle opener off the side of the fridge and popped the top off his beer. He stood there, bottle perched at his lips, watching the two of us, clearly enjoying that he still had the ability to make people squirm.

"Why didn't you tell me it was your brother who...?" she trailed off in a hushed whisper, tugging me toward my bedroom door.

"You don't need to leave the room on my account," Hutch laughed, crossing the room and perching himself on the couch, arm casually thrown across the back of the cushion. "Your secrets are safe with me, Bel."

"Stop," I scolded, holding my finger in his direction as Isobel tugged me through my bedroom doorway.

"What the hell?!?" she whispered frantically, smacking me in the chest while I tried to school my features so I didn't laugh. It wasn't very nice of me to spring it on her this way, but she never would have agreed if I told her who it was. "You're such a dick."

"He really is," Hutch called out from the other room, and I tugged my bottom lip between my teeth to hold in the laugh at the way her eyes flared with embarrassment.

"I can't believe you. Well, I can believe you're that much of a dick. But seriously? I'm supposed to ask your brother, who is your fucking identical twin, questions about his sex life? On what planet is that okay?"

"This one, Bel," he laughed, clearly still shamelessly eavesdropping, but she hadn't closed the door either. "I'm an open book. Ask me whatever questions you want."

"I hate you," she hissed at me as I pulled her into a hug, sighing in relief when her arms wrapped around my back, squeezing tightly.

"Pretty sure you don't," I exhaled into her hair, my lips grazing her forehead.

"You two ready to stop whispering about me?" Hutch yelled, drawing a soft laugh from Isobel.

"He's here for you," I whispered as she pulled back, gazing up at me with wariness in her eyes, but also a bit of trust. "I wouldn't have asked him to do this otherwise. You need answers to feel comfortable with this manuscript and he can help with that."

"Fine," she growled, but it didn't hold any conviction. "But you're getting punished for this later."

"And I'll look forward to that, *Madame Isobel*." Her lip curled up in one corner, a soft smile forming while she looked up at me.

Hutch's big mouth once again ruined the playful moment, calling out, "I've got some ideas for things you can do to him."

Isobel's nerves dissipated, her grin growing as she walked around me and back into the living room. "Let's start with that."

Hutch's laid-back nature made it easy for Isobel to relax, and he carried the conversation while we waited for dinner to be delivered. Once it came, none of us seemed to know what to say, focusing on our meals.

Temporarily sated, the three of us were lounging in the living room after we'd eaten our fill of pasta from the place Isobel loved down the street.

"Adrian's always had a thing for blondes. Although you seem to have something the ones he went after in high school did not."

"And what is that?" Isobel laughed while she sat on my lap in the armchair across from where my brother had manspread across my couch.

"Brains. Most of them only had big—"

"Fuck you," I laughed, kicking forward, my toe stinging as my shoe contacted his shin. "Not all of them were airheads. I was the nerdy one, remember? You were the one who chased after everyone who'd open their legs for you. I guess not much has changed since then."

"Ouch, you fuck. At least kick the bionic one. And I don't chase anyone. They find me."

"You're not the *Million-dollar Man,*" I scoffed while Isobel looked between the two of us. She knew Hutch had a prosthetic, but she hadn't pried past the one time I'd talked to her about it. "Maybe it's time for you to tell Isobel about your new weekend hobby."

"That is why you brought me here, isn't it?" he grinned, raising an eyebrow. "Go ahead, Isobel. Ask away."

"The scene with the client. Is that really a thing? The cuckold scene?"

Hutch sat back, rubbing his fingers along the edge of his jaw, and I watched it clench as he tried to formulate a response. I knew my brother had always been the more adventurous of the two of us. Since his marriage ended, he'd sworn off monogamy, but I didn't exactly ask him to divulge all the information about the changes to his sex life. I just knew that he had been exploring the local kink scene and dabbling in fulfilling cuckold fantasies, and mine was stagnant until a certain blonde blew up my carefully constructed professional façade.

"Cuckolding is a very real kink." His voice was low while he looked straight at her, studying her tense posture and the way she kept nervously darting her eyes away from him. "I know it's frowned upon by mainstream society, but as long as all the parties agree, watching your partner being pleasured by someone else is intense, and it turns lots of people on."

There were things my brother and I had done as teenagers before he'd been deployed the first time that I'd written off as reckless things you did in your youth, but watching your brother have sex with the girl you were casually dating wasn't something I talked about.

We'd only done it a few times, and once I got over the fact that I had to see my brother's naked ass on display, I'd enjoyed watching the girl's expressions when we'd done it. Seeing her come and knowing I wasn't the one providing it was a weird experience, but she'd been into it. Hutch loved it, suggesting it two more times before he met Lena and then he stopped screwing around, but it stuck with me. All these years later, I could still remember making eye contact with my girlfriend at the time while she rode my brother's cock.

But the thought of Isobel doing the same thing made me feel a little ferally possessive.

"So, it's something that you think Frances would provide as a dominatrix?"

"I think there are a lot of men and women who provide the same service without payment, and all parties involved really fuckin' enjoy it."

Hutch's eyes darted over to me as Isobel shifted, clearly not expecting that answer. I knew she grew up in a conservative environment on her small Iowa farm, where I doubted that sharing was a widely accepted practice. When I'd read that scene in the manuscript, I hadn't been surprised that kink was included, but clearly Isobel still was.

"And you've done this?" Isobel asked, tilting her head, her eyes nervously finding mine as Hutch's grin spread.

"Yes, sweetheart, I have fucked another man's wife while he watched, or she. Sometimes lesbians enjoy watching their partner get railed. Adds a little spice to it when she comes extra hard on my cock."

She was quiet, intently listening while she sat on my lap.

"I've fucked my brother's girlfriend while he watched, so trust me, this kink isn't something new to me. Or him. And it's certainly not something uncommon either."

Her eyes widened as she turned to face me, studying my passive expression. I wasn't ashamed of my behavior. And I wasn't sorry that I'd enjoyed it, but I still had to fight the urge to shift beneath her in my seat at her blatant shock.

"You two...?" her voice trailed off, looking between us. Hutch's casual shrug and wide grin were a stark contrast to my tight nod and heavy swallow. "Like, recently?"

"No," Hutch laughed, shaking his head. "We were seventeen the first time, and it's been a long time since that happened. Don't worry, Adrian won't try to share you." But now I was thinking about it. "At least not unless you're wanting to be shared."

"Not gonna happen, Hutch," I interrupted.

Isobel's body language shifted, and she was squirming on my lap, and glancing at me out of the corner of her eye as Hutch changed the subject to another chapter in the book. Despite knowing it violated so many different provisions of my contract, I'd sent Hutch a copy of the manuscript not long after we'd received it a few days ago, having questions of my own about the content.

He'd been impressed with the nature of Evan and Chase's manuscript, only pointing out a few things he saw as not true to his experiences in the local kink community.

I knew Chase had researched a few of her other books with a local Dom, but as far as I knew, Evan had never shown an inclination toward the kinkier side of life. Isobel had her theories about exactly how close our authors had gotten when they'd gone off the grid, but whatever was going on, the words they created together were magic.

This book blended our two genres perfectly, a strong romantic thriller plot that wove in elements of mystery and BDSM in a way that was seamless. I may have made a few jokes to Sam about it being fucking hot, but the plot and the characters were solid.

Evan had leveled up with this book, and Chase had broken out of the mold I knew Isobel hated that was forced upon the contemporary romance authors.

"I don't think he's paying attention to us," Hutch chuckled, scooting sideways and patting the cushion next to him, encouraging Isobel to join him on the couch. "Should we make out and see if that gets his attention? He seemed a little possessive when the kiss cam stopped on us."

Isobel laughed, surprisingly not disagreeing with him, and her hand briefly pressed against my thigh as she rose from my lap. "I *have* always wondered what it was like to kiss a man with a beard."

What?

"Ah, so is that your fantasy then, Bel?" Hutch laughed, pressing his shoulder into hers briefly while she perched herself on the cushion next to him. "Being taken by a roguish bearded man?"

"Not exactly." The shyness in her voice attracted my attention, and I sat up straighter, watching her expression better as she glanced at my twin out of the corner of her eye.

"Oh, sounds like there's something you're hiding. Maybe there are a few kinky fantasies in there, huh?"

"Maybe."

"So, you've never kissed a bearded man..." Hutch mused before he lifted his hand to her face, his thumb tracing her bottom lip. Isobel hesitated, freezing when her eyes found mine over his shoulder. I knew I should put a stop to his flirting, but she didn't look uncomfortable with his touch. "What other fantasies do you have? What have you always wanted to try but never had the opportunity to ask for?"

Isobel continued to stare at me over his shoulder, her eyes darting across my face while she licked her lips.

"Tell him," I commented quietly, wanting to know what she desired. "I'd like to know too."

"I've..." Her neck flexed as she swallowed, licking her lips again quickly before her eyes slipped closed. "I've fantasized about what it'd feel like to be with two men. About being watched."

"Now we're talking," Hutch laughed, his voice laced with amusement. "I think I need to hear more about this fantasy of two men. What about you, Ad? Do you want to know more?"

I did.

Rising from the chair, I walked around the end of the couch, taking a seat on the other side of Isobel.

I could sense she was nervous, but with the way she'd kept glancing at me with wide eyes, and then darting back toward Hutch, I knew she was thinking hard about something.

An irrational flare of jealousy tore through me at the thought of another man running his hands along the curves of her body. But if she wanted to fantasize about it, who was I to deny her?

"Are you comfortable sharing this with us?" Hutch asked as I placed my hand on Isobel's thigh, hers immediately covering mine. She hesitated for a moment. "It's fine if you don't want to, but I think you have both of us intrigued by your little confession."

"I'm just curious about the fantasy of it all. I don't think I could ever do it in real life, but thinking about it..." Isobel shifted, turned toward me, and looked up into my eyes. I still couldn't get over the fact that this fiercely independent—sexy as hell—woman wanted me. That she'd welcomed me into her life, and her mind and her body...and I hoped her heart. "Thinking about it excites me."

"What about it excites you?" he asked again. "We don't have to talk about specifics, but I can give you an idea of how fantasy play is a big part of the lifestyle. You up for that?"

Chapter
TWENTY-FIVE

ISOBEL

BOSTON

Adrian leaned back, his eyes serious while he stared at me, his thumb slowly stroking my cheek while they waited for my answer.

"Yeah, I think I am."

"It's all about enacting a scene," Hutch mused a few moments later. "Part of being an effective submissive or an effective dominant is learning how to immerse yourself in the role. I once heard a creator refer to it as Fuck Larping. And he was a fuckin' genius. It *is* like live-action role play, but sometimes you're naked. And the props are made for a different kind of *pillaging*."

Adrian laughed at his brother's dramatic delivery, but his humor helped take the edge off my nerves. I'd never done anything like this—talking openly about sex with men, much less the kind of sex Frances engaged in with Dominic and her clients in this book. It was intimidating to think people in real life had those kinds of experiences. People who actively brought their fantasies to life.

Of course, I'd talked about scenes with my authors, but that was all another type of fantasy with people that weren't real. As much as they could move people emotionally, and sometimes in a more carnal manner, the book boyfriends that came out of my author's heads weren't real.

"Which brings me back to this book and your questions. While it is written in a very emotional and tension-filled way, your writers pretty much nailed the kink part. Fanny makes people's fantasies a reality, and to a certain extent, that's what most people strive for in their lifestyle. Expressing and embracing what people really want. Making the fantasies other people only daydream about a reality."

"But doesn't that complicate their real lives?" Living in a fantasy world all the time wasn't practical. "You can't live in your fantasies."

"Says who?" Hutch asked, turning toward me.

Warm breath fanned across my shoulder, and I shuddered when Adrian's warm voice was in my ear. "Being with you is *my* fantasy."

Fire raced through my veins at his low declaration, and I let out a tiny moan, unable to control my reaction to him. Hutch watched my face as his brother kissed the side of my neck, curiosity in his gaze. It almost felt like Adrian was marking me, but I wasn't opposed to him making his claim on me known in front of his brother. *Again.* He hadn't exactly been subtle at the baseball game either.

"I can see the gears turning in there, Bel," Hutch murmured. "Anything else you want to ask me?"

"Don't you ever feel *ashamed* of the things you want? Aren't you afraid people will judge you if they find out what you do?"

"You shouldn't feel ashamed talking about your desires, Bel, because it's okay to want things. And no, I gave up feeling ashamed about my choices. Life is too short not to go after what you want. Fuck what other people think." He looked past me, lifting an eyebrow at his brother, before he grinned and moved his gaze back to me. "If you want two guys, go for it. Let me know if you want help and I'll make it happen."

"Alright. That's enough," Adrian growled. "I think we've got all the *help* we need from you tonight."

"Oh, come on. I was teasing. I'm not interested in your girl, Ad," he laughed. "I know I'm not the brother Isobel's in love with."

"He's... we... it's not." My eyes darted between the two of them. While I was on my way to being in love with Adrian, I wasn't ready to tell him that.

"You two can keep pretending that this is casual, but I've seen how you look at each other. You make my brother happy and I'm not about to get into the middle of that."

Adrian rose from the couch, stepping over my legs to stand in front of his brother. "Enough talking, Hutch."

"Someone seems a little possessive," Hutch teased while he took Adrian's hand to help pull himself up from the couch. "You're welcome, by the way."

"What?" Adrian frowned as he stepped back, gesturing toward the door to the apartment.

"Now you know what your girlfriend fantasizes about."

"Shut up," Adrian laughed, shaking his head.

"You two kids have fun," Hutch teased as he pulled his jacket on. "Do every fuckin' thing I would do."

"I don't think that's how the saying goes," I giggled, watching Adrian rushing his brother out of his apartment.

"Love you, bro," Adrian called before he pushed him out the door. "But get the fuck out of my apartment."

Hutch's boisterous laugh sounded from the other side of the door as Adrian crossed the living room in a few steps, stopping directly in front of me.

"Sorry about him. My brother is an idiot. If his flirting made you uncomfortable..."

"It didn't. I think it was more to get a reaction out of you than an attraction to me." Hutch had been a little suggestive, but he was still respectful of my relationship with Adrian.

"Doubt that. You're a beautiful woman, so don't sell yourself short. I know he'd be all over you if you showed an interest."

"I'm only interested in one man," I cooed, hooking my fingers into his belt.

"That's fucking right. I'll be the only one fulfilling any fantasies you've got." The growly, possessive quality of his voice should have worried me, but it made me feel wanted.

"Oh really? Even that last one?"

"Are you doubting my ability to give you what you need?" Adrian almost looked intimidating, looming in front of me, but I knew he'd do whatever I wanted. Lucky for him, he was all I wanted.

"No. But last I checked; you didn't have two penises." My fingers trailed down the front seam of his pants, the one penis he was hiding in there already thickening behind the material.

"But I'm guessing you've got something in your bag of tricks in my bedroom that could stand in for another one," he murmured, bringing his thumb to my bottom lip and pressing it inside my mouth.

"Are you saying you want to... with one of my...?" I panted, squirming against the leather cushion beneath me.

"Do I want to fuck you with a vibrator? Is that even a question?" he laughed, pressing his other hand into my hair and using it to tilt my head back.

"But aren't most men intimidated by toys?" I asked, panting as his fingers pulled the strands, my neck arching as his thumb left my mouth and his hand wrapped around the front of my throat.

"What gave you the impression that I'm one of those men?" he asked, releasing me, and leaning down to throw me over his shoulder.

"Put me down," I laughed, secretly enjoying that he was being this possessive. He was setting me down at the foot of his bed moments later, spinning me to face away from him.

"I'm never going to let another man touch you, but I'm down for acting out the kinky fantasies in that beautiful brain of yours."

"*Fuck me*," I exhaled, enjoying the way he ground his hips into mine.

"Nope, I'm not gonna fuck you yet. You wanted me to watch you with another cock tonight, remember?"

He left me standing at the end of the bed, reaching beside the nightstand to pick something up and placing my small black duffel bag onto the mattress beside me. He unzipped it and pulled the sides open, nodding to it.

"Get out your vibrator."

"But..." I hesitated, glancing between the open bag and his eyes.

"Now, Isobel."

There was something about the commanding tone in his voice that was turning me on. I reached inside the bag, pulling out a black velvet pouch. I loosened the drawstring and handed it to him.

Adrian carefully parted the opening, reaching inside to pull out the toy.

"Holy shit. What is this thing? You didn't tell me you were hiding Thor's hammer in that bag."

The toy was long, thick and black, with a loop in the handle, that Adrian was now comically using to swing the vibrator from side to side on his finger.

"Did you want me to get out something else?" I asked, reaching over to halt his motions.

"You tell me, Is," he murmured, his hand closing around mine, and pulling the toy up between us. "Is this the other cock you want me to watch you fuck?"

Holy shit.

One nod and he gently pulled the toy from my hand, gripping it in his and turning it with an appraising look on his face.

"You might want to grab some lube to take on this beast, unless you're already as excited as I think you are."

I was nervous at the prospect of him watching me with my vibrator, but his willingness to fulfill my fantasies figuratively opened the floodgates.

I grabbed the lube anyway.

Chapter
TWENTY-SIX

ADRIAN

BOSTON

ISOBEL WAS QUIET AS she led the way back to the living room, her ass swaying beneath the silky material of her dress the entire way.

"Do you want to sit in the chair?" she asked, nodding at the chair across the room.

"What I want doesn't matter right now. Where do you want me to sit?"

She nibbled on the corner of her lip, her eyes darting around the room. "I don't know," she murmured, hesitation clear in her voice. She wasn't used to asking for what she wanted. And I was willing to bet no one had ever asked her either.

"Tell me what to do, Isobel."

She took a deep breath, letting it out slowly as she extended her hand in my direction. "Give me the vibrator and go sit in the chair."

"Yes, ma'am."

I perched myself on the edge of the cushion, watching as she sat across from me on the center couch cushion, clutching the vibrator in her hand. She looked nervous, but her eyes were bright, and her cheeks were pink with arousal. I could practically smell her from here, but she was still holding back.

"You want to see how crazy you make me?" I asked, her eyes fixed on mine. She nodded, letting out another shaky exhale. "Then pretend that giant fake cock is Callum and I'll be your Dominic."

Her eyes widened as I stared back at her, silently encouraging her to let go of her inhibitions and pretend with me.

"Unzip your pants and pull yourself out, but don't touch. I want to watch what this does to you." Her voice was clear and strong as she repeated Fanny's words, and I hurried to obey, unbuckling my belt quickly before I yanked down my zipper, shifting my pants and boxer briefs down enough to free my aching cock.

Isobel shifted to her knees, untying the bow on her dress and pulling it open, revealing the sexiest lace bra and panty set I'd ever seen. The cups barely covered her nipples, and I itched to pull them down.

She rolled her shoulders before she reached down for the vibrator, and a gentle hum filled the room after she turned it on.

My fingers clenched the edge of the chair as I watched her bring the tip to her neck, slowly drawing it down her chest, in between her lace covered breasts, past her navel and stopping as it met the lace covering her pussy.

She watched my reactions as she slid it along the seam of her panties, my cock throbbing visibly as I imagined the vibrations making her wet. My eyes were transfixed by her movements as she rocked her hips into the toy, letting it rumble and hum between her legs.

I wanted to take over, to tell her to pull off her panties and sink down onto it so I could watch her make herself come, but I clenched my jaw, sealing the words in because watching her control her own pleasure was the hottest thing I'd ever seen.

Little moans escaped her mouth as Isobel played with herself, her free hand clenching her breast while she gave me a show. Her eyes closed, and she gasped as I watched, but I could tell she was getting frustrated.

I tracked every movement greedily, my cock twitching as she gave into her instincts and blindly sought pleasure. It was excruciating to hold back, but a feral groan escaped my throat when she paused and stood, frantically pushing her panties to the floor before she climbed back onto the couch, kneeling on the cushion.

She grabbed the bottle of lube from where she'd placed it on the coffee table and dripped a generous amount onto the tip of her girthy friend. Her eyes locked with mine as she brought the vibrator between her legs, slowly sinking onto it while my fingers dug into the arms of the chair.

"Fuck," she gasped as her body enveloped the toy. Her thighs shook as she let herself adjust to the size before she rose to her knees, repeating the motion over and over while I watched.

My jaw ached as I ground my teeth together, desperately trying to keep myself under control, but I couldn't keep my eyes off her. She looked so fucking sexy as she rode that big black vibrator until she was gasping. Her head fell back as she fought for breath, her body arching while her climax took over.

Her eyes were closed as she gingerly rose off the toy, collapsing back into the cushion behind her with it clutched in her hand.

Unable to hold off any longer, I stood, crossing the room in a few strides and sitting on the edge of the coffee table in front of her. Her drowsy eyes met mine as my hand settled on her knee, trembling with the pent-up need to touch her. My fingers grasped the humming toy, clenching it in my fist.

"Can you handle more?"

She nodded with wide eyes, leaning back while I pulled her dress apart further, revealing her visibly wet pussy. Pretty and pink, and all fucking mine.

"Fuck, you are drenched," I murmured, scooting forward, parting her legs and drawing my fingers through the wetness.

"Fuck," she cursed, her chest heaving—hand grasping my wrist and guiding the toy toward her. As the gentle vibrations touched her skin, her mouth dropped open, hooded eyes watching me as I dragged it slowly upward to press against her clit.

"You're going to make me come again," she moaned, her eyelids fluttering.

"I think you want me to," I chuckled, nodding down for her to watch what I was doing. My eyes were riveted as I watched the toy slowly press inside, her body greedily pulling it in, her hips wiggling against the intrusion. "Does that feel good? Me pushing this gigantic cock inside you? Does Thor make you feel good?"

"Yes," she gasped, her free hand tracing the neckline of her dress, her palm cupping her breast over the silky material.

"Do you want me to play with your tits while he fucks you?"

"Oh, fuck. Yes, oh my God," she groaned, and I perched myself on the edge of the table to get closer.

"Such pretty pink nipples." My fingers grasped the flimsy lace of her bra, slowly drawing it down until one breast was revealed, and then the other. Her nipples were firm, tight little buds, just begging for my mouth.

"You love it when I tug on them with my teeth, don't you, babe?" I murmured, doing just that, and growling when she moaned loudly.

"Don't close your eyes. Watch me while we play with you." She blinked drowsily, listening to my demand.

My cock pulsed angrily between my legs, eager to be buried inside her. It drove me insane that I could all hear how excited she was with each thrust of her big, black, battery-operated boyfriend.

Isobel's eyes tracked my every movement while I played with her, my lips and tongue tracing every millimeter of her tits. This angle was perfect because I could watch her reaction to everything I did to her, knowing she was drowning in pleasure at the attention.

This was what I loved about being with her, how fucking arousing it was to watch her drunk on pleasure and greedily taking more.

"Be a good girl and tell me how much you want it, Isobel," I whispered, slowing the pace of my hand. "How much do you want us to make you come?"

"Fuck, so much."

I pulled the vibrator out, pressing the button on the handle a few times until it was back to the lowest vibration. I knew she desperately wanted release, but it was more fun to draw it out. She'd driven me crazy by making me watch her fuck this thing. Now it was my turn to play. My eyes were torn as to what to watch—her eyes while she desperately tried to catch her breath or her wet, pink pussy, glistening with arousal.

"You're so close," I teased, tracing the toy alongside where she wanted its attention the most, watching her squirm.

"More."

"Such a greedy fucking girl," I chuckled, pressing my hand into her thigh to keep her still.

"Don't tease me," she panted, arching her back.

"So fucking needy. Do you need more, babe?"

She tried to nod but broke off into a moan after I pressed the button to increase the speed of the vibrations.

"Hmm, not sure if that was an answer," I taunted, leaning forward to latch onto one nipple, trapping it in between my teeth and slowly leaning back until she was gasping and arching her back. "For someone who's typically so mouthy, you're being awfully quiet."

"Fuck, yes. God, just touch me," she moaned as I rolled both nipples between my fingers, stopping to run my tongue over them before I started all over again. "Please."

"You did ask nicely," I laughed, drawing the toy up, then back down while I returned to teasingly biting her nipples. She would have marks tomorrow, but I had a feeling she wouldn't mind.

"Maybe I should let you come," I murmured, cupping one breast as I trailed down her stomach, holding the end of the toy at her entrance while I waited for a reaction.

"Oh, fuck, please, please, please, let me come."

Deciding to put her out of her misery, I guided the toy back inside, holding it in place with my thumb through the loop on the end, while my fingers pressed down on her clit. Her hips bucked, the toy disappearing inside her, and I leaned down to suck on her nipple while I rubbed tight circles around the little nub.

"I'm... I'm..." she gasped, her fingernails digging into my shoulders.

"You ready, babe?" I asked, pulling back and cupping the side of her neck while my other fingers kept up their insistent movements between her thighs.

"Yes, oh God, Adrian, please." She was almost desperate, her chest heaving as she hovered so close to her release.

Turning the vibrator back to the highest setting, I thrust it in and out until her climax took over. She screamed as she detonated, rocking forward and grabbing my head, holding it against her as she came.

Her heart beat frantically against my ear as she clung to me, trying to catch her breath. When she finally released me, I leaned back, righting the cups of Isobel's bra and pulling her dress closed. She reached for the tie at the side, but I stopped her, knowing it was useless because this dress was going to be on my bedroom floor in less than a minute.

Isobel was unsteady when I pulled her to stand with me. I shifted her so I could pull her into my arms, and she sighed, relaxing into my hold as I carried her to my bedroom.

"Was that everything you fantasized about?" I asked as I sat her on the edge of the bed, helping her remove the silk and lace covering her.

"No," she whispered, shaking her head. "It wasn't what I needed."

"Then what do you need?" She quietly watched my fingers while I unbuttoned my shirt, shrugging it from my shoulders before I shed the rest of my clothes.

"I need you," she whispered. "Only you."

She welcomed me with open arms and soft lips as I sunk into her, my hips pushing her into the mattress with each desperate thrust. As I came inside her, filling her as she moaned in my ear, I knew I couldn't hide the strength of my feelings anymore. I was hers. And I'd do everything in my power to keep making her desires a reality.

TWENTY-SEVEN

ISOBEL

BOSTON

TAPPING MY PEN AGAINST the edge of my desk, I tried to focus on the PDF covering the screen in front of me. Chase and Evan's book was going to print in a week. Their launch was scheduled, the tour dates had been finalized and we'd dropped the bomb that Adrian and I wouldn't be traveling with them. My intern Kristine was less than enthusiastic about going, but if she planned to go after the promotion she was up for, she needed it to keep her edge on the competition.

Adrian's intern, Sam, seemed less hesitant, but sending the two of them out by themselves made me more than a little nervous. They could handle it, and they'd be going through press training with Chase and Evan, but tours were hectic even when you knew what you were doing.

"You ready?" Adrian asked, leaning against the doorframe to my office.

"Yeah." He knew I was distracted as he stepped into the office, pressing my laptop closed and holding his hand out to help me stand.

"You sure you're okay with this?" I asked, squeezing his hand before standing and wiping my sweaty palms on my skirt.

"I already told you I was. If this is what you need to feel comfortable, I've got no problem with it. Other than the last few days."

He was making a trip to the fertility clinic with me, getting a sperm sample tested to make sure we wouldn't run into any issues later. It was my paranoia manifesting, but since he'd never fathered any children, and I'd been tested already, I wasn't leaving things to chance and wasting more time if we needed to pursue other options.

"Think they'll let you come in the room with me?" he asked, pressing his hand into the center of my back, and guiding me into the hallway, but keeping an otherwise respectful distance. Rumors had been rampant in the last month that we were fucking, and we were, but we didn't need to broadcast it.

"I was told I could help as long as none of my fluids could potentially get mixed with yours."

He leaned down, whispering in my ear as we waited for the elevator. "So I can play with your tits?"

"Such a romantic."

"That wasn't a no," he chuckled, urging me forward as the elevator doors opened. It seemed everyone else had already left for lunch as we traveled down in an empty elevator car. "I've been such a good boy and kept my hands to myself for the last three days. All I want to do is play with your nipples."

He'd been instructed to abstain from any kind of emissions for seventy-two hours before sample collection, and I was glad I'd spent most of the last three days in meetings with Sloane being briefed about my new position.

"I promise you can play with them all you want when we go home later."

"You sure you can wait that long?" he teased, stepping behind me and playfully cupping me through my thin blouse.

"Stop. A few hours won't kill you. It's not like you'll die since you haven't come for a few days."

"I'm so fuckin' horny," he whined, grinding into my ass and I couldn't hold in the laughter any longer, giggling as we reached the ground floor.

He didn't seem to think it was so funny, pouting on the short walk to our destination, even though he walked with me pressed against his side the entire time.

"Checking in for O'Neill," I said after we stepped up to the reception desk.

"What's your appointment for?"

"Relief," Adrian sighed, but it turned into a grunt when I smacked him in the stomach.

"Sample collection."

"Geez, babe. Save your hand strength. We'll need it for a different kind of beating a few minutes from now."

I rolled my eyes at his crass joke, but the receptionist bit her lip to hold in a laugh, her shoulders shaking.

"See. She thinks I'm funny," he teased, his hand creeping down to grab a handful of my ass.

For someone who claimed he'd been celibate for months before we got together, he seemed a bit pent up after only three days of abstinence. But clearly, even though he was in a dry spell, he'd given his hand a regular workout.

"I'll need to check both of your IDs if you're going in together." Thankfully, Adrian didn't make any more inappropriate jokes while we waited for her to scan our licenses.

"It'll be a few minutes. They'll call you from that door," she said, gesturing toward a door on the far side of the waiting room.

Adrian dutifully followed me, throwing his arm across the back of my chair after we settled into the tiny chairs.

"Think they'll have some porn back there?"

Shaking my head, I squeezed his knee, not wanting the other people sitting near us to listen to my desperately horny sperm provider. "Shush."

"I put your bullet vibrator in my bag when I left your place this morning," he whispered, and my eyes widened. "It's in my pocket." He paused as his fingertips caressed my shoulder. "That's not the only rocket in my pocket."

I coughed, stifling my laugh. "You're ridiculous."

"Ridiculously smart, you mean."

"Not really. We both know you're only thinking with one head right now."

Before he could respond, they called his name, and we stood, following the nurse through the door and down a hallway filled with small exam rooms. But these had an armchair, a small loveseat, and a bookcase filled with inspirational materials instead of the exam tables with stirrups on the other side of the office.

"Here is your sample collection specimen cup. Make sure both of you thoroughly wash your hands before you get things started. Manual masturbation only, no oral sex or intercourse, as it can contaminate the sample," she explained, completely unfazed. "There are visual stimulation materials provided on the bookcase. If you have a mishap and any of your sample escapes onto one of them, please throw it away before you leave."

Adrian's chest shook as he tried to hold in a laugh, and my cheeks heated as I blushed.

"Any questions?"

He opened his mouth to respond, but I reached down and pinched his thigh. "No, I think we're good."

"Sample goes in the box in the wall next to the door. Make sure the lid is closed securely. Don't use the sanitizing wipes on the specimen container. There are paper towels by the sink if you need to clean up any overflow."

Nodding, she gestured for us to enter the room. "Have fun, kids."

As the door clicked closed, Adrian burst out laughing, doubling over as he tried to control himself. "How many times a day do you think she has to repeat that?"

"Can you be serious for like two seconds? People come here because they're trying to have a baby. It's not a joke." Ignoring him, I washed my hands, stepping away to let him do the same before I stood awkwardly in the center of the room.

"I know, babe," he murmured, pulling me into his arms. "But you have to find humor in moments like this or the worrying will eat you alive. Just relax. This is one step closer to what we both want."

He swayed us gently, tucking my head into his shoulder. "But right now, the only thing I can think about is making you squirm while I stroke my cock. Take off your blouse, 'cause I'll rip it off if we don't get naked in the next twenty seconds."

Laughing, I pushed him back, pointing to the couch. He paused, pulling the vibrator out of his pocket, and pressing it into my hand. Winking as he held up the tiny remote that controlled it, he stepped backward while unbuttoning his suit pants.

I worked on the buttons of my blouse as he shrugged off his jacket, carefully laying it across the back of the chair, his cufflinks and shirt following.

"Skirt too," he instructed, pulling his pants and boxers down, shoving them to his calves before he took a seat on the loveseat, the paper covering it crinkling audibly under his weight. "Now the bra."

Reaching back, I lowered the zipper of my skirt, letting it drop to the floor and stepping free. My bra was next, his cock twitching as he watched me. Standing in front of him in only my lacy underwear and a pair of high heels should have felt awkward, but when his large hand grasped his hard cock, I felt a rush of excitement flow through me.

"Put the toy in." His voice was low and raspy, his eyelids fluttering while he stroked himself. Adrian, under normal circumstances, was hot, but staring at me with hooded eyes and his abs flexing while he pleasured himself was insane.

His eyebrow raised when I hesitated, but the feral look that replaced it when I slipped my hand inside my panties—pushing the toy into place—had my pulse racing.

"Now come here." He spread his legs, his free arm stretching across the back of the couch as he settled in, the remote clasped in his hand.

Stepping forward, I panted after he pressed the button, the gentle vibrations making me even wetter.

"Come sit on my lap."

"But we can't..." I trailed off at the stern look on his face. The man clearly had a plan.

"I didn't say facing me. Now, are you going to listen and let me tell you what I want, or are you going to make this more difficult? Turn around and sit on my knee."

Nodding, I obeyed him, sitting down on his knee. His arm wrapped around me, his palm settling on my breast, the remote still between his fingers.

"I want you to grind on my leg and make yourself come while I fuck my hand, wishing I was inside you right now."

Oh, fuck. This wasn't how I'd imagined this process going, but as he pushed the button two more times, I gasped and rocked against his leg instinctually.

"That's it, babe. Use me."

His palm massaged my nipple as my hips rocked, the friction of the lace against my clit driving me closer while his breathing became ragged behind me.

"God, you're so fucking hot," he grunted, flexing his thigh against my movements. Who would have thought humping your boyfriend's leg while he jacked off behind you would be so exhilarating? "Wish you were leaking all over my cock instead of my lap right now. I'm going to fuck you so hard later. You're going to have to lock me out of your office because all I can think about right now is bending you over your desk."

"Fuck," I moaned, my head falling back as I got closer and closer.

"Can't wait to fill you up and then watch it slide down your leg, my fingers catching it and pushing it back inside before I pull your panties back into place, knowing you're full of me while you try to concentrate on work."

His dirty words did the trick; my breath catching in my throat as I felt the pulses start.

"Fuck, babe, I can feel your thighs shaking. Come all over me. Fuck, yes..." he groaned, panting while my body hummed.

"Get the cup. I'm close."

On shaky legs, I stood, grabbing the cup, and awkwardly holding it out to him.

"Fuck, feels so good," he grunted, standing in front of me, his fist flying over his length.

My hand closed over his, eyes widening as his hand flexed. He grasped my breast, rolling my nipple between his fingers before his breathing increased.

"Now," he groaned, aiming his dick down until it was pointed at where it needed to be. "Fucking hell."

My eyes widened as his entire body flexed, his grip on my breast almost painful when he came, filling the cup in my hand. There was something so simultaneously hot and hilarious about this situation,Somehow, and my chest shook as I tried to stifle a laugh.

Adrian joined me, his body shaking with laughter while we both stared down at the cup. "Score, didn't make a mess."

"Oh my God," I giggled, screwing the lid back on and walking to the little door in the wall. Thankfully, there was a closed door on the other side, so the nurses didn't see me topless.

"Wonder what kinds of crazy shit they hear going on in these rooms..." Adrian laughed, pulling his pants up and fastening the button. He stepped toward me, backing me into the wall before sliding his hand beneath my panties. I gasped as he gently coaxed the vibrator loose, tucking it back into his pocket before bringing his fingers to his mouth. "You made such a mess in those tiny panties."

"Stop," I whined, pushing at his chest, suddenly embarrassed to be half-naked in a fertility doctor's office.

"You were just doing your duty to help me out, babe. Don't need to be embarrassed," he teased, kissing my pink cheek.

"Somehow I don't think the nurses planned on me riding your leg to completion while you promised to fuck me on my desk as a method for sperm collection."

"Then other people clearly aren't doing it right."

"Get dressed." Placing my hand on his bare chest, I pushed him back, slipping around him to get my discarded clothing from the floor. Adrian smacked my ass when he passed me, redressing with a ridiculous smile on his face.

Part of me wondered if I was insane to want to have a child with this man, but the other part of me fell a little bit further because he made me want so much more.

TWO DAYS LATER, AS I was sitting in the chair across from Sloane's desk, an alert scrolled across the screen of my watch.

Discreetly swiping open my phone as she talked, explaining the travel she had planned for me over the next three months, I clicked the new text message.

> Adrian: Sample results are in. As you already know, I'm a stud.

> Adrian: 60% normal sperm shape.

> Adrian: 3.5 out of 4 for movement. (Those little guys are wily and fast)

> Adrian: PH 7.4

> Adrian: 3 milliliters of volume collected (slightly above average)

> Adrian: 150 million swimmers (above average for my age)

> Adrian: Consistency optimal (But you already knew that)

Sloane paused as I tried to hold back laughter at his commentary. "Something you need to take care of?" she asked, nodding to my lap.

Not right now. But after work was a different story.

"No, just a text from a colleague I need to address this afternoon."

"Hmm," she hummed, smirking before she continued. It was clear the rumor mill had made its way to the executive floor to further confirm her previous hunch about Adrian and me. "Are you alright with the schedule for the week before I need you and Adrian in New York? I know you wanted to oversee the last few signings for the Rose and Evans book."

"Yeah, I'm good," I confirmed, switching over to the calendar app to input the dates and cities she needed me in.

"Kristine and Sam set to go?"

"Yeah, I think they'll be fine. Adrian has been sharing past tour plans with Sam and I've given Kristine the preliminary schedules from PR."

One of the department heads from the public relations department would travel with Chase, Evan, Kristine, and Sam for the duration of the tour to make sure things ran smoothly in my and Adrian's absence. It was hard to hand over the reins, but since I had a feeling my intern would be gone in a matter of weeks, I needed to equip her to step into her new position. It'd be selfish of me to request to keep her, even if I wasn't looking forward to training her replacement, taking on my additional job duties and trying to get pregnant.

As Sloane dove back in, I took notes, filling the notebook in my lap with more information than I'd been expecting. Part of me was panicking when I tried to picture the future, me having to travel a third of the year with a new baby. But I didn't want to give up either opportunity.

"After the first of the year, we'll need you in Chicago and Seattle for three weeks at each office for a new project, but I'll give you details later."

My heart pounded as I did the math. If I tried to get pregnant this summer—in the next two or three months—I'd likely be too far along to travel that much.

"Are there any conflicts you can think of that might prevent the start of the year being travel heavy?"

Shaking my head, my palms grew sweaty as I lied. While I wasn't pregnant now, the possibility was there, and now that we knew the only barrier preventing it was my IUD, I wasn't sure when it would be a good time to get it removed and start trying. The likelihood of conceiving quickly wasn't great with both of us being over thirty-five, but they weren't non-existent either. My OB had told me the first three months after an IUD removal would likely be months when I was very fertile as my hormones tried to regulate.

Could I risk it, or should we wait until later in the fall?

"That's all I have for today. I know you've got a lot on your plate." She extended a file folder in my direction, and I reached forward to grab it, opening the front cover. "Those are the preliminary candidates to replace the copy-editing interns should they move on. Since you'll be busy over the next month, I'm giving these to you and Adrian to look through."

On my way to the elevator, I flipped through the resumes, stopping on a familiar name. As I scanned her credentials, I hadn't realized that Andrea, the administrative assistant on our floor, had a degree in English with a certification in copy editing. She was also in graduate school for a master's degree in English and communications.

As I passed by her desk on the way to my own, I watched her move around her desk, the area meticulously organized. Maybe finding a candidate to replace Kristine wouldn't be as hard as I thought.

TWENTY-EIGHT

ISOBEL

BOSTON

Laying my head on my desk, I took a deep breath. Work had been insane over the last month, trying to get everything organized before my first trip in my new position. Chase and Evan had been in the office all week, going through training with Kristine and Sam with Di from the PR department. Their book launch was tonight, and all I wanted to do was curl up in my bed and sleep for like a week straight.

Adrian had been great, feeding me when I forgot, and giving me orgasms when I was stressed, even if I tried to tell him I didn't have time to fool around. But he'd been there, rolling with the punches when I was moody and not complaining when I fell asleep on the couch instead of joining him in bed most nights.

We'd talked about when I'd schedule my IUD removal, and I'd made an appointment for the week between my trip and the signings in New York. But I felt guilty for considering canceling the appointment. I was barely managing my workload right now. Was it really fair to add a baby to the mix?

I hadn't told him about my hesitations because he'd been so excited, leaning enthusiastically into *practicing*. He'd become obsessed with coming inside me, serious about making sure I was full of him as much as I'd allow. Don't get me wrong, it was hot, but it was also really shitty timing.

"You ready, Isobel?" Kristine asked, standing in my doorway with a small suitcase by her side, a garment bag draped over her arm. We needed to get to the hotel to prep for tonight, but I was exhausted.

"Yeah, let me grab my outfit and I'll meet you downstairs."

We rode across town in silence, both of us absorbed in our phones. "You alright?" she asked after I sighed loudly.

"Yeah, just have the sinking feeling I'm going to forget something for tonight. We need this to go off smoothly. The execs want Chase and Evan to knock this one out of the park."

"Don't worry." She patted my hand, reassuring me, and I felt guilty that I needed reassurance from my intern. "We've got this down to a science, and you've crammed me full of more information than I need to get through the next six weeks. As long as you can keep a muzzle on Adrian, tonight will be fine."

Spoiler Alert: Everything was not fine.

THREE HOURS LATER, I paced the hallway between the conference rooms and the nearly empty ballroom, freaking the fuck out. And nothing Adrian said could calm me down. He'd done enough damage tonight with an untimely reappearance of his verbal diarrhea. His brain-to-mouth filter had clearly been damaged by how much we'd had sex lately.

"I thought we were past this," I sighed, stopping as his palm clasped my upper arm, halting my movements. "Between your mouth and now Evan, this is a freaking disaster."

"It'll be okay, Is. He's done this before. He disappeared for a month after Simone fucked him up last time. We'll figure this out."

His author Evan had fled the hotel mid-anxiety attack when his emotionally abusive ex-girlfriend had snuck into the launch party pretending to be her boss. Chase had punched her in the face when she cornered the author, but after she'd been removed from the hotel, she'd run into Evan. The poor guy, who had a particularly severe case of social anxiety, had disappeared in a cab without a trace.

"This isn't all going to be okay. He's gone." Shaking my arm free from him, I resumed my pacing. "Sam has his phone, and he left by himself. Are we really going to hope that the two guys we sent after him are magically going to appear with him before he needs to leave for the airport in the morning?"

"Yeah, I think that's exactly what we're hoping for at this point. I'm sure he's fine."

"God, you're so fucking frustrating. Do you ever take anything seriously?" His brow pinched; his expression stunned as I ranted at him. "You're not even fazed by this. I don't know if I can be around you right now."

"Is," he sighed, trying to reach forward to grasp my wrist, but my throat tightened. My stomach twisted while I covered my mouth and bolted the other way down the hallway.

He followed behind me, catching me by the shoulders as I tried to yank open the outer door to the bathroom. "You alright?"

Heaving, I pushed around him, dropping to my knees in the closest stall, the contents of my stomach emptying into the toilet in front of me.

Adrian knelt behind me, gathering the hair that'd fallen out of my bun away from my face. "Babe, you're burning yourself out. We can't change what happened, but you've gotta calm down. All this stress can't be good for you. You can barely keep your eyes open half the time after work. And you're up before dawn to work on your laptop."

"Because I have to be," I whispered, pulling a few sheets of toilet paper loose and wiping my mouth before I let him pull me back into his chest.

"No, you don't. You need to let me help. Let the people at the office help. I know Sloane offered to divide up some of your open manuscripts to lighten your load. Let her. You've gotta stop trying to do everything yourself."

My lips quivered, tears springing to my eyes when he kissed my temple, not even bothered that we were sitting on the floor of a hotel bathroom a foot away from a toilet full of my vomit.

"Let's go home and get some sleep. We can come back early tomorrow and figure things out. Sam and Kristine will get Chase ready, and even though I don't really know them, we need to trust Emory and Nathan will sort out tracking down Evan."

"But what if—"

"We're going home," he told me, voice firm as he pulled me up from the floor, helping me wipe my face and wash out my mouth at the sink before he led me back to the ballroom to gather our things.

He was quiet as he drove back to my apartment building, holding my hand tightly on the center console.

"You're going to bed when we get inside, and I'll wake you up at seven so we can get to the hotel in plenty of time."

"But..."

He shook his head as he parked the car, disentangling our fingers and holding his hand in front of my chest. "Phone. You're done for the night."

"You can't just—"

"For fuck's sake, Isobel. You got yourself so worked up that you literally made yourself sick. Take a fuckin' break. Give me the phone. It's not a question. And we both know I'll take it from you if I have to."

Defeated, I pulled it out of my purse, setting it in his open palm as my lip quivered.

"I'm going to run you a bath and you're going to soak in some of that girly bubble bath you like. I'm going to make you a snack, and then you're going to bed."

"But..."

He didn't let me finish, reaching down to release my seatbelt before he climbed out of the car, walking around the hood with purposeful strides and pulling my door open.

"No arguing."

Quietly following him into the building after he punched my code in the door, I tried to let everything go. He was right. I was running myself into the ground, and I couldn't keep living like this.

By the time he unlocked my apartment door, my chest was tight, and my eyes had pooled with tears. Something had to give, and I knew what it was.

Adrian placed our bags on the bench by the front door, leaving me to take off my coat while he headed toward my bedroom. I heard the tub running as I kicked off my heels, reaching up to pull the pins out of my hair. My head ached from my bun, and my temples throbbed as I numbly headed to find Adrian, undressing as I went.

"Come here," he whispered as I appeared in the doorway in my underwear.

Wrapped in his strong arms, I let the tears fall, not knowing how to talk to him about what I'd decided I needed to let go.

THE NEXT MORNING, AS we drove back to the hotel, I stared out the window. He still hadn't given my phone back, but I had the sinking suspicion things were still a mess.

Kristine cornered me as we walked into the lobby, pulling me away from Adrian with a glare. Before she tugged me off, he pushed my fully charged phone into my hand. She hadn't liked him before, but with his dumbass comments reappearing this week, she was firmly in the camp that he needed to be shoved into a dumpster.

"Did you hear anything?"

Shaking my head, I swiped open the screen on my phone. No new text messages waiting for me. "No, but you and Sam are going to have to wing it at this point. Get Chase to Chicago and do whatever you have to do to keep things running smoothly. I'll make sure someone finds him today, and he's on a plane by tonight. We've all got too much riding on this tour going well to screw around."

"Fuck," she sighed, glancing over at Adrian's intern, Sam. "I'm sure golden boy will help me get this shitshow on the road. Spamela is disgustingly optimistic."

"You really should stop calling him that."

"Thanks for the input." Her attitude clearly rivaled mine this morning. "Since we're giving out unsolicited advice, you really should stop messing around with Dickhead."

"Kris, that's..."

"None of my business, I get it, but what the fuck, Is? I thought you had more self-respect than that."

"Since when have I tolerated you talking to me like this?" I wanted to defend him from her ire, but a small part of me used to agree with her. I wasn't sure if it still did. His behavior last night had been atrocious.

"Fine. I'll drop it. But I'm giving him hell if anything happens while we're on the road."

"Wouldn't expect anything less."

Kristine rolled her eyes before she walked away, whispering something to Chase before people started gathering their bags to head to the airport.

"You ready to go?" Adrian asked, placing his hand on the center of my back.

"Yeah, guess there isn't anything we can do right now."

Leaning down to whisper in my ear, he chuckled. "I can think of some things to keep your mind off it."

"Just...don't," I sighed, walking away to hug Chase before they left. She may have been putting on a brave face, but I knew when my author was going through the motions, and she was just on autopilot at this point. I could empathize with that.

"Can you drop me off?" I asked, Adrian's car slowing at the curb of my building. "I want to lie down. Alone."

"Are you sure? I can make you breakfast and keep you company. Help you relax for once until we have to be back at work on Monday."

His smile vanished when I shook my head, my hand reaching for the door handle as I leaned away from him. He reached across the console, placing his hand on my shoulder. "Are you sure you're alright?"

Nodding, I tried to hold back the tears that wanted to fall again. "Yeah, just need some space."

"Are we okay?" he asked, his voice concerned.

I wanted to say, of course we were, but I needed some time away from him to think about where my life was going to go from here. He'd been so on board with the idea of having a baby, and now...

Now I didn't know what to do.

"Yeah. I just want to sleep and pretend everything is normal right now." He nodded, his thumb stroking my shoulder. "I'll call you tomorrow."

"Is, I'd really like to stay with you right now. I don't like seeing you upset like this. There's stuff in my bag I can work on. I promise I won't bother you. But I don't want to leave you alone."

Leaning my head against the back of his hand, I let out a shaky sigh. "I know. But I need time."

He didn't protest when I reached for the door again, tears spilling down my cheeks while I walked away without looking back. I knew he'd wait until I was inside, but until I figured out what I wanted, I needed to be by myself. Like I always seemed to end up.

TWENTY-NINE

ADRIAN

BOSTON

"Oh, come on," I growled, watching my niece, Penelope, carefully lay out the cards in her hand, a shit-eating grin on her face that reminded me of Hutch's. "You've gotta be fuckin' kiddin' me."

"My girl knows her shit," Hutch teased, helping his daughter rake the skittles from the pot in the center of the table into the pile sitting in front of her.

"Kid is a card shark," Pops laughed, beaming as he watched his great-granddaughter. Today was a good day, but my mind still wandered to how Isobel was doing.

She'd been shaken after the whole book launch debacle, but thankfully Chase's friends had tracked Evan down and gotten him on a plane by mid-morning. Sam was keeping me apprised by text, so I assumed Kristine was doing the same, but it killed me to respect Is' wishes and give her some space.

"Quit being a pussy and take your cards." Hutch's teasing broke the trance I was in, and I laughed as Ma yelled from the other room.

"And you, Hutchins O'Neill, need to keep yah mouth shut around yah impressionable daughta'." It still amused me that after all these years, my Ma's accent had never changed. I would have thought working in an emergency room downtown would've made her adapt, but she was Southie born and bred.

"I don't think she realizes Pen goes to a public school," Hutch laughed while Pops shook his head.

"He's right," his almost thirteen-year-old agreed, "And Donny's way worse than you guys."

Hutch frowned, looking irritated as his jaw clenched. Donny had once been his best friend, but when he'd slept with Hutch's wife while he was recovering after the failed mission that took part of his leg in a hospital in Germany, that friendship had imploded even more spectacularly than an IED.

"Is that so?" he asked, and Penny's eyes widened when she realized her dad was not pleased with that information.

Deciding to change the subject, I asked Penelope about what she'd been doing lately, and her plans for summer break.

"Ma wants me to keep taking dance lessons, but ballet is boring as fuck."

"Penelope Ann O'Neill, watch yah mouth," Ma scolded from the kitchen, clearly still eavesdropping with her hawklike ears.

"I changed the box on the application for summer dance to hip hop. She'll probably lose her..." she trailed off, mouthing the word *shit*. "But since she's too busy puking up her guts right now, she won't know until the end of the summer recital. I also got Dad to enroll me in the babysittin' course at the Y. Then I can start makin' some money, so I don't have to beg her for an allowance."

"You shouldn't lie to your mother," Pops scolded, studying the cards in his hand. "Even if she is a cheating cun—"

"Liam Patrick, don't even think about it," Ma yelled again, and we all started laughing.

It wasn't a secret that no one in this household, including Pen, was a fan of Helena Parker, formerly O'Neill.

"Where's Isobel?" Hutch asked when we started playing again, skittles clinking against the surface of the dented table in the den as we all called.

"Who's Isobel?" Pops asked, looking between us.

Fuck.

"Adrian's lady friend from work. They've been bangin' out a project together," Hutch answered, smirking as he gave me an out from having to explain who she was. I was afraid to mention the baseball game, knowing he'd get agitated if he didn't remember. But he surprised me.

"Oh yeah. The one from the Sox game. You should bring her around sometime," Pops suggested, never looking up from his cards. "She was too good for you, but I liked her."

"I'll be sure to do that," I agreed, wishing he'd have more lucid days so he might meet his grandchild next year. I hated he didn't initially remember meeting Isobel, but he'd pretty much given me his seal of approval at the game that day, so I knew he'd like her.

Part of me was eager for her IUD to get removed, so we could start trying for real instead of getting in lots of practice, but the other part of me was scared shitless. What if—despite our test results—it didn't happen? If I couldn't knock her up, would she break up with me? Would she find a donor?

While I would absolutely raise another man's child if it came to that, I wanted her child to be mine.

"Your call," Hutch said, waving his hand in front of my face.

"Fold." Tossing my cards into the center of the table, I stood and shoved my phone into my pocket. "I think I'm gonna head home. Do you need me to give Pen a ride to Lena's?"

"Nah." Hutch waved me off. "I'll walk her back. It's nice out today, and it's only a few blocks."

Nodding, I popped into the kitchen to say goodbye to Ma, taking the container of leftovers she shoved into my hands.

As I headed back toward the city, I briefly thought about detouring to Isobel's apartment to make sure she'd eaten today, but knew I would see her in the morning.

EVAN CALLED TWO WEEKS into the book tour, and I hesitated to pick up, since I was waiting for Isobel to meet me for lunch.

"Hey, what's up, man? Everything going alright?" Despite the major hiccup the weekend the tour began, Evan had done surprisingly well so far. After pictures of the two authors kissing surfaced on Instagram after their first signing, I'd thought things would get dicey, but people loved it.

"I need your help," he whispered.

"What the hell is going on? Are you in trouble or something? Do I need to send bail money?"

"No," he whispered again, his voice getting louder when he continued. "Everything is fine with the tour, but I need you to arrange something in New York."

"Okay? Hit me with it. What do you need?"

"Can you arrange a dinner for the last night, after the signings downtown?"

"Yeah, we sometimes have a celebration dinner at the end of the tour, but are you sure you don't want to wait until Boston?"

"It has to be New York. I'll send you an email with what I need."

"Why all the cloak and dagger?"

"I want to propose to Chase." Stunned, I sat back in my chair, rubbing my hand over the scruff on my chin. Holy shit.

I'd questioned her motives before the tour, and he'd been quick to put me in my place, but I hadn't realized he was serious when he'd told me he wanted to marry her.

"You still there?" he asked, suddenly sounding nervous.

"Uh, yeah. Congratulations, I guess. If you send me the details this afternoon, I can get the ball rolling."

"Thank you," he sighed. "If you can arrange things on your end, I'll try to get Sam on board. As long as I can keep Kristine from killing him before then."

"Things going that well?" I laughed, knowing that my intern was more than capable of putting Isobel's in her place. Not that she'd make it easy for him.

"Everything's great so far, but after the mix-up in Denver, she's been a bit feral."

"Not surprising." She'd ripped me a new one when the rooms were mixed up at the hotel and she had to share with Sam. It broke all kinds of protocol with the company travel guidelines, but we hadn't had any other choice.

Isobel appeared in my doorway, tilting her head as she pointed at my phone. I mouthed *Evan*, and she frowned, so I knew I needed to get him off the phone to fill her in.

"I'll get everything set and email you details once everything is ready. Safe travels to your next stop."

"What's going on?" Is asked as she sat in the chair across from my desk. "Do we need to cancel lunch to fix an issue?"

"Nah, it's not anything urgent. Evan wants to propose while we're in New York. He asked me to set up a dinner. He's sending me details in an email this afternoon."

"Propose?" she whispered, eyes wide. "This soon? They barely know each other."

"Like we can talk," I chuckled, standing from my desk and sitting on the arm of the chair she occupied.

"But we've known each other for five years."

"Is, you hated me for most of that time. We've only really been together about the same amount of time as they have and we're planning to have a kid together. I don't know why you're so shocked."

As I stroked her cheek, she nodded, her eyes distant. "I guess," she finally sighed. "But it all just seems so sudden. What if things don't work out?"

I wasn't sure if she was talking about them or us, but either way, I knew things were serious for both parties. "Things will work out how they're supposed to. Have a little faith."

"I don't know if I can," she whispered, leaning her face into my palm.

"Then I'll have enough for the both of us."

Chapter
THIRTY

ISOBEL

CHICAGO

STARING AT THE PROSPECTUS on the table in front of me for Vivid's new social media push, I pinched the bridge of my nose, trying to ignore the headache I'd had for days. I'd traveled for work before, running dozens of book tours over the last seven years, but my new position wasn't remotely close to city hopping and spending most of my time in bookstores.

"Isobel, is now a good time?" Mark, the head of publishing in the Chicago office, asked, leaning through the doorway to the makeshift office they'd prepared for my brief visit.

"Yeah, I need a break from staring at these, anyway. What's going on?"

He sat across from me, placing a manila folder in front of him. "What can you tell me about Samuel Langley?"

Taken a little by surprise, I leaned back in my chair. "He's uh... He's currently the copy-editing intern of one of my colleagues."

"Adrian O'Neill, right?"

"Yeah."

"I'll cut straight to the chase. We're contemplating going after him to come run the mystery department in this office. His resume is solid, and Sloane shared his manuscript samples with me. I think he'd fit in well here, and he's got family nearby. Is there anything you'd recommend we offer to sweeten the deal?"

"Why Sam?"

He was more than qualified, but last I knew Sloane had wanted him to move up inside the Boston office. I didn't know anything about other offices having openings for copy-editing interns. But it sounded like he wasn't going to be an intern.

"Like I said, he seems like a good fit, doesn't need much training to step into the role, and Sloane said she has another intern she can offer the job in Boston to if we can convince him to move."

Fuck. Kristine was going to lose her shit. Sloane hadn't told us anything further about the hiring panel's decision because the final interviews were later this week.

"Have you talked to Adrian? He'd be able to give you a reference. Sam has been his direct report for a few years."

"I will, but I just wanted to gauge the situation before we prepared an offer package."

We'd both known there was a high possibility one of us would lose their intern, but it seemed we'd both be looking for replacements soon. Part of me wished I'd brought the candidate profiles with me so I could have Sloane schedule an interview.

"Talk to Adrian first, but I think Sam might consider it if your offer is competitive."

"Thanks, Isobel. Having you here the last few days has been great. You looking for a lateral move anytime soon?"

Shaking my head, he sighed in disappointment. "Sorry, no plans to leave Boston. But thank you for thinking of me."

"Yeah, I knew it was a long shot. And I'm pretty sure Sloane would come after me for trying, but figured I'd shoot my shot. Let me know if there's anything else you need before you head back."

He let himself out and my fingers itched to grab my phone and give Adrian a heads up. But things had been weird between us since I'd been out of the office. We still talked every night before I went to bed, but I was so exhausted from all the time changes from hopping all over the country that I usually started drifting off mid call.

I still hadn't made any decisions about what I wanted to do, and my appointment at the clinic was the day after tomorrow, so I needed to figure it out soon.

The fickle bitch that was infertility had the potential to eviscerate an otherwise stable relationship. I would know. It swiftly cut apart my marriage without hesitation, leaving me a shell of the person I once was.

The two times I'd been elated and then utterly wrecked when the spark of life inside me took a firm hold on my heart before it was snuffed out, and left scars even years later.

Was I brave enough to go through that again? Or would I always carry this ache of regret with me?

"AFTER YOU'RE DONE COLLECTING your urine sample, wipe again using these and then stay undressed from the waist down. Place the sample in the box on the wall and we'll run a quick pregnancy test. Dr. Charles will come in once we've got the results. The procedure typically takes about ten minutes. She'll give you some aftercare instructions, but you should be cleared for intercourse in a few days. Some recommend waiting for two weeks, but that's completely up to you and your partner."

The nurse placed a few hygienic wipes in my hand and left me in the exam room to do my business.

I understood why they had to do the pregnancy tests, but I'd had this IUD in for over three years with no issues. Not that my sex life had been frequent until the last six months.

After I washed my hands, I put my specimen in the box, flipping the little dial that showed the nurses a sample had been placed inside.

Adrian offered to come with me, but he couldn't be in here for the removal, so I declined, knowing he was still trying to get everything in place for Evan in New York. We'd be driving down early in the morning instead of flying since it was less than four hours. Sloane had offered to buy plane tickets, but by the time we dealt with security and luggage, it'd take nearly as long as the drive.

Sloane told me this morning about the plans she had for Sam and Kristine. He'd been the hiring committee's first choice for the opening in the fantasy department, but they were going to let Mark pitch the position in Chicago during his final interview. If he decided to take it, Kristine would get the fantasy position, and I'd requested Andrea to take her place. She'd said there was interest from another editor for her, but Adrian hadn't said anything about who he was planning to replace Sam with.

Absently flipping through my emails, I shifted on the uncomfortable paper underneath my legs, wishing they'd hurry and get this thing out of me.

My plan was to ask Adrian to use condoms for the next few months until the timing worked out better to try. I still wasn't sure how I was going to balance everything, but Leila had laid into me when I told her I was considering waiting until a time when things slowed down at work.

She'd been pissed when I mentioned it on the phone, telling me to stop doing the things I thought I needed to do to make people happy and do what I wanted.

Getting my ass handed to me by my best friend was probably the only reason I was currently sitting on this hard-as-rock exam room table with my pants off.

A knock sounded on the door, and I tossed my phone onto the pile of clothes in the chair to my right.

"Good afternoon, Isobel. How are we doing today?" Dr. Charles asked as she stepped through the door, pulling a cart behind her. From what she'd told me at my last appointment, IUD removal just required a speculum and a small device that would collapse the arms so she could pull it free. She hadn't mentioned anything about an ultrasound being needed.

"I'm good," I responded absently, watching as she uncoiled the cord on a long wand and covered it with a condom.

"We got your preliminary urine test results back, and they'll be in to collect a blood sample soon, but I just need to check something before we send you down the hall for a full scan."

"Scan of what?" I asked, my heart beating faster as she squirted the gel onto the tip of the wand and stepped toward me.

"It seems your IUD may have stopped doing its job. I'm going to do a quick transvaginal scan to see if I can locate it, and then we can talk about removal options that pose minimal risk to the fetus."

"I'm sorry...the what?"

"I guess I should have led with that," she chuckled, smiling at me while she held the ultrasound wand in the air. "Congratulations, Isobel, you're pregnant."

She kept talking, but I couldn't follow anything she said because the room started spinning and then everything went black. The last thing I remembered was the sound of her calling for a nurse.

Chapter

THIRTY-ONE

ISOBEL

BOSTON

I WAS NUMB. WALKING back to the office a few hours—and lots of tests—later, the oppressive heat coming off the sidewalks didn't even faze me.

The part of me that had craved a child for over fifteen years was elated, but the practical side knew that I had officially bitten off more than I could chew. And the insane part of it all was I didn't regret it. I was fucking terrified of what the next year would hold, but I wanted this baby. Desperately.

It was strange walking into the building after most of the people had left for the day. My thirty-minute afternoon appointment had turned into three additional hours of sitting in waiting areas for testing and then attempting to focus on all the information Dr. Charles had thrown at me.

Moderate Risk Geriatric Pregnancy, had been the thing that stood out to me the most. It could have been worse. Much worse, but so far, she seemed to think that the chances of carrying this baby to term and having minimal complications was good.

I'd had two different ultrasounds, and both showed an egg sac with a tiny speck in the center of it and nowhere in sight was my IUD. Apparently, spontaneous expulsion of the device happened in point zero five percent of women, and I was one of the lucky few.

All those months I stared at negative pregnancy test after negative pregnancy test. Having to go through two curettage procedures after my miscarriages to remove the tissue of the children who never made it to fruition and watch as my marriage crumbled. And all it had taken was a vanishing IUD and Adrian. Maybe that confirmed the universe had never wanted me to end up with Grant.

Riding the elevator up to my floor, I knew chances were good he was gone for the day, but I still needed to check. When the doors parted, Andrea sat in the reception area, studying papers spread across the surface of her desk while she chewed on the end of her pen.

"Oh shit," she exclaimed as I walked closer. She'd clearly thought she had a quiet space to work with everyone gone for the day, but right now, I was relieved to see her smiling face. "I didn't know you'd be returning today. Adrian said you had an appointment this afternoon, and I assumed, since you didn't come back, you were out for the rest of the day."

"Things didn't go exactly as planned. I just stopped in to get my laptop and the things I need to take with me when we head to New York in the morning."

"Want to take me too?" she joked, smiling widely.

"Well, not this trip, but maybe on one in the future. I saw your application for one of the copy-editing positions had made it through the initial screening."

"Oh, uh, yeah..." She looked nervous, chewing on the side of her lip as she nodded. "Actually, I had a meeting with Sloane and Adrian today. He offered me the position in the mystery department."

Well, fuck. Dickhead beat me to her.

"That's great." I tried to sound excited she'd been given the opportunity to advance, but none of the other candidates had really stood out for the position in my department. "I'm sure Adrian can show you the ropes. Despite his behavior sometimes, he's very good at his job."

"I've interacted with him enough to know he's not really that bad. A lot of the gossips in this office have a habit of taking something small and blowing it out of proportion."

Well, they were likely to have a field day when I started showing. At this point, it wouldn't be hard to guess who my baby daddy was.

"I'll let you get back to your schoolwork. Congratulations again. I know how hard you work around here, and I think you'll do great."

Would have been nice if I had gotten to her first, but clearly the timing was not on my side for anything lately.

Once I got to my office, I scanned through the emails that'd come through in my absence, noting ones I'd need to address in the next few days, and adding reminders in my calendar about upcoming deadlines or check-ins with my authors. I'd missed this part of my job while I was on the road.

> Adrian: How was your appointment? We good to go?

If he only knew that he'd already accomplished our goal. He'd been in *do-not-disturb* mode with his alerts off when I'd tried to text him earlier, clearly finalizing the details of his new intern. Until I had answers, I hadn't wanted to freak him out while I was at the clinic, but now that I did, I wasn't sure how to go about telling him.

I'd thought we'd have a few months until this happened. Was I supposed to come up with some elaborate pregnancy reveal? Or could I just blurt it out in the car in the morning? I wasn't sure what the protocol was for something like this. Especially since the last time I'd been pregnant, it'd been over before it had really sunk in.

Adrian: I've got some leftover Chinese food from having dinner with Pops. Want me to stop by? Have you eaten yet?

My stomach turned as I thought about eating anything, and now I knew why I'd been so exhausted lately. It was still early, but I should have noticed the signs. I chalked everything up to stress and hadn't been worried when my cycle was light a few weeks ago. It was never particularly heavy with the IUD in anyway, but I hadn't suspected a thing.

Dr. Charles said it'd probably dislodged during my previous cycle, and the last time I remembered checking my strings was a few days before it'd started.

Isobel: Still need to wrap up at the office and head home to finish packing. I'm exhausted. Rain check?

Adrian: Want me to bring you a chocolate croissant in the morning?

Isobel: Do you really need me to answer that question?

Adrian: I might even bring you two, so you don't try to steal mine again.

Isobel: Probably best, since I don't think I'd have room for three of them, but I can't make any promises yours will be safe in the end.

Adrian: I thought you liked having two at once.

I laughed, finally letting a little bit of my anxiety go because I knew he wasn't talking about chocolate croissants. Before I could respond, he texted me again.

Adrian: Go home and get some sleep, babe.

Isobel: So bossy.

Adrian: Just want to make sure my girl is taking care of herself.

And even more of my nerves melted away. I could do this. I would figure it out. *We* would figure it out.

"Your apartment better have burned down and you're standing in the street homeless, looking at the smoking ashes."

Laughing, I slid my toiletry case in my bag, eyeing the emergency tampon tucked in the side. Guess I wouldn't be needing that for a while.

"Good morning to you too, Leila."

"Seriously, it's six in the morning. I'm not caffeinated enough for this. But I know you wouldn't call before ten if you didn't need me. What's up? Aren't you leaving today?"

"Yeah..." I sighed.

"Oh no, I recognize that sigh. What did Dickhead do?"

"He didn't do any... Well, he didn't do anything intentionally." Cause his super sperm had clearly done something.

"Just tell me. Did I not mention the part about being under-caffeinated?"

"I'm pregnant."

Silence echoed through the speaker, and I was kind of shocked that Leila could be rendered speechless.

"Feel like I'm missing something here. Didn't you just get your IUD removed yesterday?"

"They tried, but things didn't go exactly as planned."

"How can you try to take out an IUD? It's either there or it's not." It was most decidedly not.

"That was the issue. It was not."

"Not taken out or not there?"

She was starting to sound more frantic by the moment, and it was freaking me out a little. "They did an ultrasound and couldn't find it. But they found something else inhabiting the space near where it used to be."

"You're seriously pregnant?"

"Yes," I laughed, relieved to tell someone. Adrian probably should have been the first one I told, but I needed my best friend right now. She'd been with me through all the shit with Grant, so she understood how hard this was for me.

A huge part of me was terrified that a few weeks from now I'd be sitting in a hospital heartbroken like I'd been too many times before.

"Holy shit. This is... This is, wow."

"Really fucking scary." My voice cracked as the tears appeared, one escaping down my cheek.

"Oh, honey. No, it's amazing. I'm finally going to be an auntie. And you know your kid is going to be gorgeous. That baby daddy of yours might be a bit of a dick, but he's not terrible to look at. If only he had a hot brother to sweep me off my feet."

"Um," I mumbled, not sure how to tell her he had an identical twin.

"You've been holding out on me," she laughed. "Tell me all about Dick-head's brother."

"He's not exactly your type."

"Not intending to marry the guy. Everyone is my type if they're hot enough." She wasn't wrong, her roster had some depth. With both men and women.

"You're too bossy. He's a bit too...dominant for you." Which he was. She never took orders from anyone. Hutch would be too much for her. While she liked to have a good time, Leila wouldn't survive a pleasure Dom, much less one who fucked other women in front of their partners.

"Okay, fine. Back to the original topic. How did Adrian take it? Is he impressed with himself? I'm sure he's eating this up."

"I..."

"You haven't told him yet?" she exclaimed, and I knew she was about to unleash on me. "Why did you tell me first? You know he's treated the idea of knocking you up like his new mission in life. Why haven't you said something?"

"Because I'm scared. This wasn't part of the plan. It was supposed to take months. Long enough for me to settle into this job and have fun trying. What if it happens again? I can't go through that this time. It'd break me."

She knew exactly what I was talking about. She'd been there through one of my miscarriages.

"Honey, no one can predict what will happen. But you can't let that fear stop you. That man isn't just interested in you for your ability to carry a child. You'll figure it out together."

Nodding, I tried to hold back the tears that wanted to escape. Adrian would be here to pick me up in less than a half hour and he'd know I'd been crying if I lost it right now.

"I need to finish packing. Thank you for answering the phone. I just needed to talk to you."

"Never be afraid to call me, hun. While I've never been knocked up and am now going to be religiously checking my strings before I let any dicks near my holy grail, I'll always be a sounding board for you when you need it."

"Thank you."

"And tell that man. I'm betting he's going to fuck the shit out of you when he finds out."

Zipping up my suitcase after I disconnected the call, I took a deep breath, trying to calm myself down enough to get through today. Two back-to-back signings and the dinner awaited us today, and I didn't want to draw the focus from Evan. Tonight was his grand proposal to Chase, and I knew Adrian would never keep his mouth shut if I told him before tonight.

"Hey, babe," he greeted, kissing me on the cheek before opening the passenger door to his car.

The strong, sickly sweet smell of my usual coffee order hit me as soon as I put my hand on the doorframe to step in. My stomach rolled, and I knew I'd never be able to make it four hours in the car with that smell.

"Oh, shit. I left my folder with the itinerary for today on my desk. I'll be right back."

Not giving him a chance to respond, I grabbed the cup and escaped toward my building, holding back the bile creeping up my throat while I swiped my keycard.

I looked back, making sure Adrian wasn't watching as I slipped around the corner next to the elevator and into the single stall bathroom, wrenching the lid from the cup in my hand. I turned on the water, pouring the coffee down the drain while I took shallow breaths through my mouth.

It didn't work, and my chest heaved as I escaped into the stall, retching over the bowl, but nothing came out since I hadn't eaten this morning.

Bracing my hands on the toilet seat, I tried to relax—closing my eyes and taking deep breaths. When I felt like my stomach wouldn't revolt, I retreated to the sink, washed my hands, and rinsed out my mouth before I turned off the water.

Adrian was on his phone when I walked out the front door of my building, a frown pulling at his lips as he hung up while I walked in his direction.

"Was the folder not there?" Shit. I hadn't even made it to my apartment.

"Must be in my bag."

"Where's your coffee?"

Shrugging, I brushed past him and lowered myself into my seat, thankful the coffee smell hadn't lingered. "I was thirsty."

"Yeah, you do like to guzzle the creamy stuff in the morning." He laughed at his own joke, closing the door, and walking around to the driver's side. "Your croissants are in the same place as last time."

Their existence seemed like a bomb waiting to go off. Hesitantly reaching behind his seat, I pinched the top of the paper bag, pulling it across the console and setting it in my lap like it was going to explode if I wasn't careful.

He pulled away from the curb and I carefully unfolded the top, hesitantly leaning forward to sniff the contents. Thankfully, my empty stomach growled, and I reached in to grab one, taking a bite and humming before I relaxed back into my seat.

"That sound is gonna get you into trouble," he laughed, reaching over to place his free hand on my thigh.

Covering my mouth with my hand, I swallowed enough to talk. "Keep it in your pants. We've got a busy day."

"I could always practice knocking you up in the back seat at the next rest stop."

"While that sounds so romantic, gonna pass. We don't have time." And he wouldn't need to practice until the next kid.

Fuck. This pregnancy was clearly messing with my head if I was thinking about having another baby with him while this one was still in the incubation process.

"Just wanted to make sure you knew I'd be willing to put in the effort for you."

"Thanks," I laughed, finally feeling the weight start to lift from my chest. "Nice to know how much you're willing to sacrifice to get the job done."

Now to gather the courage to tell him he'd already accomplished it.

THIRTY-TWO

ISOBEL

NEW YORK

EVAN WAS JUST AS much of a romantic as Chase. And part of me envied her right now. Adrian, Sam, and Chase's brothers had turned the courtyard in the center of The Met Cloisters into a surreal, romantic dream this morning after we'd arrived. Twinkling lights hung from the archways, and a long table set up nearby covered in lush floral arrangements and a variety of ornate platters.

The garden where he intended to propose was filled with summer flowers, the fragrance amazing, but too strong for my stomach, so I'd left the men to finish setting up the lights and rose petals Evan had requested. I waited in the main courtyard, idly flipping through my phone while some of the other guests started arriving and the sun sank in the sky.

"Isobel," Kristine greeted when she joined me, smiling for once. I'd thought she'd be desperate to escape everyone involved with the tour, but she'd readily agreed to the invitation for tonight. She didn't know the hiring committee's decision yet, so I wouldn't spoil it for her, but I was going to miss her when she moved on.

It felt like so much of my life was changing all at once, and I blinked hard when she hugged me, trying to fight off the urge to cry. Fucking hormones.

"Where's the booze?" she asked, looking over her shoulder toward where Sam was standing.

"There's some wine already open on the table. Help yourself. Everyone else should get here soon." I watched as she filled her glass and then walked over to Sam. He placed his hand in the center of her back, leaning down to whisper in her ear. When they straightened, both with wide smiles on their faces, my stomach sank. Looked like they hadn't discussed the phone conference Sam had been on this morning.

But I wasn't getting involved in that mess. I had my own life to figure out first.

"You did good," I whispered, leaning back into Adrian's chest. He'd barely left my side the entire dinner, holding my hand or my thigh when he was near and wrapping me in his arms while we chatted with guests. Evan and Chase had just disappeared, and I knew it was showtime.

Evan's dad quietly gestured for us to follow him through the path that led to the breezeway overlooking the lower gardens, where we'd wait for them to reappear.

"I just did what Evan asked me to."

"Mmhmm," I whispered, knowing that he'd done a lot more than that. He may have had a sometimes-acrimonious relationship with Evan, but it was clear he considered the young author a friend. "Take credit. You did a lot more than he expected and you know it."

Now that the sun had set, the gardens had been transformed into something out of one of Chase's novels. I was thrilled for her, but secretly wondered if that was in store for me. Adrian hadn't mentioned the future of our relationship through all of this. He'd jumped headfirst into volunteering as tribute to get me pregnant, but he'd never brought up marriage.

I wasn't even sure if it was something he wanted. He would be forty-one in a few months and had been a bachelor until this point, with no change in sight.

My story was messier. I knew how it felt to have someone you loved with your whole heart just crush it in their hands and walk away, leaving you to figure out what to do after your divorce. The love I'd felt for Grant was strong for us being so young, but what I felt for Adrian was so different.

Even though he liked to give off the impression he didn't care about people, his actions told an entirely different story. He was a good man, and I was well on my way to falling for him.

We quietly watched while Evan led Chase into the courtyard, her eyes lighting up and filling with tears as he quietly knelt on one knee behind her.

"That could be us," Adrian whispered in my ear, his hand moving to cover my stomach. Butterflies swarmed beneath it, a warm feeling spreading through me as he kissed my temple. "You let me know when you're ready for it, and I'm there."

He hadn't even told me he loved me yet, and I'd been terrified to even think about voicing the depth of my feelings, but his comment was beyond those three little words.

As the people around us cheered and cat-called the newly engaged couple below us, I knew now was the time. Reaching back to cup the side of his face, I turned to look into his eyes.

"I'm pregnant."

He seemed stunned for a moment, his fingers tightening his hold on my stomach, but then he exhaled and loosened his grip. "Seriously?"

Nodding, I tried to keep the tears from escaping my eyes, but as he tilted his head and his filled with moisture, I couldn't keep them from falling.

"Babe," he whispered, tucking his face into the side of neck. His chest heaved as he tried to keep his emotions in check, but he didn't seem upset.

Closing my eyes, I rested my hand on the back of his, letting him process the news.

"Not sure how this happened," he laughed, disbelief clear in his voice.

"Pretty sure you know how it happened," I teased, but I hadn't expected it to happen like this either. "Maybe we need to go buy some lottery tickets since chance seems to be on our side."

"I don't need lottery tickets. I feel like I already won the jackpot."

Despite all the fears that still lingered, I did too.

LEILA HAD BEEN CORRECT. Adrian indeed fucked the shit out of me once we got back to the hotel room in New York. He'd also been surprisingly discreet, not saying anything while we were still at the Cloisters that night.

Three days later—after we'd returned to Boston where he refused to let me out of sight—we were sitting in an exam room with my brand-new obstetrician.

"So," Adrian's voice was light, conversational, but I could tell from the naughty gleam in his eye he was going to say something stupid. He'd learned to read my expressions, but this was one of his I'd been familiar with for years.

"Did you have a question, Mr. O'Neill?"

"Is this something that happens regularly?"

"Pregnancy?" My OB laughed lightly. "Yeah, it happens quite often. My kids wouldn't have gotten braces if people practiced more abstinence or regular use of contraceptives."

"No, I know that happens. We're all one condom break from becoming a parent. Am I right?"

Fortunately, Dr. Reeves looked more amused by Adrian than annoyed. Depending on what he was going to say next, my response might go either way.

"I meant an IUD dislodging itself. Is that common?"

"No," she replied, her eyes briefly flashing to mine. "It's somewhere between a point zero five to eight percent chance of an IUD spontaneously migrating or dislodging. It typically happens during a woman's cycle. And if she doesn't know it happened, it significantly increases the risk of pregnancy within the first month afterward."

"Does the size of her partner impact that?"

"Not typically, but particularly rough sex could affect the placement of the device's strings that would put it at risk for migration or expulsion."

"So it's possible that a well-endowed partner could cause something like this?"

"Very small one, Mr. O'Neill," she laughed. "But it's not out of the realm of possibility."

"A very small one wouldn't have done the job." Adrian leaned toward me, cupping his hand in front of his mouth. I shook my head, squeezing his knee, but it didn't stop the Dickhead from slipping out. "Did you hear that, babe? Your IUD never stood a chance against my massive dick."

"Oh, my God. Just shut up." Part of me wanted to be surprised he'd actually said it. But as my obstetrician laughed loudly at his not so quiet comment, I knew he'd said it to take my mind off the fact this part of my plan hadn't exactly gone how I thought it would.

"Anyway, now that we've got that out of the way, would you like to know the due date of your little one?"

Adrian and I looked at each other before we nodded.

"Looks like you'll be having a baby chick right before Easter this year. He or she will make their appearance on March twentieth."

"Wonder if they'll have a cock-a-doodle-doo?" Adrian snickered, and I smacked him in the stomach with one palm while I covered my face with the other.

"Hutch told me when his ex was pregnant that babies on ultrasounds look like aliens," Adrian mused as we sat side by side on a bench outside our office building. Today was cooler, the shade of the building allowing us to sit outside until we were ready to return from our lunch break despite it being the middle of July.

"Feels pretty alien right now." Looking down at my flat stomach, I tried to imagine it getting bigger, but I also didn't want to let myself think that far ahead.

"How're you feeling? Need me to get you something bland to snack on from the bodega down the street?"

Smiling at him, I cupped his cheek and kissed him softly. He was killin' it at this attentive baby daddy thing. "I'm good for now. But thank you for offering. Hopefully, the ginger ale in my travel mug will be enough to get me through today."

Dr. Reeves had told me that the sudden onset of morning sickness was typical from ten to fifteen weeks, but it'd come in with a vengeance a bit early. If I hadn't told him while we were in New York, Adrian would have figured it out pretty quickly when I woke him up at six am heaving over the toilet the last three days. She'd sent a prescription for an anti-nausea medication to the pharmacy near my apartment building to use as needed, and I had a feeling I'd be needing it.

"If it's any consolation, your tits have been quite impressive the last few weeks," Adrian teased, laying his palm on my stomach. "Wonder how big they'll get by the time the baby's here?"

Rolling my eyes, I leaned into him as his arm wrapped around my back. "You keep letting the Dickhead out and you won't be touching them."

"I thought you liked my dickhead?" he whispered, goosebumps cropping up across my neck as his lips traced behind my ear. "In fact, I'm pretty sure I remember you screaming how much you loved it this weekend, as the headboard dented the wall in our hotel room while you rode me."

"You weren't complaining."

"You know how Dr. Reeves was telling us about possible symptoms during the second trimester?" I had a feeling I knew where this was going. "I think we need to come up with a signal, so I know when you're needing to take the edge off."

"So it's selfless? Nothing for you to gain from the increase in my hormones?"

"I'll selflessly press you up against my office window and fuck the daylights out of you whenever you need it, babe. My body is yours to command."

"Your priorities are clearly in the right place."

"Exactly. Have tah worry about the health and wellbein' of my baby mama. Don't want to leave her miserable and pent up. I'm willin' to work night and day tah make sure she's got what she needs."

"Such a pervert," I laughed, placing my hand atop his resting on my stomach. There was also something about him slipping back into his natural accent when he was saying dirty things in my ear that stirred something entirely different from my nausea.

"You wouldn't like me if I wasn't." And some small part of me agreed with him. His humor, especially the self-deprecating part, had been one of the more endearing traits that attracted me to him in the first place.

"You might possibly be right."

"Of course I am."

Chapter
THIRTY-THREE

ADRIAN

BOSTON

"Come on," Hutch urged as he slid a clear shot glass across the old, cracked countertop in Ma's kitchen—that I'd offered to replace a thousand times. "Out with it. What's goin' on?"

Blowing out a breath, I picked up the glass, knocked it back, and closed my eyes as the bourbon burned its way down my throat. "Isobel's pregnant."

"Oh, fuck. Really? Is it mine?" He laughed, slapping a palm against the side of my arm. "What am I talking about? Of course, it's mine. At least that's what the paternity test will say." Warmth spread through my chest as I looked over at his easy smile, like this didn't change everything. I'd even give him a pass on the smartass paternity comment. "That's awesome, man. Kids are a trip."

I nodded, using my fingers to spin the empty glass while I thought about the course of the last few months. I was excited. The thought of the woman I was pretty much obsessed with carrying my child was a heady feeling. It made me feel strong and virile. And also scared outta my fuckin' mind.

What now? What if she decided she didn't need me now that she'd gotten pregnant? I wasn't even sure if she loved me.

"What's wrong? It's not like you're in high school anymore. We're almost forty-one. I'm honestly surprised you don't have a dozen kids by now."

"I'm not the one that's into free love and spreading my seed around," I laughed, shaking my head at him.

"Hey," he laughed, picking at the label on the liquor bottle. "I keep my shit wrapped up. Unlike someone, apparently."

"She had an IUD, but I guess something happened and... But she'd...*we'd* been looking into her options to have a kid and..."

"Now you're gonna have a baby."

"Yeah, I'm gonna have a baby. *We're* gonna have a baby."

It was the first time I'd said it out loud like that. Not that Is was pregnant, but that I would have a kid. And the idea didn't terrify me—mostly.

"You're not gonna flake out, right? You're gonna do the right thing?"

"Thanks for the vote of confidence, asswipe. Yes, I'm going to do the right thing. I love her. And I'll love this baby, no matter what."

"Cause I'd hate to have to beat your ass if you did something stupid."

"Good luck with that," I chuckled, narrowing my eyes at him. He'd bulked up in the last month or so, and it'd likely be an unfair fight with his combat training.

"Although, I could easily just shave and then I could be Bel's Daddy."

"Shut the fuck up," I growled, narrowing my eyes at my sarcastic asshole brother. "You stay the fuck away from my girlfriend, you pervert."

"You sure that's what she wants?"

"Don't think for one second since confessed a fantasy that she'd be interested in you."

"I'm not tryin' to start a fight here, Ad. I was just yankin' yah chain. I know Isobel wants to be with you. Every time I've seen you two together, she couldn't keep her eyes off you. What happened to teasin' about you being responsible for raising another human being?"

"If you can do it, how hard can it be?"

"I was off getting shot at for half of Pen's childhood. I'm not exactly the model of fatherhood."

"But you've more than made up for it by now. That girl adores you." I just hated that the thing that brought him back to us was getting half his leg blown off.

"That's all you can do. Try to be there for them. I will never regret my time in the service, but you are lucky that you'll get to be there for your kid in all the ways I couldn't be."

"I'm gonna try." All I had to do was convince their mom I was in this for the long haul.

"When are you goin' to tell Ma?"

"Isobel doesn't even know I told you at this point. I just needed to confide in someone."

"Aw, bro, I'm so touched you chose me," he said sarcastically, and I flipped him off.

"Maybe once she's in her second trimester. She's had a few miscarriages before, so I'd hate for something to happen after we start telling people for real."

"You know Ma—and Pops for that matter—are gonna ask if you want the ring."

"I know." Taking a deep breath, I scrubbed my hand over my face. "I don't know if Is ever wants to get married again. Her ex was a dumbass who left some scars."

"Don't wait too long. Pops has been having good days lately. Might be somethin' that'd be good for him to focus on. He'd like knowin' grandma's ring had found someone who deserved it."

Nodding, I sighed. "Once we know the baby is healthy, I'll bring her over to meet everybody. I'm sure Pen will want to meet her, too."

"Pen will be fuckin' stoked to get a cousin. I'll make sure she's here when you guys are ready."

The only problem was that I wasn't sure how ready Isobel was to be an official part of my family.

TIME SEEMED TO DISAPPEAR over the next few months. Isobel was out of town half the time, and I was busy trying to train Sam's replacement after he'd taken a promotion in the Chicago office. He'd been with me so long I'd almost forgotten he was around the same age I was when I'd gotten my first big promotion. Ten years later, I'd been recruited by Vivid, and it'd changed my life. Now I felt like I was always meant to be here.

Even though I felt guilty as fuck that I'd accidentally hired Andrea out from under Isobel, she was a lifesaver. She was organized and had a good eye for detail. It was almost criminal she'd been stuck as an office administrator for the last two years.

"Is there anything else you need me to be doing while you're gone?"

Several people from the office would fly to Minneapolis today to attend Chase and Evan's engagement party. I'd come into the office to make sure my emails were caught up before we left.

Isobel was asked to be a bridesmaid, but I was worried about the timing. She was due in late March and the wedding was tentatively scheduled for Valentine's Day. Her OB had said as long as everything was going well, it wouldn't be a problem to attend, but considering she was still puking her guts out every morning with no end in sight, I wasn't so optimistic.

"Nah, I think we're set."

"How's she doing?" Andrea asked, and I didn't have to guess who she was talking about. With how much time she spent in my office, it was hard to hide Isobel's pregnancy from her for more than a few weeks. Since I had a couch in my office, Isobel had taken naps in here more than once over our lunch break, so she could make it through to the end of the day.

"Still has trouble with the morning sickness, but I think her energy is finally coming back."

"Has she tried ginger chews? A few of my clients when I was an au pair swore by them."

"She hasn't. I'll pick some up for her. We're willing to try anything at this point. She's miserable."

"Is there anything else I can do while you're gone? I don't want you to think I'm slacking off since you'll be gone."

"You're doing great. Give yourself some time to rest over the weekend. I'm sure the next few weeks will be stressful. We've got some submissions to sort through."

She nodded and then fled my office. I quickly finished packing my bags so I could meet Isobel at her place to head to the airport.

THIRTY-FOUR

ISOBEL

MINNEAPOLIS

THE FLIGHT FROM BOSTON had been rough. I'd purposefully booked our seats close to the bathroom, splurging to get seats in first class. Typically, I never sat in first class unless the airline upgraded me because of my newly earned travel status, but I'd felt so terrible lately, it was worth it to have the extra space.

"You feeling better now?" Adrian asked, glancing over at me in the passenger seat of our rental car. His hand flexed on my knee and a rush of warmth spread through me.

"A bit. Brushing my teeth and washing my face at the airport helped. Thank you for those ginger chews. They've been a game changer. But I really want to take a shower and lay down once we check in."

I was definitely at my least sexy—throwing up constantly, losing weight, other parts expanding, exhausted all the time. He'd been a saint, though. When I was in town, he took care of me. Often letting me crash in his office when I was so exhausted the words on my laptop blurred, making sure I got home every night safely and stocking foods he knew I could eat in my office and at both of our places.

The one thing I felt guilty about was we hadn't been intimate in almost a month. My libido was returning, but I was self-conscious that he didn't find me attractive anymore. I didn't want him to feel obligated to because of the baby, but part of me wanted him to initiate things, even if I ended up turning him down. I knew it was fucked up, but with how terrible I'd been feeling, I just wanted to be wanted.

"Whatever you need, babe. I can always go by myself tonight if you're not feeling up to it. Chase and Evan would understand."

"I think I'll be alright. Chase wanted the bridesmaids there so we could officially meet each other."

While we'd only officially told a handful of people, we also hadn't denied the rumors going around at work. There was already speculation that I was pregnant.

"Have you given any thought to going to see your family?"

I sighed, turning to look out the window. To say my family was less than thrilled about my pregnancy would be an understatement. I'd told them after we'd gone to the ultrasound to confirm the heartbeat, and they had expressed their disappointment in our relationship status.

"I can't. They'll come around eventually, but I can't handle their judgment right now. They don't understand why we won't get married."

Adrian was quiet for a few minutes, softly running his thumb across my inner thigh. Neither of us had brought up the subject. I wasn't sure I wanted to get married again, but Adrian would be the only person I'd want.

"We could go visit them at Thanksgiving." I knew he'd wanted to spend the holiday with his family, but the fact he offered to go with me meant a lot.

"I'd much rather spend it with your family."

"Let me know if you change your mind. I'll go with you. You shouldn't have to face that alone."

"I know you would," I answered, trying to hold back my tears. The hormones made me cry at the drop of a hat lately, and Adrian being sweet didn't help that.

"No more tears, babe. You never have to wonder where you stand with me. I'm in this for the long haul."

Except I wasn't sure if he meant only with the baby, or with me. Neither of us had said those three little words. He showed me every day that he might feel the same way I'd come to feel about him. But I was terrified to say it first.

By the time we were pulling up to the hotel, my eyelids were drooping.

"Let's get you to bed."

Glancing at the clock, I noted it was only three o'clock and calculated I'd have at least two hours to sleep before we got ready. Hopefully, that was enough to keep me from looking like a zombie.

"Do you want to wait here while I check in, or...?"

"Already have the room key loaded to my phone," I answered, yawning.

"Let me get the bags then, since you're ahead of the game." Adrian's teasing tone brought a smile to my face. "Since you'll actually let me carry your bags now without busting my balls."

"I rather like those," I quipped. Adrian paused at my wink, his eyes widening as his gaze turned more predatory.

"Noted. Glad you still enjoy them even after they've done their job."

Waiting until he opened my car door, I took his hand and followed as he led us into the hotel. He carried both our bags for the weekend effortlessly in his other hand.

When we reached the reception desk, he caged me in against the counter while he talked to the desk clerk. As his chest pressed into my back, I suddenly had visions of him fucking me against the shower wall.

When we entered the elevators, he kept glancing at me out of the corner of his eye, assessing me in a way he hadn't done for weeks. "What has you blushing so hard over there?"

Which only made my blush deepen, my entire body suddenly feeling like it was on fire.

"Nothing."

"Bullshit," he laughed, letting go of my hand to pull me into his side. "You're thinking something naughty over here, and I want to know what it is, so I can make it happen."

His rough whisper had me panting, suddenly desperate to rip his clothes off.

"Somehow I don't think you're worried about laying down so much as you are getting laid."

"Stop," I whined, shuddering as his warm breath coasted across my neck. "I just threw up an hour ago. You can't find that sexy."

"Babe, you threw up because you're carrying my baby. What's sexier than that?" I could think of about a million things, but I wouldn't tell him that. "I've been dying to touch you for weeks, but I didn't want to pressure you because you've been so tired."

"I thought you didn't want me." Fuck. I would not cry again.

"You've got about two minutes to get undressed and naked in that shower before I join you. And I'll remind you of how much I want you. Multiple times if I need to."

Adrian pressed his hand into the middle of my back when we reached our floor, walking calmly behind me.

"Why aren't you hurrying me?" I laughed, looking back at him over my shoulder.

"Just enjoying the scenery." His eyes were fixated on my ass as he talked, slowly running the tip of his tongue along his bottom lip. It was reminiscent of how he'd teased me the last time we'd been in a hotel together, even though we'd been in separate rooms back in Maine.

My fingers fumbled on the door handle as I recalled what it'd felt like to be on my knees for him the first time, and how ravenous he'd been when he followed me to my room afterward.

"You coming?" I asked, holding the door open for him.

He leaned in, wrapping his arm around my waist and pulling me into his chest. "Not yet. But you're about to be. Get in that fuckin' shower, now."

My morning sickness was nowhere to be found as I threw my purse on the couch, quickly pulling off my clothes and underwear while Adrian casually sat on the end of the bed watching.

"Two minutes," he warned, nodding toward the bathroom door.

My pulse raced as I escaped inside, closing the door but leaving it unlocked, and pulling open the glass door to the shower. Another one of the perks of my job. Hotel upgrades. The mini suites did not disappoint with a large, walk-in tiled shower with two shower heads mounted on the walls and another handheld one below.

Wetting my hair, I reached for the hotel shampoo, quickly lathering it through my hair before I rubbed myself down with body wash.

The door opened while I was rinsing my face. Large hands cupped my sensitive breasts, and a warm chest pressed into my back. "Such a good girl," he murmured, softly running his thumbs across my nipples. His touch burned, but the throbbing between my legs made the mild discomfort worth it.

"Oh God," I panted, leaning back against him while his hands roamed.

"So fuckin' wet," he growled in my ear. "I don't think you've ever been this drenched. Is the thought of me being inside you again getting you this excited?"

"Yes," I hissed when his fingertips passed over my clit, causing me to buck my hips back. He was hard against my ass, and it made me desperate to feel him. It'd felt like torture every night he wrapped himself around me but didn't try to take things further.

"We'll get there." His voice was a low whisper as he reached forward, pulling the handheld wand off the wall and turning the dial to increase the water pressure. "Want to try something first."

He turned it toward us, directing the spray toward my chest first, making me jump as it assaulted my breasts with a thumping rhythm. "Shh, it's okay. I'll make it all feel better."

"Please," I begged, desperate for him to do something to soothe this ache.

"Let's see how this feels a bit lower."

Adrian slowly lowered the spray. My stomach contracted at the sensation, but when he replaced his fingers with it, I moaned desperately while it pulsed against my clit. "Fuck."

He didn't let up, holding the showerhead inches from my pussy as his other hand toyed with my nipple. This was something we'd never done, and I suddenly wanted to hit up a hardware store to buy a new showerhead for my apartment.

"Do you like that?" he asked as I bucked against him, his hard body keeping me from moving very far. But every time my ass pressed into him, he'd groan, his dick throbbing against my lower back.

"I..."

"That's it, babe. Let go. It's been so long since you came, I bet it's going to feel so fuckin' amazing to get all that pent up tension out."

And he was absolutely right as the insistent pulsing of the water sent me over the edge, my moans echoing off the tiled walls surrounding us. Once he could tell I was sated, he finally pulled the shower head away, hanging it back up before he spun me in his arms.

"Lean against the wall and pull my hair while I make you come again with my mouth. Then I'm going to press you against these tiles and make you come all over my cock."

While I wasn't sure I could come again so soon, Adrian quickly proved me wrong. He'd made me see stars with his hands and mouth before making good on his promise to make me come again while he held me against the wall and bounced me on his cock. He groaned so loud when he came inside me, that I was sure the entire floor heard it. I was too relaxed to care, passing out within minutes after he'd dried me off and tucked me into bed.

After that weekend, I'd been insatiable. Attacking Adrian at any available opportunity. He'd even gotten his chance to bend me over my desk one night when we'd stayed late.

We were all over each other, enjoying my newly surging hormones, but I was still puking all the time, finally resulting in me needing to stop by the clinic for weekly IV infusions of electrolytes and fluids to keep me from being hospitalized.

Dr. Reeves wasn't worried so much about the baby, but as my belly grew, my exhaustion started catching up with me again.

"Are you excited about this?" I asked Adrian for about the millionth time in the last forty-eight hours.

"Of course, I'm excited, babe. We get to see what it looks like now that it'll look like an actual baby."

"And you won't be disappointed if it's not what you want?"

"Babe," he sighed, leaning in to kiss my temple. "I'm gonna love this baby no matter what gender it is."

Nodding, I acknowledged what he'd been telling me for weeks, but I was still unsure why I'd had these fleeting feelings of unease. Personally, I was more worried about the baby. Worried that there was something wrong. I was so sick all the time that I had a hard time believing it wasn't influencing its development.

Before I could start on a downward spiral, we were called back, ironically led into the ultrasound room they'd confirmed I was indeed pregnant in.

"Deep breaths, babe. Just focus on right now," Adrian said, pulling me into a hug after we were left alone. "This baby already has an awesome mama, and I feel so blessed that I get to be its dad."

Tears pricked in the corners of my eyes, and he gently brushed them away, leaning forward to kiss me softly before he helped me get settled on the exam table. Sometimes I felt like I didn't deserve him, but I didn't want to think about things changing between us.

THIRTY-FIVE

ADRIAN

BOSTON

Isobel's clammy hand shook in mine while we waited for the ultrasound tech to join us, and I hated I couldn't do more to calm her fears about everything. This pregnancy had been much harder than either of us had anticipated, but I wouldn't change a second of it because it'd brought us so much closer.

"Let's take a peek at this little one, shall we?" The tech that joined us a few moments later was very upbeat, and it seemed to help settle Isobel's nerves a bit as she tucked a towel into the top of her skirt and squirted the gel onto her exposed stomach. "Have we talked about whether we'd like to know the gender today? Since you're twenty-one weeks along, we should be able to tell if the baby cooperates."

Even though I wanted to know, I'd follow Is's lead on this one. What I'd told her was the truth. I didn't have a preference either way. My brother loved being a girl dad, and I was a little terrified to end up with a boy who'd be as much of a shit as I was growing up, but either would be good. Because it'd be a physical manifestation of my feelings for their mother.

"I'd like to know," Isobel said quietly, squeezing my hand.

We'd heard the heartbeat a few times, but there was something entirely different about seeing that little flutter on the screen. Seeing physical proof your child was alive and growing was more intense than I'd expected.

"Wow," Isobel breathed while the tech moved the wand around, taking pictures and measurements as she went, narrating the entire time. I was more focused on watching Isobel's reactions, my heart swelling as every bit of awe I felt played out across her face as well.

We'd spent months dancing around it, but I loved her so much it physically hurt to watch her struggle. And this brief reprieve from the hard parts had my confession on the tip of my tongue.

"Looks like our little one isn't shy. Are you ready for the big reveal?"

My heart pounded as I glanced between the screen and Isobel, nodding because I was too choked up to answer.

"While the baby is measuring a little on the large side for your date of conception." I fought with the urge to hurry her along, impatient to find out what our baby was so we could start talking about names. "She looks perfectly healthy. Congratulations, you're having a girl."

Isobel's eyes watered as she nodded, her lip quivering as she absorbed the news that we were going to have a little girl in a few short months. Blinking back tears, I leaned over, wrapping my arm around her back and kissing the side of her head.

"I'm going to print out some pictures for you to take home and then give you some privacy. I'll forward the images along to your OB for your next appointment."

Isobel clung to my arm as the tech let herself out of the room, tears streaming down her cheeks as soon as the door clicked shut.

"A girl," she whispered, her hand settling on her gently rounded stomach that seemed to grow every day at this point. "We're having a girl."

"We are," I whispered, kissing her cheek and letting my lips linger against her warm skin. "And I hope she grows up to be as fierce and gorgeous as her mama."

She reached up, threading her fingers through my hair to hold my head to her cheek while her chest shook, and I hoped these were happy tears. Her emotions had been up and down the last few weeks, and I hated she was away for most of it. It had to be isolating for her to be traveling while she was like this, but I'd been so busy I couldn't go with her even if I wanted to.

"Adrian, I..." Her voice cracked as it trailed off, and I knew I needed to be brave enough for both of us to confess how I felt about her.

"I love you, Is," I whispered against her cheek, my hand joining hers, my thumb sweeping across her skin. I hadn't been able to feel the baby kick yet, but I was looking forward to it. Being able to witness my baby girl moving and growing inside her.

Isobel whimpered, turning toward me, and staring into my eyes as her breath caught. I knew it was scary for her to confess her feelings for me, but I knew she felt the same way. "I love you too, Ad. So much it hurts sometimes."

Nodding, I cupped her cheek, kissing her softly until she melted into my embrace. She never had to worry about how I felt. I'd been hers for longer than she realized.

"Dude, where have you been lately?" Hutch grumbled, settling onto the barstool next to me. Pops was in the back room of the bar with his usual poker buddies. Hutch had been keeping a closer eye on him recently, so I'd made the trip out to keep him company since Isobel had flown out for work again this morning.

"Trying to recuperate."

He frowned, turning his stool to face me, wincing when his knee brushed against the bar. "What are you recuperating from? Being a fuckin' cake eater who sits in his office with a view all day?"

"Yeah, yeah, laugh it up." Placing my elbows on the bar, I let my face drop into my palms, squeezing my eyes shut.

"Seriously? Are you okay?"

"I'm fuckin' exhausted. Why didn't you tell me it was like this?"

"I'm totally lost here." He placed his hand on my shoulder, and I turned my head to face him.

"I know it's been a while, but was Lena a little bit unhinged during her second trimester?"

A look of relief crossed his face and was replaced with a naughty grin. "Those hormones giving you a run for your money?"

"Fuck, man. She's still puking her guts out every morning, but then she brushes her teeth, and she practically mauls me. I don't know if I can keep up." My brother's shoulders shook as he tried to hold back a laugh. "I think I'm chafed down there. There's nothing left. My dick lets out a poof of smoke whenever I come. Pretty sure if she was still in town a little flag would pop out of the end saying *bang* like in those old kids shows Pops used to make us watch with the fucked-up clowns."

Hutch wasn't even trying to hold back, clutching his stomach as he let out a bellow of a laugh. A few of the regulars looked over at us, but quickly returned to the basketball game on the television. "Pretty sure those flags weren't coming out of a clown's dick during those shows."

"It's not funny."

"It's pretty fuckin' funny," he chuckled. "Not that I'm picturing your dick right now, but the imagery of a little flag popping out the end with you passed out in the middle of the bed is killin' me."

"She's gonna kill me. My little girl is going to grow up without a father because he's going to be fucked to death before she's even born. I didn't know a pregnant woman could be this horny. I look in her direction and suddenly she's sending me naughty text messages and pictures of her cleavage. I seriously don't know what to do right now."

"I do." He squeezed my shoulder. "You get as much as you can handle right now. Because after that baby is born, the memories of the next few months are gonna have to tide you over when the only thing you're fuckin' is your own damn hand."

"She took four vibrators with her on her trip. Four. I watched her put four fucking goddamn vibrators in her carry-on. She had more vibrators than pairs of shoes."

"Get her to FaceTime you. That'd be pretty hot."

Smacking him, I sighed before I reached for my beer. I'd only have one since I'd need to drive him and Pops back to Ma's before I drove home later. But I needed a fuckin' drink.

"When is she planning to use them? She even took a tiny one that fits inside her panties. What's she gonna do, use it at work?"

"Again... Convince her to FaceTime you. And if you don't do that, I'll text her and she can FaceTime me."

"Fuck you, asshole. You are not going to watch my pregnant girlfriend get herself off with the four fucking vibrators she took with her."

"Wonder if she can use all four at the same time," he mused, clearly enjoying my misery. "What kinds did she take?"

"Oh, my God. I don't even know why I'm talking to you about this."

"You're the one who brought it up."

"Maybe once she gets back, she'll let you use the toys on her if your dick needs a break."

"I already have," I sighed, knowing that things had gotten a little spicier than normal before she packed for her trip. "And somehow, when I was fucking her last night, I ended up with a vibrator in my ass."

Hutch lost it, doubling over and slapping his hand on the bar top while I shook my head. If it was happening to anyone else, I would have been laughing, too. But I was too fuckin' tired.

"And? How'd that go?"

"You really want to know if I enjoyed having a little purple vibrator up my ass? Isn't that like too much information or something?"

"Since when have we had clear boundaries with each other about this kinda stuff? You know I like to fuck people's wives with them watching. This is a little bit tamer than that."

"Shh," I tried to quiet him, so he didn't broadcast that to the entire bar, but when I looked around, no one was paying any attention to us. "I'm pretty sure I blacked out and came to with her on top of me, playing with her tits."

"Sounds like a fun night to me," he laughed.

"At least I have the next three days to rest before she's back in Boston."

"Electrolytes, my brother. Go stock up on electrolytes so Is doesn't come looking for the better-looking twin to take care of her when you can't."

"I hate you."

"Yeah, I get that a lot. Doesn't sound as convincing coming from you as it does from my teenager." His face sobered as he looked at me. "How wild is that? Penny is going to have two genetic half-siblings born within a few months of each other."

"Yeah, I'd appreciate it if you didn't tell your daughter that my daughter is her sibling. That's not something we need her repeating around the neighborhood. You've got the gossips following your every move as it is. And I doubt a twelve-year-old would understand the nuances of twin genetics."

"The offer still stands if you'd like me to step in and take over as Bel's Daddy."

My middle finger was the only response I could muster as my head fell to the surface of the bar, the cool lacquered wood doing nothing to help my fatigue.

ISOBEL

BOSTON

THANKSGIVING HAD BEEN LOW key this year. With all the travel I'd done, I had no desire to return to Iowa to spend time with my family.

They didn't seem to understand that my career was my life, and while things had now changed with my pregnancy, I had no intention of staying home like my mom and sisters did with their kids. That would never be in the cards for me. I liked my job too much to give up everything I'd worked for.

Some people might think that was selfish, and there were countless women who were amazing stay-at-home moms, but I didn't expect being one of them. That didn't mean I wouldn't try to be the best mom to this baby, but she would never be encouraged to give up her dreams to fit into some antiquated female stereotype. She should be able to make her own choices without judgment. Which was why I was thankful Adrian had never even brought it up for me to stay home longer than my planned maternity leave.

We had accepted that we'd both continue to work full time and have her downstairs at the corporate daycare during the day. He hadn't even asked me if I would consider something different. The one time it came up, he'd taken my opinion and wholeheartedly supported me. He'd grown up in a household where his mother worked full-time to provide for their family, and he'd never resented her or questioned her decisions.

"Hey." Think of the handsome devil and he would appear—wearing a suit, no less. "Do you need to go home to change before tonight?"

Closing my eyes, I scrunched my nose and then slowly blinked, trying to refocus my eyes after staring at a screen for so long. "Huh?"

"Are you wearing that to the cocktail hour?" Glancing down at my casual blouse and Adrian's favorite white skirt that barely fit despite having a stretchy waistband, I frowned.

"No, but I don't need to go home. My dress is in the garment bag on the back of my door." Adrian had been at an early morning meeting with an author when I needed to come into work, so I'd just taken an Uber instead of waiting for him to get done. I felt bad enough I was relying on him for transportation to and from work every day.

He adamantly refused to let me give him any money for gas, and he got cranky when I didn't ask him first if I needed to go somewhere. I knew his heart was in the right place because he wanted to take care of me in any way he could, but sometimes the quiet to gather my thoughts before a hectic day at work was nice.

"Need some help?" he asked, stepping a few feet further into my office and reaching back to close the door. He moved to the blinds, twisted the rod to close them, and turned off the overhead lights. The click of the lock was last.

"Not the kind of help you'd clearly like to provide," I laughed as he grabbed the garment bag off the door and unzipped it while he headed in my direction.

"I'm only here to please my lady," he chuckled, draping the dress over the chair and beckoning me to stand with a crook of his finger.

"You just want to reenact a few weeks ago." While he'd threatened to bend me over my desk multiple times as a joke in the past, I may have lured him into my office a few weeks ago under false pretenses to do just that. My hormones started going haywire after twenty-three weeks and now that I was at twenty-seven weeks, things had settled back to as normal as they could get with my growing midsection.

"While I'd love to take you up on that, we need to leave in a half hour. And you know Sloane would not be impressed if we're late."

In my new capacity as her right-hand woman, Sloane had invited me—and Adrian by extension—to attend a holiday cocktail party followed by a dinner held every year for the region's publishing industry professionals. Vivid was the host this year, so she expected the attendance of several of the genre heads in the editing department.

"Think she'd be alright with us cutting out early after dinner is over?" While I appreciated the opportunity to network, I was also asleep by nine pm most nights. That was true before I got pregnant, and even more so now.

"We'll see how it goes, but I doubt we're getting out of there until she leaves."

"That's what I was afraid of," I sighed, reaching for the zipper on the back of my skirt. Adrian's eyes followed every movement as I wiggled my hips and it dropped to the floor. "Why are you staring at me like that?"

"I think you know why," he murmured, walking around to stand behind me and using his fingers to unfasten the small button on my blouse that rested at the base of my neck. "I love seeing you like this."

Cupping my belly, I arched my back and let out a heavy breath. "I'm huge. And we still have twelve weeks left. I'm going to need my own area code by the time she's born. Don't even get me started on the swollen ankles. Wearing heels makes me want to cry."

"Is, babe, stop," he chuckled, wrapping his arms around me to palm my stomach. "This is not an I love you to appease you right now. This is an I love you, period, full stop. These curves are just a bonus."

"You don't have to flatter me. I know this isn't what you're attracted to. It's fine. Just..."

"Look at me," he growled, cutting me off and pulling me back into his chest. His strong hand cupped my jaw and turned my head so I could look back at him. "That's better. Stop thinking that gaining a few pounds or your hips spreading—because you're carrying my fucking baby—are things I'm not 100 percent here for. You are still sexy as fuck."

Adrian grasped my hand and pressed it to the front of his suit pants. "You still make me hard when I think about being with you. It's you. It's not a number on a scale in a doctor's office. I'm attracted to you. I want you."

"But what happens if I never find me again once she's here? What if the me you fell in love with is gone?" That's what I was afraid of most. There were no guarantees he'd stick around for me after she was born. I knew he'd never step away from his daughter, but I wasn't owed anything. Even a ring didn't mean security, not that he'd ever brought up marriage again after New York.

"She's not. She's right here with me. I'm going to keep loving her as long as she lets me. And I'm going to do everything in my power to show her I find her to be the sexiest, smartest, most sensual woman I know. I'm still in awe of the fact that she lets me be near her every day."

Unbidden tears rose to my eyes, and I nodded. "Okay."

"Damn straight it's okay. Now step forward so I can get this blouse off and that dress wrapped around these curves. I've got a sexy girlfriend to show off."

Raising my arms above my head, he pulled the material up, carefully freeing my hair before he threw it toward my desk. His large hands flattened on either side of my belly, and he tucked his face into my neck while his thumbs rubbed softly against my skin.

She stirred and the familiar butterflies floated in my belly as our little girl wiggled, making her presence known. It was crazy that she was already over a pound. That might have been one bonus of being considered a geriatric pregnancy—I had 3D ultrasounds scheduled every four weeks.

"There she is," Adrian murmured against my neck, his hand tracing across my skin to follow her movements.

"We're going to be late if I don't get dressed," I whispered, hating that I was breaking the sweet moment with his daughter, but we needed to get moving. I knew I'd need to pee at least once before we drove across downtown to the restaurant.

Kissing my neck, he stepped away, grabbing my dress and helping me wrap it around my back before he fastened the ties at my waist. This dress showed a bit more cleavage than I was comfortable with right now, but his eyes had lit up when I tried it on at the maternity boutique two blocks away from the office a few days ago.

After I'd put my coat on—that I couldn't button anymore—he grabbed my shoulders, bending down slightly to look into my eyes. "You are going to go in there tonight and show how much of a boss babe you are. Don't let being tired or self-conscious diminish your shine. You deserve everything you have earned and never doubt it."

As I followed Adrian out my office door, I silently sent thanks to whatever cosmic forces aligned to make sure we ended up together. I never expected it, and definitely not with him, but Adrian just very well may be the love of my life.

"CAN I GET YOU a water, babe?" Adrian asked, placing his hand in the center of my back. Shaking my head, I smiled when he leaned in and kissed my cheek before he retreated.

Things had gotten crazy once we arrived at the restaurant, the cocktails portion of the party already in full swing. Sloane had almost immediately dragged me off to introduce me to people, and Adrian had kept busy talking to other editors he knew across the room.

That didn't mean he wasn't watching me like a hawk, periodically stepping in behind me and handing me a glass of water before he disappeared again. He hadn't once tried to insert himself into conversations he hadn't been invited to, and I hadn't realized how empowering that would feel. He was letting me spend the night doing the thing I loved most—talking about books and publishing—without trying to steal the attention for himself.

"Adrian seems to be keeping a pretty close eye on you tonight," one of the publishing execs at a rival publisher mused as Adrian walked away.

Sloane cut in before I could respond. "Mr. O'Neill has an excellent track record of being very attentive to things he's passionate about."

"Maybe that's why he turned down my job offer six months ago," he casually commented, and my eyebrows drew together. Adrian had never said a word about it. I wasn't sure if that was because he didn't trust me, or because he'd never considered leaving Vivid. "Now I can see maybe there was something else keeping him in his current position. It really is too bad when people let personal relationships cloud their professional decisions."

Sloane growled, not loud enough to be heard, but I knew she was holding back from laying into this jackass. Maybe Adrian hadn't considered the offer because this guy was an even bigger dick than people around the office thought Adrian was. "On that interesting note, I believe they're flagging everyone down to get dinner started. It was as lovely as it usually is to talk to you, Chip."

The man smiled, lifting his drink in my direction before he walked away. Sloane gripped my elbow, halting my movements as she leaned over. "Adrian turned it down because the offer was shit and he has much more responsibility and freedom at Vivid. Don't start thinking he stalled his career for personal reasons. I knew about the offer and matched the salary they were offering him."

Nodding, I sighed, relieved that he hadn't passed something up to stay close to me.

"Seriously, put it out of your head. It's in the past, and I'm sure he had other things on his mind at the time. Which he should have, considering..." she trailed off, gesturing at my stomach.

"What are we whispering about over here?" Adrian asked as he stepped up behind me, placing a hand on my hip.

"Just how Chip tried to poach you and insinuated that you stayed at Vivid to stay near the colleague you knocked up." My eyes widened as she blurted it out, but Adrian started laughing, his chest shaking against my back. Then I realized he hadn't hidden it from me because he was trying to keep it a secret—it just wasn't something he'd ever considered seriously.

"God, he's such a fuckin' ass. Maybe I didn't consider his offer because my boss would have been an egomaniacal sexist jerkoff. Although I appreciated the pay bump. Maybe I should try to get poached more often."

"Glad to know I'm a better supervisor than Chip. Not that it sets the bar that high. Anyway, I'll see the two of you at the office on Monday. I'm planning to take off after the speeches are over."

Sloane walked away, and I turned in Adrian's arms, grasping the plackets on his suit jacket as I looked up at him. Since I'd given up on high heels, our height difference was even more pronounced lately.

"You could have told me."

He smiled, leaning down to kiss my nose, pulling me closer with a hand on the center of my back. "It was the same week we found out you were pregnant. You were freaked out enough and I honestly never even considered it. I'm right where I want to be."

"I love you," I whispered.

He murmured the affectionate words back and his hand slid down my back to grab my ass, tucking his face into my neck. "Maybe your idea of disappearing was a good one."

Before I could agree and convince him to play hooky, a low voice from beside us sent a chill up my spine.

"Isobel, is that you?"

Adrian pulled back, tilting his head and glancing at the man standing a few feet away before giving me a questioning look.

"Oh, uh... I didn't know you were back in Boston," I stuttered as Adrian shifted to stand beside me, wrapping a protective arm around my back. My ex still worked for a local magazine, but he'd gone remote when he'd relocated to Colorado. Too bad he and his new family didn't stay there.

"Yeah, we moved back a few weeks ago. Trina's residency was over in Denver, and she got hired to take over pediatrics at a clinic near Cambridge."

"That's..." I wracked my brain, trying to recall if I knew his yoga instructor was a physician.

"She's at home with the baby right now. Lei told me you knew about the adoption and everything." I hated he was using my best friend to keep tabs on me.

"She did. That's great. Happy for you two."

He nodded, the conversation stalling. Adrian squeezed my waist and extended his hand toward Grant. "Adrian O'Neill. I'm Isobel's fiancé."

My eyes widened as he claimed me with a title we'd never discussed, but as Grant's face fell, I didn't bother to correct him. "I didn't know you were involved with anyone."

"Well, neither of us felt the need to notify people who are firmly in our past. It's kind of tacky to broadcast that stuff all over social media. The only people who need to know about the important milestones of our lives are still actively involved in it." Adrian's wrist flexed, clearly squeezing hard before letting go of Grant's hand. "How do you know Is? The only ex she's told me about is her ex-husband. But he was an ass who threw away this stunning creature, so... can't say I'm sorry he's out of the picture."

"I'm the ass," Grant replied sheepishly. "Sounds like Isobel has told you some stories about me. But you know there are two sides to every relationship and she..."

Adrian held up his hand, stopping Grant before he said anything else. "I'm gonna stop you right there. The only other thing either of us needs to say to you is thank you. If you hadn't been incapable of behaving like a real man, we wouldn't be welcoming this baby in three months."

"Is, can we...?"

"No," I interrupted, reaching down to clasp Adrian's hand. He squeezed it back, letting me finally get closure with my past. "I would say it was nice catching up with you, Grant. But I can't because you're still as much of a selfish asshole as you were over a decade ago. I'm sorry I ever tied my self-worth to how you treated me, but I've found someone who understands what it's like to be a partner. I'm not interested in investing any of my time into worrying about what people with the emotional maturity of a gnat think of me."

Grant's eyes widened as I took a breath and prepared to really give him a piece of my mind. Adrian could tell I was about to lose my shit and wrapped his arm around me, laying the final blow. "See ya later, cunt... I mean Grant."

Adrian pulled me to his side, steering me toward the exit of the restaurant, my heart beating out of my chest as I realized what I'd just said.

"Oh my God," I gasped. Adrian grabbed our coats from the coat check and helped me into mine before he tugged me out the door. "What did I just..."

But Adrian stopped me, pulling me around the corner and backing me into the bricks on the side of the building.

His mouth covered mine, and he kissed me desperately, thrusting his tongue into my mouth while his hands grabbed my ass and pulled me tightly against him.

"You stood up for yourself, and you were fucking amazing," he panted against my lips when we separated. "I fuckin' love you, babe."

"But..."

"Nope." He shook his head, reaching up to push my hair behind my ear. "No second guessing putting that asshat in his place. He was your past, but he's never going to be a part of our future."

"I love you," I whispered, leaning into his warm embrace.

He wrapped his arms around me, rocking us from side to side. One of his hands drifted to the side of my stomach and he looked down between us. "Your mama is a badass little one."

I laughed as she kicked him, tears gathering in my eyes when his met mine. "Take me home."

"Oh, you're gonna get it tonight, Isobel. Gonna fuck the thoughts of that man out of your mind for the last fuckin' time."

THIRTY-SEVEN

ISOBEL

MINNEAPOLIS

CHRISTMAS HAD COME AND gone the next week, with both Adrian and I spending the holidays with his family. I'd FaceTime'd my parents and my sisters on Christmas Day, but judging from the looks they'd given my ever-expanding midsection the entire call, I knew they still weren't thrilled with my decisions. I honestly didn't have the energy to give a fuck anymore. If they wanted to screw up the opportunity to be in my daughter's life from the beginning, I wouldn't stop them.

Pops had been teary eyed when he saw how big I'd gotten, and I hoped he'd continue to have good days so he could remember meeting his great-granddaughter in a few months.

Adrian's mother had been excited enough for everyone, politely asking to touch my belly before she cradled it in her hands and cooed at her granddaughter. It was one of the few times I was in the same room as Adrian and he wasn't touching me in some way.

When we watched television in the evenings, his hand was on my belly, or he was lying with his head in my lap whispering things to her I couldn't hear. I wanted to be annoyed that he was constantly touching me, but it was fricking adorable.

Other people touching me hadn't been so welcomed. I wasn't sure why people thought they had the right to touch pregnant women without their permission, but I'd held my tongue more than I'd have liked to over the last month.

I was days from being 36-weeks pregnant, and while Sloane had been amazing about letting me do a lot of my work remotely from my office instead of going to the other branches, I was just uncomfortable. Traveling was exhausting, but Dr. Reeves saw no reason I couldn't make one last trip over

Valentine's Day for Chase and Evan's wedding. Adrian wasn't thrilled with the idea, but I just wanted to do something that made me feel normal right now.

My morning sickness had turned into terrible heartburn, and I was convinced the baby would come out with hair down her back at this rate. The only question that wouldn't be answered until she graced us with her presence was if she'd get my fairer Scandinavian locks or Adrian's dark hair. But for all we knew, we might end up with a ginger since Adrian's Irish roots run deep.

Groaning, I tried to shift my hips toward the side of the bed to push myself upright, but there was no way I was getting up by myself.

"You alright, babe?" Adrian asked, his voice groggy as he placed his hand in the middle of my back.

"I need to pee." My voice was a broken whisper as I tried again to push myself up from the mattress. "Can you help me?"

"Of course." He didn't hesitate, scooting closer so he could sit up behind me and help maneuver me into a sitting position on the edge of the bed.

"You sure you're feeling alright? Do you need me to get you some water?"

"Just need to sit for a minute." My side ached from the pressure of my belly, and I winced as I reached my arms above my head with a yawn. I was enormous, and I still had a month to go. The doctor kept insisting that it was a good thing and meant she was growing, but I was tired of being an incubator. Being thirty-eight and pregnant was not for the faint of heart.

"Do I need to help you to the bathroom?"

"I'm okay." Sighing, I closed my eyes and tried to conjure the energy to stand. Adrian was constantly trying to anticipate what I needed, and I loved he was being such a huge part of this journey, but I felt like such a burden. At least I hadn't been placed on bed rest, or I would have completely fallen apart. "You can go back to sleep. I know it's early."

Huffing, I pushed my hands against the mattress, slowly rising to my feet. Blood rushed to my head, and I braced my hand on the bottom of my belly as I regained my equilibrium. I'd been getting vertigo when I stood up for days, but my blood pressure was still normal. My doctor had made me travel with both portable blood pressure and sugar monitors. Since I was technically still at moderate risk, I hadn't complained.

After doing my business, I washed my hands and stared at myself in the hotel bathroom mirror. Despite my exhaustion, now that I wasn't throwing up all the time, I looked more like myself. My hair was thick and shiny, my eyes looked tired, but my cheeks had filled back out.

"You alright?" Adrian asked, appearing behind me and leaning against the door frame. Since I'd traveled so much over the last seven months, he'd spent our time apart in the gym, and I hated him a little bit for looking even more fit than he'd been when everything started between us.

Physical intimacy had been difficult the last few weeks, but Adrian had taken it all in stride, taking the edge off by going down on me instead of pushing for sex. The surge of hormones that'd made me insatiable only weeks ago were overrun by my physical discomfort.

"Just trying to muster up the energy to shower and figure out how to shave my legs."

He chuckled, stepping in close and placing his hand on my belly before he leaned in to kiss my neck. I shivered, goosebumps cropping up along my back. As his lips became more insistent, our daughter made her presence known, happily rolling and kicking her father's hand. "Want me to do it?"

"Do what?" I asked, leaning back into his warm embrace.

"Shave you."

My eyes met his in the mirror, and my breath stuttered at the naked desire I saw. While I felt the least sexy I'd felt in my entire life, the way he looked at me gave me butterflies. "You'd do that?"

"Do you really have to ask that, Is? I've spent the last six months trying to make sure you're comfortable and have everything you need. Why wouldn't I shave your legs?"

"Okay," I whispered, leaning forward to grab my razor out of my toiletries bag and pressing it into his hand. "I forgot my shaving gel, but..."

"I'll use mine. Then you can smell like me. Shower first?"

Nodding, I let him undress me, then he took his clothes off. My heart beat faster as I watched him lean into the shower to turn on the water. He held out his hand, helping me step over the threshold of the glass door, and into the warm spray of the water.

I didn't even have to ask for help. Adrian pulled my shampoo off the shelf and massaged it into my scalp before he turned to me and ran his fingers through my hair to rinse it clean.

By the time he was done, I was more relaxed, my earlier discomfort fading away.

"Ready?" he asked, reaching around me to turn off the water after he'd cleaned himself.

"You sure you still want to do this?"

He chuckled, grasping my chin in his hand and tilting my head toward him. "You're going to have to let me take care of you one of these days without thinking I don't want to be doing it." His other hand cupped the side of my belly. "If you hadn't noticed, I'm a bit obsessed with you."

"Not sure I understand why," I sighed, closing my eyes to escape his intense stare.

"Because you're fucking amazing. You still love me even when I'm being an asshole, and you look insanely sexy with my baby growing inside you."

"Agree to disagree with that last one."

"Yes, we fuckin' will," he said, shifting his hand to grasp mine and pull it toward him. Placing it on his cock, he groaned quietly, and I felt my cheeks heat when I felt how hard he was. "If I didn't think you were sexy as fuck, I wouldn't be hard as a fuckin' rock right now."

My hand closed around his length, pulling up and eliciting a hiss from him, but he stalled my movements, moving it away. "Don't you want me to..." I trailed off as he pushed the shower door open and grabbed a towel off the nearby shelf.

"You're not distracting me from what we should be doing right now. If we have time after, then you can touch my cock all you want. Right now, I'm going to get on my knees and take care of you." As he noticed my smirk, he shook his head. "Shaving first. Making you scream later."

He helped dry me off, wrapping a towel around my shoulders before he reached out to grab one for himself. I felt like I had a ticket to a private peep show as I unabashedly watched him dry off, his hard cock disappearing as he finally wrapped the towel around his waist.

Reaching up, I tucked a wet curl of his hair back, my fingers lingering on the side of his face. "Thank you for loving me so much."

He nodded, leaning in, but stopping millimeters before his lips met mine. His voice was a whisper, but his words brought tears to my eyes. "It's effortless, babe. I'm the one who should be thankful you've let me into your heart. I love you so much, Is."

Adrian kissed me gently and leaned back, helping me step out of the shower ahead of him before he grabbed two more plush towels from the shelf. He laid one on the floor in front of the counter and placed the other on the edge of the waist height vanity.

"Up we go," he said with a smile, reaching down to cup the back of my thighs before he hoisted me, and settled me onto the towel at the edge of the countertop.

"You're going to throw your back out lifting me," I joked, but he narrowed his eyes, clearly not liking the way I talked about myself. It was hard not to feel self-conscious when I weighed twenty pounds more than I used to.

"I could fuck you standing up right now and not break a sweat, so don't worry about me hurting myself by lifting you up to the counter. Now sit back and be a good girl while I cover you in creamy white stuff."

Laughing, I listened, propping myself up with my arms braced against the counter behind me. Adrian pulled a small bottle of shaving cream from his toiletry kit and squirted a generous amount in his hand before smoothing it onto the lower portion of my leg.

His tongue peeked out of the corner of his mouth as he gently stroked the razor upward, the blade gently rasping against my skin as he worked. I watched transfixed as he carefully shaved my calf, briefly stopping every few strokes to swish the razor in a small cup of water next to him and wipe the razor on the towel next to him before continuing.

When he was done with the first section, he moved to the sink, rinsing my razor more thoroughly under a stream of water, refilling his cup before he dropped back down and moved to the next part. My body was humming as he carefully shaved my thighs, his large hands bracing me on the edge of the counter as he stood between my knees. My belly almost touched his when he stepped in further to gently glide the razor over my outer thighs.

He leaned in, his soft lips brushing my earlobe. "Are your legs the only thing you want me to shave?"

"I..." I trailed off as his large hand settled high on my thigh, his thumb brushing the sensitive skin I hadn't been able to reach with a razor in months.

"I'll be gentle," he whispered, his lips moving to caress the skin beneath my ear. "And when I'm done, I'll make sure to get you nice and clean."

"Mmm," I hummed, feeling way more turned on than I should at him asking to shave my pussy.

"And then when I've wiped away all the cream, I'll lick you until you're screaming my name."

"Fuck."

"That too if you want it," he chuckled, pulling away. My mouth was dry as I watched him wet a washcloth with warm water before he brought it between my legs, slowly running the damp cloth over every inch of my skin.

Adrian's eyes never left mine as he covered his fingers in shaving cream. "Lean back a bit, babe. Want to make sure I get every...little...spot covered with it."

He could cover every little spot of whatever he wanted down there. I burned from the inside out as his gentle fingers spread the cream, jumping as he grazed my clit. "Oh, God."

"Just relax. I'll take care of you. Close your eyes." His voice was a low murmur as he gently held the razor to my skin, making careful swipes, and humming as he went. Leaning back, I rested my head on the mirror, my arms aching as I held myself up. "Almost done. You're being such a good girl, holding still for me. Such a pretty, pink pussy."

When he'd finished, he dropped the razor in the sink, not bothering to rinse it. I was drowsy, drunk with pleasure and anticipation as he wet the washcloth again, wiping between my legs, cleaning every inch of my newly shaved skin before he covered it with my lotion. It'd been months since I was bare, and judging by the hungry look as he watched me, he was enjoying every second of this.

"Still with me?" he asked, licking his lips and stepping as close as he could get with my belly in the way. He leaned over me, his lips inches from mine. "Tell me how much you want it. Are you as desperate for me to touch you as I am?"

"Yes," I moaned as his fingertips traced between my legs, gently caressing my clit.

"Do you want my mouth on you?"

Nodding, I tried to sit up, but struggled with my arms shaking.

"Let's go to the bed so you're more comfortable." While I knew he was eager to make good on his promises, he also didn't want me to be uncomfortable.

I wrapped my arms around his neck, and he lifted me, effortlessly carrying me to the other room and sitting me on the end of the bed. He reached past me and pulled the pillows forward, propping me up so I didn't have to lay flat on my back since it was hard to breathe that way.

"Mmm," he whispered, dipping his fingers between my legs. This part had always been one of my favorites, watching him play with me, but my belly blocked my view. "You're so fuckin' wet, babe. I think you needed this."

He continued murmuring words of appreciation as he crouched down, his head disappearing from sight. "Oh, fuck," I moaned when his tongue pressed into my clit, curling slightly before he wrapped his lips around me and sucked.

His large hands grasped my thighs, forcing my legs wider as he devoured me, groaning loudly. It didn't take long for my orgasm to build. Warm pulses of ecstasy ran through my veins as I threw my head back and gasped while he never stopped licking.

"Fuck," he groaned, sliding his fingers inside me while I pulsed around them, making my hips squirm. "What I wouldn't give to be inside you right now."

"Yes," I moaned, reaching down and grasping the hair on the side of his head. "I need it. I want you inside me."

His eyes widened in surprise, a grin pulling at his lips when he realized I was serious.

"You want this cock?" He stood, reaching down to unfasten the towel at his waist and letting it drop to the floor. Without hesitation, he wrapped his hand around his length, pumping as he looked down at me. "Tell me how much."

"Please," I whimpered, my eyes transfixed by the movement of his hand.

"How much, Isobel?"

"So much. Please, just fuck me."

"Lean back, babe," he urged me to lean back against the stack of pillows, pulling my hips to the edge of the bed. He watched me as he bent his knees, lining up and playfully smacking the head of his dick on my clit.

Moaning, my head fell back, and I arched toward him while he pushed inside, the intrusion welcome after so many weeks apart.

"Fuckin' hell, you're so fuckin' tight," he groaned, pulling back and smoothly thrusting forward with gentle movements. His chest flexed as he held me still, his fingertips digging into the outside of my thighs while he tried to hold himself back.

"Make me come," I whimpered, trying to reach down to touch myself, but my belly was in the way.

"Fuck, yes." The sounds that came out of his mouth were almost feral as he fucked me, slowly picking up the pace, but still being careful with me. "God, I'm going to fuckin' come. Please, please..."

His thumb rubbed my clit as our moans filled the air around us, building into a crescendo that had me gripping the comforter beneath me while I pulsed around him. "Come in me," I moaned as he stared at me, watching my every expression as I came. "Fill me with it. I want to feel it. Please. Mark me."

He growled loudly, pulling me toward him as his hips faltered, his mouth dropping open and his neck flexing as he came, his hard cock pulsing inside me.

Adrian panted while he stared at me, his thumbs stroking the outside of my thighs as he carefully slipped out. He wiggled his eyebrows and shot me a satisfied smile before he disappeared into the bathroom, coming back with a warm washcloth. I hummed as he wiped me clean, enjoying the drowsy feeling lingering in my body.

Baby girl must have enjoyed the rush of endorphins as she gently wiggled inside me, turning before she settled down. Adrian watched as the skin on my belly shifted, placing his hand where it looked like her feet might be. "I know we've still got a little way to go, but I can't wait to meet her."

"Me too," I sniffled, tears pricking in the corners of my eyes as he gently caressed my skin. I was ready to start the next chapter of our lives, even if I knew it'd be challenging.

THIRTY-EIGHT

ISOBEL

MINNEAPOLIS

"WE SHOULD GET YOU ready," Adrian said after we'd both recovered from our unexpected coupling. He moved to the bag he'd abandoned by the dresser, pulling out my underwear and helping me with them before he disappeared to retrieve my dress from where he'd hung it in the closet.

It was kind of comical that he was helping me dress while he was still completely naked, but after he settled me into the chair next to the desk, I got to watch him get dressed. He looked handsome in his dark slacks and button-down shirt, a red tie completing the look.

We still had hours until the wedding, but he was escorting me to the bridal suite before he joined the men on another floor. He was the last grooms-man—paired with me—and the others were Chase's brothers, each paired with their spouses.

"I can't wait to see you later," he whispered while we rode the elevator to the fourth floor. "You're going to look stunning."

I, on the other hand, was not so sure. The dress Chase had picked out was gorgeous, a pink satin maternity wrap dress that was gathered under the bust and gently draped over my enormous belly in soft folds. But I still felt like a whale.

"Don't start getting in your head," he teased, his hand rubbing small circles on my lower back. I'd had some nerve pain lately, causing my lower back to ache constantly, and I was getting to the point where I needed to be seated more often than not. "You're a knockout, and everyone here can see it."

Rolling my eyes, I took a deep breath as the elevator settled; the doors sliding open. Adrian guided me toward the door to the suite at the end of the hallway, and I was suddenly nervous. I was going to have to spend all day letting other people touch me. Not that I didn't want to look nice for pictures, but my skin was so sensitive lately I didn't like people—other than Adrian—touching me.

I felt like I was being marched toward the Spanish Inquisition as we walked off the elevator, but it was time to get this show on the road.

Adrian knocked on the door to the bridal suite, his thumb tracing my spine through my dress as we waited.

"Is!" Chase squealed as she pulled the door open. She was covered in a plush white robe with a glass of champagne in her hand. "Everyone else is here. I had them bring up some mocktails so you can join in the fun."

"Have a good time, babe," Adrian whispered in my ear, kissing my cheek before he pressed my small clutch into my hand. "If you need me, text. I'll make sure my phone is on me at all times. I'll see you in a few hours."

Chase grinned, wiggling her eyebrows as Adrian turned and retreated down the hallway. He watched me from his place near the elevator, waving and shaking his head at Chase's obnoxious squeal.

"Get in here and tell everyone about your hunky boyfriend." Chase tugged my elbow and pulled me into the suite, guiding me to a plush chair before she told me to sit and placed a champagne flute filled with sparkling grape juice and orange juice in my hand. It tasted sickly sweet, and I winced as my stomach cramped.

The baby turned, and I pressed my hand into her until she settled back down. No one ever told you how painful it was to have a tiny foot crammed into your ribcage twenty times a day.

"Come on, spill." Chase settled into a chair facing a large mirror, a hairstylist setting to work with a curling wand.

"There's not much to spill."

The other women looked at me expectantly, Kristine smirking as she tried to hold back. She had never been on great terms with Adrian, but they'd kind of come to a truce before she moved to Chicago to work with Sam.

"Well, obviously something is going on between you and Evan's editor, because I don't think that's a giant burrito shoved under that dress," Evan's sister Kelly said with a laugh.

"We're...it's complicated." I wasn't sure how to answer their questions. We were just taking things one day at a time. Neither one of us had brought up what the next step would be besides moving in together.

My lease didn't end until April, and Adrian's until May, so we were waiting until after she was born to find a place together. I knew it wasn't ideal to split time with a newborn between two apartments, but we'd make it work. People co-parented all the time from separate households. Only they typically weren't together anymore.

"So uncomplicate it," Kristine said, shrugging before she took a sip of her mimosa. "Nana told me that when I had my head up my ass about Sam."

"I think you're in a bit of a different situation than she is," Chase's sis-ter-in-law, Elle, commented, turning toward me with a soft smile. "Trying to navigate a relationship while you're pregnant isn't easy. And not everyone wants to get married."

"Amen." Kristine lifted her glass in a toast, but I knew she'd change her tune if Sam proposed.

I wasn't sure what I would do if Adrian proposed. Despite him telling Grant we were engaged; I was too scared to broach the subject. I'd never told him I wanted to get remarried someday, and he hadn't officially asked.

"Dickhead seems to have changed over the last few months," Chase commented, looking at us through the mirror she was seated in front of. "Evan said he's been almost tolerable with the draft of his new book."

"He has. I almost feel bad I thought so poorly of him for so many years. Once he let his walls down, he was a completely different person."

"Still a dick," Kristine laughed.

"I think we all have our moments when we can be a dick. Don't you think?" Her whirlwind romance with Sam before their months long separation while she had her head up her ass was proof enough.

"We're not talking about me."

"How's it going with Sam being your boss?" Chase asked with a smirk.

"Does he treat you like his naughty employee at home?" Elle asked. Both Chase and Kelly groaned, and I laughed at their reactions.

"Sam is like another little brother," Kelly gagged and wrinkled her nose in a cringe.

Chase chimed in, wincing as she looked back at her sister-in-law. "And I don't need to know about my brother playing naughty architect with you."

"Like you're one to talk," Kelly laughed. "You forget I'm in the room and talk about spanking Evan way too much. No one needs to know that."

"Maybe you just need to get a better sex life," Chase shot back, laughing as her almost sister-in-law flipped her off.

"On that note," Kelly said flippantly. "I'm going to take the opportunity to go drink alone in my hotel room since my mother thinks I need to be sober for this lovefest. Hard pass."

"Don't you want to get dressed first?" Elle asked, as Kelly tightened the tie around her silky robe.

"Nope, if someone wants to take a peep in the hallway, I don't really care. It'd be more action than I've gotten in months."

"Our moms are on their way up, so you'd better hurry if you don't want to get caught," Chase commented as she scrolled through the texts on her phone.

"Peace out, happily settled bitches. I'm off to find my companion for the evening, Mr. Bourbon."

"Is she okay?" I asked as she shuffled out the door, cotton balls shoved between her toes while her nails dried.

"I think she's just having a hard time lately. Evan said she was dating a guy last year and something happened. But she's been closed-lipped about it. I'm afraid being around all these couples on Valentine's Day is a little too much for her right now."

"Who knows," Kristine mused. "Maybe she'll hook up with one of your cousins."

"Ew." Chase wrinkled her nose, but I knew she came from a huge family. "I'd rather not think of that. Besides, there are some other people invited from Boston I think she'd like better."

"Who?" I asked, curious as to which one of the guests who traveled here from Boston might interest Kelly. As far as I knew, she lived in Chicago.

"We'll see if anything happens," she shrugged, returning her attention to her phone as the nail technician set up her things in front of me. I was mildly excited about getting a pedicure since I could barely see my feet these days and was relieved Kelly had taken the heat off speculation about Adrian and me.

Chapter
THIRTY-NINE

ADRIAN

MINNEAPOLIS

Pulling my phone out of my pocket, I checked the screen for messages again. Isobel hadn't texted me, but I had the weird feeling that something was off with her. I was sure it was just my overprotective streak that'd flared the closer we got to the end of this pregnancy. No matter what it was, I wanted to make sure I was accessible if she needed me.

"Put the phone back in your pocket, Casanova," Chase's brother-in-law, Miguel, commanded as he shoved a shot glass into my hand.

"I'm good." I refused the glass, pressing it back in his direction. "Not planning to drink much today."

"Alright, overprotective baby daddy, if you say so."

"I don't see your husband drinking either," I pointed out, gesturing toward where Drew and Ethan were playing poker at the table in Evan's suite.

"That's because he gets horny when he's drunk and he's waiting until later," he said casually, tipping the shot back and swallowing. "And he's promised to bend me over the balcony railing later, so he's not allowed to get sloppy drunk. That privilege is left for moi."

Unsure of how to respond to that extreme over share, I just nodded. "Why don't we go see what the groom is up to?"

"He's going over his vows for the ten millionth time. Maybe you should go help him, since you're his editor and all."

Evan tended to get in his head. Especially with his writing. That's why I typically approached him with the Dickhead persona I'd carefully crafted over the years. If I coddled him and acted nicely, he'd continue to retreat into his shell. If I acted like a jackass, he'd push back and try to prove me wrong.

It'd worked out pretty well for his relationship with Chase so far. If it weren't for me sending her books to him—knowing her work would complement his writing style—he wouldn't be marrying her today. Then when he'd stood up for her before their book tour, I knew he was serious. I'd watched him retreat into himself after his ex, Simone, had manipulated him and then driven him into seclusion. He'd never told me how bad it'd gotten with her, but the fact he'd completely isolated himself for two years was enough to confirm she had completely shattered his self-confidence. If I could prevent anything like that from happening again, I'd piss him off to make a point.

"How's it goin', loverboy?" I asked, walking up behind where he was seated at the desk in the bedroom. His hair was a disaster, so I knew he was stressing over making sure his vows were perfect. He failed to account for the fact Chase thought rainbows shot out of his ass.

"Why did you never tell me how terrible my first drafts were?"

Chuckling, I glanced down at the pieces of paper he'd spread across the desk.

"Quit, you drama queen. You know you're talented. You don't need me blowing you up. It's Chase's job to blow you."

Evan growled, turning the chair to look at me. "Keep her name out of your mouth."

He bristled as my hand clasped his shoulder. "Seriously, though, calm the fuck down. You know she's gonna love whatever is in those vows. You want to know why?"

He frowned, looking vulnerable.

"Because she loves you for who you are. That's rare in a person, and you should trust that no matter what you say to her up at that altar will be perfect for you two. Just pretend the two of you are talking to each other. Everyone else doesn't matter. Because at the end of the day, she's your partner, and she loves you, perceived shortcomings and all."

"What happened to you?" he laughed, a smile breaking through.

"I fell in love."

He nodded, covering my hand with his. "Knocks you on your ass, doesn't it?"

"Absolutely. But in the best possible way."

"Thank you." His shoulders relaxed as he pushed the papers into a neat pile, placing his palm on the top of the stack.

"No problem, man. I've diffused your freakouts enough that I'm an old pro by now."

He looked back at the paper on the desk. "Do you want to read them? Make sure they're okay?"

"Nope. She's going to love whatever you wrote. My opinion doesn't matter."

A loud cheer came from the other room and we both looked toward the door. "Sounds like your brother-in-law is getting a little wild in there."

"He hasn't started stripping yet, so we're good." He looked down at his watch. "Looks like it's show time."

He stood, grabbing his suit jacket off the back of the chair and pulling it on. "Time for me to get married."

"You got this."

He nodded, passing me to head to the other room. I pulled my suit jacket off the rack by the door, ready to get this wedding over with so I could get Isobel home. We had a lot of things to prepare for in the next few weeks, and not a lot of time to accomplish it.

Adrian: How're you feeling?

Isobel: Tired.

Adrian: Have you been sitting down?

Isobel: Yes, Daddy.

Adrian: Daddy, huh? I like that. And I will be soon. Drinking your water?

Isobel: I'm okay. Back is just a little sore. Your giant child has been trying to use me as a punching bag all morning.

Adrian: It's cause she loves her mama.

Isobel: Or she enjoys torturing me like her father.

Adrian: We're heading downstairs. Meet you at the end of the aisle.

Isobel: I'll be the whale in pink.

Adrian: And you'll be a gorgeous sea creature.

Isobel: Hate you. Aren't you supposed to be complimenting me?

Adrian: Love you too. And I did. I called you gorgeous.

Once we reached the ground level where the wedding would be held in a covered atrium, the wedding planner ushered us into place. Evan looked nervous as fuck, but I knew once he saw Chase he'd be fine.

As the music from the quartet started, my eyes were fixed on the door at the back of the room. I may not have been the one getting married—yet—but I couldn't wait to see Isobel. Despite her insistence she was huge, I still loved seeing her round with my child. There was something insanely sexy about knowing we did that. We created that child because of our connection, which had only strengthened with time.

And I wanted to put a ring on her finger, but she had enough things to adjust to over the next few months. I could be patient.

The ceremony went by quickly, both authors making the wedding guests cry with their heartfelt vows. Evan killed it, and I was so proud of how he'd finally found a way to cope with his anxiety and let his true personality shine.

I hadn't realized how true that statement was as Isobel's pained whimper met my ears over the melee in the ballroom during the reception an hour later.

"Oh, God. Oh, no..."

Her hand grasped my knee, her fingers digging into my suit pants as her face morphed into a grimace.

"Babe? You okay?"

Evan's sister Kelly asked her if she was alright from her other side, and we both watched as Isobel panted, her face pinched with discomfort.

"I think my water just broke." My pulse jumped as I registered what her scared voice had said.

"Holy..." Kelly sounded panicked from her other side, looking up and making eye contact with me.

"Babe? Is she coming?" It was too early. We weren't ready for this.

"I think so..." Isobel's grip on my knee tightened, and I watched as her stomach flexed.

"But it's not time yet. We were supposed to be back home. She's not due for over a month." This was why I was afraid to come this weekend. We weren't ready for this. Especially not so far away from home.

"Grab her wrap, hot shot," Miguel said, grabbing my shoulder while I tried not to panic.

"Fuck, sorry, babe," I responded, pulling Isobel's wrap from the back of her chair and throwing it over her shoulders. "Do you think you can stand?"

"Maybe," she whimpered, her face seeming to relax after the contraction was over.

"Let's get you up then."

Things seemed to speed up as I wrapped her velvet shawl around her waist and lifted her into my arms. "I've got yah, babe." Tilting my head toward the table, I spoke to Kelly. "Grab her clutch and follow me to the front, would yah?"

As I made my way out the doors to the ballroom, a crowd was following us, including the bride and groom.

"I'm fine," Isobel whimpered, but I knew she wasn't from the terrified look on her face. "I'm so sorry."

"Don't apologize," Chase insisted as she waved away Isobel's comment. "Is there anything we can do to help?"

Isobel's worried voice nearly broke me as I carried her out the front doors of the hotel. "I didn't mean to ruin your wedding reception. I thought we still had a few weeks. My doctor said it was okay to fly."

Well...the doctor was wrong in this situation. And as amniotic fluid soaked through my suit jacket, I hoped we would make it to the hospital before our daughter made her impromptu entrance into the world.

FORTY

ADRIAN

MINNEAPOLIS

CHASE'S BROTHER DREW WAS thankfully one step ahead of us, an SUV practically squealing its way around the corner from the parking lot. He jumped out, opening the back door. "We'll get them checked in and come back to the reception. She's not going to have the baby in the back seat."

His husband Miguel seemed suddenly sober, freaking out more than I was that she was in labor. "That better be a guarantee. We're burning the car if that happens. You cannot get the smell of placenta out of leather. I'll never look at this car the same—"

His voice drifted off as I placed Isobel in the back seat, jumping in after her and slamming the door.

"Fuck," she whimpered, squeezing my hand—hard—as I sat beside her in the back seat. All I could focus on was her while the car accelerated onto the highway, heading toward what I hoped was the closest hospital.

Miguel may have been freaking out, but I didn't want to have to deliver my child in the back seat of a car either.

"Is she okay?" he asked, looking at me from the passenger seat, his eyes locked on mine.

"Is? How're you doing?" She'd clearly already had two contractions, but she seemed to relax into me as the second one let up.

"Can he drive faster? It hurts. This isn't how this was supposed to happen."

Her sniffles broke my heart, knowing she had to be terrified. We'd discussed a birth plan, had bags packed at home, Dr. Reeves' phone number programmed into both our phones. We'd toured the hospital and driven the route from both of our apartments. But nothing prepared us for this—going into labor hundreds of miles from home.

"You got this, babe. We're going to be just fine." We had to be.

"Is she..." Miguel trailed off, gesturing at Isobel like she was terrifying. "Leaking or anything? Is it sticking out of her? Don't you need to be at the other end to catch it?"

Drew smacked his husband on the arm. "She's had two contractions. I highly doubt there's a baby coming out yet. Chill the fuck out, you're freaking her out."

Isobel leaned into my side, her hand clasped tightly in mine while we took an exit marked Abbott Northwestern.

"Oh, fuck," Isobel groaned, squeezing my knee as she tensed up.

Miguel jumped out of the car like it was on fire, rushing through the Emergency Room doors. I had no idea what he said to get such a quick response, but before Drew and I could get her turned and ready to lift out of the backseat, a nurse was waiting with a wheelchair.

"How far along is she?" the nurse asked as Isobel clutched her stomach and panted through the rest of the contraction.

"Thirty-five weeks, three days."

"Do you know which obstetrician she's using? We can page them and see if they're on call."

She turned and headed toward the Emergency room doors, the three of us hustling after her.

"We were here for a wedding. Her OB and perinatologist are in Boston."

"I'll call up to labor and delivery to see who's on. Do you have her identification?"

Isobel smacked me in the stomach with her clutch, white-knuckling the arm of the wheelchair as she panted.

"I'm assuming you're Dad?" she asked while I pulled out Isobel's license and took out her small card wallet to find her insurance card.

"Yes, I'm the dad. She's had three contractions so far. Water broke about a half hour ago."

The nurse made a call using the walkie on her name badge, and two men came in to lift Isobel to a hospital bed. Another guy in a white lab coat came in moments later, rubbing his hands with sanitizer and reaching for a set of gloves out of the dispenser on the wall.

"Sound like we're having a baby tonight, folks."

"She's not supposed to be here yet." A few tears streaked down Isobel's cheek, and I sat down beside her, gripping her hand.

"Babies don't always come according to plan. We're going to get you set up with some monitors and an IV. Since your water broke, we're going to push some steroids with an antibiotic and give you something to slow down your contractions. As soon as they've got a room prepped upstairs in the baby center, we'll transfer you."

She nodded, whimpering as she squeezed my hand.

As soon as the monitor belt was strapped across her belly, the line on the screen arced and Isobel gasped, gripping my hand hard enough to turn both our knuckles white.

"Have you decided about pain intervention?" the doctor asked, watching the line on the screen arc upward. "Can you tell me on a scale of one to ten how much pain you're feeling?"

"I don't know. It feels like I'm being tortured one moment, but then it eases off and I feel okay."

"Hmm," he hummed. "Looks like you're still in the early stages of labor, so those contractions will get much stronger as she moves down the birth canal and her head drops into position."

Miguel made a gagging noise from his spot near the doorway, and I narrowed my eyes at him.

"These are going to get stronger?" Isobel whispered, wincing at the line as it continued to travel up. When I thought she'd squeeze my hand off, she said something none of us were expecting. "Who do I have to blow to get an epidural around here?"

Miguel and Drew let out surprised laughs, finally deciding they'd seen enough of this show. "On that note, we're gonna take off. Text Chase and we can make sure your rental car gets brought over sometime tonight."

I fished the keys out of my pocket, describing the car and telling him where we'd parked it.

The two of them left, and the ER doctor followed shortly afterward. He'd been completely unfazed by her uncharacteristically crass demand for pain intervention, promising to let the nurses upstairs know she wanted an epidural.

"Please tell me this is just a false alarm?" Isobel whispered as she turned her head to face me. Her once polished up-do had fallen, curls cascading down her shoulders. She looked terrified, but still beautiful.

"She'll be okay. If they thought it was an actual emergency, we'd already be in a delivery room. We'll make it work, whatever happens."

"How are we going to get her home? What if she has to go to the NICU?" Isobel's breath faltered, more tears streaming down her cheeks. "I should have listened to you. I'm a terrible mother. It was so selfish of me to want to come here this weekend. I keep trying and nothing seems to go right lately."

"Is," I whispered, cupping her cheek. "We had no way of knowing this was going to happen. We just have to trust the doctors to get her here safely. Worrying won't change anything. We'll figure this out."

THREE HOURS LATER, THE baby was still nowhere close to being born. Isobel had been settled into a private room that could double as a delivery suite as long as the baby and mom weren't in distress.

Isobel had been in pain until the anesthesiologist had come with her epidural a short while ago. Once the giant ass needle had been inserted into her spine, she'd calmed down, eventually falling asleep. Even resting, her face was drawn with worry, and I wished there was something I could do. Just waiting like this made me feel helpless.

While I'd tried to be encouraging at the time, I was just as freaked out as she was. We were nowhere close to home and had no idea if our premature baby would be stuck here after she was born.

Drifting off in the chair next to her, I tried to get some rest while she did, knowing I'd need to be strong for both of us.

FIVE HOURS LATER, THE lights in her room flickered on, and another doctor came in to check on her.

"Has she been resting alright with the epidural?"

Blinking the drowsiness out of my eyes, I squeezed Isobel's hand, watching as she winced before she awoke.

"I think so. I fell asleep, but she never woke me up."

"How're we doing, Ms. Blom?" the doctor asked, moving to the end of the bed and shifting the blankets off her legs. "I'm going to see how far along you are."

We both watched, Isobel squeezing my hand as the doctor's gloved hand disappeared beneath her hospital gown. "We're almost ready to get this show on the road. Are you feeling a lot of pressure down here?"

"Am I supposed to be?" Isobel asked with a yawn.

"I'd hope so. You're dilated to a little over nine centimeters. I'm going to go ahead and page the rest of the birth team and we can get you sitting upright to try to push."

"Already?" Isobel's panicked eyes found mine, and I tried not to look as terrified as she did.

"Looks like your daughter isn't going to hang out anymore. I'd expect she'll be here very soon. I'll get in contact with Peds and let the NICU know we will be expecting a pre-term delivery in case they need to step in."

Isobel's chin trembled as he let himself out, "NICU? She's going to need the NICU?"

"We don't know that yet. Babies born at thirty-five weeks don't always have to spend time in the NICU."

Watching her cry, I felt helpless, standing to pull her into my arms as much as I could with all the monitors attached to her. "You got this, babe. We can do this. *You* can do this."

TWO HOURS LATER, OUR daughter was born with an impressive wail, announcing her arrival. She'd been tiny at 5 lbs 4 ounces, but the doctors had assured us she was doing extremely well for a pre-term delivery.

Isobel had cried while she held her, lifting the small baby to kiss her forehead, while I watched on, completely overwhelmed with an emotion I had trouble identifying as it was one I never expected to experience. Watching the two of them together—despite being terrified, our daughter had a fight ahead of her—irrevocably changed something inside me. I couldn't imagine loving anyone more than I did at that moment.

It'd been years since I felt overwhelmed enough to cry, but my eyes watered and my chest felt like it was going to burst as she cradled our tiny bundle. She was so beautiful despite her chaotic entry to meet us, with a full head of soft, downy hair and tiny fingers and toes. She was perfect.

What felt like seconds later, the nurse had whisked her away, inspecting her before they tucked her into an enclosed bassinet. I watched helplessly as they wheeled her out of the room, hoping the nurses hadn't been blowing smoke up my ass about her being healthy. My baby girl would be strong like her mother, despite the uncertainty we faced.

Isobel had fallen asleep after they'd gotten her cleaned up, the tears only tapering off as she fell asleep. I'd been watching her, trying not to cry. She needed—they both needed—someone to be strong through this. And while it killed me, I couldn't take away Isobel's fears, but I had hope that things would turn out okay.

A nurse crept into the room, whispering to get my attention. "Is Dad ready to visit his little girl?"

"She's asleep, I can't leave her without..." Isobel didn't stir as we talked, completely exhausted.

"I can have an aide come sit until she wakes up. The doctor wanted to give her a chance to rest and recommended we hold off on moving her for a few hours. We'll need to see if she'd like to pump until they give the all-clear to nurse. If you'd like to see the baby, they've got her settled into the NICU nursery for observation. The attending physician didn't see the need to admit her to a bed yet. We'll watch her overnight and probably most of the day tomorrow. But you can go see her now if you'd like."

Nodding, I slowly slipped my hand from Isobel's, following the nurse into the hallway. The floor was quiet, which made sense considering it was the middle of the night.

The sound of beeping monitors and crying babies followed us as we walked through the hallways, my mind focused entirely on what was about to happen.

I was a dad. Part of me had wanted to wait for Is to see her, but I didn't want to leave the baby by herself. She'd had a rough entry into the world, and if her mother couldn't be with her right now, I would be.

"She's doing well so far. Her APGAR was an 8, which is high for a preemie. Definitely has a set of lungs. Which is good. If they're strong enough to cry, they're strong enough not to need a vent."

I was quiet as I listened to her talk, following when she swiped a badge next to a door and it swung open.

"She's got quite a bit of blonde hair and bright blue eyes. Longer than we thought she'd be after we got her uncurled to measure. We'll have to watch her temperature since her body fat is low."

"Do you think she'll need to be in the NICU for very long?" I knew it'd likely be weeks until we could go home with her, but I hoped she wouldn't be in the NICU that whole time.

"It depends on if she eats or not. If we need to use a GI tube, she'll probably be in here for a week or so at least, but we don't know until we try to feed her."

"Doesn't she need to be with Isobel for that?"

"We'll let Mom rest for now. They like to start preemies on a special formula first sometimes. Just to make sure they're getting the nutrients they need that mom might not be producing yet. The nurses can go over more when mom wakes up. We can give your wife something to help jumpstart her milk supply, but it may be a few weeks until the baby is ready to nurse on her own."

She stopped in front of a door with little cutouts of pink and blue baby footprints.

"We can put you in a family room, so you've got some privacy to hold her. Are you ready?"

Nodding, I followed her through the door, listening to her directions on how to wash my hands. It felt like my body was on autopilot as she led me to a quiet room with a rocking chair and told me to sit and she'd be right back.

She returned moments later with a bassinet, wheeling it into the room and plugging a monitor stand into the wall.

"Is she okay?" While she seemed to be breathing on her own, she still had several wires hanging out of the blanket she was wrapped in.

"She's great. We just need to monitor her temperature and oxygen levels, so these cords need to stay connected. I'll get you set up. Are we planning to do skin-to-skin?"

"Can I?"

She nodded, pulling my daughter out of the bassinet and carefully laying her in my arms. Tears sprung to my eyes as I gazed down at her tiny features, amazed at how light she felt. She was like a delicate little angel.

"I'll let you situate her. You can unbutton your shirt and unwrap the front of her blanket to lay her on your chest. Just don't try to stand with her. Use the call button on her cart when you need a nurse to help you get her back into the bassinet."

As I gazed down at the tiny little bundle in my arms, my throat tightened, and I felt the rest of my walls start to crumble. The same rush of warmth that flowed through me when I looked at Isobel was there, but this was something more. Something deeper.

I wanted to be a better man for this tiny little goddess in my arms, with her mother's soft blonde hair and shining blue eyes that matched my own. Her mother had the potential to break my heart, but this little girl owned it.

And I was going to try my damndest to deserve her love. And show her the man I should be, not the one I'd been hiding behind.

ADRIAN

MINNEAPOLIS

"It seems fitting that she tried to make her appearance on Valentine's Day." Technically, she'd been born on February 15th, but she'd given us a hell of a Valentine's Day.

"Why's that?"

After a moment of silence, Isobel's eyes rolled as she looked up toward me, likely recalling how we'd spent Valentine's Day the year before. Back at that publishing conference and dancing around each other with a bucket full of unresolved sexual tension.

"Because it was the first time you—"

She cut me off with a quiet growl. "You better not say it was the first time I gave you a blowjob."

"While that was quite memorable. It wasn't what I was going to say."

Her lips pursed, a look I was quite familiar with, but I continued anyway, reaching down with my fingertip to push a wayward lock of sweaty blonde hair from her forehead.

While she'd looked fucking radiant in her bridesmaid's dress last night, I think I preferred her disheveled look after having spent the last few hours bringing our daughter into the world. I knew she was a badass, but watching her earlier, I was seeing how strong she was through fresh eyes.

Even though she'd been torn between all the new obligations at work and struggling with the guilt of knowing things would look different from what we'd planned, when she looked at our daughter for the first time it was like a piece of her that'd been missing settled into place. I just hoped that I was a part of their puzzle.

"It was the first time you gave me any sort of sign that my five-year long, one-sided crush on you might be reciprocated."

Her gaze softened; the worry lines that'd been an almost constant presence for the last four months eased in a way that gave me hope we'd all get through this.

"Although if I'd known then that she was going to be the result, I'd have chased you down and knocked you up a long time ago. You were meant to be her mama, Is."

What I left unsaid was *I hope I'm meant to be yours too.*

"Can we go see her?"

"They'll make you go in the wheelchair. Please don't argue with the nurses. You just gave birth, so I don't want you hurting yourself."

"I don't care how they get me there. I just want to see her. Make sure she's okay." Her voice cracked and her chin quivered as she tried to hold back tears. "Make sure I didn't fail her."

"Is, no." Sitting down beside her, I pulled her forward until her face was buried in my neck. "You have been amazing through this whole thing. You didn't fail her. She's strong and beautiful, just like you. And she's a fighter, just like you. She'll be alright. We'll make sure she's alright."

Isobel was quiet as I called for the nurse and helped her get settled into the wheelchair. She didn't talk the entire trip to the NICU, picking at the blanket in her lap. Her silence ate at me. I knew she was beating herself up the baby had arrived earlier than planned. But there wasn't anything we could change, so we just had to roll with it.

"What did you tell them her name was?"

"I was waiting for you," I confessed, and she finally looked up at me, a faint smile pulling at her lips. We hadn't been 100 percent sure what her name was going to be, and I didn't want to take that away from her.

"Is mom ready to hold baby Blom?"

"Baby O'Neill," she whispered, reaching for my hand and squeezing tightly as the nurse picked our daughter up from the bassinet.

"She's gorgeous." Isobel's voice was reverent as the nurse placed the baby into her arms.

"She's a pretty one," the nurse agreed. "You can have Dad help get you settled with skin-to-skin if you'd like. He's an old pro."

I'd spent a half hour with her when I was here earlier until they'd needed to feed her.

"Did she eat?"

"She tried. Isn't sure how to roll her tongue yet, but she'll figure it out. If you want to nurse, you can offer the nipple to her, but don't be discouraged if she doesn't quite get a good latch. Once she's a little older, we can have the lactation consultant work with you."

The nurse quietly let herself out, and I watched Isobel take her daughter in for the second time. The first had been brief and chaotic, but this time seemed peaceful despite her melancholic mood.

"What are we going to call her?" she whispered, staring down at the sleeping bundle, a tear slowly tracking down her cheek. Her fingers trailed over her downy, white-blonde hair before she spoke.

We were waiting until she was born to see what felt like it fit. "Which one do you think fits her?" I asked, tracing a finger along the baby's hairline.

"Finley. She looks like Finley. And I know you were trying not to sway my decision, but I know Fin reminds you of your dad."

It meant fair haired warrior. Isobel had marked it as one of her favorites and a nod to my family's Irish roots—more specifically, my dad. My father's middle name had been Finn, and he'd been a fighter all his life until it was cut tragically short when I was a boy.

"He'd be proud of you," she whispered, her voice emotional. I hoped she was right. His presence in my life had been cut short, but I wanted to be the father he had never had the chance to be.

"I hope so." My voice was rough, unshed tears clogging my throat, but naming her Finley felt right. "Finley is perfect."

Reaching forward, I ran my thumb along the edge of the baby's jaw, smiling as her little lips puckered like she was sucking on something in her dreams. "She's definitely our little warrior."

ALMOST TWO WEEKS LATER, when I reentered the hospital room in the NICU, my hands full of coffee and snacks from the hospital cafeteria, Hutch was seated in the armchair in the corner. While I knew we were the same build, seeing my tiny daughter cradled in his large arms was surprising. The time we'd spent here had been filled with difficulties, but she was gradually making progress.

He traced the side of her face gently with his fingertip, likely thinking about all the moments like this he'd missed when he was overseas.

"Thank you for flying out here. I know how you feel about flying, but..." I trailed off, the exhaustion of the last few weeks settling in. We'd expected just to come here for the weekend to be in the wedding, and now we'd be here for at least another few weeks while we waited for Finley to be old enough to fly.

She'd been breathing fine on her own and working on bottle feeding, but she was still small and hadn't passed the two-hour car seat test yet.

We'd weighed our options and while it wasn't ideal, neither was a twenty-hour road trip with a newborn to get back to Boston. That'd likely turn into over thirty with how often she was feeding and the plethora of dirty diapers she seemed to go through in a day. And Isobel had been trying to pump as much as she could produce to supplement the preemie formula.

"Of course, man." He leaned down to place a kiss on the middle of Finley's forehead. She was so tiny, and she already had all the adults in her life wrapped around her little fingers. "You know Ma would be here if she could be, but with her hours at the hospital and Pops..."

"I get it. But I think it'll be good to have another adult around, at least for a few days."

"You know I'm stayin' to help you guys get back home, right?" He straightened up in the chair, hugging Fin to his chest before he offered the little bundle to me.

"You don't have to, but I think we may need help. She's calm now, but this kid has some lungs."

"Imagine that," Hutch teased as I sat back in the chair next to his and carefully cradled the baby to my shoulder. "Your kid being a grouchy loudmouth."

Isobel shifted, a small moan escaping her lips in her sleep. I felt terrible that we seemed to be trapped here, but neither of us had expected the baby to come nearly a month early.

"How's Is doing with all this?"

Closing my eyes, I sighed. I knew she was having a hard time, but I wasn't sure how to help her.

"She's trying to be strong, but this has been hard on her. She already had a lot going on at work, and now..."

"I get it, kids don't always do what you want 'em to."

I wasn't sure how much to divulge to him. The guilt she seemed to carry around with her about taking the promotion and trying to balance motherhood had weighed heavily on her. I wasn't sure there was room for me in the equation sometimes, but I loved both these women, and I wasn't ever going to willingly walk away from them.

Our dad and Hutch were stronger men than I was with how they left the country to go serve overseas and miss time with their children. They'd both made sacrifices for their families that I couldn't even imagine.

"Yah know if you guys need help during the day, I can handle it. I know everyone thinks I'm an invalid, but I can take care of a kid. With Penny in school now, my days are wide open."

"It's not that. We've got daycare in the building. Neither of us is worried about someone watching her. I think Is is more worried about the work trips she needs to take and the long hours she's used to pulling."

"Gotcha." He nodded, leaning back in his chair and crossing his ankle over his knee. The metal of his prosthetic glinted in the overhead light, and I was still shocked he flew all the way here without his cane. "Just know the offer is there if you need it."

"I appreciate it."

And I did. Having two parents who worked full-time would be a challenge, but I'd never ask Isobel to compromise her career to change that. It was a relief we'd have family close by if we needed it. Isobel's support system—even if her parents hadn't been giant assholes about the unexpected pregnancy—was halfway across the country.

"How much longer do you think she'll need to be here?"

That was the question we didn't have an answer to. Finley had been fine for the first twenty-four hours during her observational period, and we'd thought maybe we'd be able to take her home after the first week, but then she'd started refusing to eat.

When she started losing more weight than they were comfortable with, they admitted her to the NICU and started using a GI tube to feed her. Isobel had cried all night when she'd been discharged from the hospital, and we had to leave Finley behind.

She'd woken up the next morning bleary-eyed and exhausted, demanding we go back to the hospital, but I'd made her take a shower and eat breakfast before we headed back.

The nurses had warned us that NICU burnout was a possibility, but as the days wore on, Isobel had withdrawn further and further into herself. And while I tried to be strong and supportive, she almost seemed like she didn't want me here half the time.

"I think having you here will be a good distraction. She hasn't wanted to leave most nights, and she only sleeps when she gets to the point of total exhaustion."

Hutch looked over at her hunched form and shook his head. "Has she talked to anyone about it?"

"The nurses gave me the name of some counselors available in the hospital, but Isobel totally shut down when they mentioned it."

"Lena struggled with some postpartum issues when I got deployed. It's hard, man. Absolutely tears you up to see them struggling but just keep sticking with it. She may not admit that she needs your support, but don't let her push you out. It may have taken a decade for Lena to cheat on me and end our marriage, but it was never the same after Pen was born."

I wasn't convinced it'd taken Lena a decade to cheat, but he was right. The only thing I could do at this point was support Isobel. Because I wouldn't give up on her, and I couldn't see my future without her. I didn't *want* to imagine my future without her.

Chapter
FORTY-TWO

ISOBEL

MINNEAPOLIS

LEANING MY FOREHEAD AGAINST the cold tile of the shower, I let the tears stream down my cheeks. The past month had been a nightmare. Adrian kept insisting that none of this was my fault, but it sure as hell felt like it.

My body was the one that failed to keep her inside longer.

My body not producing enough milk was the reason she started losing weight and had to be put on a feeding tube.

My selfish desire to take that promotion had put me in a position where I was worried I couldn't give her the attention she'd need.

I'd brought her into this world, and I felt completely unequipped to help her navigate it.

"Is, you okay?" Adrian's voice drifted into the fog of my brain, and I reached up to wipe the tears from my eyes. I knew it upset him when I cried, but when I was alone, I couldn't hold it in anymore. "We've got about an hour before we need to head to the hospital. The nurses called and said she passed the physical and the last car seat test this morning. I booked us some tickets to go home on the direct flight from Minneapolis to Boston at six tonight."

We'd been waiting for this for days—for weeks. Finley had finally started eating on her own, but one requirement for release from the NICU was a two-hour car seat test where they monitored her heart rate and oxygen levels.

Today was the fourth time they'd done it, and I'd almost lost hope she'd be able to be discharged. It was nearly the end of March, and I'd gotten to the point where I didn't even know what day it was.

"Is?" The door closed, and I took a deep breath, trying to gather the energy to finish washing my hair.

Closing my eyes and trying to focus on my breaths, I slowly felt the tension leaving my body. Until a warm hand settled between my shoulder blades.

Adrian didn't speak as he gathered me into his arms, hugging me to his bare chest while his palm cradled the back of my head.

My shoulders shook as he held me, and I somehow appreciated that he wasn't instantly trying to figure out why I was crying. These days, I didn't even know why. Every time I thought we'd made some progress; we'd show up in her room in the morning and she'd had a rough night and the waiting continued.

Finley was more alert as the days passed, and such a sweet baby during the day. But at night, she cried, she refused to sleep, she wouldn't eat; I was terrified when we didn't have a team of nurses to step in, I'd fail her again.

Hutch and Adrian had tried to keep me distracted. They brought me snacks, and they made me take walks around the hospital if Finley was out of the room for tests. Adrian held me when I was tired, and Hutch would go buy us dinner every night, so we weren't reliant entirely on hospital cafeteria food.

Having them both here was a godsend, but I still wanted to curl up inside myself and cry until I had no tears left.

"Did you wash your hair yet?" Adrian asked, his fingers combing through the wet tangles. When I shook my head, he didn't even hesitate, lathering his hands and gently cleaning my hair, tipping me backward into the stream of the water to rinse.

My chest shook as he smoothed the conditioner into the ends, unable to hold back the tears.

"I know things seem like they're overwhelming right now, but I'm here. However you need me, I'm here." He pulled me back into his chest and let me cry, finally turning off the water when it started to cool.

He dried me off, combing my hair and wrapping me in a towel before he led me back into our room. He'd moved us from the hotel where the wedding was held into one a few blocks away from the hospital. As I stared at the polyester comforter, I finally felt relief that we'd be leaving this place. How families endured this for months was completely baffling. If I had to spend another day in this place, I wasn't sure my heart would survive it.

"I packed your suitcase. We just need to put your toiletries inside it. Hutch went and got some more preemie clothes and a backpack diaper bag. It's kind of disturbing how much my brother likes picking out pink shit with ruffles on the butt." I was only half listening as he laid an outfit next to me on the bed.

"The hospital said they can send us home with plenty of preemie formula and a note for TSA. They'll still have to inspect it, but it should be enough to get us home. Ma went and picked some up and dropped it off at my apartment. We've got preemie diapers and plenty of wipes in my carry-on. I know she hasn't really taken to the pacifier, but we picked up several to try out if she needs one on the plane."

After he finished getting dressed, he knelt in front of me on the carpet, placing his hands on my knees. "We got this, babe. Tonight, she'll be home."

Nodding, I sniffled, trying not to cry again. Adrian helped me get dressed, kissing me on the forehead when he stood after tying my shoes. I hated he had to help me get through things I never blinked an eye at before.

"Sloane wants me in the office on Monday to talk about a few things, and to get my paternity leave paperwork filled out. But I can work remotely for at least two weeks before I need to start going in a couple of days a week."

I knew there was an application for temporary leave sitting in my inbox. But I couldn't make myself open it, much less fill it out.

We'd originally planned for me to take twelve weeks of maternity leave, and five of those were already gone. I missed work. The traveling part, not so much, but I missed my authors. I missed feeling like I was doing something meaningful helping get people's stories out in the world.

I wasn't even sure how I was going to get through the next 48 hours, much less seven more weeks of feeling like I had no control over any part of my life.

"You ready to go? Hutch was going to get breakfast, so we didn't have to eat those rubbery eggs in the continental breakfast downstairs. He found a bakery that had chocolate almond croissants on the other side of the hospital. He texted that he'll meet us there. I already put his bag in the rental car."

I wasn't sure what I'd do without them being here to keep me from completely breaking down. And I hated Adrian was so worried about me. Just another thing to feel guilty about.

Going through the motions, I checked the room for any stray belongings, zipping up my suitcase after I'd stuffed everything inside.

"I need to pump," I whispered, pulling the portable pump from my carry-on bag and sitting down on the edge of the bed. Adrian disappeared with the bags as I got everything set up. The familiar tingle of my milk letting down made my stomach turn.

I felt like the baby books had lied to me as I mechanically went through the motions, tucking the cups into my nursing tank and pressing the button to turn it on. They made breastfeeding seem like this magical experience, but I just felt like a cow with raw and battered nipples. Finley had done a number on them, biting down when she couldn't get a good latch, so I'd resorted to pumping most of the time. Motherhood was out to get me. I couldn't even rely on my own body to feed my child.

Adrian returned, and I turned away, hating that even this made me want to cry. He hesitantly sat behind me on the bed, his thighs bracketing mine as he pulled me back to lean against his chest.

"You don't have to be in here while I do this. I know it's weird."

His nose skimmed the side of my neck, goosebumps following in his wake, and I winced as I felt myself let down again. "You're doing something that feeds our child. A breast pump is not going to scare me away."

His hand settled on my stomach, his thumb slowly caressing me through my thin tank top while he waited for me to finish. I felt like he'd never see me as the woman I once was after this. My body wasn't even close to being the same as before I got pregnant, and now I was just a milk dispenser. A faulty one at that.

He didn't even hesitate once I turned off the pump and disconnected the collection cups, standing to retrieve the storage bottles from the small cooler bag I carried around when we weren't at the hospital. After watching me transfer the contents, he grabbed the washable parts and disappeared into the bathroom, reappearing a few moments later with everything cleaned and tucked back into the carrying case.

"A few more hours," he murmured after pulling me into his arms, kissing my cheek before he helped me pack up the remaining things in the room.

While I was terrified to take her home, I was ready to leave this part of our journey behind.

EIGHT VERY LONG HOURS later, I was flanked by both men, walking toward the gate where we'd board the plane home. Finley had been sleeping for the last twenty minutes since we'd tucked her back into the car seat after going through security, and as long as we kept the stroller moving, she seemed content.

It was insane how much we needed for a three-hour flight to Boston. We'd checked our suitcases, but we had a diaper bag, both men had backpacks, and we had a small cooler full of breastmilk and formula that'd been treated like a bomb by TSA.

When the agent had told us we needed to dump out the unsealed bottles I'd pumped, Adrian had scared the shit out of the poor guy quoting TSA breastmilk guidelines to him. After a few tense moments, he'd let us pass, apologizing for the misunderstanding. The thought of pouring out what'd taken me hours to produce would have devastated me.

"Do you want me to sit with her on the plane?" Adrian offered as we sat down near the gate.

"She seems to be doing okay, I'll stay with her. You two will be right behind me. I'm sure it'll be fine. It's only a few hours."

Only it wasn't fine. Ninety minutes into the flight, Finley had been startled awake from the seat beside me and shrieked louder than I'd been aware a six-week-old baby could. Her ear-piercing wail had garnered the attention of everyone in the seats surrounding us, and I scrambled to free her from the straps of the car seat.

"It's okay, sweet girl. I know you're probably getting hungry."

She momentarily calmed, closing her eyes and resting her head on my chest as little puffs of air escaped her pursed lips. I stared at her, watching her eyelids flutter as a tiny fist held onto a lock of my hair. It still hardly felt real that she was mine. That I'd made her.

A few moments later, the plane dipped, hitting a pocket of turbulence, and her face scrunched, her fist tightening before she started crying again. Knowing she was probably hungry; I pulled out my nursing wrap and carefully pulled down my tank top to let her nurse. I'd already leaked onto the fabric, which seemed to be a constant problem because I let down every time she cried. Which was a lot.

Her tiny lips clasped the offered nipple, but she refused to latch, squirming and biting me until I gasped.

Adrian's hand appeared between the seats, holding one of the tiny formula bottles. Carefully tucking myself away, I turned her to cradle in my arms. I tried offering her the bottle, watching as she took two sucks and then gurgled as her distress became more evident.

My pulse started to pound when she arched her back and let out a pained squeal. Glancing at the seats around us, I saw several people had turned, watching as my daughter's whimpers turned into angry cries.

Trying every tactic I'd been taught in the hospital, I rubbed her back, offered her a pacifier, bounced her in my arms, but nothing worked as I watched her little face turn red. Listening to her broke my heart.

As tears welled in my eyes, a hand settled on my shoulder, Hutch leaning around my seat from behind me. "Let me take her. Switch me seats."

Shaking my head, I tried to sway her from side to side, patting her back.

Hutch stood, holding his hand out while he waited next to my seat in the aisle. "I wasn't asking. I can take her. You sit with Adrian."

"But..." Finley's screams didn't show any signs of stopping, and after an arched eyebrow from my boyfriend's twin, I knew we needed to try something.

Standing, I stepped out into the aisle, reluctantly laying my daughter in his arms after he'd taken my seat. He cooed at her, and I watched helplessly as she hiccupped, her cries quieting as she grasped one of his large fingers in her fist. "Go sit, I've got her."

Hesitating, I watched him effortlessly work to calm her cries, his soft voice talking to her. I was thankful he could get her settled, but it just made me feel guilty. Made me feel more like a failure at motherhood.

"Babe, come sit." Adrian extended his hand toward me, pulling me into the aisle seat, and wrapping his arm around my shoulders. "She's fine. Let him sit with her. If she gets upset again, you can switch back."

"I can't even keep her from crying."

He sighed at my quiet admission, pulling me into his chest and leaning down to whisper into my ear. "Just rest, please. You're doing the best you can. Let the baby whisperer do his thing and let me hold you."

The sun had set as we crossed the Midwest, the dark night sky visible past Adrian's shoulder through the tiny oval window. Listening to his heartbeat, I let my eyes close. Hutch's whispers to our daughter shifted into the low dulcet sounds of a children's song I couldn't quite place, and I let myself drift as the quiet sounds of the airplane carried us back home.

FORTY-THREE

ADRIAN

BOSTON

THINGS WERE FAR FROM easy as we settled into our lives back in Boston. Sloane had let me continue to work remotely three days a week, and although she protested me babying her, I think Isobel was relieved she had someone else at home to help during the day.

Finley had grown, filling out her once tiny little chicken legs and finally looking more like a healthy infant and less like a tiny preemie. She was still small, but she was thriving.

She just didn't fuckin' sleep. Which was wearing on both of us.

I tried to get up as much as possible during the night, often stealing the baby monitor from Isobel's nightstand after she'd fallen asleep, but there were still nights when neither of us seemed to calm her down.

The pediatrician insisted it was normal—that some babies simply had colicky tendencies—but as we reached the point where we'd be able to take her to the office daycare; I feared she wouldn't be ready to go.

It'd been four months since she was born, and I was also worried that Isobel would never come out of the funk she'd been in. Sloane had convinced her to take the entire 12 weeks of maternity leave before she started transitioning back to her regular hours, but Isobel was struggling with guilt that her job was pulling too much of the focus from Finley.

As the days wore on, and neither of us had solid sleep at night, we both struggled to find a routine that worked.

The days I went to the office, she was up with me at dawn, even if Finley had finally fallen asleep. By the time I returned at night with dinner, she'd be surrounded by papers on the couch, usually with Finley passed out on her chest, clearly working on days she wasn't supposed to be.

I had to cajole her into the shower more often than not, and she absolutely refused to try to go places on the weekend where she thought Finley would be exposed to too many people.

When we'd first gotten home, I understood it, because we were still on the tail end of flu season, and she was medically vulnerable. But now we were well into spring, and she rarely left the apartment. We were supposed to move into a new townhouse a few blocks from her current apartment in three weeks, and while my apartment was a sea of neatly stacked boxes, she hadn't gotten far with packing.

Dr. Reeves had broached the subject of seeing a counselor to talk to Isobel about her fears regarding being a new parent and balancing her time as a working mom, but she brushed it off, throwing away the business card when she thought I wasn't looking.

I tried to take on as much as I could, but she wouldn't let me, and I felt helpless as I watched her spiral.

But I was thankful for rare days like today. Finley had sporadically been sleeping longer at night, and last night was one of those nights. Isobel had gotten seven hours of uninterrupted sleep, and I'd made her breakfast after we'd showered. The little line between her eyebrows had softened as we went through a seemingly normal weekend routine together. Finley had been in a good mood when she'd woken up, and I hoped we were finally working toward more peaceful nights.

She was lying between us on the bed, milk drunk and content, kicking her little legs into the air as she played with my hands.

Isobel was leaning against the headboard, her laptop perched on her knees while she sifted through the backlog of work emails. I'd tried to get her to stop thinking about work during the weekends, but she worried her projects were going to fall through the cracks while she was only working part-time.

I was tired of fighting her, so I didn't argue, knowing it gave her the feeling of control that was missing when it came to her daily life right now.

Things were far from perfect, but I knew this stage was temporary. Weeks ago, we'd been trapped in a hospital with no end in sight, and now we had a healthy, mostly happy baby who was starting to thrive.

Pressing my nose into Finley's hair, I inhaled, thinking that there was no way my life could feel more complete than it did right now. Well, one more thing would make it perfect.

"Marry me," I whispered to Isobel, looking over our daughter's head to where she was sitting on the bed beside us.

"What?" Her eyes widened as she froze, her hand dropping to her side. "No. What are you talking about?"

Well, that wasn't the answer I was hoping for.

"Adrian..."

"Stop. Just stop," I urged quietly, reaching over to grasp her hand. "Hear me out."

"Are you insane?"

"Maybe," I chuckled, but the shell-shocked expression didn't move from her face as she put her laptop on her nightstand and pulled her hand out of mine. "But I can't imagine not spending every day like this. Only with a ring on your finger."

"Only a ring," she scoffed as she scooted sideways, standing at the edge of the bed for a moment before she started pacing the length of it. "You don't want to marry me."

"I..."

Her brow furrowed, and I watched tears spill from the corners of her eyes, tracking down her cheeks. "I'm a mess. You can't seriously want this forever. I can barely make it through the day under the weight of all this and you're just over there in la la land thinking about weddings and rainbows while I'm literally falling apart. Every morning, I wake up and wonder if we made a mistake. If having her was a mistake." She stared at Finley, and her voice caught as more tears fell. "And then I feel like a monster because I love her so much, but she doesn't deserve a mom who can't handle taking care of her."

"Babe." Gently placing Finley into the cot next to the bed, I walked to where Isobel was pacing, grasping her shoulders. "I don't care about any of that. All I know is that I don't want to look back on my life and regret anything. I don't want to regret telling you how I feel. I know you lo..."

"Loving you isn't the problem, Adrian. But I can't imagine getting married right now. Or maybe ever."

"I just want you to think about it. We don't have to do it right now. I need to get the ring from Pops still, and I'll wait as long as you need me to, but I want you to know how I feel."

"I can't..."

She tried to pull away, but I held tight, bending my knees to look in her eyes. "Talk to me. Please."

"Stop. Just stop. Enough. I don't want to talk about this right now. I can't. I...have too much on my plate right now and I can't manage it all. Please don't add something else for me to fail at." This time, when she tried to pull free, I released her, watching as she disappeared into the bathroom and locked the door.

The walls she'd seemed to dismantle over the last year came back up in an instant, fortified with abject terror and fucking postpartum depression. I knew I was pushing her, but I also thought we could work through this phase and come out stronger on the other side.

Clearly, I was mistaken.

Chapter
FORTY-FOUR

ADRIAN

BOSTON

Isobel had withdrawn into herself even more after I'd proposed. And my heart was breaking watching her fall apart. She'd come out of the bathroom afterward, avoiding talking to me by funneling all of her focus into catching up on work. I didn't want to pressure her, but knowing she thought she was a failure as a mother or that she'd fail at being my wife was gut wrenching.

When Monday rolled around, I'd left her apartment, returning home to swap out my clothes and head to work for a few hours. Every day that week when I came home, she was in the same place. Finley would be propped on her chest, and Isobel would be wearing the same pajamas she'd put on the night before after I'd made her take a shower. It was like she was making it her mission in life to torture herself by only focusing on work or the baby.

For someone who was so committed to making sure happy endings came to life, she was insistent on avoiding her own.

When Thursday morning rolled around, I had a meeting I couldn't skip at ten, so I was packing my things to drive downtown. Isobel was going to try to come into the office to meet with Sloane at three this afternoon while Finley spent a few hours at the daycare as a trial run.

"Are you sure you don't want me to take her?" I offered, gazing at where Finley sat in her bouncy chair in the middle of the living room. She'd been a little out of sorts and congested the last few days as the rainy weather of spring transitioned into summer. She hadn't had a bad night, but she was sleepier than usual.

Isobel still hadn't taken the time to get in the shower, making sure Finley was having a good morning, while neglecting herself. Again.

"It'll be fine," she reassured, but the shadows underneath her eyes concerned me. She wouldn't be able to keep up this pace without sleep, and I often wondered if maybe I needed to cut back on my hours to help more. She would never let me, but I still wanted to.

"I have about fifteen minutes until I have to leave if you want to go shower."

"What's the worst that can happen? She cries the entire time I'm in there like she does every other day?" she joked, but I could see through her attempt at humor for what it really was...exhaustion.

"Next time you go in, I'll get her ready in the morning. You shouldn't have to give up taking time for yourself to care for her when I can help. We can take turns getting her ready when we're both headed in."

"I know," she sighed, and I decided to drop the argument for now. Kissing both of my ladies on the cheek and crossing my fingers that Isobel wouldn't continue to disappear every time I left the apartment, I made the trek into the office. I felt like I was losing her and there was nothing I could do to stop it.

AFTER SITTING THROUGH A ninety-minute meeting—I didn't pay attention to half of—I sat down at my desk and tried to concentrate on what I needed to get done so I didn't have to work over the weekend.

"Why didn't you tell me how adorable your daughter was?" Andrea walked into my office without knocking and sat down on my couch with her tablet in her lap.

"What?"

People had requested to see pictures when I'd returned to work, and the baby announcement had somehow ended up on the shared server, but Isobel had refused to bring her into the office in person.

"She's got such tiny hands and those big blue eyes. I just want to squeeze her."

"Why are you suddenly fawning over my daughter?"

Andrea frowned, glancing at the door before she looked back at me. "Because I just saw her in the elevator. Isobel got off on two to drop her off at the daycare when I was headed back from lunch."

I closed my laptop, picking my phone up from where it'd been lying face down on the desk. "It's not even noon. She wasn't supposed to come in until this afternoon."

"Well, she's here early then. She said she had a meeting with Sloane."

Pulling open my messenger app, I opened the thread with Isobel, but there weren't any new texts.

Adrian: Are you at the office?

Isobel didn't respond right away, but my eyes widened when I saw what she texted back.

> Isobel: Sloane needed me to come in early to talk about some last-minute changes to a project she wants me to help with. I'll come to find you if I have time later.

> Adrian: Is everything okay?

> Isobel: I think so, but it's not something I can work on remotely, so I'm not sure if a slow transition back to the office is going to be possible.

When we'd talked about her returning to work, the plan had been for her to work in the office three days a week for a month, and then slowly ease back into visiting the other branches for a few days at a time. But we'd make it work if that needed to change.

> Adrian: Did Finley get settled into the daycare alright?

> Isobel: She lost her shit while I was in the shower, but she calmed down on the ride here, otherwise I wouldn't have left her. I thought about canceling my meeting, but I can't keep sitting in the apartment listening to her scream all the time.

> Adrian: Why didn't you call me? I could've come back home after my meeting if you needed help.

> Isobel: You can't always rescue me. I need to figure out how to balance my job and Fin.

> Adrian: But you shouldn't have to do it alone.

After dropping my phone back to the surface of my desk, I scrubbed my hand over my face. She was going to run herself ragged trying to take everything on by herself.

"Is everything okay?" Andrea asked, nervously perching herself on the edge of the couch.

"Yeah, Isobel's meeting got moved up," I said absently, feeling guilty for not being there to help her. If I had known Fin was going to have a rough morning, I would have insisted she let me help her more.

FOUR HOURS LATER, ISOBEL still hadn't come to find me, and I was getting worried as the end of the workday approached. It wasn't like her to completely freeze me out, but I had to trust she would come to me for help if she needed it.

> Adrian: Haven't heard from you all day. Is now a good time?

> Isobel: Heading to your office now, I need to talk to you about something. But I'm not sure you're going to like it.

Pacing behind my desk, I waited for her to arrive, wondering what I wasn't going to like about what she needed to tell me.

"Hey," she whispered as she entered my office and closed the door.

"Hey." Stepping toward her, I pulled her into my chest, sighing when she wrapped her arms around my back. "Is everything okay?"

"Yeah," she mumbled as she pulled away from me, looking down while nervously wringing her hands in front of her. She looked even more exhausted than she had been when I left this morning, and I just wanted to get Fin and take them both home.

"Can you pick Finley up from the daycare before you leave?"

Frowning, I tried to step toward her to tip her chin up, but she stepped back again. "Is everything okay? Did something happen today?"

She sniffled as she looked away, and I didn't see any tears, but her expression had me worried.

"There is a dinner meeting with an author tonight, and Sloane said I didn't need to go, but if I don't go, then she'll probably take me off the project, and I don't want her to feel like I'm not doing my job..."

"Hey." I grasped her shoulders, pulling her toward me and tucking her into my chest. "Slow down."

"There should be plenty of milk in the cooler bag if you want to take her back to your place tonight," she mumbled into my shirt. "If you don't want me to go, I won't, but..."

"Is." I coaxed her face upward, using my thumb to wipe away a tear at the corner of her eye. "Why wouldn't I want you to go to a business meeting? If you need to do this, don't feel guilty asking me to pick up my own child."

"But this was so last minute, and now I feel like I'm letting everyone down. Sloane shouldn't have to do my job for me, and if this author doesn't agree to the proposal, then why is she even keeping me around? This is important to Vivid, and it falls under my job description, and if I screw this up...”

"She's keeping you around because you're good at your job. You've just barely returned from maternity leave. Don't put so much pressure on yourself."

"And there's another meeting on Monday in New York. Sloane gave me an out to stay here, but the author she's meeting has been one of my authors for years, and if I don't go and she backs out, I'm going to feel like this is all my fault."

"Breathe," I coaxed as I rubbed her back. "If you need to go to New York for a day, it will be fine."

"I'll be gone overnight," she whispered, and tears pooled at the corners of her eyes. "I'd feel guilty leaving Fin for the first time for a work trip, and she still doesn't sleep, and you need to work too, and it wasn't supposed to be this hard..."

"Is, it'll all be fine. We'll figure this out. We knew travel was a part of this job and it's only one night. You'll be a few hours away. I'm not worried." Returning her head to my chest, her body shuddered, and I ran my hand down the back of her head. "Are you coming back to my place tonight?" I asked, hating the way she still wasn't coming to me for support. It shouldn't upset her this much to let people help her.

"I don't know how long this dinner will last."

"That's okay. I can handle picking Finley up and getting her settled for the night. Why don't you spend tonight at your apartment so you can get some sleep after you're done. Your job is important too. Don't feel guilty for asking me to help."

She stiffened in my arms, and I knew she was going to fight me on the suggestion, but her voice cracked when she spoke. "My job is the one thing I'm not supposed to be a failure at, but every day I'm gone I fall further behind."

"Then let me help you."

By the time she left my office with a promise to text later, she'd calmed down, but it was clear she was still trying to put on a brave face and do everything alone. Instead of dealing with her depression, she continued pretending to be strong, like I didn't know she spent half the time crying.

At six o'clock, I took the elevator down to the second floor, making my way to the daycare we'd toured a few months ago. Finley was cleared by her pediatrician to start, but I had worried her first day might be a rough transition.

"I'm here to pick up Finley O'Neill. She's in the infant room."

"She was great today, a little fussy after she ate, but calmed right down once we put her in the swing. I'll go grab her for you." At least one person in our family seemed to be having a good day.

I felt like I was going through the motions as I gathered her things and headed toward the elevators. Thankfully, she stayed asleep while I clicked her car seat into place in the back seat of my car.

"I guess it's just the two of us," I whispered after I started the car, turning the radio on low so I didn't startle her. "Sorry you're stuck with Daddy for the night."

She slept most of the way home, only waking up as I pulled her seat out of the car. It seemed she was just as out of sorts as I was, crying the entire ride in the elevator.

My apartment seemed rather depressing with the stacks of boxes covering a majority of the surfaces, but I was thankful I still had a freezer full of prepackaged meals.

"You hungry, Fin?"

She protested loudly when I pulled her from her car seat, but settled once I had her tucked with her head against my shoulder.

Isobel had filled the little cooler with pre-measured bottles of her milk, and I pulled one out before I tucked the rest of them into the almost barren fridge. I still had an unopened case of premixed formula in the cabinet, so we would be fine overnight.

I went through the motions of slowly heating the bottle with warm water while I bounced her against my chest. Finley finally calmed down as I sat on the couch to feed her. She watched my face as she hungrily sucked down the contents, only stopping when I pulled the empty bottle from her mouth.

Knowing she was notorious for projectile reflux and spitting up, I pulled the diaper bag closer with my foot and grabbed a burp cloth to throw over my shoulder. Rubbing her back and patting gently until she burped, I tried not to worry as the hour grew later and later with no word from her mother.

Using her as a distraction, I tucked Fin into her bouncy seat and talked to her while I heated food for myself. "Daddy kinda sucks at feeding himself when Mommy isn't around. She'd probably yell at me for eating this and tell me it wasn't fair that I look like I do and eat crap. But Mommy looks beautiful with spit up in her hair, and I like her new curves. Don't think she's going to let me touch them anytime soon, but I can be patient."

She stared up at me, and I felt like my own kid was sizing me up. "What? Don't look at me like that. I have self-control."

She made an adorable little cooing noise and then hiccupped. Poor kid had pretty much religiously gotten hiccups every night since we brought her home. It'd been adorable at first, but it usually meant she was about to lose her shit.

Thankfully, she waited to start crying until I was seated at the table. I unbuckled her and propped her up in my lap, trying to feed myself with one hand. She watched what I was doing with curious bright blue eyes, trying to grab my fork, but I was too quick for her even if it took me twice as long to eat.

I couldn't blame Isobel for feeling overwhelmed. She was there to help most of the time I was with Fin if I needed it. If I had a hard time with her around, doing it by herself when her only companion was a screaming infant had to be nearly impossible.

We watched TV for a little while after, but when she yawned and her eyes started drifting closed, I took her to my room to get ready for bed. I'd become an old pro at changing diapers and there had been a sleep sack tucked in the diaper bag. The kid almost had more clothing than I did, although my closet was mostly full of suits.

"Alright, little demon, Daddy is flying solo tonight, so I need you to try to sleep. I know I'm not the same as Mommy, but she needs a break right now. I need you to work on this whole crying thing. I know it's not your fault, but a little sleep would be nice."

While Isobel had initially scolded me for calling Finley "little demon" during one late night feeding while we were both extremely sleep deprived, the nickname had stuck. She was prone to acid reflux—which her pediatrician thought might be related to the colic—which meant she often spit up after a bottle. But this wasn't any normal spit up. The girl could have given the actress in *The Exorcist* a run for her money. We'd tried to switch formulas, and Isobel had adjusted her diet, but nothing seemed to help.

After getting Fin settled in the portable crib next to the bed, I retreated to the living room.

Isobel had been such a constant presence in my life for so long I wasn't sure what to do with myself. Most of the shows I watched on streaming were ones I'd started with her, and I'd feel like even more of a dick if I watched them without her. Baseball season had started, but we'd been so busy trying to adjust to life with a baby that I hadn't made time to watch the games, much less go to one.

Turning on ESPN for background noise, I opened my text messages, willing one to appear on the screen from Isobel so I knew she was okay, but it never came.

THE DIM GLOW OF the television was the only light in the living room when my eyes opened several hours later. I hadn't meant to fall asleep on the couch, but I also hadn't wanted to wake Finley up by going through my normal routine.

Whimpers reached my ears from my cracked open bedroom door, and I arched my back and rolled my neck from side to side while I tried to work out the soreness. I'd slept in some weird positions during all the travel I'd done when I still played ball, but I was also nearly twenty years younger back then. Now, if I slept wrong, I'd permanently injure myself. Might as well slap on a neck brace and admit that I was getting fuckin' old.

Yawning, I checked my phone, and there still weren't any notifications from Isobel. Part of me wanted to text her to see how everything went, but it was three in the morning, and if she was finally getting sleep at her place, I didn't want to disturb her.

A loud wail tore through the air, and I knew my rest for the night was likely over. Finley was hungry. And she was also pissed.

"What's wrong, sweet girl? Are we ready for a late-night snack? I get hangry sometimes too. Mommy likes to call me a dick and shove a protein bar at me, but I bet you'd rather have a bottle than one of those."

Her little face was red, her cheeks wet with tears as I pulled her up and tucked her against my shoulder. She screamed while I got her bottle ready to warm and only settled briefly while I changed her diaper.

She didn't want to stop screaming to eat, but eventually hunger won out and she sucked down the contents of her bottle. I thought she was satisfied, and I might be able to tuck her back into bed so we could get a few more hours of sleep. But, of course, things couldn't be that easy.

When I got her up to sway her, trying to see if movement would calm her down, she'd puked all over me, the smell of curdled formula mixed with breast milk saturating my clothing. I wasn't sure how one tiny bottle had multiplied inside her little body, but she covered every piece of clothing I was wearing and herself.

"You know you're supposed to keep that inside or you'll get hungry again, right? I promise I won't complain about the smells that come out of your diapers if you tone down on the projectile spit up. Deal?"

Deciding wiping both of us up would take too long, I made an executive decision. "Mommy probably wouldn't be happy with me for doing this, because it'd be a fall hazard, but I won't tell if you don't."

I stripped Fin down to her diaper, laying her on a blanket in the middle of the bed while I pulled off my clothing, my nose wrinkling at the smell. It'd only been in her stomach for ten minutes, and it didn't smell like that before it went in.

Once I was down to my briefs, I picked her up and headed to the bathroom. Trying to shower one handed with a slippery infant was challenging, but we managed to get most of the funk off.

"That's better. No more stink monster. Should we get dressed and try to eat a little bit so we can go back to sleep?"

She was in a much better mood once I'd redressed her in clean pajamas, gently drying her chaotic hair. She'd gotten a mix of my curls and Isobel's straight hair. I was glad she was a girl because her cowlicks were wild. Fin was adorable as fuck—and I wasn't just biased because she was my kid—with giant blue eyes that didn't quite fit her face, the O'Neill dimples, and her mother's button nose.

Her curious eyes followed me as I threw on a pair of sweats before I picked her back up.

Deciding it was probably safe to give her half a bottle, I settled into the couch and fed her until she fell asleep, her lips gumming the nipple when she drifted off part way through.

With all the lights off, the apartment was quiet. Her quiet sighs made it impossible to think about putting her back in the crib, so I settled back against the pillows in the corner of the couch with her tucked against my chest. Closing my eyes, I rubbed her back, drifting but not quite asleep until gentle streams of sunlight started to filter in my windows.

FORTY-FIVE

ISOBEL

BOSTON

WHEN I'D PACKED FIN up to go to the office this afternoon, I hadn't anticipated ending the day perched on a toilet seat with a breast pump attached to my chest trying not to cry. My life didn't feel like my own right now, and I couldn't even get through half a day without breaking down.

I was supposed to go and finish a business dinner with an author we were trying to woo, and I had freaking bullseye breast milk stains on the front of my now see-through blouse.

One day.

I just wanted one fucking day where I didn't feel like a failure.

One day where I could just feel normal instead of this alien version of myself that couldn't seem to do anything right.

For fuck's sake, I was crying in a restaurant bathroom stall being milked like a cow because I heard a baby crying on the other side of the restaurant and my milk let down.

The noise of the restaurant almost drowned out the sound of the pump when the door to the ladies' room opened. The door to the stall next to me closed before a voice asked, "What's that noise?"

"I don't know. It kinda sounds like you're in your room after ten every night."

"You can hear that?"

"Oh my god, I think everyone on our floor can hear it. My electric toothbrush is quieter than your vibrator."

"Seriously. What is that? It's kind of creeping me out."

Trying to ignore the commentary on my current state of being, I turned off the pump, suddenly self-conscious about leaving the stall.

"Sounds like they're done. Wish I could come that quietly," the one closest said.

"Yeah, so do I."

"Must have really needed to take the edge off if they're doing that in a bathroom stall."

Both women laughed, and I cringed while I packed away the collection bottles and re-buttoned my stained blouse. Awkwardly balancing my pump bag with my purse, I tried to put my blazer back on without dropping anything.

When I opened my door, the stall next to me did at the same time, and I made eye contact with the woman emerging before looking down and heading to the sink.

The other stall opened and another young woman in a tight, short dress joined us at the sinks.

They both eyed me as I washed my hands before rinsing off the parts to my pump. It'd be nice if these things magically cleaned themselves so I could escape right now.

"What is that?" the one closest asked, and the other smacked her in the shoulder. She turned to her friend and shrugged. "What? You're the one who thought it was a vibrator."

At this point, I wished it was a vibrator. Since I hadn't had an orgasm in over four months, and probably wouldn't ever again once Adrian decided to stop putting up with me.

"It's a breast pump."

Their mouths puckered, and they looked at me.

"Is that like a sex thing?"

"Holy shit, you're an idiot," her friend hissed.

"I don't know what a breast pump is."

"It's for milk. For a baby," I explained. "For food."

"You have to milk yourself in public when you have a baby?"

Unfortunately, sometimes yes. "Can't you just feed it with a bottle or something? Why do you have to do that here?"

"You think I enjoy milking myself in a bathroom stall? Most places don't have anywhere else for me to go. I'd probably get asked to leave if I tried to do this at the table."

She didn't answer, squinting as she watched me pack away the pump parts. "Where is your baby?"

"She's with her dad." Who I hoped didn't hate me right now. Because I hated myself enough for the both of us.

"Ah. So, he's babysitting so you can go out?"

"He's her father. It's not babysitting when it's your own kid." I hated it with a passion when people said that. Fathers were perfectly capable of watching their children while their partners left. And it wasn't fucking babysitting.

"What else are you supposed to call it?"

She stared at me expectantly, and I was baffled that we were still having this conversation in this day and age. "Parenting. Would it be babysitting if I were watching her?"

The eyes of the girl next to her widened and I think she could tell I was teetering on the edge of my sanity right now. "We should probably go, Mills. The guys are waiting."

Yeah, Mills. I'd like to wallow in self-loathing with milk stains on my shirt in a restaurant bathroom by myself.

Sloane was walking down the hall toward me as I exited the bathroom. I attempted to pull my blazer closed so she wouldn't see my predicament, but I had a feeling she saw it anyway.

"You feeling okay? You've been gone a while."

"I'm uh..." While the stains had started to dry, there was still a visible mark left behind. I would have to start carrying extra shirts with me from now on. This definitely wasn't something they told you about in the baby books.

"Oh, no worries, Is. I can cover the rest of the meeting. These things happen. I know when I was nursing, I leaked through things during meetings all the time. I finally started wearing black blouses all the time, so it wasn't as noticeable. You'll get the hang of things. Whatever you need to do to be comfortable is a priority at work. If you need to nurse during the day, feel free to pop down to the daycare and take care of it."

Sloane had always been a very supportive boss, but the fact she was more than willing to accommodate my rough start into motherhood brought tears to my eyes. I sniffled, trying to smile as I nodded, but as her expression shifted to concern, I was afraid she'd judge my ability to return to my job. But I needed something to focus on right now, desperately, because being a mother was so much harder than I thought it'd be.

"Why don't you go home and get some rest? I'm assuming Adrian has the baby right now, so let him help you. It's hard the first few months, and with her being a preemie, I'm sure it's much harder than I went through, but you will get past this. Things won't necessarily get easier, but you'll figure it out. I promise."

Unable to hold back the tears, I nodded, my throat too tight to talk. I think she could tell I was seconds away from a meltdown, and she stepped toward me, placing a comforting hand on my shoulder.

"Rest tonight. Reset for tomorrow. If you're willing to make the trip to New York with me, I'd really appreciate your help, but I understand if..."

"No," I rasped, my voice wavering. "I need to try. You didn't promote me to not do my job. I want to start getting back to what my duties should be. I need something to start going right."

"I promoted you because I know you are a very competent employee, but I also know how hard it is to navigate being a woman in the professional world. It may take some time and adjustment, but I'm not worried about your work performance. You taking care of that sweet baby is a priority now too."

Thinking about Finley and all the ways I was failing her had been my constant companion for the last few months. Adrian had tried to comfort me and give me space to work through things, but I just couldn't let go of the guilt. It followed me around like a black cloud.

"Thank you," I whispered, situating the straps of my bags on my shoulder.

"No need for a thank you. Feel free to work remotely tomorrow if you need to. Just pencil me in for a call in the afternoon to settle travel plans."

I nodded, taking a deep breath after she let go of my shoulder and skirted around me to duck into the bathroom.

Once she was gone, I fought the urge to cry, not knowing how I'd continue to balance everything. She'd tried to give me an out from the trip to New York, but I felt like not going would let her down. I just didn't want to let my family down either by leaving them.

Going home sounded like an impossible task right now, and the one place I really wanted to go seemed selfish, but I was going anyway. Because I couldn't stomach facing Adrian—or Finley—right now.

"HEY," LEILA GREETED AS her door swung open, a confused look on her face. I'd shown up unannounced, but I needed to talk to her. She might not understand the stress of motherhood, but she was always a shoulder to lean on. And someone who wasn't afraid to give me the truth. "You okay?"

"No," I whimpered, shaking my head. I was so not okay right now.

"Shit, girl, don't cry. Get your ass in here. I'll grab the wine." She stepped aside so I could enter her apartment, and walked toward the kitchen while I stood still in the entryway, trying not to turn into a blubbering mess.

"I can't drink," I mumbled, and she leaned over the counter, rolling her eyes.

"Half a glass won't hurt you. It looks like you need it right now. Go sit, don't just stand there looking like a wounded puppy."

Placing my bag down by the door, I pulled out the small cooler I stored the pumped milk inside. "Can I put this in your refrigerator?"

"What you got in there?"

"Milk."

She laughed, motioning for me to join her in the kitchen. "I'm gonna assume that it's not from a cow."

"I feel like one lately. Nobody told me I'd have to milk myself like ten times a day."

"Fin still not cooperating with the whole breast-feeding thing?" I'd talked to Leila sporadically over the last few months, and she was great about asking how

I was doing, but most of those conversations ended up with me unloading my problems on her. Yet another thing I was failing at, I was a terrible friend.

"Pretty sure she hates me. Why didn't you try to talk me out of it when I told you I wanted a baby? I'm probably the worst mother in history."

"I've never been a mother, but I know that's not true. You've gotta give yourself some grace. You've had a rough couple of months, but you're still trying. Dickhead have her right now?"

"Yeah." I bit my lip, trying not to cry again, but my eyes watered. "I pretty much dumped her on him and ran this afternoon."

"And I'm sure he was okay with that. You know he'll help when you need it. I'm kinda surprised the guy hasn't tried to put a ring on it, to be honest."

"He did."

"You're engaged, and you didn't tell me? What the hell, Is?"

Shaking my head, I reached up to wipe my cheeks, tears leaking in earnest now. "I said no. Or I think I said no. He asked me out of the blue while I was trying to go through work emails, and I panicked. I don't even know why he wants to marry me. I'm a total shit show."

"Maybe because he loves you. And he's obsessed with you, and your adorable kid."

"I know he loves Fin, but..." With how much I'd withdrawn over the last few months, and how distant I was throughout my pregnancy, I wasn't so sure about me.

How could he love me when I couldn't find anything to love about myself?

"Sit down," Leila commanded, pointing to her couch. "Sounds like you need to finally unload some of that self-loathing."

I couldn't even deny that I loathed myself. I did. No matter how much I tried to pull myself together over the last six months—hell, for the last decade—something was always there to knock me back down. I was so tired of it. I was just so tired in general. Exhaustion seemed to follow me like a black cloud.

She joined me on the couch a few minutes later, silently handing me a wineglass that was a little more than half full and sitting on the opposite end.

"I don't know where to start." My voice was a broken whisper.

"I think that's part of the problem, Is. You've been so fixated on what everyone else wants you haven't permitted yourself to just live. You may have moved on from Grant, but you never moved on from what you perceived to be a failure on your part."

Bringing my glass to my lips, I contemplated what she was saying. Maybe I was still carrying around the baggage of my failed marriage. I hated disappointing people. That was why I'd thrown myself into work for all these years. I failed Grant. I failed my marriage. I failed my parents and their expectations.

The one thing I hadn't failed at was bringing other people's stories to life. I gave other people the tools to make their dreams come true, and I was afraid to embrace mine.

"What if I can't do this?" The weight of everything was crushing me. Motherhood. My job. Being a terrible partner. Being a terrible friend.

A year ago, I'd thought Adrian and his attitude were the problem. Now he'd shown me how caring and selfless he could be. The last person I thought I'd fall for was the one person keeping me afloat, so I didn't drown. I was scared to contemplate what my life would even look like right now if I had done this on my own. But I'd failed at marriage once, so I was terrified it'd happen again, and if Adrian left me, I'd be crushed.

"What if you can? You have all the parts to create this wonderful life for yourself, and you refuse to stop beating yourself up for things that were out of your control."

"But what if they were my fault?"

"Your marriage ending was not your fault. You were dealt a shitty hand of cards, and the man who was supposed to be your partner was too much of a coward to stay when it got hard."

"It's not just him. It's everything. Finley might not have been premature if I'd been better at managing my stress. It was my body that failed her. She's so beautiful and tiny and everything I thought I ever wanted...but it's so hard. She never stops crying. All day she cries. She doesn't sleep. I don't sleep. And every time Adrian comes home, and she immediately calms down, I hate him a little more. Then I hate myself for hating him. I don't want to hate him...I..."

"You love him."

Nodding, I reached for a tissue from the box on her coffee table. "I do. But he's so much like Grant, I'm scared. What if he leaves me too?"

"Is," she sighed, moving closer. She set her glass and mine on the table and pulled me into her chest. "He may have acted like Grant initially, but from everything he's done for you, we both know he's not him. He loves you, and I bet it's killing him to see you suffering like this. You need to let him in."

Adrian had never looked at me with disgust or pity like my ex had during the end of our marriage, but I wasn't sure how long that would last. I was disgusted with myself.

"Maybe they're both better off without me."

"Girl, I love you...but shut the fuck up. You're a hot fucking mess right now, but we both know you're a badass. And I'll be damned if we let any of this pull you under. Baby girl, you're a fighter. And you're going to fight for that baby, and that man. Maybe I should have pushed you harder back then. You have to talk to someone about this. Someone who knows how to handle stuff like this."

"I'm talking to you," I mumbled into her shoulder.

"While I will always be here for you, and I know you'd do the same for me. I can't fix this for you. You have to want to fix it for yourself. Hiding from it is only going to make it harder. Tomorrow you are going to go home, and you're going to call someone because I won't let you self-destruct again. I can't lose you either."

"What if it's too late? What if Adrian hates me now? What kind of person just abandons their baby?"

"Is," she laughed, running her hand down my hair. "You've been gone for half a day. You hardly abandoned them. Maybe it'll be good for him to see what you've been dealing with."

"I should go home." I wasn't sure where that was. Adrian was at his apartment. Mine was a disaster area of half-packed boxes and the explosion of baby stuff. We were supposed to move in a few weeks, and I was so far behind it'd never happen at this rate. If that was even still the plan.

"No, you should get some fucking sleep. You're exhausted. Take one night off and everything will look clearer in the morning. I'll get you some PJs and then you're going to let yourself get some rest."

"But I can't..."

"This is gonna sound way too profound coming from me, but you can't drink from an empty cup, babe. Let the people who love you fill it."

The soothing motions of her fingers combing through my hair were bringing the exhaustion to the surface. She was right. I was so tired I didn't know how I'd even had the energy to get to work today, much less think I could make it through a business meeting. While she hadn't said it, even Sloane had looked at me like she thought I was going to fall apart in the restaurant.

"Get your skinny ass up and go take a shower. You know where everything is, and I should have something clean you can wear in the top drawer of my dresser."

Leila pulled me up from the couch, steering my weary body toward her bedroom door and playfully swatting my ass. It was the most action I'd seen in months.

"While I love you, I think we're too old, and you're too straight for me to help you shower. Go before you pass out."

The hot water felt good on my scalp as I let it wash away the things I'd been holding onto for way too long. Leila was right. Maybe it was time to let go of everything from my past so I could find a way to move forward. For Finley. For Adrian. For *myself*.

As my oldest friend tucked me into her bed, I let myself sink into the pillow, unwanted tears soaking the soft fabric.

My phone hung limply in my hand, the text thread with Adrian open. He deserved more than this, more from me. But as my fingers hovered over the screen, I hesitated. Nothing I said to him now could convey what was going on in my head.

As my eyes grew heavy and I drifted off, I vowed I'd find the strength to fight through this. Because I couldn't allow myself to go back to how things were before.

FORTY-SIX

ADRIAN

BOSTON

I WAS SURE I'D be worthless today, but since Finley did alright in the daycare yesterday, I decided we needed to go into the office instead of working remotely.

"Alright, little demon, time to get dressed so Daddy can be productive."

Finley decided not to pull another impersonation of *The Exorcist* and settled into her car seat happily for the ride downtown. She was all smiles when I got her checked into the infant room and I sighed in relief that we'd made it through a night solo without me totally screwing up.

Leaning against the back wall of the elevator, I closed my eyes as it traveled upward, trying to tune out the other people as the car filled.

"Rough night, O'Neill?" A voice teased from my right, and I peeked one eye open. Sloane was leaning against the wall beside me, hands folded across her stomach. She looked perfectly put together, as always, but I was sure I looked like a hot mess. Trying to get dressed with a clingy baby who screamed if you put her down was not easy.

"Little bit. How's your morning going?"

"Good. Good. Did Isobel get home alright last night?"

"I'm sure she did. We didn't ride in together this morning. I told her to stay at her place last night so she could actually get some sleep."

She frowned, turning toward me once enough people had gotten off so she could move. "She seemed a bit off at dinner last night, so I sent her home early. Having a newborn is rough, so I want her to take her time transitioning back in, but I appreciate her willingness to help get this rights deal to bed. She'll be a real asset in New York with me next week since she has an existing relationship with the author."

"She's eager to get back into her normal job duties. I know she's felt guilty that her maternity leave didn't go as planned."

"She has no reason to feel guilty. These things happen. I'm just glad we could accommodate her leave so you two could handle what you needed to. While it wasn't ideal, the rest of the team was able to handle your absences."

"Do you think she's ready to come back? Other than being tired, how did she seem yesterday?" Since Sloane had spent more time with her than I had, I wanted to see how much of an intervention I needed to stage when I finally tracked her down.

"Not her usual self, but that's to be expected when you're functioning on broken sleep. Honestly, she was fine all afternoon and throughout most of dinner. I think she had a minor wardrobe malfunction and seemed embarrassed about it, so I sent her home so she could change and get things situated."

She must have noticed my confusion and leaned in, circling her palm in front of her chest. "Poor thing had a leak that seeped into her blouse. I tried to tell her it happened to most of us at some point or another, but I could tell she'd been crying."

Fuck. She'd been embarrassed the first time she'd leaked through a nursing pad while we were still in the hospital, too. No one really cared. She was obviously a new mother, but she'd started hiding herself to pump after that.

"If Isobel comes with me, are you ready to go solo with Finley for a few days next week? You're welcome to work with her in your office if you need to at any point."

"I'm sure we'll manage," I replied. It'd be a battle to get Isobel to go with Sloane on this trip, but we'd manage without her because she needed to go. "She's done well in the daycare so far. I'm sure she'll be fine."

"Let me know if you guys need anything. I know some of the stodgy old execs think letting parents have flexibility while their kids are little is too new age, but I'd rather have happy, productive employees than risk people burning out or worrying about absences they can't control."

"And we appreciate that," I said as the elevator doors opened on my floor. "It was good talking to you."

"Hug that little cutie for me. I might need you to bring her to my office once we return next week for some snuggles."

As I walked to my office, I checked my phone again, frowning as I saw a text from an unfamiliar number.

> *Unknown: Is got to my place safe last night. She's sleeping in my guest bedroom, but I think she needs some time to talk through things before she goes home. Are you okay with Finley another night?*

> *Adrian: Who is this?*

> *Unknown: Leila. She showed up at my apartment last night in tears.*

It hurt that she didn't feel she could come to me, but if it meant she'd finally go talk to someone instead of retreating into herself, I had faith Leila would talk some sense into her.

FINLEY WAS ALL SMILES when I picked her up from the daycare at the end of the day. My mind was still a chaotic mess—worried about Isobel—but I knew I couldn't force her. She wouldn't leave us. I knew that in my heart. She was lost, and I hoped she'd find her way out of it without falling apart even more.

Maybe I should have pushed the issue months ago, but I'd been too scared and overwhelmed by everything going on with Finley to really process how

Isobel was crumbling before my eyes. If she didn't want to talk to someone about how she'd been feeling, I couldn't force her. She had to want to get healthy for herself.

It'd been so gradual over the last several months, and I hadn't realized how bad it had gotten until yesterday. She'd been pulling into herself bit by bit until the vibrant woman I'd fallen for was a ghost of herself.

I knew she couldn't see why I wanted to marry her, but even after her rejection, I still wanted that. Not just because we had a child together, but because I'd been falling for her for years. I wouldn't let the last nine months of our lives define her. She deserved more than that. She'd had one man who couldn't support her through hard times, and I wasn't going to be a coward like him.

Even if she never wanted to marry me, I was hers. Finley wasn't the only thing tying us together, and if she needed me to love her harder over the next few months while we tried to get through this rough spot, I would. Because I was going to need her to lean on soon, and I was afraid she'd fall apart if I couldn't hold us both afloat.

Pop's health had been declining, Hutch and I having more conversations than we would like about putting him in a care facility, but Ma was still holding out. We were both struggling through some pretty heavy things right now, but I wasn't going to let either of them push us apart. Both of us deserved to be happy. I just wished I'd done more for Isobel, so things didn't get to this point.

Finley chugged her way through a bottle once we got back to my apartment and then passed out, peacefully sleeping on my chest. I knew I should get up to feed myself, but she was only this little once. Her tiny lips quivered as I gazed at her, cataloging all the ways she looked like her mother. I was going to have to use the next thirteen years to prepare myself for when she was a teenager, because she was going to get me into trouble. With her pink pouty lips, the dimples she had started showing off when she smiled, and her deep blue eyes, she was going to be a heartbreaker.

I only hoped her mother didn't break mine.

THE BUZZING OF MY phone awoke me, and I yawned as I blindly felt across the bed to find it. The faint sounds of tiny breaths came from the crib on the other side of the room, and I hoped Fin would stay asleep for a little longer.

My phone buzzed again, and I lifted Isobel's pillow, finding it stuffed underneath.

The screen went blank as I turned it to face me, and a missed call alert popped up on the screen. Isobel had been trying to call, and I missed it.

Another alert scrolled across the screen for a voicemail before I could get it unlocked.

Since I'd accidentally fallen asleep with my glasses on, the face identification kept popping up a failure alert until I ripped them off and chucked them at my nightstand. Finley startled after they hit the surface, and I cursed that I'd woken her up.

Giving up on my phone momentarily, I scooped my grumpy girl up, holding her to my bare chest and heading toward the kitchen to make her a bottle.

"I'm sorry, sweetheart. Daddy is a mess this morning. Let's get you fed so you don't start waking the neighbors."

Normally on Saturday mornings, we'd take her for a walk to a park close to my place if we stayed here, but going without Isobel somehow felt wrong. I didn't want to do this parenting thing by myself. I knew she was worried about failing, but from what my brother had told me over the years, none of us knew what we were doing. We just had to try to mold our tiny people into good humans despite our very adult flaws.

Finley's little fist flexed in my chest hair, and I winced as she pulled, sounding as frustrated and adrift as I felt. "I know, baby girl, I miss Mommy too."

Bouncing her on my hip, I got a bottle ready and returned to the couch to feed her. Her little eyes were a carbon copy of mine, and they tracked my movements while she clung to my fingers holding the bottle. She wasn't quite ready to hold it on her own, but it was only a matter of time. Part of me wanted to fast forward to her being a little more independent, but I knew these moments were fleeting.

Sooner than I was ready for, she'd turn into the snarky teen I saw in my niece. Pen was already as tall as my Ma, and it was weird to see the little girl I used to carry around on my shoulders growing into an almost adult.

"You need to stay this little forever," I whispered, stroking her cheek. Milk leaked out of the corner of her mouth as she smiled up at me, dribbling down my bare chest. "But maybe you could also start sleeping. That'd be awesome."

I could hear my phone buzzing from the other room and knew I should go find it, but I was soaking in the quiet morning.

Fin's eyelids started drooping, her once voracious sucks turning into little lip quivers as she drifted. "Don't even think about it. It's not time for a nap yet. Maybe we should start some of that tummy time stuff I know you hate."

She squawked as I stood, bouncing her a bit as I rubbed her back. Of course, I'd made a rookie mistake and she spit up on my chest—again—sour milk embedding itself into my chest hair, but at least she hadn't pulled a full-on *Exorcist* head spin.

"Guess we're doing tummy time in the bathroom." Gathering the mat and play pillow, I balanced everything on one arm as I tried to keep her from rubbing herself in the spit-up cementing itself into my abs. Babies were gross.

"But maybe we should change your diaper first since you already made a mess of Daddy." As if on cue, she grunted, and the sound of a tiny explosion could be felt through her diaper against my arm. "That's just nasty. No wonder Mommy is worn out. You really are a little demon."

I expected her to cry at the smell, but she laughed, cementing my nickname for her even more.

Trying not to gag as I saved her from the toxic waste in her diaper, I double bagged that shit—literally—and sealed it into a Ziploc before I stashed it at the bottom of the bathroom trash can. I definitely needed to take that to the trash chute sometime soon. I'd thought I'd seen and smelled some pretty disgusting things throughout my lifetime. Hell, I'd spent time in an MLB locker room during Spring Training after playing in 90-degree heat, but nothing compared to the smell of a ripe diaper that'd been left to decay for too long.

Finley was all smiles as I propped her up on the little pillow that was tucked underneath her armpits, her eyes tracking the crinkly toys attached to the front of it as she tried to pick them up with her tiny fingers.

"Don't go anywhere," I warned her, stripping off my bottoms and climbing into the shower.

I was hopeful I'd make it through before she unleashed her scream of holy terror, but just as I was washing the shampoo from my hair, Finley let out a shriek that I was sure the neighbors could hear through the floor. Maybe I needed to invest in noise-cancellation headphones for Isobel for Mother's Day. I wasn't sure how she made it through the day with Fin with her hearing intact.

After the world's fastest shower, I grabbed a towel, wrapping it around my hips before I saved my temperamental baby from the clutches of her evil tummy time crinkly toys.

"You really need to work on your timing, kid."

As soon as I picked her up, she settled, her little baby talons scraping my chest as I carried her back into my bedroom. "Watch it," I hissed, trying to pry her tiny fingers from my chest.

She cooed as I lowered her to the mattress while I pulled out some boxer briefs from the dresser. I watched her like a hawk as I started to dress and wondered how we'd manage to do anything when this kid started to roll in the next few months. Once she was mobile, it was game over.

"Can you chill for like a minute so I can find my phone?"

She cooed again as I dropped to my knees and reached between the bed frame and my nightstand to retrieve the wayward technology.

Closing my eyes once it was in my grasp, I simultaneously prayed for a message from Isobel and also dreaded what one might say.

Leila had asked for the time to let Is work through whatever was going on, but I desperately wanted to talk to her. To hear her voice and know she was safe, even if she wasn't okay right now.

Waking the screen, I saw several text notifications waiting for me.

> Hutch: Pops is in the ER. He fell this morning but seems to be okay. Scared the shit out of me more than anything. Call me if you get this, I have a feeling we've hit the point where he needs more than Ma and I can give him.

Sitting down on the bed, I scrubbed my hand over my face, knowing he was right. It wasn't fair of any of us to ignore that we were headed toward the end of our time with him. Watching him slip further and further into himself, I knew my grandma would have been heartbroken to see him like this.

> Hutch: You know Pen would love to keep her cousin entertained while we discuss things with Ma. They're probably going to admit him for observation until at least tomorrow. While he's got a hard head, he also managed to give himself a concussion. Thankfully he didn't break anything else on the way down.

Shit.

> Adrian: Let me get some things packed up and I'll meet you at the house.

> Hutch: Isobel is welcome too. I can stop to grab lunch on my way back. Ma needs to eat something.

I hesitated, not wanting to drag my brother into whatever was going on in my personal life while he was in the thick of it with our grandfather.

> Adrian: She's taking care of some things today and leaves for New York tomorrow. It'll just be me and Fin.

> Hutch: No one to stop me from stealing some baby snuggles from my kid.

> Adrian: Not your kid, fuck face. See you in a few hours. Need me to break Pen out of Lena's?

> Hutch: She can walk over. Thankfully she wasn't home when he fell. I don't want her to see him like that.

No one wanted to see him like that. But you couldn't avoid dementia just because you didn't want to lose someone mentally before you watched them fade away physically.

Taking a deep breath, I rested my palm on Fin's stomach before I pulled open the next text message.

> Isobel: Tried to call a few times. I'm back at my apartment trying to sort through the nightmare of packing my closet so I can unbury my suitcase.

> Isobel: I'm sorry I didn't call sooner. It wasn't fair of me to just disappear.

> Isobel: I totally get it if you hate me right now. I'm trying not to hate myself. I love both of you so much.

Deciding it was easier to talk to her while I tried to get ready, I called her, and she answered on the first ring.

"Hey," her voice was quiet, but for once she didn't sound exhausted.

"Hey," I responded, using my shoulder to hold the phone to my head as I went to the dresser to find clothes to wear.

"I'm sorry," she whispered, and I could tell she was still beating herself up about prioritizing her needs.

"You don't need to apologize, babe. You shouldn't feel guilty for asking for help when you have other responsibilities you need to handle."

"But I feel bad when those responsibilities take me away from you and Fin. And now Sloane needs me to fly to New York with her for that meeting tomorrow, but I don't want you to hate me if I just leave both of you."

Sighing, I put the phone on speaker and laid it on my dresser while I pulled on my shirt. "Do you need to take this trip?"

"Well, I..." she trailed off, and I hated she was still trying to justify always putting her needs last.

"Don't make this harder than it needs to be. If you need to go to New York, then go. Fin and I will be okay. There are plenty of people who will step up to help if I need it."

"Sloane is worried my author won't agree to the new contract with the adjusted agreement on moving her books into film production. She's been with Vivid for years, and I've been her editor since the beginning. If we can't secure the film rights to her books, it'll set the California office back months in planning while we try to shuffle another project forward, which means securing the rights to another manuscript, and..."

"Then it shouldn't even be a question. Go do what you need to. It's only a few days."

The speaker rustled as I heard her take a deep breath. "After I finish packing, do you want to come over there?"

Sighing, I looked toward where Fin was trying to eat her fist in the center of the bed. "We need to head to Ma's today. Pops is in the hospital."

"Adrian, oh my God. Why didn't you lead with that? Is he okay? Do you need me to come get Finley?"

"He's got a concussion but didn't break anything. He's stable, and they're keeping him for observations. Hutch said Pen is looking forward to some one-on-one baby time, so I'm hoping it keeps them both distracted while we make some decisions."

"I'll call Sloane and tell her what's going on. We can try to reschedule..."

"No, Is. All you'd be doing is waiting around." My heart ached with how she was so willing to drop everything, but we both had things that needed our attention right now. "You're only going to be gone for a night. Go get those contracts signed and I'll let you know if things change with Pops."

She was quiet, and I knew she wanted to argue with me about staying here, but she eventually whispered, "I'm so sorry you're going through this. I hope he's going to be okay."

"Me too." He had to be.

SUNDAY I WAS TOO busy to even check my phone, scouring through websites to find places near Southie that were taking new memory care patients. Thankfully, Pops had a little nest egg tucked away since the mortgage was paid off—thanks to my salary from my single year with the Sox and some of Hutch's income while he was overseas.

Relying on a Medicare bed being open wasn't going to happen. Ma had been pulling strings where she could, getting appointments set for her and Hutch to tour some facilities first thing on Monday.

I wanted to be there to help, but Finley wasn't allowed in most of the places he could go until she was a little older. Pops' concussion was showing the promise of resolving itself, but the doctors didn't want to discharge him with how confused he still seemed.

Hutch had stuck around the house to help Pen with her cousin while I made a trip to the hospital to see him. I hated leaving Finley since she'd not slept well the night before and woke up refusing to eat and out of sorts, but Hutch had insisted he could handle a cranky baby.

When I got to the hospital, I was exhausted. I wasn't typically quick to cry but seeing him in that hospital bed gutted me. I'd grown up without a father, but this man had tried his best to make up for his son's absence. He'd been our rock for so long, encouraging us to spread our wings and find our places in life, and now we needed to be strong for him.

I never wanted Finley to grow up with only one parent. The circumstances were different than a husband killed in action, but I couldn't lose Isobel. Whatever I had to do to make sure she found her way through this depression, I would do.

My phone had been an afterthought until I arrived back at my apartment. Finley had been worn out from playing with her cousin and slept the whole way home, only briefly rousing to drink part of a bottle before I settled her back into the crib.

Isobel would only be gone a few days on her trip, but it felt like it was a lifetime away. I needed her but asking her to choose between something she needed to do for her job and shouldering my burdens when there wasn't anything for her to do to help wasn't fair. She had enough on her plate, so I needed to focus on the things on mine.

FORTY-SEVEN

ISOBEL

BOSTON

LEILA KICKED ME OUT of her apartment bright and early, with a coffee mug in my hand and a donut in the other. She had to get to work, and it was time I dealt with things I'd been avoiding as the stress of my life threatened to pull me under.

My breasts ached as I waited for my Uber to arrive, and I was thankful that my apartment was a quick ride away. Sitting down to pump once I got home, I turned my phone back on, my lips quivering as I pulled open the text messages. Adrian was worried, but I wasn't sure how to face him.

By the time I was done, I checked my phone again, noticing I had two new voicemails. Bracing myself, I pressed the play button on the first one.

"Is, please call me. I'm worried that I didn't hear from you last night, and I just want to make sure you're okay. I'm not mad, babe, I'm just concerned. Please don't push me away. I know things are hard right now, but we're going to get through this."

I sniffed as I pushed the play button on the second one, trying not to cry again. I hated I was doing this to them.

"Is, you need to talk to me. I don't want to leave things like this. Please let me know if you're okay. I'll give you space if you need it, but please don't push me away. I'm taking Fin with me into the office today, and I'll bring her back to my place tonight. Love you."

The pain in his voice killed me and it had me doing something I was scared—so damn scared—to do when it'd come up at my appointment weeks ago.

Digging through the trash can in my bathroom, I pulled out the business card I'd buried in there. Sitting on the closed toilet seat, my heart thrummed in my temples as I tried to gather the courage to type in the numbers printed.

When the phone connected, I swallowed down the panic and took a step forward instead of letting myself get sucked down by the past.

"Women's health and wellness. How may I direct your call?"

My throat was dry, but my voice came out stronger than I felt.

"Hi, my name is Isobel Blom. I need to make an appointment to see a therapist. My OB referred me to your clinic. She was worried I may have postpartum depression, and I think I'm ready to talk to someone."

I WAS ABLE TO get a last-minute appointment, thanks to a cancellation, on Friday for an initial assessment of my depression. I hadn't expected things to move so quickly, but I couldn't avoid this more than I already had. Living in denial was going to not only make me miserable, but it'd also make my family suffer.

My new psychiatrist, Dr. Stefano—who insisted I call him Garrett—was not what I'd expected, but he'd been ready to jump into things. He'd had me fill out a few assessments at the beginning of my appointment and then had made me tell him—in as much detail as I'd felt comfortable with—why I was coming to see him.

His calming demeanor had made it easier for me to divulge my fears, and I left my session on Friday, hopeful for the first time in months. After my appointment, I was anxious to tell Adrian that I'd finally talked to someone about how I'd been feeling, but I still needed a bit of time to process things on my own.

I had another appointment scheduled for next Friday to discuss possible medication options. Garrett also recommended getting a genetic test done to explore the best medication options for my body, so I'd spent half the morning waiting at the lab to have a cheek swab done.

I'd spent the evening and the next morning throwing myself into things I'd been avoiding, attempting to pack up the disaster that was my apartment.

Talking to Adrian on Saturday, I'd been ready to tell him I'd finally made a step toward coping with my life in a healthier way, but after he'd dropped the bomb of Pops in the hospital, I knew he was dealing with enough. I wanted to catch an Uber to be with them, but I knew he'd be upset if I put things on hold at work to do it.

As THE WHEELS OF the plane touched down in New York, my phone chimed from my pocket, so I pulled it out.

> Adrian: Please travel safely. Call me if you're up for talking. I just want to hear your voice.

I wanted to hear his voice too, but I was afraid of what he'd want to say to me. This weekend was the longest I'd spent away from either of them in months, and I hated I was the reason I wouldn't see them for another few days. It felt like an eternity to spend away from the two people who I loved the most.

"Everything okay?" Sloane asked as I frowned at my phone, but I didn't want to unload on her and have her doubt my ability to close this deal. She was counting on me to have my shit together, and I was determined to pretend I did until we had a signature on the contract in my bag.

"Yeah, it will be. Is there anything you need me to take care of before the meeting?"

She smiled, laying her hand on mine. "No, I know she'll be more comfortable with you here, so I want you to be well-rested for tomorrow. Go lay down or take a bath when we get to the hotel. Enjoy the quiet I know you're not getting at home right now."

She had no idea how right she was. My life was a total clusterfuck.

When I woke up to my phone alarm echoing in my too-quiet hotel room, I still had a few hours until I had to be ready for the meeting with my author, Nikki, and Sloane. It would have been the perfect time to get some rest, but a phone call interrupted it.

"Hi, is this Isobel Blom?"

"This is she," I answered absently, not entirely sure who was calling me. It was a Boston number, but it wasn't saved in my phone.

"Dr. Stefano had a last-minute cancellation for an appointment starting at 9:00. He wanted me to check to see if you'd be up for an additional session since you're a new patient."

Hesitating, I took a deep breath. Friday had been draining, but I felt good after unloading some of the things I'd been keeping inside.

"I'm out of town right now, but is he able to do a telehealth call?"

After we hung up with plans for me to log into the online portal, a few tears leaked out as I tried to fight off how overwhelmed I still felt. But I could do this. I *would* do this, because my daughter deserved more than a mother who was a broken shell of herself. I loved her too much to let this get any worse.

"How's your Monday going, Isobel?" Garrett asked, smiling at me through my computer monitor. "Were you able to get some sleep this weekend? I know you mentioned your daughter isn't a fan of sleeping last session."

Would he judge me if he knew I hadn't seen my daughter since then? I suddenly felt like even more of a terrible parent.

"I can tell by your expression that the question isn't one you want to answer. Remember, I'm here to help you talk through your issues, not judge you."

Easy enough for him to say. I was judging myself enough for everyone.

"I..." I hesitated to continue. "She was with her father the whole weekend while I stayed at my apartment."

"Are you still involved with her father? I thought you were in a romantic relationship with him."

"Yes, I am...we are. At least I hope so. Things have been hectic with me transitioning back to work, and he had a family emergency over the weekend. Now I'm in New York on a work trip. I won't see them again until late tonight. At this rate, probably tomorrow."

He tilted his head to the side, and I tried not to feel like I was under a microscope, but as his dark brown eyes assessed me, it was difficult not to squirm. "And you feel guilty because your professional obligations took your attention away from your daughter?"

Was I that easy to read?

"Pretty much. I shouldn't have dumped her on him, especially when he was dealing with his grandfather."

"Did he ask you to take your daughter while he dealt with his family situation?"

"No." I shook my head. I'd offered, but he told me to focus on myself. "He told me he was alright with me taking this trip."

"And you don't believe him?"

"Shouldn't I have dropped everything to go to them?"

"Let's reframe that. Would you have changed your plans if he asked you to?"

There wasn't any doubt in my mind that I would. "Of course."

"Then you need to trust your partner enough to communicate his needs with you. Is that something you feel comfortable doing with him? Have you shared your fears with him?"

"Which ones?" I joked, wiping my sweaty palms on my thighs. "You're going to have to be more specific. What aren't I afraid of lately?"

"Have you talked with him about *any* of your fears?"

Had I? He'd been comforting me for months, trying to take things off my plate to help me get through, but had I actually opened my mouth and talked to him? My eyes burned as I realized that while he tried to talk to me, I had internalized everything I was afraid of because if I voiced them, he might not love me anymore.

"No." My voice shook, and I tried to keep myself from crying.

"And that is upsetting to you?"

"Shouldn't it be?" I sniffed. "I feel like a terrible partner on top of a terrible parent. Maybe they both would be better off without me."

"Do you really believe that?"

I took a deep breath and tried not to let the tears overwhelm me.

"It'd make their life a lot easier if I had my shit together. He said he wanted to marry me, but when he brought it up, I panicked."

"Do you not want to marry him?"

"I do, but I'm scared. My first marriage didn't end well. He left me with some deep scars and I'm afraid of history repeating itself. With how spectacularly I'm failing at everything right now, I wouldn't want to marry me."

"Shouldn't that be something you let him decide?"

Was it really that easy? Adrian knew I was a disaster right now, and he hadn't run screaming yet.

"It sounds like instead of trying to let him help you with your problems, you're hiding them because you're afraid they'll push him away. Maybe if you both leaned on each other for support, it'd bring you closer instead of driving you apart."

"Instead, I ran away," I muttered, staring over the top of my laptop at the empty hotel room.

"Taking care of work obligations isn't running away, but if you continue to keep internalizing everything, then yes, emotionally you might be. Maybe it's time for you to run toward the people who matter to you, not away. Let them help you."

Garrett talked me through some coping strategies, such as journaling and writing my feelings down to share with Adrian if talking was too hard. I still had a lot of work ahead of me, but for once, it felt like I might be able to see a way through.

"We're often our worst critics, so you need to give yourself some grace as you navigate this new part of your life. Babies—and parenting in general—are hard, but as long as you keep trying to do your best, that's not failing. Same with relationships. Let your partner in, even if it's hard."

"I can try." I needed to try something because what I'd been doing wasn't working for anyone.

"Safe travels on your trip. Try to be kinder to yourself this week. Most people are so worried about their own struggles that they aren't going to judge you for yours. Feeling afraid and guilty won't help you move forward in life, so looking back constantly isn't where you need to be focusing your thoughts and actions. We can only move forward."

I let his words sink in long after we'd ended the call.

Chapter
FORTY-EIGHT

ISOBEL

NEW YORK

"I KNOW GIVING UP some of the creative control on your series is scary, but the screenwriter we've been working with doesn't want to change your stories, they just want to bring them to a whole new audience."

Nikki sighed, glancing between Sloane and me where we sat across from her in one of the small conference rooms at Vivid's offices in New York. Her lawyer had already raked through the contract, assuring we were giving her a fair deal on acquiring the film rights to her wildly successful small-town romance series. But she was still struggling with the fact that there was no way to avoid some things getting changed in the screenwriting process.

"Look," I sighed, leaning forward and staring straight at her. She'd been working with me for nearly my entire tenure at Vivid, so I felt like I needed to assure her she would be safe taking this monumental step with us. "I know these characters feel like your family, and you don't want someone to come in and hurt your family. Honestly, they feel like mine too after working on all your books, but that's why it's so important to share these stories with a wider audience."

"They are my family," she murmured, leaning back in her chair and crossing her arms over her chest. "But I'm not going to sell them out to make more money. That isn't fair to my characters or my readers."

"This isn't about making money, Nik. We want to preserve as much as we can of your stories during this process. Vivid has been just as much like your family for almost ten years since your agent brought me your first manuscript. I know it's hard to think about taking this step, but sometimes the things that are the scariest are the ones that will totally change your life."

She searched my face while she let my words sink in. Maybe I needed to take my own advice. I needed to stop being scared and take what I wanted from life instead of hiding from the hard parts.

My phone buzzed in the bag at my feet, distracting me, but Sloane picked up the conversation, talking to her about what the next steps were after the screenwriting process. She assured her that as the author she'd still have plenty of creative control during the project while working with the Vivid team.

My phone continued buzzing, so I reached down to slip it out of the pocket of my bag while still trying to follow the conversation.

My eyes widened as I saw I had three missed calls on the notification screen, one from the office daycare, and two from Adrian, along with half a dozen missed text messages.

Unlocking the phone, I pulled up Adrian's messages, my heart beating faster as I scrolled through them.

> *Adrian: Not sure what time your meeting is at. Can you call me when you have a chance?*

> *Adrian: I'm at a meeting with an author at a bookstore across town, but the daycare called to tell me Finley has a fever. They assured me she was okay, but she needs to be picked up.*

> *Adrian: Called Hutch, but he didn't answer. He's probably still in the meetings at the memory care center with Ma. Was able to get ahold of Andrea, and I put her on the pickup list to get Fin from daycare.*

> *Adrian: I know I should have asked you first, but we probably need to talk about having a backup plan for things like this in the future if you're going to be traveling more.*

> *Adrian: I have an appointment scheduled with the pediatrician at 4:30. I don't know when you'll see this, but please try not to worry. I'll handle this.*

But he shouldn't have to. My vision blurred as I stared at my phone, feeling helpless. My baby was sick, and I was sitting in a conference room, hours away from home. Suddenly proving myself at work didn't seem so important.

> *Adrian: I hope you're not panicking with all these messages when you get them. I just wanted to make sure you knew what was going on. I promise she's okay. Or at least Andrea said she was. She's waiting for me in my office.*

Another text came through as I was reading.

> *Adrian: Headed back to the office now to get our girl. I'll try to call you later once I know more. I love you.*

As I read the last message, I hadn't even realized that Sloane and Nikki had stopped talking.

"Is everything okay, Isobel?" Nikki asked, concern clear on her face.

As I tried to come up with an excuse, I realized that maybe this was a sign I wasn't where I needed to be right now.

"Actually, no. I'm sorry, but I need to go."

My hands gathered the papers in front of me on the table into a haphazard stack and I hastily shoved them in my bag before I went to stand.

"What's going on?" Sloane asked, placing her hand on my forearm while her eyes widened. I hoped leaving like this didn't completely derail things, but I couldn't sit here and pretend it was where I wanted to be.

"I need to get back to Boston to be with my family. Finley is sick and I know Adrian can handle a sick baby alone, but he's got enough going on with his grandfather in the hospital right now and he shouldn't have to."

I looked across the table to Nikki, expecting her to be upset that I was leaving like this, but she was smiling.

"I know you wanted me here to help you make this decision, but if it doesn't feel right, then it's your decision to make. I've loved working with you all these years, and I hope I get to continue working with you on upcoming projects. I understand if this makes you lose faith in my ability to..."

Nikki laughed, waving her hand. "Isobel, go. You know I love a good grand gesture, and it sounds like you've got one to make. Sloane can help me figure out where to sign, and I'll talk to you later."

"Are you sure? I can..."

"Go!" She pointed at the door, and I looked down at Sloane. She winked and nodded her head at the door.

I didn't even hesitate as I grabbed my things and ran down the hallway, stopping only to grab my suitcase from behind the reception desk.

Nikki was right, I had a grand gesture to make.

YOU KNOW THOSE SCENES in a movie where the hero or the heroine rushes through an airport to make a romantic gesture? Well, mine was not quite as graceful.

After I'd fled from Vivid's offices, I'd caught a cab to the airport. While we were stuck in traffic, I pulled up the flight schedules, and it looked like there was one leaving in an hour and a half that would get me into Boston three hours from now. That felt like an eternity, but it was either that or waiting for my original flight almost eight hours away.

FOUR HOURS LATER, MY Uber was pulling up to the front doors of Vivid. I was sure I looked like a hot mess from rushing through the airport, but I didn't care. I was finally where I needed to be.

Thankfully, no one was on the elevator, but it moved entirely too fucking slowly on its way to the tenth floor.

Andrea's replacement at the admin desk tilted her head as I rushed past her, heading in the opposite direction from my office. I wasn't even sure if she knew who I was because she hadn't been here for very long before I went on maternity leave.

I could hear voices as I approached Adrian's office and slowed, trying to straighten my disheveled clothes before he saw me. I didn't want to make him even more worried about me than he had been.

"Bel?" Hutch's voice carried as I stepped into the doorway and Adrian spun, Finley held to his chest.

"Hey," I whispered, hesitating before I stepped toward them. Finley's cheeks were flushed, and she looked miserable, but she was in one piece. Thank God. Moisture pooled in the corners of my eyes as I stared at her sweet little face. How could I have left her?

"Aren't you supposed to be in New York?" Adrian whispered, swaying slightly from side to side as his big palm cradled our daughter.

"Yeah, but I left early," I responded quietly, running my fingertips over her hair. She felt warm, but she was awake, so that had to be a good sign.

"Why?" he asked, stepping closer so our sides touched. "I told you she was okay. You didn't need to rush back here because she's got a bug. Babies get sick."

"I got your texts while I was in the meeting, and I knew I needed to leave."

His brow furrowed as he looked at me, and I could tell he was probably wondering if I had a mental breakdown, but I still didn't regret my decision. "What about the contract?"

"She signed. Or at least I think she did. Both she and Sloane told me to go, but she said she was going to."

But that was all background noise at this point because the center of my universe was right in front of me. The only part of my life that truly mattered. Things with my job would be there later.

"You didn't need to come. That wasn't why I texted you. I could have handled this. Kids get sick, Is. It's probably going to be frequent with her being in daycare."

"I know." I nodded, but the concerned look on his face never faded. "But I shouldn't have left with everything going on right now. I'm sorry that I screwed this all up. I know you probably hate me, and I wasn't there when you both needed me, but I'm trying to be here now."

"Um," Hutch said, clearing his throat. "Not that I'm not enjoying this adorable little family reunion, but you two do know that we're still in the room, right?"

I turned, taking in Hutch's casual lean against the couch on the other side of the room in stark contrast to Andrea who sat ramrod straight next to him looking like she wanted to be anywhere else but here.

"He's right, maybe we shouldn't do this here."

Adrian turned, leaving me standing by the door to his office while he handed off the baby to Hutch.

Now it was time for me to face my fears and tell him how I felt.

Chapter
FORTY-NINE

ADRIAN

BOSTON

"I THINK WE NEED to talk," I said to Isobel, looking back at where Hutch was holding Finley on my couch while Andrea hovered next to him.

"We got her. Go talk in her office," my brother told us, nodding toward the door.

"Are you sure, I can—"

Andrea interrupted me. "I've been a nanny for years. I'll make sure she's safe."

"I'm her uncle and I have a twelve-year-old. I think I can handle a four-month-old baby," Hutch argued, staring down my intern.

"Can you?" Andrea asked, arching an eyebrow at Hutch.

"I was a field medic and am halfway through the testing to go for my EMT certification. I'm probably a little more qualified than you to deal with a sick baby."

They continued to bicker, and I grasped Isobel's elbow, nodding toward the door. "Let's go somewhere quieter."

She looked longingly at Finley, and I knew she was worried about her, but I could tell we needed to talk without an audience. "But…"

"She's okay for a bit. They'll call us if her fever gets worse. We don't need to leave for the doctor for another twenty minutes."

Nodding, her chin quivered, but she let me lead her out the door and into the hallway. We walked silently side-by-side. I was almost desperate to hold her hand, but I didn't want to push things. She was clearly struggling right now.

By the time we reached her office, I could tell she was moments from breaking down again. I didn't like that I could tell when she was about to burst into tears. After the door closed behind us, she let out a sob that had me pulling her into my arms.

"I'm so sorry," she whispered brokenly. "I should have stayed. But I thought if I went on that trip and got her to sign that it'd make me feel like there was something I finally wasn't failing."

"You weren't failing, Is. Having a baby is hard."

"Not for you."

"Is that what you think? That it's easy for me?" Every day that she drew further and further into herself, I wondered if I wasn't being supportive enough. She refused to lean on me to take off the burden, and I often wondered if it was because she couldn't trust me. Our history wasn't the best, and while I know she saw who I was now, I'd been an asshole for years. You act like something long enough and people tend to believe it.

"You make everything look so easy. She doesn't cry as much for you. You never seem tired. Work isn't a struggle for you to balance," she blurted, barely taking a breath with unshed tears in her eyes.

"Is," I sighed, running my hand down her chaotic hair. "Every time I went back to the hotel while you were still admitted to the hospital, I cried in the shower. I cried in my car in the parking lot when I went to get dinner most nights. I didn't want you to feel like I was one more person for you to shoulder the burden for. I hated seeing you both struggle. I just didn't want you to see me upset. Being strong for you made it easier to focus on something I could control when nothing seemed to go right."

She sniffled, burrowing into my chest. Her body was practically shaking in my arms, and I hated that she'd gotten to the point where she felt like she had to run away from me.

"Do you have any idea how many terrifying scenarios went through my head when you were in labor? How terrified I was that I was going to lose one or both of you?"

"Why didn't you ever tell me this?"

"Because I didn't want to scare you. I've felt like I was losing you for months and I didn't want to make it worse."

"I'm sorry."

Leaning down to lay my cheek against her hair, I hugged her tighter to my chest. "You've been so withdrawn and upset lately. I think this is more than just adjusting to parenthood."

"You're right, it's because I didn't know how to talk to you about how I felt. I didn't want to admit how unequipped I've been to handle any of this. How much of a failure I felt like."

My heart cracked wide open at the despair in her voice. She had no idea how strong she was. How in awe of her I was most days.

"Asking for help doesn't make you a failure. And admitting you may have postpartum depression doesn't make you weak. It makes you human. The longer you let yourself suffer, the harder it will be. We've gotta break this cycle. We need to get you in to talk to someone."

"I have been," she mumbled into my shirt, her fingers tracing the wet spot her tears had left behind. "I went to talk to someone on Friday, and I actually talked to him this morning, too. Then I went to the meeting, knowing I'd rather be here instead. It didn't seem like it was going well, but then my phone started buzzing..."

"And you saw all my text messages," I deduced, knowing it had to have freaked her out. I didn't want to burden her, but I also didn't want her to find out through a voicemail from the daycare that Fin was sick and radio silence from me.

"I wish I would've been here."

"Is." I hated she continued to second guess herself. "You can't be everywhere for everyone all the time. Sometimes our jobs are going to take us away from home, and we need to be there to support each other without freaking out. You can't run home every time something happens."

"I didn't just come home early for her," she whispered. "You may have thought I was being an overly reactive parent, but you were part of my reasoning, too. I'm sorry I wasn't there for *you*. I shut you out because I was afraid you would leave."

"You may have shut me out, but, Is..." Pulling her back from me, I grasped her shoulders and leaned down to look into her eyes. I wanted her to know I meant the next words I told her. "I'm not leaving."

"I know you're not. And I need to believe you when you tell me things. When you told me you wanted to marry me a few weeks ago, I panicked instead of talking to you about it. Then I was so worried you'd change your mind that I refused to bring it up again. But..." She averted her gaze, but I saw the tear slip down her cheek.

"I meant what I asked you a few weeks ago. If you wanted to, I'd marry you today," I whispered, using my fingertips to tilt her face back toward me. "Well, maybe tomorrow since we need to go to the pediatrician and I'm sure the courthouse closes at 5."

"Ask me again when I'm not so much of a shit show," she whispered back, her palm rising to cup my jaw.

"I'm not waiting *that* long," I teased, but she smiled, so I was considering it a win.

She may be lost now, but she wouldn't be forever. Isobel had finally taken my hand to find her way out of the darkness, and I was ready for both of us to find the light. Together.

Epilogue
PART ONE

ISOBEL

BOSTON

ADRIAN PROPOSED AGAIN AT the end of the summer, and this time I said yes without hesitation.

The man deserved a medal for putting up with me some days, but he had his moments as well. Like when he met my parents for the first time when they'd been in Boston to meet their granddaughter when she turned 6 months old, and he told them that if they couldn't accept their daughter or ours that they could fuck right off back to Iowa. I agreed with him a thousand percent, but I was afraid it'd be the thing that finally severed my relationship with my parents.

Thankfully, my father had been impressed by his protective streak and was not offended. My mother tried to hold a grudge, but he won her over too with how dedicated he was to Finley. It would have been nice if they'd attempted to meet her sooner, but their behavior wasn't something I could—or wanted to—control. I wouldn't keep them from their grandchild, but I wasn't letting them make me feel guilty for my choices any longer.

Garrett and I had still been meeting weekly, but I'd finally let go of the past and started to enjoy my present. Baby steps had gotten me to a place where I felt healthier asking for help and giving myself grace when I needed it.

Finley was getting huge, no longer the tiny fragile baby who was born a month early, and now topping out the growth charts. She'd started talking too, and of course, her first word had been 'Dada', closely followed by 'shit', but neither of us was taking credit for that one. At least it hadn't been Dickhead.

She was walking now too, which was fun since she seemed to have a well-developed sense of adventure—meaning she liked to randomly run off in public to make adults catch her.

"You ready?" Adrian asked, wrapping his arms around me from behind. His hand settled on my stomach, and I tried not to let the butterflies overwhelm me. Or send me to the bathroom again.

"I thought you weren't supposed to see me until later?"

"You're not in your dress yet, and we've got the next thirty minutes alone. Are you saying you want me to leave?"

I was in that awkward transitional phase where I was a combination of terribly nauseous and horny. We hadn't told anyone we were pregnant again, but my growing midsection was going to clue people in as soon as I wore something other than high-waisted skirts and dresses to work. There was only so much I could do to conceal the two little people who'd surprised us with their appearance a few months ago.

"I literally just threw up three minutes ago."

"And you brushed your teeth and used mouthwash. I don't see what the problem is here. Are you saying you don't want me to make you come before I'm kicked out of this room? It'd add to that whole blushing bride look."

"You're terrible."

"And you're gorgeous." His hands started to slowly draw up the flowy sundress I'd tossed on earlier when Hutch had come to retrieve his niece so we could get ready for the wedding.

"Are you still going to be this attracted to me once I'm not pregnant again? You seem to have a bit of a pregnancy fetish," I laughed as his fingers slid underneath my panties, slowly pressing inside me.

"Are you forgetting how you keep getting pregnant? Pretty sure I just can't keep my hands off you, period."

We hadn't planned this pregnancy, but birth control failures seemed on brand for our relationship. This time it hadn't been a vanishing IUD. Instead, we'd had an acute case of food poisoning that had apparently rendered my birth control pills ineffective.

"Well, enjoy the next few months without condoms, because until you take care of things on your end, admittance is denied. We're not risking ending up with more than three." I would be forty by the end of the year, and there was no way we would be trying to handle a toddler and twin babies without ensuring we wouldn't have any more surprise additions.

"Nothing like talk of my balls getting snipped to turn me on, babe," he laughed, pressing his erection into me from behind.

"Doesn't seem to have had much of an effect."

"That's because I'm imagining fucking your tits. Have you seen them lately?"

"You're such a romantic. Did you put that in your vows?"

"Yup," he whispered into my neck. "Right next to the part about expecting anal on my birthday."

"Good luck with that one. Although you seemed to enjoy it when I shoved that vibrator up your ass when I was pregnant with Fin."

"I thought we agreed not to talk about that."

"You told Hutch," I laughed. "Pretty sure he's gonna be teasing you about that until the day you die."

"Can we not talk about my brother when I'm trying to get in your pants?"

Humming, I pressed his fingers into me harder. "I guess."

Adrian growled, his teeth nipping my throat as he tugged my panties down. "Take off this dress and put your palms on the dresser so I can remind you who this pussy belongs to. We'll see if you're still thinking about anyone but me when my cum is running down your leg underneath your wedding dress."

"Maybe I should reconsider that fantasy I used to have..."

"Don't test me, Isobel, or I'll make sure you're so turned on you can't focus on the officiant and are desperate to get me alone so I can finish you off."

"Have you been reading the manuscripts on my computer again?" I laughed as I braced myself against the dresser, watching his reflection in the mirror while he angrily ripped off his clothing.

He stepped in close, his warm chest pressing against my back, his cock sliding between my legs. "This is all me, babe. Now push that ass out so I can make you scream my name before we need to get ready. You're going to be my wife the next time I fuck you."

PART TWO

ADRIAN

BOSTON

PART OF ME WANTED to freeze time as I watched Isobel walk down the aisle toward me, her arm linked with her father's. Isobel's best friend Leilani was standing on the other side of the officiant as maid of honor, next to her sisters—who Isobel had reluctantly included in the ceremony.

Hutch was standing next to me, too busy staring at his date in the third row to pay attention to Isobel, but that fucker could keep his eyes off my wife. Penelope stood at the end of the line on my side, holding onto Finley's hand.

A small crowd of our friends and family had gathered at a wedding venue in a fourth-floor historic library. Being surrounded by books while I married the love of my life seemed àpropos. It also wasn't far from where I'd originally suggested we get married—Fenway Park. But since it was technically during the season, and the Sox had a home game tomorrow, that idea was quickly dismissed.

I had convinced her to get our engagement photos taken there before the season started instead. She insisted we didn't need them since this was her second marriage, but I told her they were an opportunity to get family photos taken while Finley was still little. And it was really fuckin' cool to see my little girl toddling around with a tiny baseball bat on a field I'd briefly had the honor of playing on.

We'd also brought along the rest of my family. Pops got a kick out of sitting in the dugout with his other great-granddaughter while we got our photos taken, and then we had an extended family one taken since we weren't sure how much longer Pops would hold out before he joined his wife.

He was currently sitting in the front row with Ma and her new boyfriend, having been sprung from the memory care facility to attend the wedding.

"Damn, she looks hot," Hutch whispered when his attention returned to my wedding and not his much, much younger date. Or whatever she was. I was staying out of their relationship. It was bad enough he'd slept with Finley's nanny.

"I have no problem punching you in the balls in front of all these people if you disrespect my wife again."

"She's already confiscated yours, so I guess at least one of us has balls. And she's not your wife yet. Plenty of time for her to change her mind." He paused for a second and I thought he'd drop the teasing. "Do her boobs look bigger?"

I growled, suddenly wanting to prioritize kicking my brother's ass for making comments about my pregnant fiancée, who was minutes from becoming my wife.

"She's pregnant again, isn't she?"

"Just announce it to the entire room," I hissed, throwing my elbow into his side.

"Is it mine?" he asked in a hushed whisper, trying not to laugh.

The officiant side-eyed us as Penny not so subtly shushed her father.

"No, dickwad. *They're* mine."

"Nice. Super sperm is at it again." Hutch patted my back as Isobel stepped forward, clasping my outstretched hand with a loaded look between my brother and me.

"Do I even want to know?" she whispered, smiling at me.

"You're gorgeous," I replied, hoping to distract her. "Some might even say you look like a *blushing* bride."

"Behave," she warned before she turned to face the officiant, and my dumbass brother snickered from behind me.

It was hard to pay attention to the ceremony as I was too busy watching Isobel. For years, I thought she was just an unattainable woman that I was destined to admire from afar who hated my guts. While she still wasn't always happy with my sporadic bouts of foot-in-mouth disease, I knew she loved me—and our growing family—with her whole heart.

And I was honored that I finally got to call her mine in every sense.

"...by the power vested in me from the state of Massachusetts, I now pronounce you husband and wife. You may—"

"I got it from here," I interrupted, stepping forward to pull Isobel into my arms. Unable to wait any longer, I captured her lips to the laughter of our family and friends. Even though it took a long time to get here, everything had turned out better than I ever dreamed it could when I'd met her in that copy room almost seven years earlier.

THE END

Also By E.L. KOSLO

THE DIRTY WORDS SERIES

Foreplay on Words (Amazon)

Book One of The Dirty Words Series
Evan and Chase
Preview of Foreplay on Words: https://BookHip.com/WCJHJGA

Mark my Words (Amazon)

Book Two of The Dirty Words Series
Sam and Kristine
Preview of Mark my Words: https://BookHip.com/QHWGXTZ

Bound by Words (Amazon)

Book Three of The Dirty Words Series
Nathan and Kelly
Preview of Bound by Words: https://BookHip.com/NRRHRBN

More Than Words (Amazon)

Book Four of The Dirty Words Series
Adrian and Isobel
Preview of More Than Words: https://BookHip.com/TARMSTL

MASKED MEN OF SAGE SPRINGS

Accidental Abduction (Amazon)

Book One in the Masked Men of Sage Springs Series
Hudson and Charley
Preview of Accidental Abduction: https://bookhip.com/CDPWXAB
Coming to audio soon!

Illicit Illustration (Amazon)

Book Two in the Masked Men of Sage Springs Series
Reid and Hazel
Preview of Illicit Illustration: https://bookhip.com/CDPWXAB

Smokin' Situation (Amazon)

Book Three in the Masked Men of Sage Springs Series
Annie and Tristan
Preview of Smokin' Situation: https://bookhip.com/FCDAKTZ

STANDALONES

The Midnight Voyeur (Amazon)

Now available in Duet audio featuring Branden Davis-Butler, Cole Eubanks
and Troy Duran: https://books2read.com/themidnightvoyeur
(Wide at all audio retailers)
Spicy, taboo, reverse age-gap, stand-alone – Ginny
Preview The Midnight Voyeur: https://BookHip.com/SZXGKKQ

The Mystery Correspondent (Amazon)

Steamy Christmas novella, stand-alone – Ryder and Stella
Preview of The Mystery Correspondent: https://BookHip.com/XPBVAMB

Meet Him at the Altar

New Adult coming of age, written like a romcom/mystery
Kendall & The Groom
Preview of Meet Him at the Altar available on ELKoslo.com

Social Media

Website: ELKoslo.com

Instagram: @elkoslo_writes
Threads: @elkoslo_writes
TikTok: @elkoslowrites & @elkosloauthor

Facebook: E.L. Koslo
Page: EL Koslo Romance Writer
Private Reader Group: E.L. Koslo's Dirty Words Brigade

Pinterest: @elkoslo

X: @ELKoslo
BlueSky: https://bsky.app/profile/elkoslowrites.bsky.social

Amazon: amazon.com/author/e.l.koslo

Linktree: linktr.ee.Elkoslo

Newsletter: https://elkoslo.beehiiv.com/

About
E.L. KOSLO

FIND THE FUNNY IN YOUR LIFE.

E.L. writes spicy romantic comedies with a variety of cinnamon roll heroes and strong heroines. She grew up in the midwest US, married her college sweetheart, now lives in one of those flyover states with her four spirited children and emotional support/writing companion Bernedoodle, Quinn. Banter and second-hand embarrassment are her jam, so be prepared to laugh with or at her characters.

Her novels combine her love of steamy romance, awkward but loveable leading males, and headstrong heroines with a dash of humor and a little bit of kink.

www.ingramcontent.com/pod-product-compliance
Lightning Source LLC
Chambersburg PA
CBHW021211310726
48971CB00006B/1529